THE AUTHORS

Although Edith Œnone Somerville (1858-1949) and Violet Martin ('Martin Ross', 1862-1915) were second cousins, they did not meet until 1886. Their upbringings had been very different. Edith grew up in the Somerville family mansion at Drishane, County Cork, while from the age of ten Violet had lived in Dublin. From their first meeting, a deep and enduring sympathy sprang up between them, and they were to live and work together at Drishane until Violet's death, completing sixteen works of fiction and several travel books. After the good reception of their first joint work, *An Irish Cousin*, in 1889, Violet wrote to Edith: 'To write with you doubles the triumph and the enjoyment, having first halved the trouble and anxiety.' So close was their collaboration that when Violet died in 1915, Edith continued to write in their joint names.

Today Somerville and Ross are perhaps best known for *Some Experiences of an Irish R.M.* (1899) and its sequel, *Further Experiences of an Irish R.M.* (1908). But their greatest work, and their own favourite, was *The Real Charlotte* (1894). The astringent yet affectionate irony with which Somerville and Ross portray Victorian Ireland, and the depth of their psychological insight, have made their works popular with generations of readers.

THE REAL CHARLOTTE

E. Œ. Somerville and Martin Ross

New Introduction by
Molly Keane

THE HOGARTH PRESS
LONDON

Published in 1988 by
The Hogarth Press
30 Bedford Square, London WCIB 3RP

First published by Ward & Downey 1894
This edition first published by Chatto & Windus 1972
Copyright © 1984 by Sir Patrick Coghill, Bart.
New Introduction copyright © Molly Keane 1988

British Library Cataloguing in Publication Data

Somerville, E. Œ
The real Charlotte
Rn: Violet Florence Martin   I. Title
823'.8[F] PR6037.06

ISBN 0 7012 0803 1

Printed in Finland by
Werner Söderström Oy

INTRODUCTION

If *The Real Charlotte*, a novel written by two young and virgin ladies between the years 1888 and 1890, was still an embryo awaiting its birth in 1988, it would, on publication, be almost a certainty for the Booker Prize, the American Book of the Month Choice, and most probably, for the script of an important film travesty.

Delightful and justly popular as are the subsequent writings of Edith Somerville and Martin Ross, it is in *The Real Charlotte* that their genius, a force that seems intangible even to themselves, has been most ruthlessly expended. The book is a superb piece of architecture, constructed with as much intricate skill as a good detective story, each and every strand complete in itself, its probability only to be perceived and accepted in the inevitable ending. Characters, each one of them necessary, and each a living, breathing individual, throng the story, and are as much people of today as of that long past yesterday. We would not have one fewer, they all concern us in their degree. There is not a superficial glimpse of place or person; there are no lesser, stooge characters, each and every one holds, in his or her own strength and necessity to the plot, our absolute curiosity and understanding.

Places have the same wholeness as human beings – we walk the lengths of the cool, high rooms of Bruff, the family seat of the Dysarts, not yet under any threat of oblivion, though the family's reliance on a dishonest agent may be a portent in those later years of a much maligned Ascendancy. In *The Real Charlotte* we too assume, as the predestined course of events, that the gentle Dysart family should continue endlessly to inherit.

Tally-Ho Lodge, home of the villainess Charlotte Mullen, with its cat-infested meanness, its shouting whispering barefoot servants, 'the soft clinging tread of bare feet was audible in the hall', has a personality almost stronger than that of Bruff. Nothing in the house is extraneous to the story – the cats have their importance several times over; they are Charlotte's love objects. Even the age-old cockatoo, chained to his perch on the kitchen dresser, in one phrase, croaked from the past, saves his authors a page of possibly tedious racontage, concerning characters who carry a background importance, but whom the reader is not to meet.

Beneath the flow of its events and circumstances – whether these events are moments of high and irresistible comedy; whether they concern the many different kinds of loving as there are lovers in that fatal summer; or, most hauntingly, follow the slow diplomatic growth of Charlotte's maturing cruelty – we are held and convinced of an absolute truthfulness.

Briefly, the plot concerns the rise and fall of the adorable vulgarian, Francie Fitzpatrick (Eliza Doolittle before her time), fatally transplanted from a lower middle-class Dublin background to county society in the Anglo-Ireland of the 1880s where her beauty and charm capture all hearts; most tragically her own is captured too. Her final destruction is owing to the consuming jealousy and spite of her terrifying cousin, the Real Charlotte – the plot intertwines the lives of these two women, opposites in every possible way.

First we meet Francie. The book opens in Dublin with a scene of high comedy where the future is ghosted in laughter. Here the heroine, Francie, that lower-class Dublin nymphette, shows her true character, that of the bold audacious child whose audacity, charm and beauty are, a few years later, to captivate the strict society of the Anglo-Irish world until – a bird caught between hands – she is fatally subject to the love that destroys her.

Francie's beauty is never emphasised. It is snatched lightly in moments passing like a breeze through the story – a hatless head, blonde curls bunched high and full of raindrops. Yet we are as fully aware and as troubled by it as by that of Tolstoy's Anna Karenina in her velvet and sables as she moves in comfortable elegance, and talks with the old Countess in a railway carriage – we are caught in Anna's grave intention; we see the stoop of her neck. In the same way, we are convinced of Francie's absolute youth and beauty. Anna and Francie have the same helpless acceptance and subjection to love. They are both powerless in their constancy to the wrong man. In this they are sisters in misfortune. But it is Francie, when deserted and despairing, who carries her sorrows with twice the *panache*. There is no remission of her love for Hawkins. The angry heart can find no flaw in him except that he has wounded it. We recognise her courage, her wonderful impertinence, her strong and supple nature transcending the vulgarity of her clothes and her Dublin accent. Those were the days when vulgarity and 'not speaking proper' formed as much of a bar to acceptance as today they can be a cherished maintenance of individuality.

Miss Charlotte Mullen, the Real Charlotte, is the finest non-heroine in the history of the novel. The progress of her evil-doing is told with something close to sympathy, or at least with a complete understanding of the motives driving her. Our interest in her never lessens. Her story has the compulsive underwater purpose of a fish going upriver to spawn. A terrifying capacity for cruelty – the very bones of greed and cruelty – exists in Charlotte, the ugly disappointed woman. Even in a passing description of black hair growing low on her forehead we are aware of an inborn streak of criminality.

At the same time as we are repelled by her, we know that she is a helplessly driven and deprived woman. Her tenderness for the detestable Roddy Lambert – a perpetual haunting from her youth – is made evident when she eyes him with a curious guarded tenderness . . . 'and some vibration of the strong incongruous tremor that passed through her as she spoke reached Lambert's ignorant perception and startled it' . . . this while discussing some prosaic financial arrangement, an arrangement for his benefit. Her unfulfilled erotic memories are always strengthened by his perpetual presence and physical attraction. She turns her eyes towards him and the provocative look in them comes as straight as it ever did from Francie, or as ever it has been projected from the curbed heart of woman. The past and its lasting power live in the air between them.

Another side of her personality lies in her relationship with her cats. There is nothing witch-like about it, it is her only selfless emotion – a starved tenderness explicit in her touch and voice: 'My heart's love . . .' as a terrible tom-cat springs up to the refuge of her shoulder. Such moments reveal an uncanny understanding of the ugly merciless woman, driven to extremities of evil: to the point where she is helpless to delay a climax which will defeat her as utterly as her betrayal destroys its victim.

Perhaps the leading male character in the book is Roddy Lambert, Francie's most persistent lover. In the opening paragraphs four lines of dialogue convey his unchangeable vulgarity and meanness. Confident, loud, mean and dishonest, he betrays himself in every word and action; even his movements, as Somerville and Ross describe them, are repellent. Merciless to the tenants in his power, vain and extravagant, he is driven to easy dishonesty through his accumulated debts, where his needs are Charlotte's opportunities. 'Charlotte understood business matters' – a formula which conveys to his mind much flexibility in money affairs.

Although they dislike and despise him, the authors can portray Lambert's adoration of Francie without any disgust, suppressing the condemnation they feel in their recognition of its complete reality, and sympathising with his failure to possess or understand anything of her youth and gaiety of spirit. They are generous too with his ample good looks, his glossy dark head, 'his eyes turning with sombre reproach', 'Charlotte's heart tightened at the sight of Lambert on a young horse . . . at the ease of seat, at the squareness of shoulder that had so often captivated her taste'. Love or hate or jealousy fits each character like a part of their own skin.

Gerald Hawkins, the heartless, attractive soldier, is the *homme fatal* in Francie's life. Inevitably he loves and rides away. He rides back again: not for the Happy Ending, but to precipitate disaster. Hawkins' effect on happy, carefree Francie is immediate and mortal. He is different, as though he belonged to a higher human species from her many previous Dublin admirers, or from any man she has previously found attractive.

The very texture of his clothes, the scent of his handkerchief, breathes to her his high estate. In our day of blue jeans and open-necked shirts, it is difficult to accept the fact that clothes and their wearing could mark such a sharp division in social class. Oddly enough, when we are given an exact description of Mr Hawkins, that faithless dandy, dressing for the dinner party at Bruff, we are sensible of the glamour to which Francie succumbed. We, too, see and understand how spruce and well turned-out he was – even to the monogrammed silk hander-chief, taken out of a crimson silk sachet – we have another hint of his devastating *chic* when we hear the smart rattle of his polo-cart speeding along to dinner and an evening of heartless, uncalculating mischief.

If there are two characters in the book particularly set apart for their creators' deepest understanding and consideration, they must be Christopher Dysart and Francie. Opposites in every sense, their values are extremes of difference; that Francie should become for Christopher irresistible appears equally unlikely as her refusal of his offer of marriage. Then we understand his blind suffering as clearly as later we share in relief of his disillusionment.

It can happen that a character overtakes his set importance in a book. Though obviously their man for all time (what a mate for Martin Ross!), and for us one of the most dear and touching men in fiction, Christopher is never given more attention than his weight and place in the story deserves. His absolute charm is conveyed as we read of the slow, unmeditated advance of his love and courtship, so unlike Hawkins' lively assault, when a kiss in the crook of an arm almost amounts to a deflowering. In contrast, we see only a delayed, almost derisory interest on Christopher's part, when the turn of a cheek is viewed at leisure through the exquisite boredom of a choir practice. Later, in a long, formal after-dinner hour (when Francie is a very misfit guest at Bruff), the cool Northern music his sister is playing wakes in him a recognition of the same wild quality in Francie.

Following on this hint of romance comes a scene of high comedy when Francie's impudent and lively comments on his sacred photograph album alert him to an unsuspected possibility in the pleasure of her company. She makes him laugh. and laugh again. This is one of the many episodes in the book when laughter carries the shadow of future unhappiness. The slow growth of his love for Francie is told with a Chekhovian realisation of its hopelessness. In the aftermath, his recovery from love, and our realisation of his relief, goes a step further with equal validity.

The Real Charlotte is an unsurpassed example of a fusion between two lively minds. Edith Œnone Somerville and Violet Martin (Martin Ross) were cousins with the same Anglo-Irish background. Their values and their spoken language would have had an ingrown similarity. It was a period when talk – good talk – was of essential importance, and a talent to amuse was an invaluable asset. A degree of diligence was a requisite for its proper memorising – minds were stretched to entertain in ways large and small. My own aunts were of the same generation as Edith Somerville and Martin Ross, and I can remember my Aunt Bijou – a talented musician and artist – being wildly applauded for her imitation of a rabbit eating lettuce. That is very much by the way; but it is easy to imagine how receptive to entertainment were the inhabitants of those great, isolated country houses. After-dinner dancing needed music – the piano was for human hands. The quiet lamp-lit rooms knew few other interruptions of their silence – minds had worlds enough and time to fulfil their leisure in the spacious hours luxuriant around them. In that age of white, green-lined parasols, an endless expense of time was acceptable.

Gifted talkers seldom make entertaining writers; like actors, their talent evaporates in a previous achievement, a premature success. Edith and Martin are exceptions to the rule. They record, sometimes with Wildean humour, the grace and wit with which English was then spoken by the establishment. They laugh with, and at, their Familiars – such as Lady Dysart – with a remorseless acerbity, curbed in their deep understanding of Julia Duffy and Norry the Boat. The variations of speech in every class and voice are acutely audible, their different rhythms faultlessly captured. Characters think as well as speak in their own voices – the beautiful language then spoken by the peasant and servant classes must have been familiar poetry to them both. Edith's musician's ear could have memorised it like notes in music. But how did they capture the sharp vulgarity of Francie's Dublin accent?

Much of Martin's girlhood was spent in Dublin when Ross, the family house in Co. Galway, was an uninhabited vacuum. It was then that she absorbed the pattern of Dublin speech. Sunday School, as an institution, permeated all classes of society, and the book opens with a post-Sunday School escapade, a delirium of high spirits set down in classical prose. No cheap fun. Comedy without a touch of the absurd. Born and brought up, as both the young women were, in a strict and different world, a world of unquestioned convention, how did they grasp and sympathise with the pitfalls those conventions would provide for an innocent like Francie? Careless and ignorant of the social code as it then was, Francie's mistakes, her failures to please, are as touching to us when we read of them as is her beauty – our anxiety for her never lessens.

Although given without a flicker of sentimentality, their descriptions of scenery are poignantly effective. A summer afternoon lives on in 'streaks of light lying like dreams across lake water.' What could be more astringent than 'the distant struggle of the Connemara Mountains'? They have a wonderful way of mixing weather and mood, summer and love: 'the sounds of summer in the air strengthened and deepened in a blush . . . the golden green light that filtered through the leaves of the lime moved like water over the white dress.' Beyond the polite slumberous hour of a summer afternoon – lawn tennis and afternoon tea in a garden – the story pushes on, unhesitatingly, compulsive and entertaining. Always we feel that shiver of expectancy of – what next?

'I take my stand on Charlotte,' Martin said when further work was proposed. She must have realised their extraordinary achievement, and may have doubted if they could ever touch it again. Perhaps it was Martin who held the rapier pen. Her critical faculty was, possibly, the sharper of the two. But it is Edith, one feels sure, who had the stronger force of invention. Her superb mastery of a story goes on without Martin's collaboration; but there are some passages in her later writing when the acerbity is a thought softened. As an artist, and as a musician, the impulse to show and tell all must have needed an excessive, lone discipline.

Sympathy is only absent, and their steely perception barbed and unkind, when their objects are the upward social struggles of the middle classes. It has to be remembered how, at that time, a two-handled sword came down between the landed and commercial worlds of Ireland. Refinement was what they found repulsively laughable – as John Betjeman was to do so many years later – yet it is to Francie, coming as she does from the lower strata of that unattractive society, that they give a brilliant edge, disallowing any snobbish intention.

The book is so modern in outlook, its people so belong to today, that it is only when some small description of forgotten fashion or custom of manners strikes one, that thoughts skip backwards 100 years . . . when Lady Dysart, that sharp-tongued *grande dame*, rustles in, wearing a sombrely sumptuous widow's gown, unties her bonnet strings and flings them back over each shoulder, that we feel surprised she is not bareheaded. Hats are worn by every woman on all occasions, except dinner and bed. Francie trims a picture hat with dog roses in preparation for a windy day's sailing on the lake. Christian names are used sparingly – Hawkins is *never* Gerald, Lambert is *never* Roddy, Miss Hope-Drummond invariably addresses and speaks of Christopher as Mister Dysart, and Captain Cursitor is Captain Cursitor to the end. The slow pace of horse-drawn transport is taken for granted. So is the bright romantic jingle of a carriage.

None of this dating comes between us and our living companionship with every character in the story. A surge of life as strong today as yesterday keeps its inescapable grip on the reader. Perhaps it is due to Somerville and Ross's clinical forces of observation that their genius is set free to seize on the brief moment of truth – the moment that holds the very breath of love, or hate, jealousy, or death.

Molly Keane, Dysert, Ardmore, Co. Waterford August 1987

1

An August Sunday afternoon in the north side of Dublin. Epitome of all that is hot, arid, and empty. Tall brick houses, browbeating each other in gloomy respectability across the white streets; broad pavements, promenaded mainly by the nomadic cat; stifling squares, wherein the infant of unfashionable parentage is taken for the daily baking that is its substitute for the breezes and the press of perambulators on the Bray Esplanade or the Kingston pier. Few towns are duller out of the season than Dublin, but the dullness of its north side neither waxes nor wanes; it is immutable, unchangeable, fixed as the stars. So at least it appears to the observer whose impressions are only eye-deep, and are derived from the emptiness of the streets, the unvarying dirt of the window panes, and the almost forgotten type of ugliness of the window curtains.

But even an August Sunday in the north side has its distractions for those who know where to seek them, and there are some of a sufficiently ingenuous disposition to find in Sunday-school a social excitement that is independent of fashion, except so far as its slow eddies may have touched the teacher's bonnet. Perhaps it is peculiar to Dublin that Sunday-school, as an institution, is by no means reserved for children of the poorer sort only, but permeates all ranks, and has as many recruits from the upper and middle as from the lower classes. Certainly the excellent Mrs Fitzpatrick, of Number O, Mountjoy Square, as she lay in mountainous repose on the sofa in her dining room, had no

1

thought that it was derogatory to the dignity of her daughters and her niece to sit, as they were now sitting, between the children of her grocer, Mr Mulvany, and her chemist, Mr Nolan. Sunday-school was, in her mind, an admirable institution that at one and the same time cleared her house of her offspring, and spared her the complications of their religious training, and her broad, black satin-clad bosom rose and fell in rhythmic accord with the snores that were the last expression of Sabbath peace and repose.

It was nearly four o'clock, and the heat and dull clamour in the schoolhouse were beginning to tell equally upon teachers and scholars. Francie Fitzpatrick had yawned twice, though she had a sufficient sense of politeness to conceal the action behind her Bible; the pleasure of thrusting out in front of her, for the envious regard of her fellows, a new pair of side spring boots, with mock buttons and stitching, had palled upon her; the spider that had for a few quivering moments hung uncertainly above the gor-geous bonnet of Miss Bewley, the teacher, had drawn itself up again, staggered, no doubt, by the unknown tropic growths it found beneath; and the silver ring that Tommy Whitty had crammed upon her gloved finger before school, as a mark of devotion, had become perfectly immovable and was a source of at least as much anxiety as satisfaction. Even Miss Bewley's powers of exposition had melted away in the heat; she had called out her catechetical reserves, and was reduced to a dropping fire of questions as to the meaning of Scriptural names, when at length the superintendent mounted the rostrum and tapped thrice upon it. The closing hymn was sung, and then, class by class, the hot, tired children clattered out into the road.

On Francie rested the responsibility of bringing home her four small cousins, of ages varying from six to eleven, but this duty did not seem to weigh very heavily on her. She had many acquaint-ances in the Sunday-school, and with Susie Brennan's and Fanny Hemphill's arms round her waist, and Tommy Whitty in close attendance, she was in no hurry to go home. Children are, if un-consciously, as much influenced by good looks as their elders, and even the raw angularities of fourteen, and Mrs Fitzpatrick's taste in hats, could not prevent Francie from looking extremely pretty and piquante, as she held forth to an attentive audience on the charms of a young man who had on that day partaken of an early dinner at her Uncle Fitzpatrick's house.

Francie's accent and mode of expressing herself were alike deplorable; Dublin had done its worst for her in that respect, but unless the reader has some slight previous notion of how dreadful

2

a thing is a pure-bred Dublin accent, it would be impossible for him to realise in any degree the tone in which she said:

'But oh! Tommy Whitty! wait till I tell you what he said about the excursion! He said he'd come to it if I'd promise to stay with him the whole day; so now, see how grand I'll be! And he has a long black mustash!' she concluded, as a side thrust at Tommy's smooth, apple cheeks.

'Oh, indeed, I'm sure he's a bewty without paint,' returned the slighted Tommy, with such sarcasm as he could muster; 'but unless you come in the van with me, the way you said you would, I'll take me ring back from you and give it to Lizzie Jemmison! So now!'

'Much I care!' said Francie, tossing her long golden plait of hair, and giving a defiant skip as she walked; 'and what's more, I can't get it off, and nobody will till I die! and so now yourself!'

Her left hand was dangling over Fanny Hemphill's shoulder, and she thrust it forward, starfish-wise, in front of Tommy Whitty's face. The silver ring glittered sumptuously on its background of crimson silk glove, and the sudden snatch that her swain made at it was as much impelled by an unworthy desire to repossess the treasure as by the pangs of wounded affection.

'G'long, ye dirty fella'!' screamed Francie, in high good humour, at the same moment eluding the snatch and whirling herself free from the winding embrace of the Misses Hemphill and Brennan; 'I dare ye to take it from me!'

She was off like a lapwing down the deserted street, pursued by the more cumbrous Tommy, and by the encouraging yells of the children, who were trooping along the pavement after them. Francie was lithe and swift beyond her fellows, and on ordinary occasions Tommy Whitty, with all his masculine advantage of costume and his two years of seniority, would have found it as much as he could do to catch her. But on this untoward day the traitorous new side spring boots played her false. That decorative band of white stitching across the toes began to press upon her like a vice, and, do what she would, she knew that she could not keep her lead much longer. Strategy was her only resource. Swinging herself round a friendly lamp post, she stopped short with a suddenness that compelled her pursuer to shoot past her, and with an inspiration whose very daring made it the more delirious, she darted across the street, and sprang into a milk cart that was waiting at a door. The meek white horse went on at once, and, with a breathless, goading hiss to hasten him, she tried to gather up the reins. Unfortunately, however, it happened that these were under his tail, and the more she tugged at them the tighter he clasped them to him, and the more lively became his trot. In spite of an irrepressible alarm as to the end of the adventure, Francie still retained sufficient presence of mind to put out her tongue at her baffled enemy, as, seated in front of the milk cans, she clanked past him and the other children. There was a chorus, in tones varying from admiration to horror, of, 'Oh, *look* at Francie Fitzpatrick!' and then Tommy Whitty's robuster accents, 'Ye'd better look out! the milkman's after ye!'

Francie looked round, and with terror beheld that functionary in enraged pursuit. It was vain to try blandishments with the horse, now making for his stable at a good round trot; vainer still to pull at the reins. They were nearing the end of the long street, and Francie and the milkman, from their different points of view, were feeling equally helpless and despairing, when a young man came round the corner, and apparently taking in the situation at a glance, ran out into the road, and caught the horse by the bridle.

'Well, upon my word, Miss Francie,' he said, as Miss Fitzpatrick hurriedly descended from the cart. 'You're a nice young lady! What on earth are you up to now?'

'Oh, Mr Lambert – ' began Francie; but having got thus far in her statement, she perceived the justly incensed milkman close upon her, and once more taking to her heels, she left her rescuer to return the stolen property with what explanations he could. Round the corner she fled, and down the next street, till a convenient archway offered a hiding place, and sheltering there, she laughed, now that the stress of terror was off her, till her blue eyes streamed with tears.

Presently she heard footsteps approaching, and peering cautiously out, saw Lambert striding along with the four Fitzpatrick children dancing round him; in their anxiety to present each a separate version of the escapade. The milkman was not to be seen, and Francie sallied forth to meet the party, secretly somewhat abashed, but resolved to bear an undaunted front before her cousins.

The 'long black mustash', so adroitly utilized by Francie for the chastening of Tommy Whitty, was stretched in a wide smile as she looked tentatively at its owner. 'Will he tell Aunt Tish?' was the question that possessed her as she entered upon her explanation. The children might be trusted. Their round, white-lashed eyes had witnessed many of her exploits, and their allegiance had never faltered; but this magnificent grown-up man, who talked to Aunt Tish and Uncle Robert on terms of equality, what

4

trouble might he not get her into in his stupid desire to make a good story of it? 'Botheration to him!' she thought, 'why couldn't he have been somebody else?'

Mr Roderick Lambert marched blandly along beside her, with no wish to change places with anyone agitating his bosom. His handsome brown eyes rested approvingly on Francie's flushed face, and the thought that mainly occupied his mind was surprise that Nosey Fitzpatrick should have had such a pretty daughter. He was aware of Francie's diffident glances, but thought they were due to his good looks and his new suit of clothes, and he became even more patronizing than before. At last, quite unconsciously, he hit the dreaded point.

'Well, and what do you think your aunt will say when she hears how I found you running away in the milk cart?'

'I don't know,' replied Francie, getting very red.

'Well, what will you say to me if I don't tell her?'

'Oh, Mr Lambert, sure you won't tell mamma!' entreated the Fitzpatrick children, faithful to their leader. 'Francie'd be killed if mamma thought she was playing with Tommy Whitty!'

They were nearing the Fitzpatrick mansion by this time, and Lambert stood still at the foot of the steps and looked down at the small group of petitioners with indulgent self-satisfaction.

'Well, Francie, what'll you do for me if I don't tell?'

Francie walked stiffly up the steps.

'I don't know.' Then with a defiance that she was far from feeling, 'You may tell her if you like!'

Lambert laughed easily as he followed her up the steps.

'You're very angry with me now, aren't you? Well, never mind, we'll be friends, and I won't tell on you this time.'

2

The east wind was crying round a small house in the outskirts of an Irish country town. At nightfall it had stolen across the grey expanse of Lough Moyle, and given its first shudder among the hollies and laurestinas that hid the lower windows of

Tally Ho Lodge from the too curious passer-by, and at about two o'clock of the November night it was howling so inconsolably in the great tunnel of the kitchen chimney, that Norry the Boat, sitting on a heap of turf by the kitchen fire, drew her shawl closer about her shoulders, and thought gruesomely of the Banshee.

The long trails of the monthly roses tapped and scratched against the window panes, so loudly sometimes that two cats, dozing on the rusty slab of a disused hothearth, opened their eyes and stared, with the expressionless yet wholly alert scrutiny of their race. The objects in the kitchen were scarcely more than visible in the dirty light of a hanging lamp, and the smell of paraffin filled the air. High presses and a dresser lined the walls, and on the top of the dresser, close under the blackened ceiling, it was just possible to make out the ghostly sleeping form of a cockatoo. A door at the end of the kitchen opened into a scullery of the usual prosaic, not to say odorous kind, which was now a cavern of darkness, traversed by twin green stars that moved to and fro as the lights move on a river at night, and looked like anything but what they were, the eyes of cats prowling round a scullery sink.

The tall, yellow-faced clock gave the gurgle with which it was accustomed to mark the half-hour, and the old woman, as if reminded of her weariness, stretched out her arms and yawned loudly and dismally.

She put back the locks of greyish-red hair that hung over her forehead, and, crouching over the fireplace, she took out of the embers a broken-nosed teapot, and proceeded to pour from it a mug of tea, black with long stewing. She had taken a few sips of it when a bell rang startlingly in the passage outside, jarring the silence of the house with its sharp outcry. Norry the Boat hastily put down her mug, and scrambled to her feet to answer its summons. She groped her way up two cramped flights of stairs that creaked under her as she went, and advanced noiselessly in her stockinged feet across a landing to where a chink of light came from under a door.

The door was opened as she came to it, and a woman's short thick figure appeared in the doorway.

'The mistress wants to see Susan,' this person said in a rough whisper; 'is he in the house?'

'I think he's below in the scullery,' returned Norry; 'but, my Law! Miss Charlotte, what does she want of him? Is it light in her head she is?'

'What's that to you? Go fetch him at once,' replied Miss

Charlotte, with a sudden fierceness. She shut the door, and Norry crept downstairs again, making a kind of groaning and lamenting as she went.

Miss Charlotte walked with a heavy step to the fireplace. A lamp was burning dully on a table at the foot of an old-fashioned bed, and the high footboard threw a shadow that made it difficult to see the occupant of the bed. It was an ordinary little shabby bedroom; the ceiling, seamed with cracks, bulged down till it nearly touched the canopy of the bed. The wall-paper had a pattern of blue flowers on a yellowish background; over the chimney shelf a filmy antique mirror looked strangely refined in the company of the Christmas cards and discoloured photographs that leaned against it. There was no sign of poverty, but everything was dingy, everything was tasteless, from the worn Kidderminster carpet to the illuminated text that was pinned to the wall facing the bed.

Miss Charlotte gave the fire a frugal poke, and lit a candle in the flame provoked from the sulky coals. In doing so some ashes became embedded in the grease, and taking a hair-pin from the ponderous mass of brown hair that was piled on the back of her head, she began to scrape the candle clean. Probably at no moment of her forty years of life had Miss Charlotte Mullen looked more startlingly plain than now, as she stood, her squat figure draped in a magenta flannel dressing gown, and the candle light shining upon her face. The night of watching had left its traces upon even her opaque skin. The lines about her prominent mouth and chin were deeper than usual; her broad cheeks had a flabby pallor; only her eyes were bright and untired, and the thick yellow-white hand that manipulated the hair-pin was as deft as it was wont to be.

When the flame burned clearly she took the candle to the bedside, and bending down, held it close to the face of the old woman who was lying there. The eyes opened and turned towards the overhanging face: small, dim, blue eyes, full of the stupor of illness, looking out of the pathetically commonplace little old face with a far-away perplexity.

'Was that Francie that was at the door?' she said in a drowsy voice that had in it the lagging drawl of intense weakness.

Charlotte took the tiny wrist in her hand, and felt the pulse with professional attention. Her broad, perceptive finger-tips gauged the forces of the little thread that was jerking in the thin network of tendons, and as she laid the hand down she said to herself, 'She'll not last out the turn of the night.'

'Why doesn't Francie come in?' murmured the old woman again in the fragmentary, uninflected voice that seems hardly spared from the unseen battle with death.

'It wasn't her you asked me for at all,' answered Charlotte. 'You said you wanted to say good-bye to Susan. Here, you'd better have a sip of this.'

The old woman swallowed some brandy and water, and the stimulant presently revived unexpected strength in her.

'Charlotte,' she said, 'it isn't cats we should be thinking of now. God knows the cats are safe with you. But little Francie, Charlotte; we ought to have done more for her. You promised me that if you got the money you'd look after her. Didn't you now, Charlotte? I wish I'd done more for her. She's a good little thing – a good little thing – ' she repeated dreamily.

Few people would think it worth their while to dispute the wandering futilities of an old dying woman, but even at this eleventh hour Charlotte could not brook the revolt of a slave.

'Good little thing!' she exclaimed, pushing the brandy bottle noisily in among a crowd of glasses and medicine bottles, 'a strapping big woman of nineteen! You didn't think her so good the time you had her here, and she put Susan's father and mother in the well!'

The old lady did not seem to understand what she had said.

'Susan, Susan!' she called quaveringly, and feebly patted the crochet quilt.

As if in answer, a hand fumbled at the door and opened it softly. Norry was standing there, tall and gaunt, holding in her apron, with both hands, something that looked like an enormous football.

'Miss Charlotte!' she whispered hoarsely, 'here's Susan for ye. He was out in the ashpit, an' I was hard set to get him, he was that wild.'

Even as she spoke there was a furious struggle in the blue apron.

'God in Heaven! ye fool!' ejaculated Charlotte. 'Don't let him go!' She shut the door behind Norry. 'Now, give him to me.'

Norry opened her apron cautiously, and Miss Charlotte lifted out of it a large grey tom-cat.

'Be quiet, my heart's love,' she said, 'be quiet.'

The cat stopped kicking and writhing, and, sprawling up on to the shoulder of the magenta dressing gown, turned a fierce grey face upon his late captor. Norry crept over to the bed, and put back the dirty chintz curtain that had been drawn forward to keep out the draught of the door. Mrs Mullen was lying very still; she

8

had drawn her knees up in front of her, and the bedclothes hung
sharply from the small point that they made. The big living old
woman took the hand of the other old woman who was so nearly
dead, and pressed her lips to it.

'Ma'am, d'ye know me?'

Her mistress opened her eyes.

'Norry,' she whispered, 'give Miss Francie some jam for her
tea tonight, but don't tell Miss Charlotte.'

'What's that she's saying?' said Charlotte, going to the other
side of the bed. 'Is she asking for me?'

'No, but for Miss Francie,' Norry answered.

'She knows as well as I do that Miss Francie's in Dublin,' said
Charlotte roughly: ' 'twas Susan she was asking for last. Here,
a'nt, here's Susan for you.'

She pulled the cat down from her shoulder, and put him on the
bed, where he crouched with a twitching tail, prepared for flight
at a moment's notice.

He was within reach of the old lady's hand, but she did not
seem to know that he was there. She opened her eyes and looked
vacantly round.

'Where's little Francie? You mustn't send her away, Charlotte;
you promised you'd take care of her; didn't you, Charlotte?'

'Yes, yes,' said Charlotte quickly, pushing the cat towards the
old lady; 'never fear, I'll see after her.'

Old Mrs Mullen's eyes, that had rested with a filmy stare on her
niece's face, closed again, and her head began to move a little
from one side to the other, a low monotonous moan coming from
her lips with each turn. Charlotte took her right hand and laid it
on the cat's brindled back. It rested there, unconscious, for some
seconds, while the two women looked on in silence, and then the
fingers drooped and contracted like a bird's claw, and the moan-
ing ceased. There was at the same time a spasmodic movement of
the gathered-up knees, and a sudden rigidity fell upon the small
insignificant face.

Norry the Boat threw herself upon her knees with a howl, and
began to pray loudly. At the sound the cat leaped to the floor, and
the hand that had been placed upon him in the only farewell his
mistress was to take, dropped stiffly on the bed. Miss Charlotte
snatched up the candle, and held it close to her aunt's face. There
was no mistaking what she saw there, and, putting down the
candle again, she plucked a large silk handkerchief from her
pocket, and, with some hideous preliminary heavings of her
shoulders, burst into transports of noisy grief.

9

3

A damp winter and a chilly spring had passed in their usual mildly disagreeable manner over that small Irish country town which was alluded to in the beginning of the last chapter. The shop windows had exhibited their usual zodiacal succession, and had progressed through red comforters and woollen gloves to straw hats, tennis shoes, and coloured Summer Numbers. The residents of Lismoyle were already congratulating each other on having 'set' their lodgings to the summer visitors; the steamer was plying on the lake, the militia was under canvas, and on this very fifteenth of June, Lady Dysart of Bruff was giving her first lawn-tennis party.

Miss Charlotte Mullen had taken advantage of the occasion to emerge from the mourning attire that since her aunt's death had so misbecome her sallow face, and was driving herself to Bruff in the phaeton that had been Mrs Mullen's, and a gown chosen with rather more view to effect than was customary with her. She was under no delusion as to her appearance, and, early recognizing its hopeless character, she had abandoned all super-fluities of decoration. A habit of costume so defiantly simple as to border on eccentricity had at least two advantages; it freed her from the absurdity of seeming to admire herself, and it was cheap. During the late Mrs Mullen's lifetime Charlotte had studied economy. The most reliable old persons had, she was wont to reflect, a slippery turn in them where their wills were concerned, and it was well to be ready for any contingency of fortune. Things had turned out very well after all; there had been one inconvenient legacy – that 'Little Francie' to whom the old lady's thoughts had turned, happily too late for her to give any practical emphasis to them – but that bequest was of the kind that may be repudiated if desirable. The rest of the disposition had been admirably convenient, and, in skilled hands, something might even be made of that legacy. Miss Mullen thought a great deal about her legacy and the steps she had taken with regard to it as she drove to Bruff. The horse that drew her ancient phaeton moved with a dignity befitting his eight and twenty years; the three miles of level lakeside road between Lismoyle and Bruff were to him a serious undertaking, and by the time he had arrived at his destination, his mistress's active mind had pursued many pleasant mental paths to their utmost limit.

This was the first of the two catholic and comprehensive entertainments that Lady Dysart's sense of her duty towards her neighbours yearly impelled her to give, and when Charlotte, wearing her company smile, came down the steps of the terrace to meet her hostess, the difficult revelry was at its height. Lady Dysart had cast her nets over a wide expanse, and the result was not encouraging. She stood, tall, dark, and majestic, on the terrace, surveying the impracticable row of women that stretched, forlorn of men, along one side of the tennis grounds, much as Cassandra might have scanned the beleaguering hosts from the ramparts of Troy; and as she advanced to meet her latest guest, her strong, clear-eyed face was perplexed and almost tragic.

'How do you do, Miss Mullen?' she said in tones of unconcealed gloom. 'Have you ever seen so few men in your life? and there are five and forty women! I cannot imagine where they have all come from, but I know where I wish they would take themselves to, and that is to the bottom of the lake!'

The large intensity of Lady Dysart's manner gave unintended weight to her most trivial utterance, and had she reflected very deeply before she spoke, it might have occurred to her that this was not a specially fortunate manner of greeting a female guest. But Charlotte understood that nothing personal was intended; she knew that the freedom of Bruff had been given to her, and that she could afford to listen to abuse of the outer world with the composure of one of the inner circle.

'Well, your ladyship,' she said, in the bluff, hearty voice which she felt accorded best with the theory of herself that she had built up in Lady Dysart's mind, 'I'll head a forlorn hope to the bottom of the lake for you, and welcome; but for the honour of the house you might give me a cup o' tay first!'

Charlotte had many tones of voice, according with the many facets of her character, and when she wished to be playful she affected a vigorous brogue, not perhaps being aware that her own accent scarcely admitted of being strengthened.

This refinement of humour was probably wasted on Lady Dysart. She was an Englishwoman, and, as such, was constitutionally unable to discern perfectly the subtle grades of Irish vulgarity. She was aware that many of the ladies on her visiting list were vulgar, but it was their subjects of conversation and their opinions that chiefly brought the fact home to her. Miss Mullen, *au fond*, was probably no less vulgar than they, but she was never dull, and Lady Dysart would suffer anything rather than dullness. It was less than nothing to her that Charlotte's mother was reported to have been in her youth a national schoolmistress, and her grandmother a barefooted country girl. These facts of Miss Mullen's pedigree were valued topics in Lismoyle, but Lady Dysart's serene radicalism ignored the inequalities of a lower class, and she welcomed a woman who could talk to her on spiritualism, or books, or indeed on any current topic, with a point and agreeability that made her accent, to English ears, merely the expression of a vigorous individuality. She now laughed in response to her visitor's jest, but her eye did not cease from roving over the gathering, and her broad brow was still con-tracted in calculation.

'I never knew the country so bereft of men or so peopled with girls! Even the little Barrington boys are off with the militia, and everyone about has conspired to fill their houses with women, and not only women but dummies!' Her glance lighted on the long bench where sat the more honourable women in midge bitten-dullness. 'And there is Kate Gascogne in one of her reveries, not hearing a word that Mrs Waller is saying to her –'

With Lady Dysart intention was accomplishment as nearly as might be. She had scarcely finished speaking before she began a headlong advance upon the objects of her diatribe, making a short cut across the corner of a lawn-tennis court, and scarcely observ-ing the havoc that her transit wrought in the game. Charlotte was less rash. She steered her course clear of the tennis grounds, and of the bench of matrons, passed the six Miss Beatties with a com-prehensive 'How are ye, girls?' and took up her position under one of the tall elm trees.

Under the next tree a few men were assembled, herding to-gether for mutual protection after the manner of men, and laying down the law to each other about road sessions, the grand jury, and Irish politics generally. They were a fairly representative trio: a country gentleman with a grey moustache and a loud voice in which he was announcing that nothing would give him greater pleasure than to pull the rope at the execution of a certain English statesman; a slight, dejected-looking clergyman, who vied with Major Waller in his denunciations, but chastenedly, like an echo in a cathedral aisle; and a smartly dressed man of about thirty-five, of whom a more detailed description need not be given, as he has been met with in the first chapter, and the six

12

years after nine-and-twenty do little more than mellow a man's taste in checks, and sprinkle a grey hair or two on his temples.

Miss Mullen listened for a few minutes to the melancholy pessimisms of the archdeacon, and then, interrupting Major Waller in a fine outburst on the advisability of martial law, she thrust herself and her attendant cloud of midges into the charmed circle of the smoke of Mr Lambert's cigarette.

'Ho! do I hear me old friend the Major at politics?' she said, shaking hands effusively with the three men. 'I declare I'm a better politician than any one of you! D'ye know how I served Tom Casey, the land-leaguing plumber, yesterday? I had him mending my tank, and when I got him into it I whipped the ladder away, and told him not a step should he budge till he sang "God save the Queen!" I was arguing there half an hour with him in water up to his middle before I converted him, and then it wasn't so much the warmth of his convictions as the cold of his legs made him tune up. I call that practical politics!'

The speed and vigour with which this story was told would have astounded anyone who did not know Miss Mullen's powers of narration, but Mr Lambert, to whom it seemed specially addressed, merely took his cigarette out of his mouth and said, with a familiar laugh:

'Practical politics, by Jove! I call it a cold water cure. Kill or cure like the rest of your doctoring, eh! Charlotte?'

Miss Mullen joined with entire good humour in the laugh that followed.

'Oh, th' ingratitude of man!' she exclaimed. 'Archdeacon, you've seen his bald scalp from the pulpit, and I ask you, now, isn't that a fresh crop he has on it? I leave it to his conscience, if he has one, to say if it wasn't my doctoring gave him that fine black thatch he has now!'

The archdeacon fixed his eyes seriously upon her; Charlotte's playfulness always alarmed and confused him.

'Do not appeal to me, Miss Mullen,' he answered, in his refined, desponding voice; 'my unfortunate sight makes my evidence in such a matter worth nothing; and, by the way, I meant to ask you if your niece would be good enough to help us in the choir? I understand she sings.'

Charlotte interrupted him.

'There's another of you at it!' she exclaimed. 'I think I'll have to advertiss it in the *Irish Times* that, whereas my first cousin, Isabella Mullen, married Johnny Fitzpatrick, who was no relation of mine, good, bad, or indifferent, their child is my first cousin once removed, and *not* my niece!'

Mr Lambert blew a cloud of smoke through his nose.

'You're a nailer at pedigrees, Charlotte,' he said with a patronage that he knew was provoking; 'but as far as I can make out the position, it comes to mighty near the same thing; you're what they call her Welsh aunt, anyhow.'

Charlotte's face reddened, and she opened her wide mouth for a retort, but before she had time for more than the champings as of a horse with a heavy bit, which preceded her more incisive repartees, another person joined the group.

'Mr Lambert,' said Pamela Dysart, in her pleasant, anxious voice, 'I am going to ask you if you will play in the next set, or if you would rather help the Miss Beatties to get up a round of golf? How do you do, Miss Mullen? I have not seen you before; why did you not bring your niece with you?'

Charlotte showed all her teeth in a forced smile as she replied, 'I suppose you mean my cousin, Miss Dysart; she won't be with me till the day after tomorrow.'

'Oh, I'm so sorry,' replied Pamela, with the sympathetic politeness that made strangers think her manner too good to be true; 'and Mr Lambert tells me she plays tennis so well.'

'Why, what does he know about her tennis playing?' said Charlotte, turning sharply towards Lambert.

The set on the nearer court was over, and the two young men who had played in it strolled up to the group as she spoke. Mr Lambert expanded his broad chest, gave his hat an extra tilt over his nose, and looked rather more self-complacent than usual as he replied:

'Well, I ought to know something about it, seeing I took her in hand when she was in short petticoats – taught her her paces myself, in fact.'

Mr Hawkins, the shorter of the two players who had just come up, ceased from mopping his scarlet face, and glanced from Mr Lambert to Pamela with a countenance devoid of expression, save that conferred by the elevation of one eyebrow almost to the roots of his yellow hair. Pamela's eyes remained unresponsive, but the precipitancy with which she again addressed herself to Mr Lambert showed that a disposition to laugh had been near.

Charlotte turned away with an expression that was the reverse of attractive. When her servants saw that look they abandoned excuse or discussion; when the Lismoyle beggars saw it they checked the flow of benediction and fled. Even the archdeacon, through the religious halo that habitually intervened between him and society, became aware that the moment was not propitious for speaking to Miss Mullen about his proposed changes in the choir, and he drifted away to think of diocesan matters, and to forget as far as possible that he was at a lawn-tennis party.

Outside the group stood the young man who had been playing in the set with Mr Hawkins. He was watching through an eyeglass, the limp progress of the game in the other court, and was even making praiseworthy attempts to applaud the very feeble efforts of the players. He was tall and slight, with a near-sighted stoop, and something of an old-fashioned, eighteenth century look about him that was accentuated by his not wearing a moustache, and was out of keeping with the flannels and brilliant blazer that are the revolutionary protest of this age against its orthodox clothing. It did not seem to occur to him that he was doing anything un-usual in occupying himself, as he was now doing, in picking up balls for the Lismoyle curate and his partner; he would have thought it much more remarkable had he found in himself a preference for doing anything else. This was an occupation that demanded neither interest nor conversation, and of a number of disagreeable duties he did not think that he had chosen the worst.

Charlotte walked up to him as he stood leaning against a tree, and held out her hand.

'How d'ye do, Mr Dysart?' she said with marked politeness. All trace of combat had left her manner, and the smile with which she greeted him was sweet and capacious. 'We haven't seen you in Lismoyle since you came back from the West Indies.'

Christopher Dysart let his eyeglass fall, and looked apologetic as he enclosed her well filled glove in his long hand, and made what excuses he could for not having called upon Miss Mullen.

'Since Captain Thesiger has got this new steamlaunch I can't call my soul my own; I'm out on the lake with him half the day, and the other half I spend with a nail-brush trying to get the blacks off.'

He spoke with a hesitation that could hardly be called a stam-mer, but was rather a delaying before his sentence, a mental rather than a physical uncertainty.

'Oh, that's a very poor excuse,' said Charlotte with loud affabil-ity, 'deserting your old friends for the blacks a second time! I thought you had enough of them in the last two years! And you know you promised – or your good mother did for you – that you'd come and photograph poor old Mrs Tommy before she died. The poor thing's so sick now we have to feed her with a baby's bottle.'

Christopher wondered if Mrs Tommy were the cook, and was on the point of asking for further particulars, when Miss Mullen continued:

'She's the great-great-grandmother of all me cats, and I want you to immortalize her; but don't come till after Monday, as I'd like to introduce you to my cousin, Miss Fitzpatrick; did you hear she was coming?'

'Yes, Mr Lambert told us she was to be here next week,' said Christopher, with an indescribable expression that was not quite amusement, but was something more than intelligence.

'What did he say of her?'

Christopher hesitated; somehow what he remembered of Mr Lambert's conversation was of too free and easy a nature for repetition to Miss Fitzpatrick's cousin.

'He – er – seemed to think her very – er – charming in all ways,' he said rather lamely.

'So it's talking of charming young ladies you and Roddy Lambert are when he comes to see you on estate business!' said Charlotte archly, but with a rasp in her voice. 'When my poor father was your father's agent, and I used to be helping him in the office, it was charming young cattle we talked about, and not young ladies.'

Christopher laughed in a helpless way.

'I wish you were at the office still, Miss Mullen; if anyone could understand the Land Act I believe it would be you.'

At this moment there was an upheaval among the matrons; the long line rose and broke, and made for the grey stone house whose windows were flashing back the sunlight through the trees at the end of the lawn-tennis grounds. The tedious skirmish with midges, and the strain of inactivity, were alike over for the present, and the conscience of the son of the house reminded him that he ought to take Miss Mullen in to tea.

16

4

There was consternation among the cats at Tally Ho Lodge; a consternation mingled with righteous resentment. Even the patriarchal Susan could scarcely remember the time that the spare bedroom had been anything else than a hospital, a nursery, and a secure parliament house for him and his descendants; yet now, in his old age, and when he had, after vast consideration of alternatives, allocated to himself the lowest shelf of the wardrobe as a sleeping place, he was evicted at a moment's notice, and the folded-away bed curtains that had formed his couch were even now perfuming the ambient air as they hung out of the window over the hall door. Susan was too dignified to give utterance to his wounded feelings; he went away by himself, and sitting on the roof of the fowl house, thought unutterable things. But his great-niece, Mrs Bruff, could not emulate his stoicism. Followed by her five latest kittens, she strode through the house, uttering harsh cries of rage and despair, and did not cease from her lamentations until Charlotte brought the whole party into the drawing room, and established them in the waste-paper basket.

The worst part about the upheaval, as even the youngest and least experienced of the cats could see, was that it was irrevocable. It was early morning when the first dull blow of Norry's broom against the wainscot had startled them with new and strange apprehension, and incredulity had grown to certainty, till the final moment when the sight of a brimming pail of water urged them to panic-struck flight. It may be admitted that Norry the Boat, who had not, as a rule, any special taste for cleanliness, had seldom enjoyed anything more than this day of turmoil, this routing of her ancient enemies. Miss Charlotte, to whom on ordinary occasions the offended cat never appealed in vain, was now bound by her own word. She had given orders that the spare room was to be 'cleaned down', and cleaned down it surely should be. It was not, strictly speaking, Norry's work. Louisa was house- and parlour-maid; Louisa, a small and sullen Protestant orphan of unequalled sluggishness and stupidity, for whose capacity for dealing with any emergency Norry had a scorn too deep for any words that might conveniently be repeated here. It was not likely that Louisa would be permitted to join in the ardours of the campaign, but even Bid Sal, Norry's own special kitchen-slut and co-religionist, was not allowed to assist.

Norry the Boat, daughter of Shaunapickeen, the ferryman (whence her title), and of Carroty Peg, his wife, was a person with whom few would have cared to co-operate against her will. On this morning she wore a more ferocious aspect than usual. Her roughly-waving hair, which had never known the dignity of a cap, was bound up in a blue duster, leaving her bony forehead bare; dust and turf-ashes hung in her grizzled eyebrows, her arms were smeared with black-lead, and the skirt of her dress was girt about her waist, displaying a petticoat of heavy Galway flannel, long thin legs, and enormous feet cased in countrymen's laced boots. It was fifteen years now, Norry reflected, while she scrubbed the floor and scraped the candle drippings off it with her nails, since Miss Charlotte and the cats had come into the house, and since then the spare room had never had a visitor in it. Nobody had stayed in the house in all those years except little Miss Francie, and for her the cot had been made up in her great-aunt's room; the old high-sided cot in which her grandmother had slept when she was a child. The cot had long since migrated into the spare room, and from it Norry had just ejected the household effects of Mrs Bruff and her family, with a pleasure that was mitigated only by the thought that Miss Francie was a young woman now, and would be likely to give a good deal more trouble in the house than even in the days when she stole the cockatoo's sopped toast for her private consumption, and christened the tomcat Susan against everyone's wishes except her great-aunt's.

Norry and the cockatoo were now the only survivors of the old *régime* at Tally Ho Lodge, in fact the cockatoo was regarded in Lismoyle as an almost prehistoric relic, dating, at the lowest computation, from the days when old Mrs Mullen's fox-hunting father had lived there, and given the place the name that was so remarkably unsuited to its subsequent career. The cockatoo was a sprightly creature of some twenty shrieking summers on the day that the two Miss Butlers, clad in high-waisted, low-necked gowns, were armed past his perch in the hall by their father, and before, as it seemed to the cockatoo, he had more than half-finished his morning doze, they were back again, this time on the arms of the two young men who, during the previous five months, had done so much to spoil his digestion by propitiatory dainties at improper hours. The cockatoo had no very clear recollection of the subsequent departure of Dr Mullen and his brother, the attorney, with their brides, on their respective honeymoons, owing to the fact that Mr Mullen, the agent, brother of the two bridegrooms, had prised open his beak, and compelled him to drink the healths of the happy couples in the strongest and sweetest whisky punch.

The cockatoo's memory after this climax was filled with vague comings and goings, extending over unknown tracts of time. He remembered two days of disturbance, on each of which a long box had been carried out of the house by several men, and a crowd of people, dressed in black, had eaten a long and clattering meal in the dining room. He had always remembered the second of these occasions with just annoyance, because, in manoeuvring the long box through the narrow hall, he had been knocked off his perch, and never after that day had the person whom he had been taught to call 'Doctor' come to give him his daily lump of sugar.

But the day that enunciated itself most stridently from the cockatoo's past life was that on which the doctor's niece had, after many short visits, finally arrived with several trunks, and a wooden case from which, when opened, sprang four of the noisome creatures whom Miss Charlotte, their owner, had taught him to call 'pussies'. A long era of persecution then began for him, of robbery of his food, and even attacks upon his person. He had retaliated by untiring mimicry, by delusive invitations to food in the manner of Miss Charlotte, and lastly, by the strangling of a too-confiding kitten, whom he had lured, with maternal mewings, within reach of his claws. That very day Miss Charlotte's hand avenged the murder, and afterwards conveyed him, a stiff guilty lump of white feathers, to the top of the kitchen press, from thenceforth never to descend, except when long and patient picking had opened a link of his chain, or when, on fine days, Norry fastened him to a branch of the tall laurel that overhung the pigstye. Norry was his only friend, a friendship slowly cemented by a common hatred of the cats and Louisa; indeed, it is probable that but for occasional conversation with Norry he would have choked from his own misanthropic fury, helpless, lonely spectator as he was of the secret gluttonies of Louisa and the maddening domestic felicity of the cats.

But on this last day of turbulence and rout he had been forgotten. The kitchen was sunny and stuffy, the blue-bottles were buzzing their loudest in the cobwebby window, one colony of evicted kittens was already beginning to make the best of things in the turf heap, and the leaves of the laurel outside were gleaming tropically against the brilliant sky, with no one to appreciate them except the pigs. When it came to half past twelve o'clock the cockatoo could no longer refrain, and fell to loud and prolonged screamings. The only result at first was a brief stupefaction on the part of the kittens, and an answering outcry from the fowl in the yard; then, after some minutes, the green baize cross-door opened, and a voice bellowed down the passage:

'Biddy! Bid Sal!' (*fortissimo*), 'can't ye stop that bird's infernal screeching?' There was dead silence, and Miss Mullen advanced into the kitchen and called again.

'Biddy's claning herself, Miss Mullen,' said a small voice from the pantry door.

'That's no reason you shouldn't answer!' thundered Charlotte; 'come out here yourself and put the cockatoo out in the yard.'

Louisa the orphan, a short, fat, white-faced girl of fourteen, shuffled out of the pantry with her chin buried in her chest, and her round terrified eyes turned upwards to Miss Charlotte's face.

'I'd be in dhread to ketch him,' she faltered.

Those ladies who considered Miss Mullen 'eccentric, but so kind hearted, and so clever and agreeable', would have been considerably surprised if they had heard the terms in which she informed Louisa that she was wanting in courage and intelligence; but Louisa's face expressed no surprise, only a vacancy that in some degree justified her mistress's language. Still denouncing her retainers, Miss Charlotte mounted nimbly upon a chair, and seizing the now speechless cockatoo by the wings, carried him herself out to the yard and fastened him to his accustomed laurel bough.

She did not go back to the kitchen, but, after a searching glance at the contents of the pigs' trough, went out of the yard by the gate that led to the front of the house. Rhododendrons and laurels made a dark green tunnel about her, and, though it was June, the beech leaves of last November lay rotting on each side of the walk. Opposite the hall door the ground rose in a slight slope, thickly covered with evergreens, and topped by a lime tree, on whose lower limbs a flock of black turkeys had ranged themselves in sepulchral meditation. The house itself was half stifled with ivy, monthly roses, and virginian creeper; everywhere was the same unkempt profusion of green things, that sucked the sunshine into themselves, and left the air damp and shadowed. Charlotte had the air of thinking very deeply as she walked slowly along with her hands in the pockets of her black alpaca apron.

The wrinkles on her forehead almost touched the hair that grew so low down upon it as to seem like a wig that had been pulled too far over the turn of the brow, and she kept chewing at her heavy underlip as was her habit during the processes of unobserved thought. Then she went into the house, and, sitting down at the davenport in the dining room, got out a sheet of her best notepaper, and wrote a note to Pamela Dysart in her strong, commercially clear hand.

Afternoon tea had never flourished as an institution at Tally Ho Lodge. Occasionally, and of necessity, a laboured repast had been served at five o'clock by the trembling Louisa; occasions on which the afternoon caller had not only to suffer the spectacle of a household being shaken to its foundations on her behalf, but had subsequently to eat of the untempting fruit of these struggles. On the afternoon, however, of the day following that of the cleansing of the spare room, timely preparations had been made. Half the round table in the centre of the drawing room had been covered with a cloth, and on it Louisa, in the plenitude of her zeal, had prepared a miniature breakfast; loaf, butter-cooler, and knives and forks, a truly realistic touch being conferred by two egg cups standing in the slop basin. A vase of marigolds and pink sweet-pea stood behind these, a fresh heap of shavings adorned the grate, the piano had been opened and dusted, and a copy of the 'Indiana Waltzes' frisked on the desk in the breeze from the open window.

Charlotte sat in a low armchair and surveyed her drawing room with a good deal of satisfaction. Her fingers moved gently through the long fur at the back of Mrs Bruff's head, administering, almost unconsciously, the most delicately satisfactory scratching about the base of the wide, sensitive ears, while her eyes wandered back to the pages of the novel that lay open on her lap. She was a great and insatiable reader, surprisingly well acquainted with the classics of literature, and unexpectedly lavish in the purchase of books. Her neighbours never forgot to mention, in describing her, the awe-inspiring fact that she 'took in the English *Times* and the *Saturday Review*, and read every word of them,' but it was hinted that the bookshelves that her own capable hands had put up in her bedroom held a large proportion of works of fiction of a startlingly advanced kind, 'and', it was generally added in tones of mystery, 'many of them French'.

It was half past five o'clock, and the sharpest of several showers that had fallen that day had caused Miss Mullen to get up and shut the window, when the grinding of the gate upon the gravel at the end of the short drive warned her that the expected guest was arriving. As she got to the hall door one of those black leather band-boxes on wheels, known in the south and west of Ireland as 'jingles' or inside cars, came brushing under the arch of wet evergreens, and she ran out on to the steps.

'Well, my dear child, welcome to Tally Ho!' she began in tones of effusive welcome, as the car turned and backed towards the doorstep in the accustomed way, then seeing through the half-closed curtains that there was nothing inside it except a trunk and a bonnet box, 'Where in the name of goodness is the young lady, Jerry? Didn't you meet her at the train?'

'I did, to be sure,' replied Jerry; 'sure she's afther me on the road now. Mr Lambert came down on the thrain with her, and he's dhrivin' her here in his own thrap.'

While he was speaking there was the sound of quick trotting on the road, and Miss Mullen saw a white straw hat and a brown billycock moving swiftly along over the tops of the evergreens. A dog-cart with a white-faced chestnut swung in at the gate, and Miss Fitzpatrick's hat was immediately swept off her head by a bough of laburnum. Its owner gave a shrill cry and made a snatch at the reins, with the idea apparently of stopping the horse.

'No, you don't,' said Mr Lambert, intercepting the snatch with his whip hand; 'you're going to be handed over to your aunt just as you are.'

Half a dozen steps brought them to the door, and the chestnut pulled up with his pink nose almost between the curtains of the inside car. It was hard to say whether Miss Mullen had heard Lambert's remark, which had certainly been loud enough to enable her to do so, but her only reply was an attack upon the carman.

'Take your car out o' that, ye great oaf!' she vociferated, 'can't ye make way for your betters?' Then with a complete change of voice, 'Well, me dear Francie, you're welcome, you're welcome.'

The greeting was perceptibly less hearty than that which had been squandered on the trunk and bonnet box; but an emotion *réchauffé* necessarily loses flavour. Francie had jumped to the ground with a reckless disregard of the caution demanded by the steps of a dog-cart, and stooping her hatless head, kissed the hard cheek that Charlotte tendered for her embrace.

'Thank you very much, I'm very glad to come,' she said, in a voice whose Dublin accent had been but little modified by the six years that had lightly gone over her since the August Sunday when she had fled from Tommy Whitty in the milkman's cart.

22

'And look at me the show I am without my hat! And it's all his fault!' with a lift of her blue eyes to Lambert, 'he wouldn't let me stop and pick it up.'

Charlotte looked up at her with the wide smile of welcome still stiff upon her face. The rough golden heap of curls on the top of Francie's head was spangled with raindrops and her coat was grey with wet.

'Well, if Mr Lambert had had any sense,' said Miss Mullen, 'he'd have let you come in the covered car. Here, Louisa, go fetch Miss Fitzpatrick's hat.'

'Ah, no, sure she'll get all wet,' said Francie, starting herself before the less agile Louisa could emerge from behind her mistress and running down the drive.

'Did you come down from Dublin today, Roddy?' said Charlotte.

'Yes, I did,' answered Mr Lambert, turning his horse as he spoke; 'I had business that took me up to town yesterday, so it just happened that I hit off Francie. Well, good evening. I expect Lucy will be calling round to see you tomorrow or next day.'

He walked his horse down the drive, and as he passed Francie returning with her hat he leaned over the wheel and said something to her that made her shake her head and laugh. Miss Charlotte was too far off to hear what it was.

5

It was generally felt in Lismoyle that Mr Roderick Lambert held an unassailable position in society. The Dysart agency had always been considered to confer brevet rank as a country gentleman upon its owner, apart even from the intimacy with the Dysarts which it implied; and as, in addition to these advantages, Mr Lambert possessed good looks, a wife with money, and a new house at least a mile from the town, built under his own directions and at his employer's expense, Lismoyle placed him unhesitatingly at the head of its visiting list. Of course his wife was placed there too, but somehow or other Mrs Lambert was a person of far less consequence than her husband. She had had the money certainly, but that quality was a good deal overlooked by the Lismoyle people in their admiration for the manner in which her husband spent it. It was natural that they should respect the captor rather than the captive, and, in any case, Mr Roderick Lambert's horses and traps were more impressive facts than the Maltese terrier and the shelf of patent medicines that were Mrs Lambert's only extravagances.

Possibly, also, the fact that she had no children placed her at a disadvantage with the matrons of Lismoyle, all of whom could have spoken fearlessly with their enemies in the gate; it deprived conversation with her of the antiphonal quality, when mother answers unto mother of vaccination and teething-rash, and the sins of the nursery maids are visited upon the company generally.

'Ah, she's a poor peenie-weenie thing!' said Mrs Baker, who was usually the mouthpiece of Lismoyle opinion, 'and it's no wonder that Lambert's for ever flourishing about the country in his dog-trap, and she never seeing a sight of him from morning till night. I'd like to see Mr Baker getting up on a horse and galloping around the roads after bank hours instead of coming in for his cup of tea with me and the girls!'

Altogether the feeling was that Mrs Lambert was a failure, and in spite of her undoubted amiability, and the creditable fact that Mr Lambert was the second husband that the eight thousand pounds ground out by her late father's mills had procured for her, her spouse was regarded with a certain regretful pity as the victim of circumstance.

In spite of his claims upon the sympathy of Lismoyle, Mr Lambert looked remarkably well able to compete with his lot in life, as he sat smoking his pipe in his dinner costume of carpet slippers and oldest shooting coat, a couple of evenings after Francie's arrival. As a rule the Lamberts preferred to sit in their dining room. The hard magnificence of the blue rep chairs in the drawing room appealed to them from different points of view; Mrs Lambert holding that they were too good to be used except by 'company', while Mr Lambert truly felt that no one who was not debarred by politeness from the power of complaint would voluntarily sit upon them. An unshaded lamp was on the table, its ugly glare conflicting with the soft remnants of June twilight that stole in between the half-drawn curtains; a tumbler of whisky and water stood on the corner of the table beside the comfortable leather-covered armchair in which the master of the house was reading his paper, while opposite to him, in a basket chair, his wife was conscientiously doing her fancy work. She was a short woman with confused brown eyes and distressingly sloping shoulders; a woman of the turkey hen type, dejected and timorous in voice, and an habitual wearer of porous plasters. Her toilet for the evening consisted in replacing by a white cashmere shawl the red knitted one which she habitually wore, and a languid untidiness in the pale brown hair that hung over her eyes intimated that she had tried to curl her fringe for dinner.

Neither were speaking; it seemed as if Mr Lambert were placidly awaiting the arrival of his usual after-dinner sleep; the Maltese terrier was already snoring plethorically on his mistress's lap, in a manner quite disproportioned to his size, and Mrs Lambert's crochet needles were moving more and more slowly through the mazes of the 'bosom friend' that she was making for herself, the knowledge that the minute hand of the black marble clock was approaching the hour at which she took her post-prandial pill alone keeping her from also yielding to the soft influences of a substantial meal. At length she took the box from the little table beside her, where it stood between a bottle of smelling salts and a lump of camphor, and having sat with it in her hand till the half hour was solemnly boomed from the chimney-piece, swallowed her pill with practised ease. At the slight noise of replacing the box, her husband opened his eyes.

'By the way, Lucy,' he said in a voice that had no trace of drowsiness in it, 'did Charlotte Mullen say what she was going to do tomorrow?'

'Oh, yes, Roderick,' replied Mrs Lambert a little anxiously, 'indeed, I was wanting to tell you – Charlotte asked me if I could drive her over to Mrs Waller's tomorrow afternoon. I forgot to ask you before if you wanted the horses.'

Mr Lambert's fine complexion deepened by one or two shades.

'Upon my soul, Charlotte Mullen has a good cheek! She gets as much work out of my horses as I do myself. I suppose you told her you'd do it?'

'Well, what else could I do?' replied Mrs Lambert with tremulous crossness; 'I'm sure it's not once in the month I get outside the place, and, as for Charlotte, she has not been to the Wallers' since before Christmas, and you know very well old Captain couldn't draw her eight miles there and eight miles back any more than the cat.'

'Cat be hanged! Why the devil can't she put her hand in her pocket and take a car for herself?' said Lambert, uncrossing his legs and sitting up straight; 'I suppose I'll hear next that I'm not to order out my own horses till I've sent round to Miss Mullen to know if she wants them first! If you weren't so infernally under her thumb you'd remember there were others to be consulted besides her.'

'I'm not under her thumb, Roderick; I beg you'll not say such a thing,' replied Mrs Lambert huffily, her eyes blinking with resentment. 'Charlotte Mullen's an old friend of mine, and yours too, and it's a hard thing I can't take her out driving without remarks being passed, and I never thought you'd want the horses. I thought you said you'd be in the office all tomorrow,' ended the poor turkey hen, whose feathers were constitutionally incapable of remaining erect for any length of time.

Lambert did not answer immediately. His eyes rested on her flushed face with just enough expression in them to convey to her that her protest was beside the point. Mrs Lambert was apparently used to this silent comment on what she said, for she went on still more apologetically:

'If you like, Roderick, I'll send Michael over early with a note to Charlotte to tell her we'll go some other day.'

Mr Lambert leaned back as if to consider the question, and began to fill his pipe for the second time.

'Well,' he said slowly, 'if it makes no difference to you, Lucy, I'd be rather glad if you did. As a matter of fact I have to ride out to Gurthnamuckla tomorrow, on business, and I thought I'd take Francie Fitzpatrick with me there on the black mare. She's no great shakes of a rider, and the black mare is the only thing I'd like to put her on. But, of course, if it was for your own sake and not Charlotte's that you wanted to go to the Wallers', I'd try and manage to take Francie some other day. For the matter of that I might put her on Paddy; I daresay he'd carry a lady.'

Mr Lambert's concession had precisely the expected effect. Mrs Lambert gave a cry of consternation:

'Roderick! you wouldn't! Is it put that girl up on that mad little savage of a pony! Why, it's only yesterday, when Michael was driving me into town, and Mr Corkran passed on his tricycle, he tore up on to his hind heels and tried to run into Ryan's public house! Indeed, if that was the way, not all the Charlottes in the world would make me go driving tomorrow.'

'Oh, all right,' said Lambert graciously; 'if you'd rather have it that way, we'll send a note over to Charlotte.'

'Would you mind – ' said Mrs Lambert hesitatingly. 'I mean, don't you think it would be better if – supposing you wrote the note? She always minds what you say, and, I declare, I don't know how in the world I'd make up the excuse, when she'd settled the whole thing, and even got me to leave word with the sweep to do her drawing room chimney that's thick with jackdaws' nests, because the family'd be from home all the afternoon.'

'Why, what was to happen to Francie?' asked Lambert quickly.

'I think Charlotte said she was to come with us,' yawned Mrs Lambert, whose memory for conversation was as feeble as the part she played in it; 'they had some talk about it, at all events. I wouldn't be sure but Francie Fitzpatrick said first she'd go for a walk to see the town – yes, so she did, and Charlotte told her what she was going for was to try and see the officers, and Francie said maybe it was, or maybe she'd come and have afternoon tea with you. They had great joking about it, but I'm sure, after all, it was settled she was to come with us. Indeed,' continued Mrs Lambert meditatively, 'I think Charlotte's quite right not to have her going through the town that way by herself; for, I declare, Roderick, that's a lovely girl.'

'Oh, she's well able to take care of herself,' said Lambert, with the gruff deprecation that is with some people the method of showing pleasure at a compliment. 'She's not such a fool as she looks, I can tell you,' he went on, feeling suddenly quite companionable; 'the Fitzpatricks didn't take such wonderful care of her that Charlotte need be bothering herself to put her in cotton wool at this time of day.'

Mrs Lambert crocheted on in silence for a few moments, inwardly counting her stitches till she came to the end of the row, then she withdrew the needle and scratched her head ruminatingly with it.

'Isn't it a strange thing, Roderick, what makes Charlotte have anyone staying in the house with her? I never remember such a thing to happen before.'

'She has to have her, and no thanks to her. Old Fitzpatrick's been doing bad business lately, and the little house he's had to take at Bray is a tight fit for themselves and the children; so, as he said to me, he thought it was time for Charlotte to do something for her own cousin's child, and no such great thanks to her either, seeing she got every halfpenny the old woman had.'

Mrs Lambert realised that she was actually carrying on a conversation with her husband, and nervously cast about in her mind for some response that should be both striking and stimulating.

'Well, now, if you want my opinion,' she said, shutting both her eyes and shaking her head with the peculiar arch sagacity of a dull woman, 'I wouldn't be surprised if Charlotte wasn't so sorry to have her here after all. Maybe she thinks she might snap up one of the officers – or there's young Charley Flood – or, Roderick!' Mrs Lambert almost giggled with delight and excitement – 'I wouldn't put it past Charlotte to be trying to ketch Mr Dysart.'

Roderick laughed in a disagreeable way.

'I'd wish her joy of him if she got him! A fellow that'd rather stick at home there at Bruff having tea with his sister than go down like any other fellow and play a game of pool at the hotel! A sort of chap that says,.if you offer him a whisky and soda in a friendly way, "Th – thanks – I don't c – care about anything at this t – t – time of day." I think Francie'd make him sit up!' Mr Lambert felt his imitation of Christopher Dysart's voice to be a success, and the shrill burst of laughter with which Mrs Lambert greeted it gave him for the moment an unusual tinge of respect for her intelligence. 'That's about the size of it, Lucy – what?'

'Oh, Roderick, how comical you are!' responded the dutiful turkey hen, wiping her watery eyes; 'it reminds me of the days when you used to bè talking of old Mr Mullen and Charlotte fighting in the office till I'd think I was listening to themselves.'

'God help the man that's got to fight with Charlotte, anyhow!' said Lambert, finishing his whisky and water as if toasting the sentiment; 'and talking of Charlotte, Lucy, you needn't mind about writing that note to her; I'll go over myself and speak to her in the morning.'

'Oh, yes, Roderick, 'twill be all right if you see herself, and you might say to her that I'll be expecting her to come in to tea.'

Mr Lambert, who had already taken up his newspaper again, merely grunted an assent. Mrs Lambert patiently folded her small bony hands upon her dog's back, and closing her eyes and opening her mouth, fell asleep in half a dozen breaths.

Her husband read his paper for a short time, while the subdued duet of snoring came continuously from the chair opposite. The clock struck nine in its sonorous, gentlemanlike voice, and at the sound Lambert threw down his paper as if an idea had occurred to him. He got up and went over to the window, and putting aside the curtains, looked out into the twilight of the June evening. The world outside was still awake, and the air was tender with the remembrance of the long day of sunshine and heat; a thrush was singing loudly down by the seringa bush at the end of the garden; the cattle were browsing and breathing audibly in the field beyond, and some children were laughing and shouting on the road. It seemed to Lambert much earlier than he had thought, and as he stood there, the invitation of the summer evening began

28

to appeal to him with seductive force; the quiet fields lay grey and mysterious under the pale western glow, and his eye travelled several times across them to a distant dark blot – the clump of trees and evergreens in which Tally Ho Lodge lay buried.

He turned from the window at last, and coming back into the lamplit room, surveyed it and its unconscious occupants with a feeling of intolerance for their unlovely slumber. His next step was the almost unprecedented one of changing his slippers for boots, and in a few minutes he had left the house.

6

Norry the Boat toiled up the back stairs with wrath in her heart. She had been listening for some minutes with grim enjoyment to cries from the landing upstairs; unavailing calls for Louisa, interspersed with the dumb galvanic quiver of a bell-less bellwire, and at last Francie's voice at the angle half way down the kitchen stairs had entreated her to find and despatch to her the missing Protestant orphan. Then Norry had said to herself, while she lifted the pot of potatoes off the fire, 'Throuble-the-house! God knows I'm heart-scalded with the whole o' yees!' And then aloud, 'She's afther goin' out to the dhryin' ground to throw out a few aper'ıns to blaych.'

'Well, I *must* have somebody; I can't get my habit on,' the voice had wailed in reply. 'Couldn't you come, Norry?'

As we have said, Norry ascended the stairs with wrath in her heart, as gruesome a lady's maid as could well be imagined, with an apron mottled with grease spots, and a stale smell of raw onions pervading her generally. Francie was standing in front of the dim looking glass with which Charlotte chastened the vanity of her guests, trying with stiff and tired fingers to drag the buttons of a brand new habit through the unyielding buttonholes that tailors alone have the gift of making, and Norry's anger was forgotten in prayerful horror, as her eyes wandered from the hard felt hat to the trousered ankle that appeared beneath the skimpy and angular skirt.

'The Lord look down in pity on thim that cut that petticoat!'
she said: 'Sure it's not out in the sthreets ye're goin' in the like o'
that! God knows it'd be as good for ye to be dhressed like a man
altogether!'

'I wouldn't care what I was dressed like if I could only make
the beastly thing meet,' said Francie, her face flushed with heat
and effort; 'wasn't I the fool to tell him to make it tight in the
waist!'

The subsequent proceedings were strenuous, but in the end
successful, and finally Miss Fitzpatrick walked stiffly downstairs,
looking very slender and tall, with the tail of the dark green habit
– she had felt green to be the colour consecrated to sport – drawn
tightly round her, and a silver horse-shoe brooch at her throat.

Charlotte was standing at the open hall door talking to Mr
Lambert.

'Come along, child,' she said genially, 'you've been so long
adorning yourself that nothing but his natural respect for the
presence of a lady kept this gentleman from indulging in abusive
language.'

Charlotte, in her lighter moods, was addicted to a ponderous
persiflage, the aristocratic foster-sister of her broader peasant
jestings in the manner of those whom she was fond of describing
as 'the *bar purple*'.

Mr Lambert did not trouble himself to reply to this sally. He
was looking at the figure in the olive-green habit that was advanc-
ing along the path of sunlight to the doorway, and thinking that
he had done well to write that letter on the subject of the riding
that Francie might expect to have at Lismoyle. Charlotte turned
her head also to look at the radiant, sunlit figure.

'Why, child, were you calling Norry just now to melt you
down and pour you into that garment? I never saw such a waist!
Take care and don't let her fall off, Roddy, or she'll snap in two!'
She laughed loudly and discordantly, looking to Mr Lambert's
groom for the appreciation that was lacking in the face of his
master; and during the arduous process of getting Miss Fitzpatrick into her saddle she remained on the steps, offering facetious suggestions and warnings, with her short arms akimbo, and
a smile that was meant to be jovial accentuating the hard lines of
her face.

At last the green habit was adjusted, the reins placed properly
between Francie's awkward fingers, and Mr Lambert had
mounted his long-legged young chestnut and was ready to start.

'Don't forget Lucy expects you to tea, Charlotte,' he said as he settled himself in his saddle.

'And don't you forget what I told you,' replied Charlotte, sinking her voice confidentially; 'don't mind her if she opens her mouth wide; it'll take less to shut it than ye'd think.'

Lambert nodded and rode after Francie, who, in compliance with the wishes of the black mare, had hurried on towards the gate. The black mare was a lady of character, well mannered but firm, and the mere sit of the saddle on her back told her that this was a case when it would be well to take matters into her own control; she accordingly dragged as much of the reins as she required from Francie's helpless hands, and by the time she had got on to the high road had given her rider to understand that her position was that of tenant at will.

They turned their backs on the town, and rode along the dazzling, dusty road, that radiated all the heat of a blazing afternoon.

'I think he did you pretty well with that habit,' remarked Lambert presently. 'What's the damage to be?'

'What do you think?' replied Francie gaily, answering one question with another after the manner of her country.

'Ten?'

'Ah, go on! Where'd I get ten pounds? He said he'd only charge me six because you recommended me, but I can tell him he'll have to wait for his money.'

'Why, are you hard up again?'

Francie looked up at him and laughed with unconcern that was not in the least affected.

'Of course I am! Did you ever know me that I wasn't?'

Lambert was silent for a moment or two, and half unconsciously his thoughts ran back over the time, six years ago now, when he had first met Francie. There had always been something exasperating to him in her brilliant indifference to the serious things of life. Her high spirits were as impenetrable as a coat of mail; her ignorance of the world was at once sublime and enraging. She had not seemed in the least impressed by the fact that he, whom up to this time she had known as merely a visitor at her uncle's house, a feature of the lawn-tennis tournament week, and a person with whom to promenade Merrion Square while the band was playing, was in reality a country gentleman, a J.P., and a man of standing, who owned as good horses as anyone in the county. She even seemed as impervious as ever to the pathos of his position in having thrown himself and his good looks away upon a plain woman six or seven years older than himself. All these things passed quickly through his mind, as if they found an accustomed groove there, and mingled acidly with the disturbing subconsciousness that the mare would inevitably come home with a sore back if her rider did not sit straighter than she was doing at present.

'Look here, Francie,' he said at last, with something of asperity, 'it's all very fine to humbug now, but if you don't take care you'll find yourself in the county court some fine day. It's easier to get there than you'd think,' he added gloomily, 'and then there'll be the devil to pay, and nothing to pay him with; and what'll you do then?'

'I'll send for you to come and bail me out!' replied Francie without hesitation, giving an unconsidered whack behind the saddle as she spoke. The black mare at once showed her sense of the liberty by kicking up her heels in a manner that lifted Francie a hand's-breadth from her seat, and shook her foot out of the stirrup. 'Gracious!' she gasped, when she had sufficiently recovered herself to speak; 'what did he do? Did he buck-jump? Oh, Mr Lambert – ' as the mare, satisfied with her protest, broke into a sharp trot, 'do stop him; I can't get my foot into the stirrup!'

Lambert, trotting serenely beside her on his tall chestnut, watched her precarious bumpings for a minute or two with a grin, then he stretched out a capable hand, and pulled the mare into a walk.

'Now, where would you be without me?' he inquired.

'Sitting on the road,' replied Francie. 'I never felt such a horrid rough thing – and look at Mrs Lambert looking at me over the wall! Weren't you a cad that you wouldn't stop him before!'

In the matter of exercise, Mrs Lambert was one of those people who want but little here below, nor want that little long. The tour of the two acres that formed the demesne of Rosemount was generally her limit, and any spare energy that remained to her after that perambulation was spent in taking weeds out of the garden path with a ladylike cane-handled spud. This implement was now in her gauntleted hand, and she waved it feebly to the riders as they passed, while Muffy stood in front of her and barked with asthmatic fury.

'Make Miss Fitzpatrick come in to tea on her way home, Roderick,' she called, looking admiringly at the girl with kind eyes that held no spark of jealousy of her beauty and youth. Mrs Lambert was one of the women who sink prematurely and un-

32

resistingly into the sloughs of middle age. For her there had been no intermediary period of anxious tracking of grey hairs, of fevered energy in the playing of lawn tennis and rounders; she had seen, with a feeling too sluggish to be respected as resignation, her complexion ascend the scale of colour from passable pink to the full sunset flush that now burned in her cheeks and spanned the sharp ridge of her nose; and she still, as she had always done, bought her expensive Sunday bonnet as she would have bought a piece of furniture, because it was handsome, not because it was becoming. The garden hat which she now wore could not pretend to either of these qualifications, and, as Francie looked at her, the contrast between her and her husband was as conspicuous as even he could have wished.

Francie's first remark, however, after they had passed by, seemed to show that her point of view was not the same as his.

'Won't she be very lonely there all the afternoon by herself?' she asked, with a backward glance at the figure in the garden hat.

'Oh, not she!' said Lambert carelessly, 'she has the dog and she'll potter about there as happy as possible. She's all right.' Then after a pause, in which the drift of Francie's question probably presented itself to him for the first time, 'I wish everyone was as satisfied with their life as she is.'

'How bad you are!' returned Francie, quite unmoved by the gloomy sentimental roll of Mr Lambert's eyes. 'I never heard a man talk such nonsense in my life!'

'My dear child,' said Lambert, with paternal melancholy, 'when you're my age – '

'Which I sha'n't be for the next fifteen years – ' interrupted Francie.

Mr Lambert checked himself abruptly, and looked cross.

'Oh, all right! If you're going to sit on me every time I open my mouth, I'd better shut up.'

Francie with some difficulty brought the black mare beside the chestnut, and put her hand for an instant on Lambert's arm.

'Ah now, don't be angry with me!' she said, with a glance whose efficacy she had often proved in similar cases; 'you know I was only funning.'

'I m not in the least angry with you,' replied Lambert coldly, though his eyes turned in spite of himself to her face.

'Oh, I know very well you're angry with me,' rejoined Francie, with unfeigned enjoyment of the situation; 'your mustash always gets as black as a coal when you're angry.'

The adornment referred to twitched, but its owner said nothing.

'There now, you're laughing!' continued Francie, 'but it's quite true; I remember the first time I noticed that, was the time you brought Mrs Lambert up to town about her teeth, and you took places at the Gaiety for the three of us – and oh! do you remember – ' leaning back and laughing whole-heartedly, 'she couldn't get her teeth in in time, and you wanted her to go without any, and she wouldn't, for fear she might laugh at the pantomime, and I had promised to go to the Dalkey Band that night with the Whittys, and then when you got up to our house and found you'd got the three tickets for nothing, you were so mad that when I came down into the parlour I declare I thought you'd been dyeing your mustash! Aunt Tish said afterwards it was because your face got so white, but *I* knew it was because you were in such a passion.'

'Well, I didn't like chucking away fifteen shillings a bit more than anyone else would,' said Lambert.

'Ah, well, we made it up, d'ye remember?' said Francie, regarding him with a laughing eye, in which there was a suspicion of sentiment; 'and after all, you were able to change the tickets to another night, and it was "Pinafore", and you laughed at me so awfully, because I cried at the part where the two lovers are saying goodbye to each other, and poor Mrs Lambert got her teeth in in a hurry to go with us, and she couldn't utter the whole night for fear they'd fall out.'

Perhaps the allusions to his wife's false teeth had a subtly soothing effect on Mr Lambert. He never was averse to anything that showed that other people were as conscious as he was of the disparity between his own admirable personal equipment and that of Mrs Lambert; it was another admission of the great fact that he had thrown himself away. His eyebrows and moustache became less truculent, he let himself down with a complete sarcasm on Francie's method of holding her whip, and, as they rode on, he permitted to himself the semi-proprietary enjoyment of an agent in pointing out boundaries, and landmarks, and improvements.

They had ridden at first under a pale green arch of roadside trees, with fields on either side full of buttercups and dog-daisies, a land of pasture and sleek cattle and neat stone walls. But in the second or third mile the face of the country changed. The blue lake that had lain in the distance like a long slab of *lapis lazuli*, was within two fields of them now, moving drowsily in and out

34

of the rocks, and over the coarse gravel of its shore. The trees had dwindled to ragged hazel and thorn bushes; the fat cows of the comfortable farms round Lismoyle were replaced by lean, dishevelled goats, and shelves and flags of grey limestone began to contest the right of the soil with the thin grass and the wiry brushwood. We have said grey limestone, but that hard-worked adjective cannot at all express the cold, pure blueness that these boulders take, under the sky of summer. Some word must yet be coined in which neither blue nor lilac shall have the supremacy, and in which the steely purple of a pigeon's breast shall not be forgotten.

The rock was everywhere. Even the hazels were at last squeezed out of existence, and inland, over the slowly swelling hills, it lay like the pavement of some giant city, that had been jarred from its symmetry by an earthquake. A mile away, on the farther side of this iron belt, a clump of trees rose conspicuously by the lake side, round a two-storeyed white house, and towards these trees the road wound its sinuous way. The grass began to show in larger and larger patches between the rocks, and the indomitable hazels crept again out of the crannies, and raised their low canopies over the heads of the browsing sheep and goats. A stream, brown with turf-mould, and fierce with battles with the boulders, made a boundary between the stony wilderness and the dark green pastures of Gurthnamuckla. It dashed under a high-backed little bridge with such excitement that the black mare, for all her intelligence, curved her neck, and sidled away from the parapet towards Lambert's horse.

Just beyond the bridge, a repulsive-looking old man was sitting on a heap of stones, turning over the contents of a dirty linen pouch. Beside him were an empty milk can, and a black and white dog which had begun by trying to be a collie, and had relapsed into an indifferent attempt at a greyhound. It greeted the riders with the usual volley of barking, and its owner let fall some of the coppers that he was counting over, in his haste to strike at it with the long stick that was lying beside him.

'Have done! Sailor! Blasht yer sowl! Have done!' then, with honeyed obsequiousness, 'Yer honour's welcome, Mr Lambert.'

'Is Miss Duffy in the house?' asked Lambert.

'She is, she is, yer honour,' he answered, in the nasal mumble peculiar to his class, getting up and beginning to shuffle after the horses; 'but what young lady is this at all? Isn't she very grand, God bless her!'

'She's Miss Fitzpatrick, Miss Mullen's cousin, Billy,' answered

Lambert graciously; approbation could not come from a source too low for him to be susceptible to it.

The old man came up beside Francie, and, clutching the skirt of her habit, blinked at her with sly and swimming eyes.

'Fitzpathrick is it? Begob I knew her grannema well; she was a fine hearty woman, the Lord have mercy on her! And she never seen me without she'd give me a shixpence or maybe a shillin'.'

Francie was skilled in the repulse of the Dublin beggar, but this ancestral precedent was something for which she was not prepared. The clutch tightened on her habit and the disgusting old face almost touched it, as Billy pressed close to her, mouthing out incomprehensible blessings and entreaties. She felt afraid of his red eyes and clawing fingers, and she turned helplessly to Lambert.

'Here, be off now, Billy, you old fool!' he said; 'we've had enough of you. Run and open the gate.'

The farm-house, with its clump of trees, was close to them, and its drooping iron entrance gate shrieked resentfully as the old man dragged it open.

7

Miss Julia Duffy, the tenant of Gurthnamuckla, was a woman of few friends. The cart track that led to her house was covered with grass, except for two brown ruts and a narrow footpath in the centre, and the boughs of the sycamores that grew on either side of it drooped low as if ignoring the possibility of a visitor. The house door remained shut from year's end to year's end, contrary to the usual kindly Irish custom; in fact, its rotten timbers were at once supported and barricaded by a diagonal beam that held them together, and was itself beginning to rot under its shroud of cobwebs. The footpath skirted the duckpond in front of the door, and led round the corner of the house to what had been in the palmy days of Gurthnamuckla the stableyard, and wound through its weedy heaps of dirt to the kitchen door.

Julia Duffy, looking back through the squalors of some sixty years, could remember the days when the hall door used to stand open from morning till night, and her father's guests were many and thirsty, almost as thirsty as he, though perhaps less persistently so. He had been a hard-drinking Protestant farmer, who had married his own dairy woman, a Roman Catholic, dirty, thriftless, and a cousin of Norry the Boat; and he had so disintegrated himself with whisky that his body and soul fell asunder at what was considered by his friends to be the premature age of seventy-two. Julia had always been wont to go to Lismoyle church with her father, not so much as a matter of religious as of social conviction. All the best bonnets in the town went to the parish church, and to a woman of Julia's stamp, whose poor relations wear hoods and shawls over their heads and go to chapel, there is no salvation out of a bonnet. After old John Duffy's death, however, bonnets and the aristocratic way of salvation seemed together to rise out of his daughter's scope. Chapel she despised with all the fervour of an Irish Protestant, but if the farm was to be kept and the rent paid, there was no money to spare for bonnets. Therefore Julia, in defiance of the entreaties of her mother's priest and her own parson, would have nothing of either chapel or church, and stayed sombrely at home. Marriage had never come near her; in her father's time the necessary dowry had not been forthcoming, and even her ownership of the farm was not enough to counterbalance her ill-looks and her pagan habits.

As in a higher grade of society science sometimes steps in when religion fails, so, in her moral isolation, Julia Duffy turned her attention to the mysteries of medicine and the culture of herbs. By the time her mother died she had established a position as doctor and wise woman, which was immensely abetted by her independence of the ministrations of any church. She was believed in by the people, but there was no liking in the belief; when they spoke to her they called her Miss Duffy, in deference to a now impalpable difference in rank as well as in recognition of her occult powers, and they kept as clear of her as they conveniently could. The payment of her professional services was a matter entirely in the hands of the people themselves, and ranged, according to the circumstances of the case, from a score of eggs or a can of buttermilk, to a crib of turf or 'the makings' of a homespun flannel petticoat. Where there was the possibility of a fee it never failed; where there was not, Julia Duffy gave her 'yerreb tay' (i.e. herb tea) and Holloway's pills without question or hesitation.

No one except herself knew how vital these offerings were to her. The farm was still hers, and, perhaps, in all her jealous unsunned nature, the only note of passion was her feeling for the twenty acres that, with the house, remained to her of her father's possessions. She had owned the farm for twenty years now, and had been the abhorrence and the despair of each successive Bruff agent. The land went from bad to worse; ignorance, neglect, and poverty are a formidable conjunction even without the moral support that the Land League for a few years had afforded her, and Miss Duffy tranquilly defied Mr Lambert, offering him at intervals such rent as she thought fitting, while she sub-let her mossy, deteriorated fields to a Lismoyle grazier. Perhaps her nearest approach to pleasure was the time at the beginning of each year when she received and dealt with the offers for the grazing; then she tasted the sweets of ownership, and then she condescended to dole out to Mr Lambert such payment 'on account' as she deemed advisable, confronting his remonstrances with her indisputable poverty, and baffling his threats with the recital of a promise that she should never be disturbed in her father's farm, made to her, she alleged, by Sir Benjamin Dysart, when she entered upon her inheritance.

There had been a time when a barefooted serving girl had suffered under Miss Duffy's rule; but for the last few years the times had been bad, the price of grazing had fallen, and the mistress's temper and the diet having fallen in a corresponding ratio, the bondwoman had returned to her own people and her father's house, and no successor had been found to take her place. That is to say, no recognised successor. But, as fate would have it, on the very day that 'Moireen Rhu' had wrapped her shawl about her head, and stumped, with cursings, out of the house of bondage, the vague stirrings that regulate the peram-bulations of beggars had caused Billy Grainy to resolve upon Gurthnamuckla as the place where he would, after the manner of his kind, ask for a walletful of potatoes and a night's shelter. A week afterwards he was still there, drawing water, bringing in turf, feeding the cow, and receiving, in return for these offices, his board and lodging and the daily dressing of a sore shin which had often coerced the most uncharitable to hasty and nauseated alms-giving. The arrangement glided into permanency, and Billy fell into a life of lazy routine that was preserved from stagnation by a daily expedition to Lismoyle to sell milk for Miss Duffy, and to do a little begging on his own account.

Gurthnamuckla had still about it some air of the older days, when Julia Duffy's grandfather was all but a gentleman and her drunken father and dairymaid mother were in their cradles. The tall sycamores that bordered the cart track were witnesses to the time when it had been an avenue, and the lawn-like field was yellow in spring with the daffodils of a former civilization. The tops of the trees were thick with nests, and the grave cawing of rooks made a background of mellow, serious respectability that had its effect even upon Francie. She said something to this intent as she and Lambert jogged along the grass by the track.

'Nice!' returned her companion with enthusiasm, 'I should think it was! I'd make that one of the sweetest little places in the country if I had it. There's no better grass for young horses anywhere, and there's first-class stabling. I can tell you you're not the only one that thinks it's a nice place,' he continued, 'but this old devil that has it won't give it up; she'd rather let the house rot to pieces over her head than go out of it.'

They rode past the barricaded hall door, and round the corner of the house into the yard, and Lambert called for Miss Duffy for some time in vain. Nothing responded except the turkey cock, who answered each call with an infuriated gobble, and a donkey, who, in the dark recesses of a cow house, lifted up his voice in heartrending rejoinder. At last a window fell down with a bang in the upper storey, and the mistress of the house put out her head. Francie had only time to catch a glimpse of a thin dirty face, a hooked nose, and unkempt black hair, before the vision was withdrawn, and a slipshod step was heard coming downstairs.

When Miss Duffy appeared at her kitchen door, she had flung a shawl round her head, possibly to conceal the fact that her crinkled mat of hair held thick in it, like powder, the turf ashes of many sluttish days. Her stained and torn black skirt had evidently just been unpinned from about her waist, and was hitched up at one side, showing a frayed red Galway petticoat, and that her feet had recently been thrust into her boots was attested by the fact that their laces trailed on the ground beside her. In spite of these disadvantages, however, it was with a manner of the utmost patronage that she greeted Mr Lambert.

'I would ask you and the young leedy to dismount,' she continued, in the carefully genteel voice that she clung to in the wreck of her fortunes, 'but I am, as you will see,' she made a gesture with a dingy hand, 'quite "in dishabilly", as they say; I've been a little indisposed, and – '

'Oh, no matter, Miss Duffy,' interrupted Lambert, 'I only wanted to say a few words to you on business, and Miss Fitzpatrick will ride about the place till we're done.'

Miss Duffy's small black eyes turned quickly to Francie.

'Oh, indeed, is that Miss Fitzpatrick? My fawther knew her grandfawther. I am much pleased to make her acquaintance.'

She inclined her head as she spoke, and Francie, with much disposition to laugh, bowed hers in return; each instant Miss Duffy's resemblance, both in feature and costume, to a beggar woman who frequented the corner of Sackville Street, was becoming harder to bear with fortitude, and she was delighted to leave Lambert to his *tête-à-tête* and ride out into the lawn, among the sycamores and hawthorns, where the black mare immediately fell to devouring grass with a resolve that was quite beyond Francie's power to combat.

She broke a little branch off a low-growing ash tree, to keep away the flies that were doing their best to spoil the pleasure of a perfect afternoon, and sat there, fanning herself lazily, while the mare, with occasional impatient tugs at the reins and stampings at the flies, cropped her way onwards from one luscious tuft to another. The Lismoyle grazier's cattle had collected themselves under the trees at the farther end of the lawn, where a swampy pool still remained of the winter encroachments of the lake. In the sunshine at the other side of the wall, a chain of such pools stretched to the broad blue water, and grey limestone rocks showed above the tangle of hemlock and tall spikes of magenta foxgloves. A white sail stood dazzlingly out in the turquoise blue of a band of calm, and the mountains on the farther side of the lake were palely clothed in thinnest lavender and most ethereal green.

It might have been the unexpected likeness that she had found in Julia Duffy to her old friend the beggar woman that took Francie's thoughts away from this idyll of perfected summer to the dry, grey Dublin streets that had been her uttermost horizon a week ago. The milkman generally called at the Fitzpatricks' house at about this hour; the clank of his pint measure against the area railings, even his pleasantries with Maggie the cook, relative to his bestowing an extra 'sup for the cat', were suddenly and sharply present with her. The younger Fitzpatrick children would be home from school, and would be raging through the kitchen seeking what they might devour in the interval before the six

o'clock dinner, and she herself would probably have been engaged in a baking game of tennis in the square outside her uncle's
house. She felt very sorry for Aunt Tish when she thought of that
hungry gang of sons and daughters and of the evil days that had
come upon the excellent and respectable Uncle Robert, and the
still more evil days that would come in another fortnight or so,
when the whole bursting party had squeezed themselves into a
little house at Bray, there to exist for an indefinite period on Irish
stew, strong tea, and a diminished income. There was a kind of
understanding that when they were 'settled' she was to go back
to them, and blend once more her five and twenty pounds a year
with the Fitzpatrick funds; but this afternoon, with the rich
summer stillness and the blaze of buttercups all about her, and
the unfamiliar feeling of the mare's restless shoulder under her
knee, she was exceedingly glad that the settling process would
take some months at least. She was not given to introspection,
and could not have said anything in the least interesting about
her mental or moral atmosphere; she was too uneducated and
too practical for any self-communings of this kind; but she was
quite certain of two things, that in spite of her affection for the
Fitzpatricks she was very glad she was not going to spend the
summer in Dublin or Bray, and also, that in spite of certain
bewildering aspects of her cousin Charlotte, she was beginning to
have what she defined to herself as 'a high old time'.

It was somewhere about this period in her meditations that she
became aware of a slight swishing and puffing sound from the
direction of the lake, and a steam launch came swiftly along close
under the shore. She was a smart-looking boat, spick and span
as white paint and a white funnel with a brass band could make
her, and in her were seated two men; one, radiant in a red and
white blazer, was steering, while the other, in clothes to which
even distance failed to lend enchantment, was menially engaged in
breaking coals with a hammer. The boughs of the trees intervened
exasperatingly between Francie and this glittering vision, and the
resolve to see it fully lent her the power to drag the black mare
from her repast, and urge her forward to an opening where she
could see and be seen, two equally important objects.

She had instantly realized that these were those heroes of
romance, 'the Lismoyle officers', the probabilities of her alliance
with one of whom had been the subject of some elegant farewell
badinage on the part of her bosom friend, Miss Fanny Hemphill.
Francie's acquaintance with the British army had hitherto been
limited to one occasion when, at a Sandymount evening band

41

performance, 'one of the officers from Beggars' Bush Barracks' –
so she had confided to Miss Hemphill – had taken off his hat to
her, and been very polite until Aunt Tish had severely told him
that no true gentleman would converse with a lady without she
was presented to him, and had incontinently swept her home. She
could see them quite plainly now, and from the fact that the man
who had been rooting among the coals was now sitting up, evidently at the behest of the steersman, and looking at her, it was
clear that she had attracted attention too. Even the black mare
pricked her ears, and stared at this new kind of dragon-fly
creature that went noisily by, leaving a feathery smear on the air
behind it, and just then Mr Lambert rode out of the stableyard,
and looked about him for his charge.

'Francie!' he called with perceptible impatience; 'what are you
at down there?'

The steam launch had by this time passed the opening, and
Francie turned and rode towards him. Her hat was a good deal
on the back of her head, and her brilliant hair caught the sunshine; the charm of her supple figure atoned for the crookedness
of her seat, and her eyes shone with an excitement born of the
delightful sight of soldiery.

'Oh, Mr Lambert, weren't those the officers?' she cried, as he
rode up to her; 'which was which? Haven't they a grand little
steamer?'

Lambert's temper had apparently not been improved by his
conversation with Julia Duffy; instead of answering Miss Fitzpatrick he looked at her with a clouded brow, and in his heart he
said, 'Damn the officers!'

'I wonder which of them is the captain?' continued Francie; 'I
suppose it is the little fair one; he was much the best dressed, and
he was making the other one do all the work.'

Lambert gave a scornful laugh.

'I'll leave you to find that out for yourself. I'll engage it won't
be long before you know all about them. You've made a good
start already.'

'Oh, very well,' replied Francie, letting fall both the reins in
order to settle her hat: 'some day you'll be asking me something,
and I won't tell you, and then you'll be sorry.'

'Someday you'll be breaking your neck, and then *you'll* be
sorry,' retorted Lambert, taking up the fallen reins.

They rode out of the gate of Gurthnamuckla in silence, and
after a mile of trotting, which was to Francie a period of mingled
pain and anxiety, the horses slackened of their own accord, and

42

began to pick their way gingerly over the smooth sheets of rock that marked the entry of the road into the stony tract mentioned in the last chapter. Francie took the opportunity for a propitiatory question.

'What were you and the old woman talking about all that time? I thought you were never coming.'

'Business,' said Lambert shortly; then viciously, 'if any conversation with a woman can ever be called business.'

'Oho! then you couldn't get her to do what you wanted!' laughed Francie; 'very good for you too! I think you always get your own way.'

'Is that your opinion?' said Lambert, turning his dark eyes upon her; 'I'm sorry I can't agree with you.'

The fierce heat had gone out of the afternoon as they passed along the lonely road, through the country of rocks and hazel bushes; the sun was sending low flashes into their eyes from the bright mirror of the lake; the goats that hopped uncomfortably about in the enforced and detested *téte-à-téte* caused by a wooden yoke across their necks, cast blue shadows of many-legged absurdity on the warm slabs of stone; a carrion crow, swaying on the thin topmost bough of a thorn bush, a blot in the mellow afternoon sky, was looking about him if haply he could see a wandering kid whose eyes would serve him for his supper; and a couple of miles away, at Rosemount, Mrs Lambert was sending down to be kept hot what she and Charlotte had left of the Sally Lunn.

Francie was not sorry when she found herself again under the trees of the Lismoyle highroad, and in spite of the injuries which the pommels of the saddle were inflicting upon her, and the growing stiffness of all her muscles, she held gallantly on at a sharp trot, till her hair pins and her hat were loosed from their foundations, and her green habit rose in ungainly folds. They were nearing Rosemount when they heard wheels behind them. Lambert took the left side of the road, and the black mare followed his example with such suddenness, that Francie, when she had recovered her equilibrium, could only be thankful that nothing more than her hat had come off. With the first instinct of woman she snatched at the coils of hair that fell down her back and hung enragingly over her eyes, and tried to wind them on to her head again. She became horribly aware that a waggonette with several people in it had pulled up beside her, and, finally, that a young man with a clean-shaved face and an eyeglass was handing her her hat and taking off his own.

Holding in her teeth the few hair pins that she had been able to save from the wreck, she stammered a gratitude that she was far from feeling; and when she heard Lambert say, 'Oh, thank you, Dysart, you just saved me getting off,' she felt that her discomfiture was complete.

8

Christopher Dysart was a person about whom Lismoyle and its neighbourhood had not been able to come to a satisfactory conclusion, unless, indeed, that conclusion can be called satisfactory which admitted him to be a disappointment. From the time that, as a shy, plain little boy he first went to school, and, after the habit of boys, ceased to exist except in theory and holidays, a steady undercurrent of interest had always set about him. His mother was so charming, and his father so delicate, and he himself so conveniently contemporary with so many daughters, that although the occasional glimpses vouchsafed of him during his Winchester and Oxford career were as discouraging as they were brief, it was confidently expected that he would emerge from his boyish shyness when he came to take his proper place in the county and settle down at Bruff. Thus Lady Eyrefield, and Mrs Waller, and their like, the careful mothers of those contemporaneous daughters, and thus also, after their kind, the lesser ladies of Lismoyle.

But though Christopher was now seven and twenty he seemed as far from 'taking his place in the county' as he had ever been. His mother's friends had no particular fault to find with him; that was a prominent feature in their dissatisfaction. He was quite good looking enough for an eldest son, and his politeness to their daughters left them nothing to complain of except the discouraging fact that it was exceeded by his politeness to themselves. His readiness to talk when occasion demanded was undisputed, but his real or pretended dullness in those matters of local interest, which no one except an outsider calls gossip, made conversation with him a hollow and heartless affair. One of his most exasperating points was that he could not be referred to any known type. He was 'between the sizes', as shopmen say of gloves. He was not smart and aggressive enough for the soldiering type, nor sporting enough for the country gentleman, but neither had he the docility and attentiveness of the ideal curate; he could not even be lightly disposed of as an eccentricity, which would have been some sort of consolation.

'If I ever could have imagined that Isabel Dysart's son would have turned out like this,' said the Dowager Lady Eyrefield, in a moment of bitterness, 'I should not have given myself the trouble of writing to Castlemore about taking him out as his secretary. I thought all those functions and dinner parties would have done something for him, but though they polished up his manners, and improved that most painful and unfortunate stutter, he's at heart just as much a stick as ever.'

Lismoyle was, according to its lights, equally nonplussed. Mrs Baker had, indeed, suggested that it was sending him to these grand English universities, instead of to Trinity College, Dublin, that had taken thè fun out of him in the first going off, and what finished him was going out to those Barbadoes, with all the blacks bowing down to him, and his liver growing the size of I don't know what with the heat. Mrs Corkran, the widow of the late rector of Lismoyle, had, however, rejoined that she had always found Mr Dysart a most humble-minded young man on the occasions when she had met him at his cousin Mrs Gascogne's, and by no means puffed up with his rank or learning. This proposition Mrs Baker had not attempted to dispute, but none the less she had felt it to be beside the point. She had not found that Christopher's learning had disposed him to come to her tennis parties, and she did not feel humility to be a virtue that graced a young man of property. Certainly, in spite of his humility, she could not venture to take him to task for his neglect of her entertainments as she could Mr Hawkins; but then it is still more certain that Christopher would not, as Mr Hawkins had often done, sit down before her, as before a walled town, and so skilfully entreat her that in five minutes all would have been forgiven and forgotten.

It was, perhaps, an additional point of aggravation that, dull and unprofitable though he was considered to be, Christopher had amusements of his own in which the neighbourhood had no part. Since he had returned from the West Indies, his three-ton cutter with the big Una sail had become one of the features of the lake, but though a red parasol was often picturesquely visible above the gunwale, the knowledge that it sheltered his sister deprived it of the almost painful interest that it might otherwise have had, and at the same time gave point to a snub that was unintentionally effective and comprehensive. There were many sunny mornings on which Mr Dysart's camera occupied commanding positions in the town, or its outskirts, while its owner photographed groups of old women and donkeys, regardless of the fact that Miss Kathleen Baker, in her most becoming hat, had taken her younger sister from the schoolroom to play a showy game of lawn tennis in the garden in front of her father's villa, or was, with Arcadian industry, cutting buds off the roses that dropped their pink petals over the low wall on to the road. It was quite inexplicable that the photographer should pack up his camera and walk home without taking advantage of this artistic opportunity beyond a civil lift of his cap; and at such times Miss Baker would re-enter the villa with a feeling of contempt for Mr Dysart that was almost too deep for words.

She might have been partially consoled had she known that on a June morning not long after the latest of these repulses, her feelings were fully shared by the person whom, for the last two Sundays, she had looked at in the Dysart pew with a respectful dislike that implied the highest compliment in her power. Miss Evelyn Hope-Drummond stood at the bow-window of the Bruff drawing room and looked out over the gravelled terrace, across the flower garden and the sunk fence, to the clump of horse chestnuts by the lake side. Beyond these the cattle were standing knee-deep in the water, and on the flat margin a pair of legs in white flannel trousers was all that the guest, whom his mother delighted to honour, could see of Christopher Dysart. The remainder of him wrestled beneath a black velvet pall wth the helplessly wilful legs of his camera, and all his mind, as Miss Hope-Drummond well knew, was concentrated upon cows. Her first visit to Ireland was proving less amusing than she had expected, she thought, and as she watched Christopher she wished fervently that she had not offered to carry any of his horrid things across the park for him. In the flower garden below the terrace she could see Lady Dysart and Pamela in deep consultation over an infirm rose-tree; a wheelbarrow full of pans of seedlings sufficiently indicated what their occupation would be for the rest of the morning, and she felt it was of a piece with the absurdities of Irish life that the ladies cf the house should enjoy doing the gardener's work for him. The strong scent of heated Gloire de Dijon roses came through the window, and suggested to her how well one of them would suit with her fawn-coloured Redfern gown, and she leaned out to pick a beautiful bud that was swaying in the sun just within reach.

'Ha – a – ah! I see ye, missy! Stop picking my flowers! Push, James Canavan, you devil, you! Push!'

A bath-chair, occupied by an old man in a tall hat, and pushed by a man also in a tall hat, had suddenly turned the corner of the house, and Miss Hope-Drummond drew back precipitately to avoid the uplifted walking-stick of Sir Benjamin Dysart.

'Oh, fie, for shame, Sir Benjamin!' exclaimed the man who had been addressed as James Canavan. 'Pray, cull the rose, miss,' he continued, with a flourish of his hand; 'sweets to the sweet!'

Sir Benjamin aimed a backward stroke with his oak stick at his attendant, a stroke in which long practice had failed to make him perfect, and in the exchange of further amenities the party passed out of sight. This was not Miss Hope-Drummond's first meeting with her host. His bath-chair had daily, as it seemed to her, lain in wait in the shrubberies, to cause terror to the solitary, and discomfiture to *tête-à-têtes*; and on one morning he had stealthily protruded the crook of his stick from the door of his room as she went by, and all but hooked her round the ankle with it.

'Really, it is disgraceful that he is not locked up,' she said to herself crossly, as she gathered the contested bud, and sat down to write letters; 'but in Ireland no one seems to think anything of anything!'

It was very hot down in the garden where Lady Dysart and Pamela were at work; Lady Dysart kneeling in the inadequate shade of a parasol, whose handle she had propped among the pans in the wheelbarrow, and Pamela weeding a flowerbed a few yards away. It was altogether a scene worthy in its domestic simplicity of the Fairchild Family, only that instead of Mr Fairchild, 'stretched on the grass at a little distance with his book', a bronze-coloured dachshund lay roasting his long side in the sun; and also that Lady Dysart, having mistaken the young chickweed in a seedling pan for the asters that should have been there, was filling her bed symmetrically with the former, an imbecility that Mrs Sherwood would never have permitted in a parent. The mother and daughter lifted their heads at the sound of the conflict on the terrace.

'Papa will frighten Evelyn into a fit,' observed Pamela, rubbing a midge off her nose with an earthy gardening glove; 'I wish James Canavan could be induced to keep him away from the house.'

'It's all right, dear,' said Lady Dysart, panting a little as she straightened her back and surveyed her rows of chickweed; 'Christopher is with her, and you know he never notices anyone else when Christopher is there.'

Lady Dysart had in her youth married, with a little judicious coercion, a man thirty years older than herself, and after a long and, on the whole, extremely unpleasant period of matrimony, she was now enjoying a species of Indian summer, dating from six years back, when Christopher's coming of age and the tenants' rejoicings thereat, had caused such a paroxysm of apoplectic jealousy on the part of Christopher's father as, combining with the heat of the day, had brought on a 'stroke'. Since then the bath-chair and James Canavan had mercifully intervened between him and the rest of the world, and his offspring were now able to fly before him with a frankness and success impossible in the old days.

Pamela did not answer her mother at once.

'Do you know I'm afraid Christopher isn't with her,' she said, looking both guilty and perturbed.

Lady Dysart groaned aloud.

'Why, where is he?' she demanded. 'I left Evelyn helping him to paste in photographs after breakfast; I thought that would have been nice occupation for them for at least two hours; but as for Christopher –' she continued, her voice deepening to declamation, 'it is quite hopeless to expect anything from him. I should rather trust Garry to entertain anyone. The day *he* took her out in the boat they weren't in till six o'clock!'

'That was because Garry ran the punt on the shallow, and they had to wade ashore and walk all the way round.'

'That has nothing to say to it; at all events they had something to talk about when they came back, which is more than Christopher has when he has been out sailing. It is *most* disheartening; I ask nice girls to the house, but I might just as well ask nice boys – Oh, of course, yes – ' in answer to a protest from her daughter; 'he *talks* to them; but you know quite well what I mean.'

This complaint was not the first indication of Lady Dysart's sentiments about this curious son whom she had produced. She was a clever woman, a renowned solver of the acrostics in her society paper, and a holder of strong opinions as to the prophetic meaning of the Pyramids; but Christopher was an acrostic in a strange language, an enigma beyond her sphere. She had a vague but rooted feeling that young men were normally in love with somebody, or at least pretending to be so; it was, of course, an excellent thing that Christopher did not lose his heart to the wrong people, but she would probably have preferred the agitation of watching his progress through the most alarming flirtations to the security that deprived conversation with other mothers of much of its legitimate charm.

'Well, there was Miss Fetherstone,' began Pamela after a moment of obvious consideration.

'Miss Fetherstone!' echoed Lady Dysart in her richest contralto, fixing eyes of solemn reproach upon her daughter, 'do you suppose that for one instant I thought there was anything in that? No baby, no *idiot* baby, could have believed in it!'

'Well, I don't know,' said Pamela; 'I think you and Mrs Waller believed in it, at least I remember you both settling what your wedding presents were to be!'

'*I* never said a word about wedding presents, it was Mrs Waller! Of course she was anxious about her own niece, just as *anybody* would have been under the circumstances.' Lady Dysart here became aware of something in Pamela's expression that made her add hurriedly, 'Not that I ever had the faintest shadow of belief in it. Too well do I know Christopher's platonic philanderings; and you see the affair turned out just as I said it would.'

Pamela refrained from pursuing her advantage.

'If you like I'll make him come with Evelyn and me to the choir practice this afternoon,' she said after a pause. 'Of course he'll hate it, poor boy, especially as Miss Mullen wrote to me the other day and asked us to come to tea after it was over.'

'Oh, yes!' said Lady Dysart with sudden interest and forgetfulness of her recent contention, 'and you will see the new importation whom we met with Mr Lambert the other day. What a charming young creature she looked! "The fair one with the golden locks" was the only description for her! And yet that miserable Christopher will only say that she is "chocolate-boxey!" Oh! I have no patience with Christopher's affectation!' she ended, rising from her knees and brushing the earth from her extensive lap with a gesture of annoyance. She began to realize that the sun was hot and luncheon late, and it was at this unpropitious moment that Pamela, having finished the flowerbed she had been weeding, approached the scene of her mother's labours.

'Mamma,' she said faintly, 'you have planted the whole bed with chickweed!'

9

It had been hard work pulling the punt across from Bruff to Lismoyle with two well-grown young women sitting in the stern; it had been a hot walk up from the landing place to the church, but worse than these, transcendently worse, in that it involved the suffering of the mind as well as the body, was the choir practice. Christopher's long nose drooped despondingly over his Irish church hymnal, and his long back had a disconsolate hoop in it as he leaned it against the wall in his place in the backmost row of the choir benches. The chants had been long and wearisome, and the hymns were proving themselves equally enduring. Christopher was not eminently musical or conspicuously religious, and he regarded with a kind of dismal respect and surprise the fervour in Pamela's pure profile as she turned to Mrs Gascogne and suggested that the hymn they had just gone through twice should be sung over again. He supposed it was because she had High Church tendencies that she was able to stand this sort of thing, and his mind drifted into abstract speculations as to how people could be as good as Pamela was and live.

In the interval before the last hymn he derived a temporary solace from finding his own name inscribed in dull red characters in the leaf of his hymnbook, with, underneath in the same colour, the fateful inscription, 'Written in blood by Garrett Dysart'. The thought of his younger brother utilizing pleasantly a cut finger and the long minutes of the archdeacon's sermon, had for the moment inspired Christopher with a sympathetic amusement, but he had relapsed into his pristine gloom. He knew the hymn perfectly well by this time, and his inoffensive tenor joined mechanically with the other voices, while his eyes roamed idly over the two rows of people in front of him. There was nothing suggestive of ethereal devotion about Pamela's neighbours. Miss Mullen's heaving shoulders and extended jaw spoke of nothing but her determination to outscream everyone else; Miss Hope-Drummond and the curate, on the bench in front of him, were singing

50

primly out of the same hymnbook, the curate obviously frightened, Miss Hope-Drummond as obviously disgusted. The Misses Beattie were furtively eyeing Miss Hope-Drummond's costume; Miss Kathleen Baker was openly eyeing the curate, whose hymnbook she had been wont to share at happier choir practices, and Miss Fitzpatrick, seated at the end of the row, was watching from the gallery window with unaffected interest the progress of the usual weekly hostilities between Pamela's dachshund and the sexton's cat, and was not even pretending to occupy herself with the business in hand. Christopher's eyes rested on her appraisingly, with the minute observation of short sight, fortified by an eyeglass, and was aware of a small head with a fluffy halo of conventionally golden hair, a straight and slender neck, and an appleblossom curve of cheek; he found himself wishing that she would turn a little further round.

The hymn had seven verses, and Pamela and Mrs Gascogne were going inexorably through them all; the schoolmaster and schoolmistress, an estimable couple, sole prop of the choir on wet Sundays, were braying brazenly beside him, and this was only the second hymn. Christopher's D sharp melted into a yawn, and before he could screen it with his hymnbook, Miss Fitzpatrick looked round and caught him in the act. A suppressed giggle and a quick lift of the eyebrows instantly conveyed to him that his sentiments were comprehended and sympathized with, and he as instantly was conscious that Miss Mullen was following the direction of her niece's eye. Lady Dysart's children did not share her taste for Miss Mullen; Christopher vaguely felt some offensive flavour in the sharp smiling glance in which she included him and Francie, and an unexplainable sequence of thought made him suddenly decide that her niece was as second-rate as might have been expected.

Never had the choir dragged so hopelessly; never had Mrs Gascogne and Pamela compelled their victims to deal with so many and difficult tunes, and never at any previous choir practice had Christopher registered so serious a vow that under no pretext whatever should Pamela entice him there again. They were all sitting down now, while the leaders consulted together about the Kyrie, and the gallery cushions slowly turned to stone in their well-remembered manner. Christopher's ideas of church going were inseparably bound up with those old gallery cushions. He had sat upon them ever since, as a small boy, he had chirped a treble beside his governess, and he knew every knob in their anatomy. There is something blighting to the devotional tenden-

51

cies in the atmosphere of a gallery. He had often formulated this theory for his own exculpation, lying flat on his back in a punt in some shady backwater, with the Oxford church bells reminding him reproachfully of Lismoyle Sundays, and of Pamela – the faithful, conscientious Pamela – whipping up the pony to get to church before the bell stopped. Now, after a couple of months' renewed acquaintance with the choir, the theory had hardened into a tedious truism, and when at last Christopher's long legs were free to carry him down the steep stairs, the malign influence of the gallery had brought their owner to the verge of free thought.

He did not know how it had happened or by whose disposition of the forces it had been brought about, but when Miss Mullen's tea party detached itself from the other members of the choir at the churchyard gate, Pamela and Miss Hope-Drummond were walking on either side of their hostess, and he was behind with Miss Fitzpatrick.

'You don't appear very fond of hymns, Mr Dysart,' began Francie at once, in the pert Dublin accent that, rightly or wrongly, gives the idea of familiarity.

'People aren't supposed to look about them in church,' replied Christopher with the peculiar suavity which, combined with his disconcerting infirmity of pausing before he spoke, had often baffled the young ladies of Barbadoes, and had acquired for him the reputation, perhaps not wholly undeserved, of being a prig.

'Oh, I daresay!' said Francie; 'I suppose that's why you sit in the back seat, that no one'll see you doing it!'

There was a directness about this that Lismoyle would not have ventured on, and Christopher looked down at his companion with an increase of interest.

'No; I sit there because I can go to sleep.'

'Well, and do you? and who do you get to wake you?' – her quick voice treading sharply on the heels of his quiet one. 'I used always to have to sit beside Uncle Robert in church to pinch him at the end of the sermon.'

'*I* find it very hard to wake at the end of the sermon too,' remarked Christopher, with an experimental curiosity to see what Miss Mullen's unexpected cousin would say next.

'Do y' indeed?' said Francie, flashing a look at him of instant comprehension and complete *sang froid*. 'I'll lend the school-mistress a hat pin if you like! What on earth makes men so sleepy in church I don't know,' she continued; 'at our church in Dublin I used to be looking at them. All the gentlemen sit in the corner seat next the aisle, because they're the most comfortable, y' know, and from the minute the clergyman gives out the text – ' she made a little gesture with her hand, showing thereby that half the buttons were off her glove – 'they're snoring!'

How young she was, and how pretty, and how inexpressibly vulgar! Christopher thought all these things in turn, while he did what in him lay to continue the conversation in the manner expected of him. The effort was perhaps not very successful, as, after a few minutes, it was evident that Francie was losing her first freedom of discourse, and was casting about for topics more appropriate to what she had heard of Mr Dysart's mental and literary standard.

'I hear you're a great photographer, Mr Dysart,' she began. 'Miss Mullen says you promised to take a picture of her and her cats, and she was telling me to remind you of it. Isn't it awfully clever of you to be able to do it?'

To this form of question reply is difficult, especially when it is put with all the good faith of complete ignorance. Christopher evaded the imbecilities of direct response.

'I shall think myself awfully clever if I photograph the cats,' he said.

'Clever!' she caught him up with a little shriek of laughter. 'I can tell you you'll want to be clever! Are you able to photograph up the chimney or under Norry's bed? for that's where they always run when a man comes into the house, and if you try to stop them they'd claw the face off you! Oh, they're terrors!'

'It's very good of you to tell me all this in time,' Christopher said, with a rather absent laugh. He was listening to Miss Mullen's voice, and realizing, for the first time, what it would be to live under the same roof with her and her cats; and yet this girl seemed quite light-hearted and happy. 'Perhaps, on the whole, I'd better stay away?' he said, looking at her, and feeling in the sudden causeless way in which often the soundest conclusions are arrived at, how vast was the chasm between her ideal of life and his own, and linking with the feeling a pity that would have been self sufficient if it had not also been perfectly simple.

'Ah! don't say you won't come and take the cats!' Francie exclaimed.

They reached the Tally Ho gate as she spoke, and the others were only a step or two in front of them. Charlotte looked over her shoulder with a benign smile.

'What's this I hear about taking my cats?' she said jovially. 'You're welcome to everything in my house, Mr Dysart, but I'll set the police on you if you take my poor cats!'

'Oh, but I assure you – '

'He's only going to photo them,' said Christopher and Francie together.

'Do you hear them, Miss Dysart?' continued Charlotte, fumbling for her latch key, 'conspiring together to rob a poor lone woman of her only livestock!'

She opened the door, and as her visitors entered the hall they caught a glance of Susan's large, stern countenance regarding them with concentrated suspicion through the rails of the staircase.

'My beauty-boy!' shouted his mistress, as he vanished upstairs. 'Steal him if you can, Mr Dysart!'

Miss Hope-Drummond looked rather more uninterested than is usual in polite society. When she had left the hammock, slung in the shade beside the tennis ground at Bruff, it had not been to share Mr Corkran's hymnbook; still less had it been to walk from the church to Tally Ho between Pamela and a woman whom, from having regarded as merely *outrée* and incomprehensible, she had now come to look upon as rather impertinent. Irish society was intolerably mixed, she decided, as she sniffed the various odours of the Tally Ho hall, and, with some sub-connection of ideas, made up her mind that photography was a detestable and silly pursuit for men. While these thoughts were passing beneath her accurately curled fringe, Miss Mullen opened the drawing-room door, and, as they walked in, a short young man in light grey clothes arose from the most comfortable chair to greet them.

There was surprise and disfavour in Miss Mullen's eye as she extended her hand to him.

'This is an unexpected pleasure, Mr Hawkins,' she said.

'Yes,' answered Mr Hawkins cheerfully, taking the hand and doing his best to shake it at the height prescribed by existing fashion, 'I thought it would be; Miss Fitzpatrick asked me to come in this afternoon; didn't you?' addressing himself to Francie. 'I got rather a nasty jar when I heard you were all out, but I thought I'd wait for a bit. I knew Miss Dysart always gives 'em fits at the choir practice. All the same, you know, I should have begun to eat the cake if you hadn't come in.'

The round table in the middle of the room was spread, in Louisa's accustomed fashion, as if for breakfast, and in the centre was placed a cake, coldly decked in the silver paper trappings that it had long worn in the grocer's window.

' 'Twas well for you you didn't!' said Francie, with, as it seemed to Christopher, a most familiar and challenging laugh.

'Why?' inquired Hawkins, looking at her with a responsive eye. 'What would you have done?'

'Plenty,' returned Francie unhesitatingly; 'enough to make you sorry anyway!'

Mr Hawkins looked delighted, and was opening his mouth for a suitable rejoinder, when Miss Mullen struck in sharply:

'Francie, go tell Louisa that I suppose she expects us to stir our tea with our fingers, for there's not a spoon on the table.'

'Oh, let me go,' said Hawkins, springing to open the door; 'I know Louisa; she was very kind to me just now. She hunted all the cats out of the room.' Francie was already in the hall, and he followed her.

The search for Louisa was lengthy, involving much calling for her by Francie, with falsetto imitations by Mr Hawkins, and finally a pause, during which it might be presumed that the pantry was being explored. Pamela brought her chair nearer to Miss Mullen, who had begun wrathfully to stir her tea with the sugar tongs, and entered upon a soothing line of questions as to the health and number of the cats; and Christopher, having cut the grocer's cake, and found that it was the usual conglomerate of tallow, sawdust, bad eggs, and gravel, devoted himself to thick bread and butter, and to conversation with Miss Hope-Drummond. The period of second cups was approaching, when laughter, and a jingle of falling silver in the hall, told that the search for Louisa was concluded, and Francie and Mr Hawkins re-entered the drawing room, the latter endeavouring, not unsuccessfully, to play the bones with four of Charlotte's best electroplated teaspoons, while his brown boots moved in the furtive rhythm of an imaginary breakdown. Miss Mullen did not even raise her eyes, and Christopher and Miss Hope-Drummond continued their conversation unmoved; only Pamela acknowledged the histrionic intention with a sympathetic but nervous smile. Pamela's finger was always instinctively on the pulse of the person to whom she was talking, and she knew better than either Francie or Hawkins that they were in disgrace.

'I'd be obliged to you for those teaspoons, Mr Hawkins, when you've quite done with them,' said Charlotte, with an ugly look at the chief offender's self-satisfied countenance; 'it's a good thing no one except myself takes sugar in their tea.'

'We couldn't help it,' replied Mr Hawkins, unabashed; 'Louisa was out for a walk with her young man, and Miss Fitzpatrick and I had to polish up the teaspoons ourselves.'

Charlotte received this explanation and the teaspoons in silence as she poured out the delinquents' tea; there were moments when she permitted herself the satisfaction of showing disapproval if she felt it. Francie accepted her cousin's displeasure philosophically, only betraying her sense of the situation by the expressive eye which she turned towards her companion in disgrace over the rim of her teacup. But Mr Hawkins rose to the occasion. He gulped his tepid and bitter cup of tea with every appearance of enjoyment, and having arranged his small moustache with a silk handkerchief, addressed himself undauntedly to Miss Mullen.

'Do you know, I don't believe you have ever been out in our tea-kettle, Miss Mullen. Captain Cursiter and I are feeling very hurt about it.'

'If you mean by "tea-kettle" that steamboat thing that I've seen going about the lake,' replied Charlotte, making an effort to resume her first attitude of suave and unruffled hospitality, and at the same time to administer needed correction to Mr Hawkins, 'I certainly have not. I have always been taught that it was manners to wait till you're asked.'

'I quite agree with you, Miss Mullen,' struck in Pamela; 'we also thought that for a long time, but we had to give it up in the end and ask ourselves! You are much more honoured than we were.'

'Oh, I say, Miss Dysart, you know it was only our grovelling humility,' expostulated Hawkins, 'and you always said it dirtied your frock and spoiled the poetry of the lake. You quite put us off taking anybody out. But we've pulled ourselves together now, Miss Mullen, and if you and Miss Fitzpatrick will fix an afternoon to go down the lake, perhaps if Miss Dysart says she's sorry we'll let her come too, and even, if she's very good, bring whoever she likes with her.'

Mr Hawkins' manner towards ladies had precisely that tone of self-complacent gallantry that Lady Dysart felt to be so signally lacking in her own son, and it was not without its effect even upon Charlotte. It is possible had she been aware that this special compliment to her had been arranged during the polishing of the teaspoons, it might have lost some of its value; but the thought of steaming forth with the Bruff party and 'th' officers', under the very noses of the Lismoyle matrons, was the only point of view that presented itself to her.

'Well, I'll give you no answer till I get Mr Dysart's opinion. He's the only one of you that knows the lake,' she said more graciously. 'If *you* say the steamboat is safe, Mr Dysart, and you'll come and see we're not drowned by these harum-scarum soldiers, I've no objection to going.'

Further discussion was interrupted by a rush and a scurry on the gravel of the garden path, and a flying ball of fur dashed up the outside of the window, the upper half of which was open, and suddenly realizing its safety, poised itself on the sash, and crooned and spat with a collected fury at Mr Hawkins' bull-terrier, who leaped unavailingly below.

'Oh! me poor darling Bruffy!' screamed Miss Mullen, springing up and upsetting her cup of tea; 'she'll be killed! Call off your dog, Mr Hawkins!'

As if in answer to her call, a tall figure darkened the window, and Mr Lambert pushed Mrs Bruff into the room with the handle of his walking stick.

'Hullo, Charlotte! Isn't that Hawkins' dog?' he began, putting his head in at the window; then, with a sudden change of manner as he caught sight of Miss Mullen's guests, 'oh – I had no idea you had anyone here,' he said, taking off his hat to as much of Pamela and Miss Hope-Drummond as was not hidden by Charlotte's bulky person, 'I only thought I'd call round and see if Francie would like to come out for a row before dinner.'

10

Washerwomen do not, as a rule, assimilate the principles of their trade. In Lismoyle, the row of cottages most affected by ladies of that profession was, indeed, planted by the side of the lake, but except in winter, when the floods sent a muddy wash in at the kitchen doors of Ferry Row, the customers' linen alone had any experience of its waters. The clouds of steam from the cauldrons of boiling clothes ascended from morning till night, and hung in beads upon the sooty cobwebs that draped the rafters; the food and wearing apparel of the laundresses and their vast families mingled horribly with their professional apparatus, and, outside in the road, the filthy children played among puddles that stagnated under an iridescent scum of soap suds. A narrow strip of goose-nibbled grass divided the road from the lake shore, and at almost any hour of the day there might be seen a slatternly woman or two kneeling by the water's edge, pounding the wet linen on a rock with a flat wooden weapon, according to the immemorial custom of their savage class.

The Row ended at the ferry pier, and perhaps one reason for the absence of self-respect in the appearance of its inhabitants lay in the fact that the only passers-by were the country people on their way to the ferry, which here, where the lake narrowed to something less than a mile, was the route to the Lismoyle market generally used by the dwellers on the opposite side. The coming of a donkey-cart down the Row was an event to be celebrated with hooting and stone-throwing by the children, and, therefore, it can be understood that when, on a certain still, sleepy afternoon Miss Mullen drove slowly in her phaeton along the line of houses, she created nearly as great a sensation as she would have made in Piccadilly.

Miss Mullen had one or two sources of income which few people knew of, and about which, with all her loud candour, she did not enlighten even her most intimate friends. Even Mr Lambert might have been surprised to know that two or three householders in Ferry Row paid rent to her, and that others of them had money dealings with her of a complicated kind, not easy to describe, but simple enough to the strong financial intellect of his predecessor's daughter. No account books were taken with her on these occasions. She and her clients were equally equipped with the absolutely accurate business memory of the Irish peasant, a memory that in few cases survives education, but, where it exists, may be relied upon more than all the generations of ledgers and account books.

Charlotte's visits to Ferry Row were usually made on foot, and were of long duration, but her business on this afternoon was of a trivial character, consisting merely in leaving a parcel at the house of Dinny Lydon, the tailor, and of convincing her washer-woman of iniquity in a manner that brought every other washer-woman to the door, and made each offer up thanks to her most favoured saint that she was not employed by Miss Mullen.

The long phaeton was at last turned, with draggings at the horse's mouth and grindings of the fore-carriage: the children took their last stare, and one or two ladies whose payments were in arrear emerged from their back gardens and returned to their washing tubs. If they flattered themselves that they had been for-gotten, they were mistaken; Charlotte had given a glance of grim amusement at the deserted washing tubs, and as her old phaeton rumbled slowly out of Ferry Row, she was computing the number of customers, and the consequent approximate income of each defaulter.

To the deep and plainly expressed chagrin of the black horse, he was not allowed to turn in at the gate of Tally Ho, but was urged along the road which led to Rosemount. There again he made a protest, but, yielding to the weighty arguments of Charlotte's whip, he fell into his usual melancholy jog, and took the turn to Gurthnamuckla with dull resignation. Once steered into that lonely road, Charlotte let him go at his own pace, and sat passive, her mouth tightly closed, and her eyes blinking quickly as she looked straight ahead of her with a slight furrow of concentration on her low forehead. She had the unusual gift of thinking out in advance her line of conversation in an interview, and, which is even less usual, she had the power of keeping to it. By sheer strength of will she could force her plan of action upon other people, as a conjurer forces a card, till they came to believe it was of their own choosing; she had done it so often that she was now confident of her skill, and she quite understood the inevitable advantage that a fixed scheme of any sort has over indefinite opposition. When the clump of trees round Gurthnamuckla rose into view, Charlotte had determined her order of battle, and was free to give her attention to outward circumstances. It was a long time since she had been out to Miss Duffy's farm, and as the stony country began to open its arms to the rich, sweet pastures, an often repressed desire asserted itself, and Charlotte heaved a sigh that was as romantic in its way as if she had been sweet and twenty, instead of tough and forty.

Julia Duffy did not come out to meet her visitor, and when Charlotte walked into the kitchen she found that the mistress of the house was absent, and that three old women were squatted on the floor in front of the fire, smoking short clay pipes, and holding converse in Irish that was punctuated with loud sniffs and coughs. At sight of the visitor the pipes vanished in the twinkling of an eye, and one of the women scrambled to her feet.

'Why, Mary Holloran, what brings you here?' said Charlotte, recognising the woman who lived in the Rosemount gate lodge.

'It was a sore leg I have, yer honour, miss,' whined Mary Holloran; 'it's running with me now these three weeks, and I come to thry would Miss Duffy give me a bit o' a plashther.'

'Take care it doesn't run away with you altogether,' replied Charlotte facetiously; 'and where's Miss Duffy herself?'

'She's sick, the craythure,' said one of the other women, who, having found and dusted a chair, now offered it to Miss Mullen;

'she have a wakeness like in her head, and an impression on her heart, and Billy Grainy came afther Peggy Roche here, the way she'd mind her.'

Peggy Roche groaned slightly, and stirred a pot of smutty gruel with an air of authority.

'Could I see her, d'ye think?' asked Charlotte, sitting down and looking about her with sharp appreciation of the substantial excellence of the smoke blackened walls and grimy woodwork. 'There wouldn't be a better kitchen in the country,' she thought, 'if it was properly done up.'

'Ye can, asthore, ye can go up,' replied Peggy Roche, 'but wait a while till I have the sup o' grool hated, and maybe yerself'll take it up to herself.'

'Is she eating nothing but that?' asked Charlotte, viewing the pasty compound with disgust.

'Faith, 'tis hardly she'll ate that itself.' Peggy Roche rose as she spoke, and, going to the dresser, returned with a black bottle. 'As for a bit o' bread, or a pratie, or the like o' that, she couldn't use it, nor let it past her shest; with respects to ye, as soon as she'd have it shwallied it'd come up as simple and as pleashant as it wint down.' She lifted the little three-legged pot off its heap of hot embers, and then took the cork out of the black bottle with nimble, dirty fingers.

'What in the name of goodness is that ye have there?' demanded Charlotte hastily.

Mrs Roche looked somewhat confused, and murmured something about 'a wheeshy suppeen o' shperits to wet the grool.'

Charlotte snatched the bottle from her, and smelt it.

'Faugh!' she said, with a guttural at the end of the word that no Saxon gullet could hope to produce; 'it's potheen! that's what it is, and mighty bad potheen too. D'ye want to poison the woman?'

A loud chorus of repudiation arose from the sick-nurse and her friends.

'As for you, Peggy Roche, you're not fit to tend a pig, let alone a Christian. You'd murder this poor woman with your filthy fresh potheen, and when your own son was dying, you begrudged him the drop of spirits that'd have kept the life in him.'

Peggy flung up her arms with a protesting howl.

'May God forgive ye that word, Miss Charlotte! If 'twas the blood of me arrm, I didn't begridge it to him; the Lord have mercy on him – '

60

'Amen! amen! You would not, asthore,' groaned the other women.

' – but doesn't the world know it's mortial sin for a poor craythur to go into th' other world with the smell of dhrink on his breath!'

'It's mortial sin to be a fool,' replied Miss Mullen, whose medical skill had often been baffled by such winds of doctrine; 'here, give me the gruel. I'll go give it to the woman before you have her murdered.' She deftly emptied the pot of gruel into a bowl, and, taking the spoon out of the old woman's hand, she started on her errand of mercy.

The stairs were just outside the door, and making their dark and perilous ascent in safety, she stood still in a low passage into which two or three other doors opened. She knocked at the first of these, and, receiving no answer, turned the handle quietly and looked in. There was no furniture in it except a broken wooden bedstead; innumerable flies buzzed on the closed window, and in the slant of sunlight that fell through the dim panes was a box from which a turkey reared its red throat, and regarded her with a suspicion born, like her chickens, of long hatching. Charlotte closed the door and noiselessly opened the next. There was nothing in the room, which was of the ordinary low-ceiled cottage type, and after a calculating look at the broken flooring and the tattered wall-paper, she went quietly out into the passage again. 'Good servants' room,' she said to herself, 'but if she's here much longer it'll be past praying for.'

If she had been in any doubt as to Miss Duffy's whereabouts, a voice from the room at the end of the little passage now settled the matter. 'Is that Peggy?' it called.

Charlotte pushed boldly into the room with the bowl of gruel.

'No, Miss Duffy, me poor old friend, it's me, Charlotte Mullen,' she said in her most cordial voice: 'they told me below you were ill, but I thought you'd see me, and I brought your gruel up in my hand. I hope you'll like it none the less for that!'

The invalid turned her night-capped head round from the wall and looked at her visitor with astonished, bloodshot eyes. Her hatchety face was very yellow, her long nose was rather red, and her black hair thrust itself out round the soiled frill of her night-cap in dingy wisps.

'You're welcome, Miss Mullen,' she said, with a pitiable attempt at dignity; 'won't you take a cheer?'

'Not till I've seen you take this,' replied Charlotte, handing her the bowl of gruel with even broader *bonhomie* than before.

61

Julia Duffy reluctantly sat up among her blankets, conscious almost to agony of the squalor of all her surroundings, conscious even that the blankets were of the homespun, madder-dyed flannel such as the poor people use, and taking the gruel, she began to eat it in silence. She tried to prop herself in this emergency with the recollection that Charlotte Mullen's grandfather drank her grandfather's port wine under this very roof, and that it was by no fault of hers that she had sunk while Charlotte had risen; but the worn-out boots that lay on the floor where she had thrown them off, and the rags stuffed into the broken panes in the window, were facts that crowded out all consolation from bygone glories.

'Well, Miss Duffy,' said Charlotte, drawing up a chair to the bedside, and looking at her hostess with a critical eye, 'I'm sorry to see you so sick; when Billy Grainy left the milk last night he told Norry you were laid up in bed, and I thought I'd come over and see if there was anything I could do for you.'

'Thank ye, Miss Mullen,' replied Julia stiffly, sipping the nauseous gruel with ladylike decorum, 'I have all I require here.'

'Well, ye know, Miss Duffy, I wanted to see how you are,' said Charlotte, slightly varying her attack; 'I'm a bit of a doctor, like yourself. Peggy Roche below told me you had what she called "an impression on the heart", but it looks to me more like a touch of liver.'

The invalid does not exist who can resist a discussion of symptoms, and Miss Duffy's hauteur slowly thawed before Charlotte's intelligent and intimate questions. In a very short time Miss Mullen had felt her pulse, inspected her tongue, promised to send her a bottle of unfailing efficacy, and delivered an exordium on the nature and treatment of her complaint.

'But in deed and in truth,' she wound up, 'if you want my opinion, I'll tell you frankly that what ails you is you're just rotting away with the damp and loneliness of this place. I declare that sometimes when I'm lying awake in my bed at nights, I've thought of you out here by yourself, without an earthly creature near you if you got sick, and wondered at you. Why, my heavenly powers! ye might die a hundred deaths before anyone would know it!'

Miss Duffy picked up a corner of the sheet and wiped the gruel from her thin lips.

'If it comes to that, Miss Mullen,' she said with some resump-

62

tion of her earlier manner, 'if I'm for dying I'd as soon die by myself as in company; and as for damp, I thank God this house was built by them that didn't spare money on it, and it's as dry this minyute as what it was forty years ago.'

'What! Do you tell me the roof's sound?' exclaimed Charlotte with genuine interest.

'I have never examined it, Miss Mullen,' replied Julia coldly, 'but it keeps the rain out, and I consider that suffeecient.'

'Oh, I'm sure there's not a word to be said against the house,' Charlotte made hasty reparation; 'but, indeed, Miss Duffy, I say – and I've heard more than myself say the same thing – that a delicate woman like you has no business to live alone so far from help. The poor Archdeacon frets about it, I can tell ye. I believe he thinks Father Heffernan'll be raking ye into his fold! And I can tell ye,' concluded Charlotte, with what she felt to be a certain rough pathos, 'there's plenty in Lismoyle would be sorry to see your father's daughter die with the wafer in her mouth!'

'I had no idea the people in Lismoyle were so anxious about me and my affairs,' said Miss Duffy. 'They're very kind, but I'm able to look afther my soul without their help.'

'Well, of course, everyone's soul is their own affair; but, ye know, when no one ever sees ye in your own parish church – well, right or wrong, there are plenty of fools to gab about it.'

The dark bags of skin under Julia Duffy's eyes became slowly red, a signal that this thrust had gone home. She did not answer, and her visitor rose, and moving towards the hermetically sealed window, looked out across the lawn over Julia's domain. Her roundest and weightiest stone was still in her sling, while her eye ran over the grazing cattle in the fields.

'Is it true what I hear, that Peter Joyce has your grazing this year?' she said casually.

'It is quite true,' answered Miss Duffy, a little defiantly. A liver attack does not predispose its victims to answer in a Christian spirit questions that are felt to be impertinent.

'Well,' returned Charlotte, still looking out of the window, with her hands deep in the pockets of her black alpaca coat, 'I'm sorry for it.'

'Why so?'

Julia's voice had a sharpness that was pleasant to Miss Mullen's ear.

'I can't well explain the matter to ye now,' Charlotte said, turning round and looking portentously upon the sick woman, 'but I have it from a sure hand that Peter Joyce is bankrupt, and will be in the courts before the year is out.'

When, a short time afterwards, Julia Duffy lay back among her madder blankets and heard the last sound of Miss Mullen's phaeton wheels die away along the lake road, she felt that the visit had at least provided her with subject for meditation.

11

Mr Roderick Lambert's study window gave upon the flower garden, and consequently the high road also came within the sphere of his observations. He had been sitting at his writing table, since luncheon time, dealing with a variety of business, and seldom lifting his glossy black head except when some sound in the road attracted his attention. It was not his custom to work after a solid luncheon on a close afternoon, nor was it by any means becoming to his complexion when he did so; but the second post had brought letters of an unpleasant character that required immediate attention, and the flush on his face was not wholly due to hot beef-steak pie and sherry. It was not only that several of Sir Benjamin's tenants had attended a Land League meeting the Sunday before, and that their religious director had written to inform him that they had there pledged themselves to the Plan of Campaign. That was annoying, but as the May rents were in he had no objection to their amusing themselves as they pleased during the summer; in fact, from a point of view on which Mr Lambert dwelt as little as possible even in his own mind, a certain amount of nominal disturbance among the tenants might not come amiss. The thing that was really vexing was the crass obstinacy of his wife's trustees, who had acquainted him with the fact that they were unable to comply with her wish that some of her capital should be sold out.

It is probably hardly necessary to say that the worthy turkey hen had expressed no such desire. A feeble, 'to be sure, Roderick dear; I daresay it'd be the best thing to do; but you know I don't understand such things,' had been her share of the transaction, and Mr Lambert knew that the refusal of her trustees to make the desired concession would not ruffle so much as a feather; but he wished he could be as sure of the equanimity of his coachbuilder, one of whose numerous demands for payment was lying upon the table in front of him; while others, dating back five years to the period of his marriage, lurked in the pigeon-holes of his writing table.

Mr Lambert, like other young gentlemen of fashion, but not of fortune, had thought that when he married a well-to-do widow, he ought to prove his power of adjusting himself to circumstances by expending her ready money in as distinguished a manner as possible. The end of the ready money had come in an absurdly short time, and, paradoxical as it may seem, it had during its brief life raised a flourishing following of bills which had in the past spring given Mr Lambert far more trouble than he felt them to be worth, and though he had stopped the mouths of some of the more rapacious of his creditors, he had done so with extreme difficulty and at a cost that made him tremble. It was especially provoking that the coachbuilder should have threatened legal proceedings about that bill just now, when, in addition to other complications, he happened to have lost more money at the Galway races than he cared to think about, certainly more than he wished his wife and her relations to know of.

Early in the afternoon he had, with an unregarding eye, seen Charlotte drive by on her way to Gurthnamuckla; but after a couple of hours of gloomy calculation and letter writing, the realization that Miss Mullen was not at her house awoke in him, coupled with the idea that a little fresh air would do him good. He went out of the house, some unconfessed purpose quickening his step. He hesitated at the gate while it expanded into determination, and then he hailed his wife, whose poppy-decked garden hat was painfully visible above the magenta blossoms of a rhododendron bush.

'Lucy! I wouldn't be surprised if I fetched Francie Fitzpatrick over for tea. She's by herself at Tally Ho. I saw Charlotte drive by without her a little while ago.'

When he reached Tally Ho he found the gate open, an offence always visited with extremest penalties by Miss Mullen, and as he walked up the drive he noticed that, besides the broad wheel-tracks of the phaeton, there were several thin and devious ones, at some places interrupted by footmarks and a general appearance of a scuffle; at another heading into a lilac bush with apparent precipitancy, and at the hall door circling endlessly and crookedly with several excursions on to the newly-mown plot of grass.

'I wonder what perambulator has been running amuck in here. Charlotte will make it hot for them, whoever they were,' thought Lambert, as he stood waiting for the door to be opened, and watched through the glass of the porch door two sleek tortoise-shell cats lapping a saucer of yellow cream in a corner of the hall. 'By Jove! how snug she is in this little place. She must have a pot of money put by; more than she'd ever own up to, I'll engage!'

At this juncture the door opened, and he was confronted by Norry the Boat, with sleeves rolled above her brown elbows, and stockinged feet untrammelled by boots.

'There's noan of them within,' she announced before he had time to speak. 'Miss Charlotte's gone dhriving to Gurthnamuckla, and Miss Francie went out a while ago.'

'Which way did she go, d'ye know?'

'Musha, faith! I do *not* know what way did she go,' replied Norry, her usual asperity heightened by a recent chase of Susan, who had fled to the roof of the turf-house with a mackerel snatched from the kitchen table. 'I have plinty to do besides running afther her. I heard her spakin' to one outside in the avenue, and with that she clapped the hall-doore afther her and she didn't come in since.'

Lambert thought it wiser not to venture on the suggestion that Louisa might be better informed, and walked away down the avenue trying hard not to admit to himself his disappointment.

He turned towards home again in an objectless way, thoroughly thwarted, and dismally conscious that the afternoon contained for him only the prospect of having tea with his wife and finishing his letters afterwards. His step became slower and slower as he approached his own entrance gates, and he looked at his watch.

'Confound it! it's only half past four. I can't go in yet;' then, a new idea striking him, 'perhaps she went out to meet Charlotte. I declare I might as well go a bit down the road and see if they're coming back yet.'

He walked for at least half a mile under the trees, whose young June leaves had already a dissipated powdering of white limestone dust, without meeting anything except a donkey with a pair of creaking panniers on its back, walking alone and discreetly at its own side of the road, as well aware as Mr Lambert that its owner was dallying with a quart of porter at a roadside public house a mile away. The turn to Gurthnamuckla was not far off when the distant rumble of wheels became at last audible; Lambert had only time to remember angrily that, as the Tally Ho phaeton had but two seats, he had had his walk for nothing, when the bowed head and long melancholy face of the black horse came in sight, and he became aware that Charlotte was without a companion.

Her face had more colour in it than usual as she pulled up beside him, perhaps from the heat of the afternoon and the no small exertion of flogging her steed, and her manner when she spoke was neither bluff nor hearty, but approximated more nearly to that of ordinary womankind than was its wont. Mr Lambert noticed none of these things; and, being a person whose breeding was not always equal to annoying emergencies, he did not trouble to take off his hat or smile appropriately as Charlotte said –

'Well, Roddy, I'd as soon expect to see your two horses sitting in the dog-cart driving you as to see you as far from home as this on your own legs. Where are you off to?'

'I was taking a stroll out to meet you, and ask you to come back and have tea with Lucy,' replied Mr Lambert, recognizing the decree of fate with a singularly bad grace. 'I went down to Tally Ho to ask you, and Norry told me you had gone to Gurthnamuckla.'

'Did you see Francie there?' said Charlotte quickly.

'No; I believe she was out somewhere.'

'Well, you were a very good man to take so much trouble about us,' she replied, looking at him with an expression that softened the lines of her face in a surprising way. 'Are you too proud to have a lift home now?'

'Thank you, I'd sooner walk – and –' casting about for an excuse – 'you mightn't like the smell of my cigar under your nose.'

'Come, now, Roddy,' exclaimed Charlotte, 'you ought to know me better than that! Don't you remember how you used to sit smoking beside me in the office when I was helping you to do your work? In fact, I wouldn't say that there hadn't been an occasion when I was guilty of a cigarette in your company myself!'

She turned her eyes towards him, and the provocative look in them came as instinctively and as straight as ever it did from Francie's, or as ever it has been projected from the curbed heart of woman. But, unfair as it may be, it is certain that if Lambert had seen it, he would not have been attracted by it. He, however, did not look up.

'Well, if you don't mind going slow, I'll walk beside you,' he said, ignoring the reminiscence. 'I want to know whether you did better business with Julia Duffy than I did last week.'

The soft look was gone in a moment from Charlotte's face.

'I couldn't get much satisfaction out of her,' she replied; 'but I think I left a thorn in her pillow when I told her Peter Joyce was bankrupt.'

'I'll take my oath you did,' said Lambert, with a short laugh. 'I declare I'd be sorry for the poor old devil if she wasn't such a bad tenant, letting the whole place go to the mischief, house and all.'

'I tell you the house isn't in such a bad way as you think; it's dirt ails it more than anything else.' Charlotte had recovered her wonted energy of utterance. 'Believe me, if I had a few workmen in that house for a month you wouldn't know it.'

'Well, I believe you will, sooner or later. All the same, I can't see what the deuce you want with it. Now, if *I* had the place, I'd make a pot of money out of it, keeping young horses there, as I've often told you. I'd do a bit of coping, and making hunters to sell. There's no work on earth I'd like as well.'

He took a long pull at his cigar, and expelled a sigh and a puff of smoke.

'Well, Roddy,' said Charlotte, after a moment's pause, speaking with an unusual slowness and almost hesitancy, 'you know I wouldn't like to come between you and your fancy. If you want the farm, in God's name take it yourself!'

'Take it myself! I haven't the money to pay the fine, much less to stock it. I tell you what, Charlotte,' he went on, turning round and putting his hand on the splash-board of the phaeton as he walked, 'you and I are old pals, and I don't mind telling you it's the most I can do to keep going the way I am now. I never was so driven for money in my life,' he ended, some vague purpose, added to the habit of an earlier part of his life, pushing him on to be confidential.

'Who's driving you, Roddy?' said Charlotte, in a voice in which a less preoccupied person than her companion might have noticed a curiously gentle inflection.

It is perhaps noteworthy that while Mr Lambert's lips replied with heartfelt irritation, 'Oh, they're all at me, Langford the coachbuilder, and everyone of them,' one section of his brain was asking the other how much ready money old Mrs Mullen had had to leave, and was receiving a satisfactory answer.

There was a pause in the conversation. It was so long now since the black horse had felt the whip, that, acting on the presumption that his mistress had fallen asleep, he fell into an even more slumbrous crawl without any notice being taken.

'Roddy,' said Charlotte at last, and Lambert now observed how low and rough her voice was, 'do you remember in old times once or twice, when you were put to it for a five pound note, you made no bones about asking a friend to help you? Well, you know I'm a poor woman' – even at this moment Charlotte's caution asserted itself – 'but I daresay I could put my hand on a couple of hundred, and if they'd be any use to you – '

Lambert became very red. The possibility of some such climax as this had floated in a sub-current of thought just below the level of formed ideas, but now that it had come, it startled him. It was an unheard of thing that Charlotte should make such an offer as this. It gave him suddenly a tingling sense of power, and at the same time a strange instinct of disgust and shame.

'Oh, my dear Charlotte,' he began awkwardly, 'upon my soul you're a great deal too good. I never thought of such a thing – I – I – ' he stammered, wishing he could refuse, but casting about for words in which to accept.

'Ah, nonsense. Now, Roddy, my dear boy,' interrupted Charlotte, regaining her usual manner as she saw his embarrassment, 'say no more about it. We'll consider it a settled thing, and we'll go through the base business details after tea.'

Lambert said to himself that there was really no way out of it. If she was so determined the only thing was to let her do as she liked; no one could say that the affair was of his seeking.

'And, you know,' continued Charlotte in her most jocular voice, before he could frame a sentence of the right sort, 'who knows, if I get the farm, that we mightn't make a joint-stock business out of it, and have young horses there, and all the rest of it!'

'You're awfully good, Charlotte,' said Lambert, with an emotion in his voice that she did not guess to be purely the result of inward relief and exultation; 'I'm awfully obliged to you – you always were a – a true friend – some day, perhaps, I'll be able to show you what I think about it,' he stammered, unable to think of anything else to say, and, lifting his hand from the splash-board, he put it on hers, that lay in her lap with the reins in it, and pressed it for a moment. Into both their minds shot simultaneously the remembrance of a somewhat similar scene, when, long ago, Charlotte had come to the help of her father's pupil, and he had expressed his gratitude in a more ardent manner – a manner that had seemed cheap enough to him at the time, but that had been more costly to Charlotte than any other thing that had ever befallen her.

'You haven't forgotten old times any more than I have,' he went on, knowing very well that he was taking now much the same simple and tempting method of getting rid of his obligation that he had once found so efficacious, and to a certain extent enjoying the thought that he could still make a fool of her. 'Ah, well!' he sighed, 'there's no use trying to get those times back, any more than there is in trying to forget them.' He hesitated. 'But, after all, there's many a new tune played on an old fiddle! Isn't that so?' He was almost frightened at his own daring as he saw Charlotte's cheek burn with a furious red, and her lips quiver in the attempt to answer.

Upon their silence there broke from the distance a loud scream, then another, and then a burst of laughter in a duet of soprano and bass, coming apparently from a lane that led into the road a little farther on – a smooth and secluded little lane, bordered thickly with hazel bushes – a private road, in fact, to a model farm that Mr Lambert had established on his employer's property. From the mouth of this there broke suddenly a whirling vision of whiteness and wheels, and Miss Fitzpatrick, mounted on a tricycle and shrieking loudly, dashed across the highroad and collapsed in a heap in the ditch. Lambert started forward, but long before he could reach her the Rev. Joseph Corkran emerged at full speed from the lane, hatless, with long flying coat-tails, and, with a skill born of experience, extricated Francie from her difficulties.

'Oh, I'm dead!' she panted. 'Oh, the horrible thing! What good were you that you let it go?' unworthily attacking the equally exhausted Corkran. Then, in tones of consternation, 'Goodness! Look at Mr Lambert and Charlotte! Oh, Mr Lambert,' as Lambert came up to her, 'did you see the toss I got? The dirty thing ran away with me down the hill, and Mr Corkran was so tired running he had to let go, and I declare I thought I was killed – and you don't look a bit sorry for me!'

'Well, what business had you to get up on a thing like that?' answered Lambert, looking angrily at the curate. I wonder, Corkran, you hadn't more sense than to let a lady ride that machine.'

'Well, indeed, Mr Lambert, I told Miss Fitzpatrick it wasn't as easy as she thought,' replied the guilty Corkran, a callow youth from Trinity College, Dublin, who had been as wax in Francie's hands, and who now saw, with unfeigned terror, the approach of Charlotte. 'I begged of her not to go outside Tally Ho, but – but – I think I'd better go back and look for my hat –' he ended abruptly, retreating into the lane just as Charlotte drew up the black horse and opened her mouth to deliver herself of her indignation.

12

The broad limestone steps at Bruff looked across the lawn to the lake, and to the south. They were flanked on either hand by stone balustrades which began and ended in a pot of blazing scarlet geraniums, and on their topmost plateau on this brilliant 1st of July, the four Bruff dogs sat on their haunches and gazed with anxious despondency in at the open hall door. For the last half hour Max and Dinah, the indoor dogs, had known that an expedition was toward. They had seen Pamela put on a hat that certainly was not her garden one, and as certainly lacked the veil that betokened the abhorred ceremony of church-going. They knew this hat well, and at the worst it usually meant a choir practice; but taken in connection with a blue serge skirt and the packing of a luncheon basket, they almost ventured to hope it portended a picnic on the lake. They adored picnics. In the first place, the outdoor dogs were always left at home, which alone would have imparted a delicious flavour to any entertainment; and in the second, all dietary rules were remitted for the occasion, and they were permitted to raven unchecked upon chicken bones, fat slices of ham, and luscious leavings of cream when the packing-up time came. There was, however, mingled with this enchanting prospect, the fear that they might be left behind, and from the sounding of the first note of preparation they had never let Pamela out of their sight. Whenever her step was heard through the long passages, there had gone with it the scurrying

71

gallop of the two little waiters on providence, and when her arrangements had culminated in the luncheon basket, their agitation had become so poignant that a growling game of play under the table, got up merely to pass the time, turned into an acrimonious squabble, and caused their ejection to the hall-door steps by Lady Dysart. Now, sitting outside the door, they listened with trembling to the discussion that was going on in the hall, and with the selfconsciousness of dogs were convinced that it was all about themselves.

'No, I cannot allow Garry to go,' exclaimed Lady Dysart, her eyes raised to the ceiling as if to show her remoteness from all human entreaty; 'he is *not* over the whooping-cough; I heard him whooping this morning in his bedroom.'

The person mentioned ceased from a game of fives with a tennis ball that threatened momentarily to break the windows, and said indignantly, 'Oh, I say, Mother, that was only the men in the yard pumping. That old pump makes a row just like whooping-cough.'

Lady Dysart faltered for a moment before this ingenious falsehood, but soon recovered herself.

'I don't care whether it was you or the pump that whooped, it does not alter the fact of your superfluity at a picnic.'

'I think Captain Cursiter and Mr Hawkins wanted him to stoke,' said Pamela from the luncheon basket.

'I have no doubt they do, but they shall not have him,' said Lady Dysart with the blandness of entire decision, though her eyes wavered from her daughter's face to her son's; 'they're very glad indeed to save their own clothes and spoil his.'

'Well, then, I'll go with Lambert,' said Garry rebelliously.

'You will do nothing of the sort!' exclaimed Lady Dysart; 'whatever I may do about allowing you to go with Captain Cursiter, nothing shall induce me to sanction any plan that involves your going in that most dangerous yacht. Christopher himself says she is over-sparred.' Lady Dysart had no idea of the meaning of the accusation, but she felt the term to be good and telling. 'Now, Pamela, will you promise me to stay with Captain Cursiter all the time?'

'Oh, yes, I will,' said Pamela, laughing; 'but you know in your heart that he would much rather have Garry.'

'I don't care what my heart knows,' replied Lady Dysart magnificently, 'I know what my mouth says, and that is that you must neither of you stir out of the steam launch.'

At this descent of his mother into the pit so artfully dug for her, Garry withdrew to attire himself for the position of stoker, and Pamela discreetly changed the conversation.

It seemed a long time to Max and Dinah before their fate was decided, but after some last moments of anguish on the pier they found themselves, the one coiled determinedly on Pamela's lap, and the other smirking in the bow in Garry's arms, as Mr Hawkins sculled the second relay of the Bruff party out to the launch. The first relay, consisting of Christopher and Miss Hope-Drummond, was already on its way down the lake in Mr Lambert's five-ton boat, with every inch of canvas set to catch the light and shifty breeze that blew petulantly down from the mountains, and ruffled the glitter of the lake with dark blue smears. The air quivered hotly over the great stones on the shore, drawing out the strong aromatic smell of the damp weeds and the bog-myrtle, and Lady Dysart stood on the end of the pier, and wrung her hands as she thought of Pamela's complexion.

Captain Cursiter was one of the anomalous soldiers whose happiness it is to spend as much time as possible in a boat, dressed in disreputable clothes, with hands begrimed and blistered with oil or ropes as the case may be, and steaming or sailing to nowhere and back again with undying enthusiasm. He was a thin, brown man, with a moustache rather lighter in colour than the tan of his face, and his beaky nose, combined with his disposition to flee from the haunts of men, had inspired his friends to bestow on him the pet name of 'Snipey'. The festivity on which he was at present embarked was none of his seeking, and it had been only by strenuous argument, fortified by the artful suggestion that no one else was really competent to work the boat, that Mr Hawkins had got him into clean flannels and the conduct of the expedition. He knew neither Miss Mullen nor Francie, and his acquaintance with the Dysarts, as with other dwellers in the neighbourhood, was of a slight and unprogressive character, and in strong contrast to the manner in which Mr Hawkins had become at Bruff and elsewhere what that young gentleman was pleased to term 'the gated infant'. During the run from Lismoyle to Bruff he had been able to occupy himself with the affairs of the steam launch; but when Hawkins, his prop and stay, had rowed ashore for the Dysart party, the iron had entered into his soul.

As the punt neared the launch, Mr Hawkins looked round to take his distance in bringing her alongside, and recognized with one delighted glance the set smile of suffering politeness that denoted that Captain Cursiter was making himself agreeable to the ladies. Charlotte was sitting in the stern with a depressing air of Sunday-outness about her, and a stout umbrella over her head. It was not in her nature to feel shy; the grain of it was too coarse and strong to harbour such a thing as diffidence, but she knew well enough when she was socially unsuccessful, and she was already aware that she was going to be out of her element on this expedition. Lambert, who would have been a kind of connecting link, was already far in the offing. Captain Cursiter she mentally characterized as a poor stick. Hawkins, whom she had begun by liking, was daily – almost hourly – gaining in her disfavour, and from neither Pamela, Francie, nor Garry did she expect much entertainment. Charlotte had a vigorous taste in conversation, and her idea of a pleasure party was not to talk to Pamela Dysart about the choir and the machinery of a school feast for an hour and a half, and from time to time to repulse with ill-assumed politeness the bird-like flights of Dinah on to her lap. Francie and Mr Hawkins sat forward on the roof of the little cabin, and apparently entertained one another vastly, judging by their appearance and the fragments of conversation that from time to time made their way aft in the environment of a cloud of smuts. Captain Cursiter, revelling in the well-known restrictions that encompass the man at the wheel, stood serenely aloof, steering among the hump-backed green islands and treacherous shallows, and thinking to himself that Hawkins was going ahead pretty fast with that Dublin girl.

Mr Hawkins had been for some time a source of anxiety to his brother officers, who disapproved of matrimony for the young of their regiment. Things had looked so serious when he was quartered at Limerick that he had been hurriedly sent on detachment to Lismoyle before he had time to 'make an example of himself', as one of the most unmarried of the majors observed, and into Captain Cursiter's trusted hands he had been committed, with urgent instructions to keep an eye on him. Cursiter's eye was renowned for its blighting qualities on occasions such as these, and his jibes at matrimony were looked on by his brother officers as the most finished and scathing expressions of proper feeling on the subject that could be desired; but it was agreed that he would have his hands full.

The launch slid smoothly along with a low clicking of the machinery, cutting her way across the reflections of the mountains in pursuit of the tall, white sail of the *Daphne*, that seemed each moment to grow taller, as the yacht was steadily overhauled by her more practical comrade. The lake was narrower here,

74

where it neared the end of its twenty-mile span, and so calm that the sheep and cattle grazing on the brown mountains were reflected in its depths, and the yacht seemed as incongruous in the midst of them as the ark on Mount Ararat. The last bend of the lake was before them; the *Daphne* crept round it, moved mysteriously by a wind that was imperceptible to the baking company on the steam launch, and by the time the latter had churned her way round the fir-clad point, the yacht was letting go her anchor near the landing place of a large wooded island.

At a picnic nothing is of much account before luncheon, and the gloom of hunger hung like a pall over the party that took ashore luncheon baskets, unpacked knives and forks, and gathered stones to put on the corners of the tablecloth. But such a hunger is Nature's salve for the inadequacy of human beings to amuse themselves; the body comes to the relief of the mind with the compassionate superiority of a good servant, and confers inward festivity upon many a dull dinner party. Max and Dinah were quite of this opinion. They had behaved with commendable fortitude during the voyage, though in the earlier part of it a shuddering dejection on Max's part had seemed to Pamela's trained eye to forebode seasickness, but at the lifting of the luncheon basket into the punt their self-control deserted them. The succulent trail left upon the air, palpable to the dog-nose as the smoke of the steam launch to the human eye, beguiled them into efforts to follow, which were only suppressed by their being secretly immured in the cabin by Garry. No one but he saw the two wan faces that yearned at the tiny cabin windows, as the last punt load left for the land, and when at last the wails of the captives streamed across the water, anyone but Garry would have repented of the cruelty. The dogs will never forget it to Captain Cursiter that it was he who rowed out to the launch and brought them ashore to enjoy their fair share of the picnic, and their gratitude will never be tempered by the knowledge that he had caught at the excuse to escape from the conversation which Miss Hope-Drummond, notwithstanding even the pangs of hunger, was proffering to him.

There is something unavoidably vulgar in the aspect of a picnic party when engaged in the culminating rite of eating on the grass. They may feel themselves to be picturesque, gipsy-like, even romantic, but to the unparticipating looker-on, not even the gilded dignity of champagne can redeem them from being a mere group of greedy, huddled backs, with ugly trimmings of paper, dirty plates, and empty bottles. But at Innishochery the only passers-by were straight-flying wild-duck or wood-pigeons, or an occasional seagull lounging up from the distant Atlantic, all observant enough in their way, but not critical. It is probable they did not notice even the singular ungracefulness of Miss Mullen's attitude, as she sat with her short legs uncomfortably tucked away, and her large jaws moving steadily as she indemnified herself for the stupidity of the recent trip. The champagne at length had its usual beneficent effect upon the conversation. Charlotte began to tell stories about her cats and her servants to Christopher and Pamela, with admirable dramatic effect and a sense of humour that made her almost attractive. Miss Hope-Drummond had discovered that Cursiter was one of the Lincolnshire Cursiters, and, with mutual friends as stepping-stones, was working her way on with much ability; and Francie was sitting on a mossy rock, a little away from the tablecloth, with a plate of cherry pie on her lap, Mr Hawkins at her feet, and unlimited opportunities for practical jestings with the cherry stones. Garry and the dogs were engaged in scraping out dishes and polishing plates in a silence more eloquent than words; Lambert alone, of all the party, remained impervious to the influences of luncheon, and lay on his side with his eyes moodily fixed upon his plate, only responding to Miss Mullen's frequent references to him by a sarcastic grunt.

'Now I assure you, Miss Dysart, it's perfectly true,' said Charlotte, after one of these polite rejoinders. 'He's too lazy to say so, but he knows right well that when I complained of my kitchen maid to her mother, all the good I got from her was that she said, "Would ye be agin havin' a switch and to be switchin' her!" That was a pretty way for me to spend my valuable time.' Her audience laughed; and inspired by another half glass of champagne, Miss Mullen continued, 'But big a fool as Bid Sal is, she's a Solon beside Donovan. He came to me th' other day and said he wanted "little Johanna for the garden". "Little *who*?" says I; "Little Johanna," says he. "Ye great, lazy fool," says I, "aren't ye big enough and ugly enough to do that little pick of work by yerself without wanting a girl to help ye?" And after all,' said Charlotte, dropping from the tones of fury in which she had rendered her own part in the interview, 'all he wanted was some guano for my early potatoes!'

Lambert got up without a smile, and sauntering down to the lake, sat down on a rock and began to smoke a cigar. He could not laugh as Christopher and even Captain Cursiter did, at

Charlotte's dramatization of her scene with her gardener. At an earlier period of his career he had found her conversation amusing, and he had not thought her vulgar. Since then he had raised himself just high enough from the sloughs of Irish middle class society to see its vulgarity, but he did not stand sufficiently apart from it to be able to appreciate the humorous side, and in any case he was at present little disposed to laugh at anything. He sat and smoked morosely for some time, feeling that he was making his dissatisfaction with the entertainment imposingly conspicuous; but his cigar was a failure, the rock was far from comfortable, and his bereaved friends seemed to be enjoying themselves rather more than when he left them. He threw the cigar into the water in front of him, to the consternation of a number of minnows, who had hung in the warm shallow as if listening, and now vanished in a twinkling to spread among the dark resorts of the elder fishes the tale of the thunderbolt that fell in their midst, while Lambert stalked back to the party under the trees.

Its component parts were little altered, saving that Miss Hope-Drummond had, by the ingenious erection of a parasol, isolated herself and Christopher from the others, and that Garry had joined himself to Francie and Hawkins, and was, in company with the latter, engaged in weaving stalks of grass across the insteps of Miss Fitzpatrick's open-worked stockings.

'Just look at them, Mr Lambert,' Francie called out in cheerful complaint. 'They're having a race to see which of them will finish their bit of grass first, and they won't let me stir, though I'm nearly mad with the flies!'

She had a waving branch of mountain-ash in her hand; the big straw hat that she had trimmed for herself with dog-roses the night before was on the back of her head; her hair clustered about her white temples, and the colour that fighting the flies had brought to her face lent a lovely depth to eyes that had the gaiety and the soullessness of a child. Lambert had forgotten most of his classics since he had left school, and it is probable that even had he remembered them it would not have occurred to him to regard anything in them as applicable to modern times. At all events Francie's dryad-like fitness to her surroundings did not strike him, as it struck another more dispassionate onlooker, when an occasional lift of the Hope-Drummond parasol revealed the white-clad figure, with its woody background, to Christopher.

'It seems to me you're well able to take care of yourself,' was Lambert's reply to Miss Fitzpatrick's appeal. He turned his back upon her, and interrupted Charlotte in the middle of a story by asking her if she would walk with him across the island and have a look at the ruins of Ochery Chapel.

One habit at least of Mr Lambert's school life remained with him. He was still a proficient at telling tales.

13

Innishochery Island lay on the water like a great green bouquet, with a narrow grey lace edging of stony beach. From the lake it seemed that the foliage stood in a solid impenetrable mass, and that nothing but the innumerable wood-pigeons could hope to gain its inner recesses; even the space of grass which, at the side of the landing place, drove a slender wedge up among the trees, had still the moss-grown stumps upon it that told it had been recovered by force from the possession of the tall pines and thick hazel and birch scrub. The edge of the wedge narrowed into a thread of a path which wound its briary way among the trees with such sinuous vagueness, and such indifference to branches overhead and rocks underfoot, that to follow it was both an act of faith and a penance. Near the middle of the island it was interrupted by a brook that slipped along whispering to itself through the silence of the wood, and though the path made a poor shift to maintain its continuity with stepping stones, it expired a few paces farther on in the bracken of a little glade.

It was a glade that had in some elfish way acquired an expression of extremest old age. The moss grew deep in the grass, lay deep on the rocks; stunted birch trees encircled it with pale twisted arms hoary with lichen, and, at the farther end of it, a grey ruined chapel, standing over the pool that was the birthplace of the stream, fulfilled the last requirement of romance. On this hot summer afternoon the glade had more than ever its air of tranced meditation upon other days and superiority to the outer world, lulled in its sovereignty of the island by the monotone of humming insects, while on the topmost stone of the chapel a magpie gabbled and cackled like a court jester. Christopher thought, as he sat by the pool smoking a cigarette, that he had done well in staying behind under the pretence of photographing the yacht from the landing place, and thus eluding the rest of the party. He was only intermittently unsociable, but he had always had a taste for his own society, and, as he said to himself, he had been going strong all the morning, and the time had come for solitude and tobacco.

He was a young man of a reflective turn, and had artistic aspirations which, had he been of a hardier nature, would probably have taken him further than photography. But Christopher's temperament held one or two things unusual in the amateur. He had the saving, or perhaps fatal power of seeing his own handiwork with as unflattering an eye as he saw other people's. He had no confidence in anything about himself except his critical ability, and as he did not satisfy that, his tentative essays in painting died an early death. It was the same with everything else. His fastidious dislike of doing a thing indifferently was probably a form of conceit, and though it was a higher form than the common vanity whose geese are all swans, it brought about in him a kind of deadlock. His relations thought him extremely clever, on the strength of his university career and his intellectual fastidiousness, and he himself was aware that he was clever, and cared very little for the knowledge. Half the people in the world were clever nowadays, he said to himself with indolent irritability, but genius was another affair; and, having torn up his latest efforts in water-colour and verse, he bought a camera, and betook himself to the more attainable perfection of photography.

It was delightful to lie here with the delicate cigarette smoke keeping the flies at bay, and the grasshoppers whirring away in the grass, like fairy sewing machines, and with the soothing knowledge that the others had been through the glade, had presumably done the ruin thoroughly, and were now cutting their boots to pieces on the water-fretted limestone rock as they scrambled round from the shore to the landing place. This small venerable wood, and the boulders that had lain about the glade through sleepy centuries till the moss had smothered their outlines, brought to Christopher's mind the enchanted country through which King Arthur's knights rode; and he lay there mouthing to himself fragments of half remembered verse, and wondering at the chance that had reserved for him this backwater in a day of otherwise dubious enjoyment. He even found himself piecing together a rhyme or two on his own account; but, as is

79

often the case, inspiration was paralysed by the overwhelming fulness of the reality; the fifth line refused to express his idea, and the interruption of lyric emotion caused by the making and lighting of a fresh cigarette proved fatal to the prospects of the sonnet. He felt disgusted with himself and his own futility. When he had been at Oxford not thus had the springs of inspiration ceased to flow. He had begun to pass the period of water-colours then, but not the period when ideas are as plenty and as full of novelty as leaves in spring, and the knowledge has not yet come that they, like the leaves, are old as the world itself.

For the past three or four years the social exigencies of Government House life had not proved conducive to fervour of any kind, and now, while he was dawdling away his time at Bruff, in the uninterested expectation of another appointment, he found that he not only could not write, but that he seemed to have lost the wish to try.

'I suppose I am sinking into the usual bucolic stupor,' he said to himself, as he abandoned the search for the vagrant rhyme. 'If I could only read the *Field*, and had a more spontaneous habit of cursing, I should be an ideal country gentleman.'

He crumpled into his pocket again the envelope on the back of which he had been scribbling, and told himself that it was more philosophic and more simple to enjoy things in the homely, pre-historic manner, without trying to express them elaborately for the benefit of others. He was intellectually effete, and what made his effeteness more hopeless was that he recognized it himself. 'I am perfectly happy if I let myself alone,' was the sum of his reflections. 'They gave me a little more culture than I could hold, and it ran over the edge at first. Now I think I'm just about sufficiently up in the bottle for Lismoyle form.' He tilted his straw hat over his nose, shut his eyes, and, leaning back, soon felt the delicious fusion into his brain of the surrounding hum and soft movement that tells of the coming of out-of-door summer sleep.

It is deplorable to think of the figure Christopher must cut in the eyes of those whose robuster taste demands in a young man some more potent and heroic qualities, a gentlemanly hardihood in language and liquor, an interesting suggestion of moral obliquity, or, at least, some hereditary vice on which the character may make shipwreck with magnificent helplessness. Christopher, with his preference for his sister's society, and his lack of interest in the majority of manly occupations, from hunting to music halls, has small claim to respect or admiration. The invertebrate-ness of his character seemed to be expressed in his attitude, as he

80

lay, supine, under the birch trees, with the grass making a luxurious couch for his lazy limbs, and the faint breeze just stirring about him. His sleep was not deep enough to still the breath of summer in his ears, but it had quieted the jabber of the magpie to a distant purring, and he was fast falling into the abyss of unconsciousness, when a gentle, regular sound made itself felt, the fall of a footstep and the brushing of a skirt through the grass. He lay very still, and cherished an ungenial hope that the white-stemmed birches might mercifully screen him from the invader. The step came nearer, and something in its solidity and determination gave Christopher a guess as to whose it was, that was speedily made certainty by a call that jarred all the sleepy enchantment of the glade.

'Fran-cie!'

Christopher shrank lower behind a mossy stone, and wildly hoped that his unconcealable white flannels might be mistaken for the stem of a fallen birch.

'Fran-cie!'

It had come nearer, and Christopher anticipated the inevitable discovery by getting up and speaking.

'I'm afraid she's not here, Miss Mullen. She has not been here for half an hour at least.' He did not feel bound to add that when he first sat down by the pool he had heard Miss Fitzpatrick's and Mr Hawkins' voices in high and agreeable altercation on the opposite side of the island to that taken by the rest of the party.

The asperity that had been discernible in Miss Mullen's summons to her cousin vanished at once.

'My goodness me! Mr Dysart! To think of your being here all the time, "Far from the madding crowd's ignoble strife!" Here I am hunting for that naughty girl to tell her to come and help to make tea, instead of letting your poor sister have all the trouble by herself.'

Charlotte was rather out of breath, and looked hot and annoyed, in spite of the smile with which she lubricated her remark.

'Oh, my sister is used to that sort of thing,' said Christopher, 'and Miss Hope-Drummond is there to help, isn't she?'

Charlotte had seated herself on a rock, and was fanning herself with her pocket-handkerchief; evidently going to make herself agreeable, Christopher thought, with an irritability that lost no detail of her hand's ungainly action.

'I don't think Miss Hope-Drummond is much in the utilitarian line,' she said, with a laugh that was as slighting as she dared to make it. 'Hers is the purely ornamental, I should imagine. Now, I will say for poor Francie, if she was there, no one would work harder than she would, and, though I say it that shouldn't, I think she's ornamental too.'

'Oh, highly ornamental,' said Christopher politely. 'I don't think there can be any doubt about that.'

'You're very good to say so,' replied Charlotte effusively; 'but I can tell you, Mr Dysart, that poor child has had to make herself useful as well as ornamental before now. From what she tells me, I suspect there were few things she didn't have to put her hand to before she came down to me here.'

'Really!' said Christopher, as politely as before, 'that was very hard luck.'

'You may say that it was!' returned Charlotte, planting a hand on each knee with elbows squared outwards, as was her wont in moments of excitement, and taking up her parable against the Fitzpatricks with all the enthusiasm of a near relation. 'Her uncle and aunt are very good people in their way, I suppose, but beyond feeding her and putting clothes on her back, I don't know what they did for her.'

Charlotte had begun her sentence with comparative calm, but she had gathered heat and velocity as she proceeded. She paused with a snort, and Christopher, who had never before been privi- leged to behold her in her intenser moments, said, without a very distinct idea of what was expected of him:

'Oh, really, and who are these amiable people?'

'Fitzpatricks!' spluttered Miss Mullen, 'and no better than the dirt under my poor cousin Isabella Mullen's feet. It's through *her* Francie's related to me, and not through the Fitzpatricks at all. *I'm* no relation of the Fitzpatricks, thank God! My father's brother married a Butler, and Francie's grandmother was a Butler too – '

'It's very intricate,' murmured Christopher; 'it sounds as if she ought to have been a parlour maid.'

'And that's the only connection I am of the Fitzpatricks,' con- tinued Miss Mullen at lightning speed, oblivious of interruption; 'but Francie takes after her mother's family and her grand- mother's family, and your poor father would tell you if he was able, that the Butlers of Tally Ho were as well known in their time as the Dysarts of Bruff!'

'I'm sure he would,' said Christopher feebly, thinking as he spoke that his conversations with his father had been wont to treat of more stirring and personal topics than the bygone glories of the Butlers.

'Yes, indeed, as good a family as any in the county. People laugh at me, and say I'm mad about family and pedigree; but I declare to goodness, Mr Dysart, I think the French are right when they say, "*bong song ne poo mongtir*," and there's nothing like good blood after all.'

Charlotte possessed the happy quality of believing in the purity of her own French accent, and she felt a great satisfaction in rounding her peroration with a quotation in that tongue. She had, moreover, worked off some of the irritation which had, from various causes, been seething within her when she met Christopher; and when she resumed her discourse it was in the voice of the orator, who, having ranted out one branch of his subject, enters upon the next with almost awful quietness.

'I don't know why I should bore you about a purely family matter, Mr Dysart, but the truth is, it cuts me to the heart when I see your sister – your charming sister – yes, and Miss Hope-Drummond too – not that I'd mention her in the same breath with Miss Dysart – with every advantage that education can give them, and then to think of that poor girl, brought up from hand to mouth, and her little fortune that should have been spent on herself going, as I may say, to fill the stomachs of the Fitzpatricks' brood!'

Christopher raised himself from the position of leaning against a tree, in which he had listened, not without interest, to the recital of Francie's wrongs.

'I don't think you need apologize for Miss Fitzpatrick,' he said, rather more coldly than he had yet spoken. He had ceased to be amused by Miss Mullen; eccentricity was one thing, but vulgar want of reserve was another; he wondered if she discussed her cousin's affairs thus openly with all her friends.

'It's very kind of you to say so,' rejoined Miss Mullen eagerly, 'but I know very well you're not blind, any more than I am, and all my affection for the girl can't make me shut my eyes to what's unladylike or bad style, though I know it's not her fault.'

Christopher looked at his watch surreptitiously.

'Now I'm delaying you in a most unwarrantable way,' said Charlotte, noting and interpreting the action at once, 'but I got so hot and tired running about the woods that I had to take a rest. I was trying to get a chance to say a word to your sister about Francie to ask her to be kind to her, but I daresay it'll come to the same thing now that I've had a chat with you,' she concluded, rising from her seat and smiling with luscious affability.

A little below the pond two great rocks leaned towards each other, and between them a hawthorn bush had pressed itself up to the light. Something like a path was trodden round the rocks, and a few rags impaled on the spikes of the thorn bush denoted that it marked the place of a holy well. Conspicuous among these votive offerings were two white rags, new and spotless, and altogether out of keeping with the scraps of red flannel and dirty frieze that had been left by the faithful in lieu of visiting cards for the patron saint of the shrine. Christopher and Charlotte's way led them within a few yards of the spot; the latter's curiosity induced her, as she passed, to examine the last contributions to the thorn bush.

'I wonder who has been tearing up their best pocket handkerchiefs for a wish?' said Christopher, putting up his eye-glass and peering at the rags.

'Two bigger fools than the rest of them, I suppose,' said Miss Mullen shortly; 'we'd better hurry on now, Mr Dysart, or we'll get no tea.'

She swept Christopher in front of her along the narrow path before he had time to see that the last two pilgrims had determined that the saint should make no mistake about their identity and had struck upon the thorn bush the corners of their handkerchiefs, one of them, a silken triangle, having on it the initials G. H., while on the other was a large and evidently home-embroidered F.

14

Late that afternoon, when the sun was beginning to stoop to the west, a wind came creeping down from somewhere back of the mountains, and began to stretch tentative cats' paws over the lake. It had pushed before it across the Atlantic, a soft mass of orange-coloured cloud, that caught the sun's lowered rays, and spread them in a mellow glare over everything. The lake turned to a coarse and furious blue; all the rocks and tree stems became like red gold, and the polished brass top of the funnel of the steam launch looked as if it were on fire as Captain Cursiter turned the *Serpolette*'s sharp snout to the wind, and steamed at full speed round Ochery Point. The yacht had started half an hour before on her tedious zig-zag journey home, and was already far down to the right, her sails all aglow as she leaned aslant like a skater, swooping and bending under the freshening breeze.

It was evident that Lambert wished to make the most of his time, for almost immediately after the *Daphne* had gone about with smooth precision, and had sprung away on the other tack, the party on the launch saw a flutter of white, and a top-sail was run up.

'By Jove! Lambert didn't make much on that tack,' remarked Captain Cursiter to his brother-in-arms, as with an imperceptible pressure of the wheel he serenely headed the launch straight for her destination. 'I don't believe he's done himself much good with that top-sail either.'

Mr Hawkins turned a sour eye upon the *Daphne*, and said laconically, 'Silly ass; he'll smother her.'

'Upon my word, I don't think he'll get in much before nine o'clock tonight,' continued Cursiter; 'it's pretty nearly dead in his teeth, and he doesn't make a hundred yards on each tack.'

Mr Hawkins slammed the lid of the coal bunker, and stepped past his chief into the after-part of the launch.

'I say, Miss Mullen,' he began with scarcely suppressed malignity, 'Captain Cursiter says you won't see your niece before tomorrow morning. You'll be sorry you wouldn't let her come home in the launch after all.'

'If she hadn't been so late for her tea,' retorted Miss Mullen, Mr Lambert could have started half an hour before he did.'

'Half an hour will be neither here nor there in this game. What Lambert ought to have done was to have started after luncheon, but I think I may remind you, Miss Mullen, that you took him off to the holy well then.'

Well, and if I did, I didn't leave my best pocket handkerchief hanging in rags on the thorn bush, like some other people I know of!' Miss Mullen felt that she had scored, and looked for sympathy to Pamela, who, having, as was usual with her, borne the heat and burden of the day in the matter of packings and washings-up, was now sitting, pale and tired, in the stern, with Dinah solidly implanted in her lap, and Max huddled miserably on the seat beside her. Miss Hope-Drummond, shrouded in silence and a long plaid cloak, paid no attention to anyone or anything. There are few who can drink the dregs of the cup of pleasuring with any appearance of enjoyment, and Miss Hope-Drummond was not one of them. The alteration in the respective crews of the yacht and the steam launch had been made by no wish of hers, and it is probable that but for the unexpected support that Cursiter had received from Miss Mullen, his schemes for Mr Hawkins' welfare would not have prospered. The idea had indeed occurred to Miss Hope-Drummond that the proprietor of the launch had perhaps a personal motive in suggesting the exchange, but when she found that Captain Cursiter was going to stand with his back to her, and steer, she wished that she had not yielded her place in the *Daphne* to a young person whom she already thought of as '*that* Miss Fitzpatrick', applying in its full force the demonstrative pronoun that denotes feminine animosity more subtly and expressively than is in the power of any adjective. Hawkins she felt was out of her jurisdiction and unworthy of attention, and she politely ignored Pamela's attempts to involve her in conversation with him. Her neat brown fringe was out of curl; long strands of hair blew unbecomingly over her ears; her feet were very cold, and she finally buried herself to the nose in a fur boa that gave her the effect of a moustached and bearded Russian noble, and began, as was her custom during sermons and other periods of tedium, to elaborate the construction of a new tea-gown.

To do Mr Hawkins justice, he, though equally illtreated by fate, rose superior to his disappointment. After his encounter with Miss Mullen he settled confidentially down in the corner beside Pamela, and amused himself by pulling Dinah's short fat tail, and puffing cigarette smoke in her face, while he regaled her mistress with an assortment of the innermost gossip of Lismoyle.

On board the *Daphne* the aspect of things was less comfortable. Although the wind was too much in her teeth for her to make much advance for home, there was enough to drive her through the water at a pace that made the long tacks from side to side of the lake seem as nothing, and to give Francie as much as she could do to keep her big hat on her head. She was sitting up on the weather side with Lambert, who was steering; and Christopher, in the bows, was working the head sails, and acting as movable ballast when they went about. At first, while they were beating out of the narrow channel of Ochery, Francie had found it advisable to lie in a heap beneath a tarpaulin, to avoid the onslaught of the boom at each frequent tack, but now that they were out on the open lake, with the top-sail hoisted, she had risen to her present position, and, in spite of her screams as the sharp squalls came down from the mountains and lifted her hat till it stood on end like a rearing horse, was enjoying herself amazingly. Unlike Miss Hope-Drummond, she was pre-eminently one of those who come home unflagging from the most prolonged outing, and today's entertainment, so far from being exhausting, had verified to the utmost her belief in the charms of the British officer, as well as Miss Fanny Hemphill's prophecies of her success in such quarters. Nevertheless she was quite content to return in the yacht; it was salutary for Mr Hawkins to see that she could do without him very well, it took her from Charlotte's dangerous proximity, and it also gave her an opportunity of appeasing Mr Lambert, who, as she was quite aware, was not in the best of tempers. So far her nimble tongue had of necessity been idle. Christopher's position in the bows isolated him from all conversation of the ordinary pitch, and Lambert had been at first too much occupied with the affairs of his boat to speak to her, but now, as a sharper gust nearly snatched her hat from her restraining hand, he turned to her.

'If it wasn't that you seem to enjoy having that hat blown inside out every second minute,' he said chillingly, 'I'd offer to lend you a cap.'

'What sort is it?' demanded Francie. 'If it's anything like that old deerstalker thing you have on your head now, I wouldn't touch it with the tongs!'

Lambert's only reply was to grope under the seat with one hand, and to bring out a red knitted cap of the conventional sailoring type, which he handed to Francie without so much as looking at her. Miss Fitzpatrick recognized its merits with half a glance, and, promptly putting it on her head, stuffed the chef-d'œuvre of the night before under the seat among the deck-swabs and ends of rope that lurked there. Christopher, looking aft at the moment, saw the change of headgear, and it was, perhaps, characteristic of him that even while he acknowledged the appropriateness of the red cap of liberty to the impertinence of the brilliant face beneath it, he found himself reminded of the extra supplement, in colours, of any Christmas number – indubitably pretty, but a trifle vulgar.

In the meantime the object of this patrónizing criticism, feeling herself now able to give her undivided attention to conversation, regarded Mr Lambert's sulky face with open amusement, and said:

'Well, now, tell me what made you so cross all day. Was it because Mrs Lambert wasn't out?'

Lambert looked at her for an instant without speaking. 'Ready about,' he called out. 'Mind your head! Lee helm!'

The little yacht hung and staggered for a moment, and then, with a diving plunge, started forward, with every sail full and straining. Francie scrambled with some difficulty to the other side of the tiny cockpit, and climbed up on to the seat by Mr Lambert, just in time to see a very fair imitation of a wave break on the weather bow and splash a sparkling shower into Christopher's face.

'Oh, Mr Dysart! are you drowned?' she screamed ecstatically.

'Not quite,' he called back, his hair hanging in dripping points on his forehead as he took off his cap and shook the water out of it. 'I say, Lambert, it's beginning to blow pretty stiff; I'd take that top-sail off her, if I were you.'

'She's often carried it in worse weather than this,' returned Lambert; 'a drop of water will do no one any harm.'

Mr Lambert in private, and as much as possible in public, affected to treat his employer's son as a milksop, and few things annoyed him more than the accepted opinion on the lake that there was no better man in a boat than Christopher Dysart. His secret fear that it was true made it now all the more intolerable that Christopher should lay down the law to him on a point of seamanship, especially with Francie by, ready in that exasperating way of hers to laugh at him on the smallest provocation.

'It'll do him no harm if he does get a drop of water over him,' he said to her in a low voice, forgetting for the moment his attitude of disapproval. 'Take some of the starch out of him for once!' He took a pull on the main sheet, and, with a satisfied upward look at the top-sail in question, applied himself to conversation. The episode had done him good, and it was with almost fatherly seriousness that he began:

'Now, Francie, you were telling me a while ago that I was cross all day. I'm a very old friend of yours, and I don't mind saying that I was greatly put out by the way' – he lowered his voice – 'by the way you were going on with that fellow Hawkins.'

'I don't know what you mean by "going on",' interrupted Francie, with a slight blush. 'What's the harm in talking to him if he likes to talk to me?'

'Plenty of harm,' returned Lambert quickly, 'when he makes a fool of you the way he did today. If you don't care that Miss

Dysart and the rest of them think you know no better than to behave like that, *I* do!'

'Behave like what?'

'Well, for one thing, to let him and Garry Dysart go sticking grass in your stockings that way after luncheon; and for another to keep Miss Dysart waiting tea for you for half an hour, and your only excuse to be to tell her that he was "teaching you to make ducks and drakes" the other side of the island.' The fatherly quality had died out of his voice, and the knuckles of the hand that held the tiller grew white from a harder grip.

Francie instinctively tucked away her feet under her petticoats. She was conscious that the green pattern still adorned her insteps and that tell-tale spikes of grass still projected on either side of her shoes.

'How could I help it? It was just a silly game that he and Garry Dysart made up between them; and as for Miss Dysart being angry with me, she never said a word to me. She was awfully good; and she and her brother had kept the teapot hot for me, and everything.' She looked furtively at Christopher, who was looking out at the launch, now crossing their path some distance ahead. 'It was more than *you'd* have done for me!'

'Yes, very likely it was; but I wouldn't have been laughing at you in my sleeve all the time as they were, or at least as he was, anyhow!'

'I believe that's a great lie,' said Francie unhesitatingly; 'and I don't care a jack-rat what he thought, or what you think either! Mr Hawkins is a very nice young man, and I'll talk to him just as much as I like! And he's coming to tea at Tally Ho tomorrow; and what's more, I asked him! So now!'

'Oh, all right!' said Lambert, in such a constrained voice of anger, that even Francie felt a little afraid of him. 'Have him to tea by all means; and if I were you I should send him down to Limerick and have Miss M'Carthy up to meet him!'

'What are you saying? Who's Miss M'Carthy?' asked Francie, with a disappointing sparkle of enjoyment in her eyes.

'She's the daughter of a George's Street tobacconist that your friend Mr Hawkins was so sweet about a couple of months ago that they packed him off here to be out of harm's way. Look out, Dysart, I'm going about now,' he continued without giving Francie time to reply. 'Lee-helm!'

'Oh, I'm sick of you and your old "lee-helm"!' cried Francie, as she grovelled again in the cockpit to avoid the swing of the boom. 'Why can't you go straight like Captain Cursiter's steamer, instead of bothering backwards and forwards, sideways, like this? And you always do it just when I want to ask you something.'

This complaint, which was mainly addressed to Mr Lambert's canvas yachting shoes, received no attention. When Francie came to the surface she found that the yacht was at a more uncomfortable angle than ever, and with some difficulty she established herself on the narrow strip of deck, outside the coaming, with her feet hanging into the cockpit.

'Now, Mr Lambert,' she began at once, 'you'd better tell me Miss M'Carthy's address, and all about her, and perhaps if you're good I'll ask you to meet her too.'

As she spoke, a smart squall struck the yacht, and Lambert luffed her hard up to meet it. A wave with a ragged white edge flopped over her bows, wetting Christopher again, and came washing aft along the deck behind the coaming.

'Look out aft there!' he shouted. 'She's putting her nose into it! I tell you that top-sail's burying her, Lambert.'

Lambert made no answer to either Francie or Christopher. He had as much as he could do to hold the yacht, which was snatching at the tiller like a horse at its bit, and ripping her way deep through the waves in a manner too vigorous to be pleasant. It was about seven o'clock, and though the sun was still some height above the dark jagged wall of the mountains, the clouds had risen in a tawny fleece across his path, and it was evident that he would be seen no more that day. The lake had turned to indigo. The beds of reeds near the shore were pallid by contrast as they stooped under the wind; the waves that raced towards the yacht had each an angry foam-crest, having, after the manner of lake waves, lashed themselves into a high state of indignation on very short notice, and hissed and effervesced like soda water all along the lee-gunwale of the flying yacht. A few seagulls that were trying to fight their way back down to the sea, looked like fluttering scraps of torn white paper against the angry bronze of the clouds, and the pine trees on the point, under the lee of which they were scudding, were tossing like the black plumes of a hearse.

Lambert put the yacht about, and headed back across the lake.

'We did pretty well on that tack, Dysart,' he shouted. 'We ought to get outside Screeb Point with the next one, and then we'll get the wind a point fairer, and make better weather of it the rest of the way home.'

He could see the launch, half a mile or so beyond the point, ploughing steadily along on her way to Lismoyle, and in his heart he wished that Francie was on board of her. He also wished that Christopher had held his confounded tongue about the top-sail. If he hadn't shoved in his oar where he wasn't wanted, he'd have had that top-sail off her twenty minutes ago; but he wasn't going to stand another man ordering him about in his own boat.

'Look here, Francie,' he said, 'you must look out for yourself when I'm going about next time. It's always a bit squally round this point, so you'd better keep down in the cockpit till we're well on the next tack.'

'But I'll get all wet down there,' objected Francie, 'and I'd much rather stay up here and see the fun.'

'You talk as if it was the top of a tram in Sackville Street,' said Lambert, snatching a glance of provoked amusement at her unconcerned face. 'I can tell you it will take a good deal more holding on to than that does. Promise me now, like a good child,' he went on, with a sudden thrill of anxiety at her helplessness and ignorance, 'that you'll do as I tell you. You *used* to mind what I said to you.'

He leaned towards her as he spoke, and Francie raised her eyes to his with a laugh in them that made him for the moment forgetful of everything else. They were in the open water in the centre of the lake by this time. And in that second a squall came roaring down upon them.

'Luff!' shouted Christopher, letting go the head sheets. 'Luff, or we're over!'

Lambert let go the main sheet and put the tiller hard down with all the strength he was master of, but he was just too late. In that moment, when he had allowed his thoughts to leave his steering, the yacht had dragged herself a thought beyond his control. The rough hand of the wind struck her, and, as she quivered and reeled under the blow, another and fiercer gust caught hold of her, and flung her flat on her side on the water.

Before Christopher had well realized what had happened, he had gone deep under water, come to the surface again, and was swimming, with a vision before him of a white figure with a red cap falling headlong from its perch. He raised himself and shook the water out of his eyes, and swimming a stroke or two to get clear of the mast, with its sails heaving prone on the water like the pinions of a great wounded bird, he saw over the shoulders of the hurrying waves the red cap and the white dress drifting away to leeward. Through the noise of the water in his ears, and the confusion of his startled brain, he heard Lambert's voice shouting frantically he did not know what; the whole force of his nature was set and centred on overtaking the red cap, to which each stroke was bringing him nearer and nearer as it appeared and reappeared ahead of him between the steely backs of the waves. She lay horribly still, with the water washing over her face; and as Christopher caught her dress, and turned, breathless, to try to fight his way back with her to the wrecked yacht, he seemed to hear a hundred voices ringing in his ears and telling him that she was dead. He was a good and practised swimmer, but not a powerful one. His clothes hung heavily about him, and with one arm necessarily given to his burden, and the waves and wind beating him back, he began to think that his task was more than he would be able to accomplish. He had up to this, in the intensity of the shock and struggle, forgotten Lambert's existence, but now the agonized shouts that he had heard came back to him, and he raised himself high in the water and stared about with a new anxiety. To his intense relief he saw that the yacht was still afloat, was, in fact, drifting slowly down towards him, and in the water not ten yards from him was her owner, labouring towards him with quick splashing strokes, and evidently in a very exhausted state. His face was purple-red, his eyes half starting out of his head, and Christopher could hear his hard breathing as he slowly bore down upon him.

'She's all right, Lambert!' Christopher cried out, though his heart belied the words. 'I've got her! Hold hard; the yacht will be down on us in a minute.'

Whether Lambert heard the words or no was not apparent. He came struggling on, and as soon as he got within reach, made a snatch at Francie's dress. Christopher had contrived to get his left arm round her waist, and to prop her chin on his shoulder, so that her face should be above the water, and, as Lambert's weight swung on him, it was all he could do to keep her in this position.

'You'll drown us all if you don't let go!' Uttermost exertion and want of breath made Christopher's voice wild and spasmodic. 'Can't you tread water till the boat gets to us?'

Lambert still speechlessly and convulsively dragged at her, his breath breaking from him in loud gasps, and his face working.

'Good God, he's gone mad!' thought Christopher; 'we're all done for if he won't let go.' In desperation he clenched his fist, with the intention of hitting Lambert on the head, but just as he gathered his forces for this extreme measure something struck him softly in the back. Lambert's weight had twisted him round so that he was no longer facing the yacht, and he did not know how near help was. It was the boom of the *Daphne* that had touched him like a friendly hand, and he turned and caught at it with a feeling of more intense thankfulness than he had known in all his life.

The yacht was lying over on her side, half full of water, but kept afloat by the air-tight compartments that Mrs Lambert's terrors had insisted on, and that her money had paid for, when her husband had first taken to sailing on the lake. Christopher was able with a desperate effort to get one knee on to the submerged coaming of the cockpit, and catching at its upper side with his right hand, he recovered himself and prepared to draw Francie up after him.

'Come, Lambert, let go!' he said threateningly, 'and help me to get her out of the water. You need not be afraid, you can hold on to the boat.'

Lambert had not hitherto tried to speak, but now with the support that the yacht gave him, his breath came back to him a little.

'Damn you!' he spluttered, the loud sobbing breaths almost choking him, 'I'm not afraid! Let her go! Take your arm from round her, I can hold her better than you can. Ah!' he shrieked, suddenly seeing Francie's face, as Christopher, without regarding what he said, drew her steadily up from his exhausted grasp, 'she's dead! you've let her drown!'

His head fell forward, and Christopher thought with the calm of despair, 'He's going under, and I can't help him if he does. Here, Lambert! man alive, don't let go! There! do you hear the launch whistling? They're coming to us!'

Lambert's hand, with its shining gold signet-ring, was gripping the coaming under water with a grasp that was already mechanical. It seemed to Christopher that it had a yellow, drowned look about it. He put out his foot, and, getting it under Lambert's chin, lifted his mouth out of the water. The steam launch was whistling incessantly, in long notes, in short ones, in jerks, and he lifted up his voice against the forces of the wind and the hissing and dashing of the water to answer her. Perhaps it was the dull weight on his arm and the stricken stillness of the face that lay in utter unconsciousness on his shoulder, but he scarcely recognized his own voice, it was broken with such a tone of stress and horror. He had never before heard such music as Hawkins' shout hailing him in answer, nor seen a sight so heavenly fair as the bow of the *Serpolette* cutting its way through the thronging waves to their rescue. White faces staring over her gunwale broke into a loud cry when they saw him hanging, half-spent, against the tilted deck of the *Daphne*. It was well, he thought, that they had not waited any longer. The only question was whether they were not even now too late. His head swam from excitement and fatigue, his arms and knees trembled, and when at last Francie, Lambert, and finally he himself, were lifted on board the launch, it seemed the culminating point of a long and awful nightmare that Charlotte Mullen should fling herself on her knees beside the bodies of her cousin and her friend, and utter yell after yell of hysterical lamentation.

15

'Sausages and bacon, Lady Dysart! Yes, indeed, that was his breakfast, and that for a man who – if you'll excuse the expression, Lady Dysart, but, indeed, I know you're such a good doctor that I'd like you to tell me if it was quite safe – who was vomiting lake water for half an hour after he was brought into the house the night before.'

'Do you really mean that he came down to breakfast?' asked Lady Dysart, with the flattering sincerity of interest that she bestowed on all topics of conversation, but especially on those that related to the art and practice of medicine. 'He ought to have stayed in bed all day to let the system recover from the shock.'

'Those were the very words I used to him, Lady Dysart,' returned Mrs Lambert dismally; 'but indeed all the answer he made was, "Fiddle-de-dee!" He wouldn't have so much as a cup of tea in his bed, and you may think what I suffered, Lady Dysart, when I was down in the parlour making the breakfast and getting his tray ready, when I heard him in his bath overhead – just as if he hadn't been half drowned the night before. I didn't tell you that, Mrs Gascogne,' she went on, turning her watery gaze upon the thin refined face of her spiritual directress. 'Now if it was me such a thing happened to, I'd have that nervous dread of water that I couldn't look at it for a week.'

'No, I am sure you would not,' answered Mrs Gascogne with

the over-earnestness which so often shipwrecks the absent-minded; 'of course you couldn't expect him to take it if it wasn't made with really boiling water.'

Mrs Lambert stared in stupefaction, and Lady Dysart, far from trying to cloak her cousin's confusion, burst into a delightful laugh.

'Kate! I don't believe you heard a single word that Mrs Lambert said! You were calculating how many gallons of tea will be wanted for your school feast.'

'Nonsense, Isabel!' said Mrs Gascogne hotly, with an indignant and repressive glance at Lady Dysart, 'and how was it – ' turning to Mrs Lambert, 'that he – a – swallowed so much lake water?'

'He was cot under the sail, Mrs Gascogne. He made a sort of a dash at Miss Fitzpatrick to save her when she was falling, and he slipped someway, and got in under the sail, and he was half choked before he could get out!' A tear of sensibility trickled down the good turkey-hen's red beak. 'Indeed, I don't know when I've been so upset, Lady Dysart,' she quavered.

'Upset!' echoed Lady Dysart, raising her large eyes dramatically to the cut glass chandelier, 'I can well believe it! When it came to ten o'clock and there was no sign of them, I was simply *raging* up and down between the house and the pier like a mad bull robbed of its whelps!' She turned to Mrs Gascogne, feeling that there was a biblical ring in the peroration that demanded a higher appreciation than Mrs Lambert could give, and was much chagrined to see that lady concealing her laughter behind a handkerchief.

Mrs Lambert looked bewilderingly from one to the other, and, feeling that the ways of the aristocracy were beyond her comprehension, went on with the recital of her own woes.

'He actually went down to Limerick by train in the afternoon – he that was half drowned the day before, and a paragraph in the paper about his narrow escape. I haven't had a wink of sleep those two nights, what with palpitations and bad dreams. I don't believe, Lady Dysart, I'll ever be the better of it.'

'Oh, you'll get over it soon, Mrs Lambert,' said Lady Dysart cheerfully; 'why I had no less than three children – '

'Calves,' murmured Mrs Gascogne, with still streaming eyes.

'Children,' repeated Lady Dysart emphatically, 'and I thought they were every one of them drowned!'

'Oh, but a *husband*, Lady Dysart,' cried Mrs Lambert with orthodox unction, 'what are children compared to the husband?'

95

'Oh – er – of course not,' said Lady Dysart, with something less than her usual conviction of utterance, her thoughts flying to Sir Benjamin and his bath chair.

'By the way,' struck in Mrs Gascogne, 'my husband desired me to say that he hopes to come over tomorrow afternoon to see Mr Lambert, and to hear all about the accident.'

Mrs Lambert looked more perturbed than gratified. 'It's very kind of the Archdeacon I'm sure,' she said nervously; 'but Mr Lambert – ' (Mrs Lambert belonged to the large class of women who are always particular to speak of their husbands by their full style and title) 'Mr Lambert is most averse to talking about it, and perhaps – if the Archdeacon didn't mind – '

'That's just what I complain of in Christopher,' exclaimed Lady Dysart, breaking with renewed vigour into the conversation. 'He was *most* unsatisfactory about it all. Of course, when he came home that night, he was so exhausted that I spared him. I said, "Not one word will I allow you to say tonight, and I *command* you to stay in bed for breakfast tomorrow morning!" I even went down at one o'clock, and pinned a paper on William's door, so that he shouldn't call him. Well – ' Lady Dysart, at this turning-point of her story, found herself betrayed into saying 'My dear', but had presence of mind enough to direct the expression at Mrs Gascogne. 'Well, my dear, when I went up in the morning, craving for news, he was most confused and unsatisfactory. He pretended he knew nothing of how it had happened, and that after the upset they all went drifting about in a sort of a knot till the yacht came down on top of them. But, of course, something more must have happened to them than *that*! It really was the greatest pity that Miss Fitzpatrick got stunned by that blow on the head just at the beginning of the whole business. *She* would have told us all about it. But men never can describe anything.'

'Oh, well, I assure you, Lady Dysart,' piped the turkey hen, 'Mr Lambert described to me all that he possibly could, and he said Mr Dysart gave every assistance in his power, and was the greatest help to him in supporting that poor girl in the water; but the townspeople were so very inquisitive, and really annoyed him so much with their questions, that he said to me this morning he hoped he'd hear no more about it, which is why I took the liberty of asking Mrs Gascogne that the Archdeacon wouldn't mention it to him.'

'Oh, yes, yes,' said Mrs Gascogne very politely, recalling herself with difficulty from the mental excursion on which she had started when Lady Dysart's unrelenting eye had been removed. 'I am sure he will – a – be delighted. I think, you know, Isabel, we ought – '

Lady Dysart was on her feet in a moment. 'Yes, indeed, we ought!' she responded briskly. 'I have to pick up Pamela. Goodbye, Mrs Lambert; I hope I shall find you looking better the next time I see you, and remember, if you cannot sleep, that there is no opiate like an open window!'

Mrs Lambert's exclamation of horror followed her visitors out of the room. Open windows were regarded by her as a necessary housekeeping evil, akin to twigging carpets and whitewashing the kitchen, something to be got over before anyone came downstairs. Not even her reverence for Lady Dysart would induce her to tolerate such a thing in any room in which she was, and she returned to her woolwork, well satisfied to let the July sunshine come to her through the well-fitting plate-glass windows of her hideous drawing room.

'The person I do pity in the whole matter,' remarked Lady Dysart, as the landau rolled out of the Rosemount gates and towards Lismoyle, 'is Charlotte Mullen. Of course, that poor excellent little Mrs Lambert got a great shock, but that was nothing compared with seeing the sail go flat down on the water, as the people in the launch did. In the middle of all poor Pamela's own fright, when she was tearing open one of the luncheon baskets to get some whisky out, Charlotte went into raging hysterics, and *roared*, my dear! And then she all but fainted on to the top of Mr Hawkins. Who would ever have thought of her breaking down in that kind of way?'

'Faugh!' said Mrs Gascogne, 'disgusting creature!'

'Now, Kate, you are always saying censorious things about that poor woman. People can't help showing their feelings sometimes, no matter how ugly they are! All that I can tell you is,' said Lady Dysart, warming to fervour as was her wont, 'if you had seen her this afternoon as I did, with the tears in her eyes as she described the whole thing to me, and the agonies she was in about that girl, you would have felt sorry for her.'

Mrs Gascogne shot a glance, bright with intelligence and amusement, at her cousin's flushed handsome face, and held her peace. With Mrs Gascogne, to hold her peace was to glide into the sanctuary of her own thoughts, and remain there oblivious of all besides; but the retribution that would surely have overtaken her at the next pause in Lady Dysart's harangue was averted by the stopping of the carriage at Miss Mullen's gate.

Francie lay back on her sofa after Pamela Dysart had left her.

She saw the landau drive away towards Bruff, with the sun twinkling on the silver of the harness, and thought with an ungrudging envy how awfully nice Miss Dysart was, and how lovely it would be to have a carriage like that to drive about in. People in Dublin, who were not half as grand as the Dysarts, would have been a great deal too grand to come and see her up in her room like this, but here everyone was as friendly as they could be, and not a bit stuck-up. It was certainly a good day for her when she came down to Lismoyle, and in spite of all that Uncle Robert had said about old Aunt Mullen's money, and how Charlotte had feathered her own nest, there was no denying that Charlotte was not a bad old thing after all. Her only regret was that she had not seen the dress that Miss Dysart had on this afternoon before she had got herself that horrid ready-made pink thing, and the shirt with the big pink horse-shoes on it. Fanny Hemphill's hitherto unquestioned opinion in the matter of costume suddenly tottered in her estimation, and, with the loosening of that buttress of her former life, all her primitive convictions were shaken.

The latch of the gate clicked again, and she leaned forward to see who was coming. 'What nonsense it is keeping me up here this way!' she said to herself; 'there's Roddy Lambert coming in, and won't he be cross when he finds that there's only Charlotte for him to talk to! I *will* go down tomorrow, no matter what they say, but I suppose it will be ages before the officers call again now.' Miss Fitzpatrick became somewhat moody at this reflection, and tried to remember what it was that Mr Hawkins had said about 'taking shooting leave for the 12th'; she wished she hadn't been such a fool as not to ask him what he had meant by the 12th. If it meant the 12th of July, she mightn't see him again till he came back, and goodness knows when that would be. Roddy Lambert was all very well, but what was he but an old married man. 'Gracious!' she interrupted herself aloud with a little giggle, 'how mad he'd be if he thought I called him that!' and Hawkins was really a very jolly fellow. The hall door opened again; she heard Charlotte's voice raised in leave-taking, and then Mr Lambert walked slowly down the drive and the hall door slammed. 'He didn't stay long,' thought Francie; 'I wonder if he's cross because I wasn't downstairs? He's a very cross man. Oh, look at him kicking Mrs Bruff into the bushes! It's well for him Charlotte's coming upstairs and can't see him!'

Charlotte was not looking any the worse for what she had gone through on the day of the accident; in fact, as she came into the room, there was an air of youthfulness and good spirits about her that altered her surprisingly, and her manner towards her cousin was geniality itself.

'Well, my child!' she began, 'I hadn't a minute since dinner to come and see you. The doorstep's worn out with the world and his wife coming to ask how you are; and Louisa doesn't know whether she's on her head or her heels with all the clean cups she's had to bring in!'

'Well, I wish to goodness I'd been downstairs to help her,' said Francie, whirling her feet off the sofa and sitting upright; 'there's nothing ails me to keep me stuck up here.'

'Well, you shall come down tomorrow,' replied Charlotte soothingly; 'I'm going to lunch with the Bakers, so you'll have to come down to do your manners to Christopher Dysart. His mother said he was coming to inquire for you tomorrow. And remember that only for him the pike would be eating you at the bottom of the lake this minute! Mind that! You'll have to thank him for saving your life.'

'Mercy on us!' cried Francie; 'what on earth will I say to him?'

'Oh, you'll find plenty to say to him! They're as easy as me old shoe, all those Dysarts; I'd pity no one that had one of them to talk to, from the mother down. Did you notice at the picnic how Pamela and her brother took all the trouble on themselves? That's what I call breeding, and not sitting about to be waited on like that great lazy hunks, Miss Hope-Drummond! I declare I loathe the sight of these English fine ladies, and my private belief is that Christopher Dysart thinks the same of her, though he's too well bred to show it. Yes, my poor Susan,' fondling with a large and motherly hand the cat that was sprawling on her shoulder; 'he's a real gentleman, like yourself, and not a drop of dirty Saxon blood in him. *He* doesn't bring his great vulgar bulldog here to worry my poor son – '

'What did Mr Lambert say, Charlotte?' asked Francie, who began to be a little bored by this rhapsody. 'Was he talking about the accident?'

'Very little,' said Charlotte, with a change of manner; 'he only said that poor Lucy, who wasn't there at all, was far worse than any of us. As I told him, you, that we thought was dead, would be down tomorrow, and not worth asking after. Indeed we were talking about business most of the time – ' She pressed her face down on the cat's grey back to hide an irrepressible smile of recollection. 'But that's only interesting to the parties concerned.'

16

Francie felt an unexpected weakness in her knees when she walked downstairs next day. She found herself clutching the stair-rail with an absurdly tight grasp, and putting her feet down with trembling caution on the oil-cloth stair covering, and when she reached the drawing room she was thankful to subside into Charlotte's armchair, and allow her dizzy head to recover its equilibrium. She thought very little about her nerves; in fact, was too ignorant to know whether she possessed such things, and she gave a feeble laugh of surprise at the way her heart jumped and fluttered when the door slammed unexpectedly behind her. The old green sofa had been pulled out from the wall and placed near the open window, with the Dublin *Express* laid upon it; Francie noticed and appreciated the attention, and noted, too, that an armchair, sacred to the use of visitors, had been planted in convenient relation to the sofa. 'For Mr Dysart, I suppose,' she thought, with a curl of her pretty lip; 'he'll be as much obliged to her as I am.' She pushed the chair away, and debated with herself as to whether she should dislodge the two cats who, with faces of frowning withdrawal from all things earthly, were heaped in simulated slumber in the corner of the sofa. She chose the armchair, and, taking up the paper, languidly read the list of places where bands would play in the coming week, and the advertisement of the anthem at St Patrick's for the next day.

How remote she felt from it all! How stale appeared these cherished amusements! Most people would think the Lismoyle choir a poor substitute for the ranks of white surplices in the chancel of St Patrick's, with the banners of the knights hanging above them, but Francie thought it much better fun to look down over the edge of the Lismoyle gallery at the red coats of Captain Cursiter's detachment, than to stand crushed in the nave of the cathedral, even though the most popular treble was to sing a solo, and though Mr Thomas Whitty might be waiting on the steps to disentangle her from the crowd that would slowly surge up them into the street. A heavy booted foot came along the passage, and

100

the door was opened by Norry, holding in her grimy hand a tumbler containing a nauseous looking yellow mixture.

'Miss Charlotte bid me give ye a bate egg with a half glass of whisky in it whenever ye'd come downstairs.' She stirred it with a black kitchen fork, and proffered the sticky tumbler to Francie, who took it, and swallowed the thin, flat liquid which it contained with a shudder of loathing. 'How bad y'are! Dhrink every dhrop of it now! An empty sack won't stand, and ye're as white as a masheroon this minute. God knows it's in yer bed ye should be, and not shtuck out in a chair in the middle of the flure readin' the paper!' Her eye fell on the apparently unconscious Mrs and Miss Bruff. 'Ha, ha! thin! how cosy the two of yez is on yer sofa! Walk out, me Lady Ann!'

This courtesy-title, the expression of Norry's supremest contempt and triumph, was accompanied by a sudden onslaught with the hearth brush, but long before it could reach them the ladies referred to had left the room by the open window.

The room was very quiet after Norry had gone away. Francie took the evicted holding of the cats, and fell speedily into a doze induced by the unwonted half glass of whisky. Her early dinner, an unappetizing meal of boiled mutton and rice pudding, was but a short interlude in the dullness of the morning; and after it was eaten, a burning tract of afternoon extended itself between her and Mr Dysart's promised visit. She looked out of the window at the sailing shreds of white cloud high up in the deep blue of the sky, at the fat bees swinging and droning in the purple blossoms of the columbine border, at two kittens playing furiously in the depths of the mignonette bed; and regardless of Charlotte's injunctions about the heat of the sun, she said to herself that she would go out into the garden for a little. It was three o'clock and her room was as hot as an oven when she went up to get her hat; her head ached as she stood before the glass and arranged the wide brim to her satisfaction, and stuck her best paste pin into the sailor's knot of her tie. Suddenly the door burst unceremoniously open, and Norry's grey head and filthy face were thrust round the edge of it.

'Come down, Miss Francie!' she said in a fierce whisper; 'give over making shnouts at yerself in the glass and hurry on down! Louisa isn't in, and sure I can't open the doore the figure I am.'

'Who's there?' asked Francie, with flushing cheeks.

'How would I know? I'd say 'twas Misther Lambert's knock whatever. Sich gallopin' in and out of the house as there is these two days! Ye may let in this one yerself!'

When Francie opened the hall door she was both relieved and disappointed to find that Norry had been right in the matter of the knock. Mr Lambert was apparently more taken by surprise than she was. He did not speak at once, but, taking her hand, pressed it very hard, and when Francie, finding the silence slightly embarrassing, looked up at him with a laugh that was intended to simplify the situation, she was both amazed and frightened to see a moisture suspiciously like tears in his eyes.

'You – you look rather washed out,' he stammered.

'You're very polite! Is that all you have to say to me?' she said, slipping her hand out of his, and gaily ignoring his tragic tone. 'You and your old yacht nearly washed me out altogether! At all events, you washed the colour out of me pretty well.' She put up her hands and rubbed her cheeks. 'Are you coming in or going out? Charlotte's lunching at the Bakers', and I'm going into the garden till tea-time, so now you can do as you like.'

'I'll come into the garden with you,' he said, stepping aside to let her pass out. 'But are you sure your head is well enough for you to go out in this sun?'

'Sun your granny!' responded Francie, walking gingerly across the gravel in her high heeled house shoes; 'I'm as well as ever I was.'

'Well, you don't look it,' he said with a concerned glance at the faint colour in her cheeks and the violet shadows under her eyes. 'Come and sit down in the shade; it's about all you're good for.'

A path skirted the flower beds and bent round the evergreen-covered slope that rose between the house and the road, and at the bend a lime tree spread its flat, green boughs lavishly over the path, shading a seat made of half-rotten larch poles that extended its dilapidated arms to the passer-by.

'Well now, tell me all about it,' began Lambert as soon as they had sat down. 'What did you feel like when you began to remember it all? Were you very angry with me?'

'Yes, of course, I was angry with you, and I am now this minute, and haven't I a good right, with my new hat at the bottom of the lake?'

'I can tell you we were both pretty nearly at the bottom of the lake along with it,' said Lambert, who disapproved of this frivolous way of treating the affair. 'I don't suppose I ever was nearer death than I was when the sail was on top of me.'

Francie looked at him for one instant with awestruck eyes, and Lambert was congratulating himself on having made her realize the seriousness of the situation, when she suddenly burst out laughing.

'Oh!' she apologized, 'the thought just came into my head of the look of Mrs Lambert in a widow's cap, and how she'd adore to wear one! You know she would, now don't you?'

'And I suppose you'd adore to see her in one?'

'Of course I would!' She gave him a look that was equivalent to the wag of the tail with which a dog assures the obtuse human being that its worrying and growling are only play. 'You might know that without being told. And now perhaps you'll tell me how poor Mrs Lambert is? I hear she was greatly upset by the fright she got about you, and indeed you're not worthy of it.'

'She's much better, thank you.'

He looked at Francie under his lowered lids, and tried to find it in his heart to wish that she could sometimes be a little more grown up and serious. She was leaning back with her hat crushed against a trunk of the tree, so that its brim made a halo round her face, and the golden green light that filtered through the leaves of the lime moved like water over the white dress. If he had ever heard the story of 'Undine' it might have afforded him the comforting hypothesis that this delicate, cool, youthful creature, with her provoking charm, could not possibly be weighted with the responsibility of a soul; but an unfortunate lack of early culture denied to Mr Lambert this excuse for the levity with which she always treated him – a man fifteen years older than she was, her oldest friend, as he might say, who had always been kind to her ever since she was a scut of a child. Her eyes were closed; but an occasional quiver of the long lashes told him that she had no intention of sleeping; she was only pretending to be tired, 'out of tricks,' he thought angrily. He waited for a moment or two, and then he spoke her name. The corners of her mouth curved a little, but the eyelashes were not raised.

'Are you tired, or are you shamming?'

'Shamming,' was the answer, still with closed eyes.

'Don't you think you could open your eyes?'

'No.'

Another short period of silence ensued, and the sound of summer in the air round them strengthened and deepened, as the colour strengthens and deepens in a blush. A wasp strayed in under the canopy of the lime and idled inquisitively about Francie's hat and the bunch of mignonette in her belt, but she lay so still under this supreme test that Lambert thought she must be really asleep, and taking out his handkerchief prepared to rout

103

the invader. At the same moment there came a sound of wheels and a fast-trotting horse on the road; it neared them rapidly, and Miss Fitzpatrick leaped to her feet and put aside the leaves of the lime just in time to see the back of Mr Hawkins' head as his polo cart spun past the Tally Ho gate.

'I declare I thought it was Mr Dysart,' she said, looking a little ashamed of herself; 'I wonder where in the name of fortune is Mr Hawkins going?'

'I thought you were so dead asleep you couldn't hear anything,' said Lambert, with a black look; 'he's not coming here, anyhow.'

She dropped back into the corner of the seat again as if the start forward had tired her.

'Oh! I was so frightened at the wasp, and I wouldn't let on!'

'I wonder why you're always so unfriendly with me now,' began Lambert suddenly, fixing his eyes upon her; 'there was once on a time when we were great friends, and you used to write to me, and you'd say you were glad to see me when I went up to town, but now you're so set up with your Dysarts and your officers that you don't think your old friends worth talking to.'

'Oh!' Francie sat up and faced her accuser valiantly, but with an inwardly-stricken conscience. 'You know that's a dirty, black lie!'

'I came over here this afternoon,' pursued Lambert, 'very anxious about you, and wanting to tell you how sorry I was, and how I accused myself for what had happened – and how am I treated? You won't so much as take the trouble to speak to me. I suppose if I was one of your swell new friends – Christopher Dysart, for instance, who you are looking out for so hard – it would be a very different story.'

By the time this indictment was delivered, Francie's face had more colour in it than it had known for some days; she kept her eyes on the ground and said nothing.

'I knew it was the way of the world to kick a fellow out of the way when you had got as much as you wanted out of him, and I suppose as I am an old married man I have no right to expect anything better, but I did think you'd have treated *me* better than this!'

'Don't,' she said brokenly, looking up at him with her eyes full of tears; 'I'm too tired to fight you.'

Lambert took her hand quickly. 'My child,' he said, in a voice rough with contrition and pity, 'I didn't mean to hurt you; I didn't know what I was saying.' He tenderly stroked the hand that lay limply in his. 'Tell me you're not vexed with me.'

'No,' said Francie, with a childish sob; 'but you said horrid things to me – '

'Well, I never will again,' he said soothingly. 'We'll always be friends, won't we?' with an interrogatory pressure of the hand. He had never seen her in such a mood as this; he forgot the inevitable effect on her nerves of what she had gone through, and his egotism made him believe that this collapse of her usual supple hardihood was due to the power of his reproaches.

'Yes,' she answered, with the dawn of a smile.

'Till the next time, anyhow,' continued Lambert, still holding her hand in one of his, and fumbling in his breast pocket with the other. 'And now, look here what I brought you to try and make up to you for nearly drowning you.' He gently pulled her hand down from her eyes, and held up a small gold bangle, with two horse-shoes in pearls on it. 'Isn't that a pretty thing?'

Francie looked at it incredulously, with the tears still shining on her eyelashes.

'Oh, Mr Lambert, you don't mean you got that for me? I *couldn't* take it. Why, it's real gold!'

'Well, you've got to take it. Look what's written on it.'

She took it from him, and saw engraved inside the narrow band of gold her own name and the date of the accident.

'Now, you see it's yours already,' he said. 'No, you mustn't refuse it,' as she tried to put it back into his hand again. 'There,' snapping it quickly on to her wrist, 'you must keep it as a sign you're not angry with me.'

'It's like a policeman putting on a handcuff,' said Francie, with a quivering laugh. 'I've often seen them putting them on the drunken men in Dublin.'

'And you'll promise not to chuck over your old friends?' said Lambert urgently.

'No, I won't chuck them over,' she replied, looking confidingly at him.

'Not for anybody?' He weighted the question with all the expression he was capable of.

'No, not for anybody,' she repeated, rather more readily than he could have wished.

'And you're sure you're not angry with me?' he persisted, 'and you like the bangle?'

She had taken it off to re-examine it, and she held it up to him.

'Here, put it on me again, and don't be silly,' she said, the old spirit beginning to wake in her eyes.

'Do you remember when you were a child the way you used

to thank me when I gave you anything?' he asked, pressing her hand hard.

'But I'm not a child now!'

Lambert, looking in her face, saw the provoking smile spread like sunshine from her eyes to her lips, and, intoxicated by it, he stooped his head and kissed her.

Steps came running along the walk towards them, and the fat face and red head of the Protestant orphan appeared under the boughs of the lime tree.

'A messenger from Bruff's afther bringing this here, Miss France,' she panted, tendering a letter in her fingers, 'an' Miss Charlotte lef' me word I should get tea when ye'd want it, an' will I wet it now?'

Christopher had shirked the expression of Miss Fitzpatrick's gratitude.

17

'My Dearest Fanny,

'Although I'm nearly dead after the bazaar I must write you a line or two to tell you what it was like. It was scrumshous. I wore my white dress with the embroidery the first day and the pink dress that you and I bought together the second day and everybody liked me best in the white one. It was fearful hot and it was great luck it was at the flower stall Mrs Gascogne asked me to sell. Kathleen Baker and the Beatties had the refreshments and if you saw the colour of their faces with the heat at teatime I declare you'd have to laugh. The Dysarts brought in a lovely lot of flowers and Mr Dysart was very nice helping me to tie them up. You needn't get on with any of your nonsense about him, he'd never think of flirting with me or anyone though he's fearfully polite and you'd be in fits if you saw the way Miss Hopedrummond the girl I told you about was running after him and anyone could see he'd sooner talk to his sister or his mother and I don't wonder for their both very nice which is more than she is. Roddy

106

Lambert was there of course and poor Mrs L. in a puce dress and everybody from the whole country round. Mr Hawkins was grand fun. Nothing would do him but to come behind the counter with me and Mrs Gascogne and go on with the greatest nonsense selling buttonholes to the old ladies and making them buy a lot of old rotten jeranium cuttings that was all Charlotte would give to the stall. The second day it was only just the townspeople that were there and I couldn't be bothered selling to them all day and little thanks you get from them. The half of them came thinking they'd get every thing for nothing because it was the last day and you'd hear them fighting Mrs Gascogne as if she was a shop-woman. I sat up in the gallery with Hawkins most of the evening and he brought up tea there and strawberries and Charlotte was shouting and roaring round the place looking for me and nobody knew where we were. 'Twas lovely – '

At this point Miss Fitzpatrick became absorbed in meditation, and the portrayal on the blotting paper of a profile of a conventionally classic type, which, by virtue of a moustache and a cigarette, might be supposed to represent Mr Hawkins. She did not feel inclined to give further details of her evening, even to Fanny Hemphill. As a matter of fact she had in her own mind pressed the possibilities of her acquaintance with Mr Hawkins to their utmost limit, and it seemed to her not impossible that soon she might have a good deal more to say on the subject; but, nevertheless, she could not stifle a certain anxiety as to whether, after all, there would ever be anything definite to tell. Hawkins was more or less an unknown quantity; his mere idioms and slang were the language of another world. It was easy to diagnose Tommy Whitty or Jimmy Jemmison and their fellows, but this was a totally new experience, and the light of previous flirtations had no illuminating power. She had, at all events, the satisfaction of being sure that on Fanny Hemphill not even the remotest shadow of an allusion would be lost, and that, whatever the future might bring forth, she would be eternally credited with the subjugation of an English officer.

The profile with the moustache and the cigarette was repeated several times on the blotting paper during this interval, but not to her satisfaction; her new bangle pressed its pearly horse-shoes into the whiteness of her wrist and hurt her, and she took it off and laid it on the table. It also, and the circumstances of its bestowal, were among the things that she had not seen fit to mention to the friend of her bosom. It was nothing of course; of no more significance than the kiss that had accompanied it, except that she had been glad to have the bangle, and had cared nothing for the kiss: but that was just what she would never be able to get Fanny Hemphill to believe.

The soft, clinging tread of bare feet became audible in the hall, and a crack of the dining room door was opened.

'Miss Francie,' said a voice through the crack, 'th' oven's hot.'

'Have you the eggs and everything ready, Bid?' asked Francie, who was adding a blotted smoke wreath to the cigarette of the twentieth profile.

'I have, Miss,' replied the invisible Bid Sal, 'an' Norry says to be hurrying, for 'tis short till Miss Charlotte'll be comin' in.'

Francie closed the blotter on her half-finished letter, and pursued the vanishing figure to the kitchen. Norry was not to be seen, but on the table were bowls with flour, eggs, and sugar, and beside them was laid a bunch of twigs, tied together like a miniature birch rod. The making of a sponge cake was one of Francie's few accomplishments, and putting on an apron of dubious cleanliness, lent by Louisa, she began operations by breaking the eggs, separating the yolks from the whites, and throwing the shells into the fire with professional accuracy of aim.

'Where's the egg whisk, Bid?' she demanded.

''Tis thim that she bates the eggs with, Miss,' answered Bid Sal in the small, bashful voice by which she indicated her extreme humility towards those in authority over her, handing the birch rod to Francie as she spoke.

'Mercy on us! What a thing! I'd be all night beating them with that!'

'Musha, how grand ye are!' broke in Norry's voice from the scullery, in tones of high disdain; 'if ye can't bate eggs with that ye'd betther lave it to thim that can!' Following her words came Norry herself, bearing an immense saucepanful of potatoes, and having hoisted it on to the fire, she addressed herself to Bid Sal. 'Get out from undher me feet out o' this! I suppose it's to make cakes ye'd go, in place of feedin' the pigs! God knows I have as much talked since breakfast as'd sicken an ass, but, indeed, I might as well be playin' the pianna as tellin' yer business to the likes o' ye.'

A harsh yell at this point announced that a cat's tail had been trodden on, but, far from expressing compunction, Norry turned with fury upon the latest offender, and seizing from a corner beside the dresser an ancient carriage whip, evidently secreted for the purpose, she flogged the whole assemblage of cats out of the kitchen. Bid Sal melted away like snow in a thaw, and Norry, snatching the bowl of eggs from Francie, began to thrash them with the birch rod, scolding and grumbling all the time.

'That ye may be happy!' (This pious wish was with Norry always ironical.) 'God knows ye should be ashamed, filling yer shtummucks with what'll sicken thim, and dhraggin' the people from their work to be runnin' afther ye!'

'I don't want you to be running after me,' began Francie humbly.

'Faith thin that's the thruth!' returned the inexorable Norry; 'if ye have thim off'cers running afther ye ye're satisfied. Here, give me the bowl till I butther it. I'd sooner butther it meself than to be lookin' at ye doin' it!'

A loud cough, coming from the scullery, of the peculiarly doleful type affected by beggars, momentarily interrupted this tirade.

'*Sha'se mick*, Nance! Look at that, now, how ye have poor Nance the Fool waitin' on me till I give her the empty bottle for Julia Duffy.'

Francie moved towards the scullery door, urged by a natural curiosity to see what manner of person Nance the Fool might be, and saw, squatted on the damp flags, an object which could only be described as a bundle of rags with a cough in it. The last characteristic was exhibited in such detail at the sight of Francie that she retired into the kitchen again, and ventured to suggest to Norry that the bottle should be given as soon as possible, and the scullery relieved of Nance the Fool's dreadful presence.

'There it is for her on the dhresser,' replied Norry, still furiously whipping the eggs; 'ye can give it yerself.'

From the bundle of rags, as Francie approached it, there issued a claw, which snatched the bottle and secreted it, and Francie just caught a glimpse, under the swathing of rags, of eyes so inflamed with crimson that they seemed to her like pools of blood, and heard mouthings and mumblings of Irish which might have been benedictions, but, if so, were certainly blessings in disguise.

'That poor craythur walked three miles to bring me the bottle I have there on the dhresser. It's yerr'b tay that Julia Duffy makes for thim that has the colic.' Norry was softening a little as the whites of the eggs rose in stiff and silvery froth. 'Julia's a cousin of me own, through the mother's family, and she's able to docthor as good as e'er a docthor there's in it.'

'I don't think I'd care to have her doctoring me,' said Francie, mindful of the touzled head and dirty face that had looked down upon her from the window at Gurthnamuckla.

'And little shance ye'd have to get her!' retorted Norry; ''tis little she regards the likes o' you towards thim that hasn't a Christhian to look to but herself.' Norry defiantly shook the foam from the birch rod, and proceeded with her eulogy of Julia Duffy. 'She's as wise a woman and as good a scholar as what's in the country, and many's the poor craythure that's prayin' hard for her night and morning for all she done for thim. B'leeve you me, there's plinty would come to her funeral that'd be follyin' their own only for her and her doctherin'.'

'She has a very pretty place,' remarked Francie, who wished to be agreeable, but could not conscientiously extol Miss Duffy; 'it's a pity she isn't able to keep the house nicer.'

'Nice! What way have she to keep it nice that hasn't one but herself to look to! And if it was clane itself, it's all the good it'd do her that they'd throw her out of it quicker.'

'Who'd throw her out?'

'I know that meself.' Norry turned away and banged open the door of the oven. 'There's plinty that's ready to pull the bed from undher a lone woman if they're lookin' for it for theirselves.'

The mixture had by this time been poured into its tin shape, and, having placed it in the oven, Francie seated herself on the kitchen table to superintend its baking. The voice of conscience told her to go back to the dining room and finish her letter, but she repressed it, and, picking up a kitten that had lurked unsuspected between a frying-pan and the wall during the rout of its relatives, she proceeded to while away the time by tormenting it, and insulting the cockatoo with frivolous questions.

Miss Mullen's weekly haggle with the butcher did not last quite as long as usual this Friday morning. She had, in fact, concluded it by herself taking the butcher's knife, and, with jocose determination, had proceeded to cut off the special portion of the 'rack' which she wished for, in spite of Mr Driscoll's protestations that it had been bespoke by Mrs Gascogne. Exhilarated by this success, she walked home at a brisk pace, regardless of the heat, and of the weight of the rusty black tourist's bag which she always wore, slung across her shoulders by a strap, on her expeditions into the town. There was no one to be seen in the house when she came into it, except the exiled cats, who were sleeping moodily in a patch of sunshine on the hall mat, and after some passing endearments, their mistress went on into the dining room, in which, by preference, as well as for economy, she sat in the mornings. It had, at all events, one advantage over the drawing room, in possessing a sunny french window, opening on to the little grass-garden – a few untidy flowerbeds, with a high, unclipped hedge surrounding them, the resort of cats and their breakfast dishes, but for all that a pleasant outlook on a hot day. Francie had been writing at the dinner table, and Charlotte sat down in the chair that her cousin had vacated and began to add up the expenses of the morning. When she had finished, she opened the blotter to dry her figures, and saw, lying in it, the letter that Francie had begun.

In the matter of reading a letter not intended for her eye, Miss Mullen recognized only her own inclinations, and the facilities afforded to her by fate, and in this instance one played into the hands of the other. She read the letter through quickly, her mouth set at its grimmest expression of attention, and replaced it carefully in the blotting case where she found it. She sat still, her two fists clenched on the table before her, and her face rather redder than even the hot walk from Lismoyle had made it.

There had been a good deal of information in the letter that was new to her, and it seemed important enough to demand much consideration. The reflection on her own contribution to the bazaar did not hurt her in the least, in fact it slightly raised her opinion of Francie that she should have noticed it; but that ingenuous confidence about the evening spent in the gallery was another affair. At this point in her reflections, she became aware that her eye was attracted by something glittering on the green baize of the dinner table, half hidden under two or three loose sheets of paper. It was the bangle that she remembered having seen on Francie's wrist, and she took it up and looked curiously at the double horse-shoes as she appraised its value. She never thought of it as being real – Francie was not at all above an effective imitation – and she glanced inside to see what the mark might be. There was the eighteen-carat mark sure enough, and there also was Francie's name and the date, July 1st, 189–. A moment's reflection enabled Charlotte to identify this as the day of the yacht accident, and another moment sufficed for her to determine that the giver of the bangle had been Mr Hawkins. She was only too sure that it had not been Christopher, and certainly no glimmer of suspicion crossed her mind that the first spendings from her loan to Mr Lambert were represented by the bangle.

She opened the blotter, and read again that part of the letter that treated of Christopher Dysart. 'P'yah!' she said to herself, 'the little fool! what does she know about him?' At this juncture, the wheezing of the spring of the passage door gave kindly signal of danger, and Charlotte deftly slipped the letter back into the blotter, replaced the bangle under the sheets of paper, and was standing outside the french window when Francie came into the room, with flushed cheeks, a dirty white apron, and in her hands a plate bearing a sponge cake of the most approved shade of golden brown. At sight of Charlotte she stopped guiltily, and, as the latter stepped in at the window, she became even redder than the fire had made her.

'Oh – I've just made this, Charlotte – ' she faltered; 'I bought the eggs and the butter myself; I sent Bid for them, and Norry said – she thought you wouldn't mind – '

On an ordinary occasion Charlotte might have minded considerably even so small a thing as the heating of the oven and the amount of flour and sugar needed for the construction of the cake; but a slight, a very slight sense of wrong-doing, conspired with a little confusion, consequent on the narrowness of her escape, to dispose her to compliance.

'Why, me dear child, why would I mind anything so agreeable to me and all concerned as that splendour of a cake that I see there? I declare I never gave you credit for being able to do anything half as useful! 'Pon me honour, I'll give a tea party on the strength of it.' Even as she spoke she had elaborated the details of a scheme of which the motor should be the cake that Francie's own hand had constructed.

The choir practice was poorly attended that afternoon. A long and heavy shower, coming at the critical moment, had combined with a still longer and heavier luncheon party given by Mrs Lynch, the solicitor's wife, to keep away several members. Francie had evaded her duties by announcing that her only pair of thick boots had gone to be soled, and only the most ardent mustered round Mrs Gascogne's organ bench. Of these was Pamela Dysart, faithful, as was her wont, in the doing of what she had undertaken; and as Charlotte kicked off her goloshes at the gallery door, and saw Pamela's figure in its accustomed place, she said to herself that consistency was an admirable quality. Her approbation was still warm when she joined Pamela at the church door after the practice was over, and she permitted herself the expression of it.

'Miss Dysart, you're the only young woman of the rising generation in whom I place one ha'porth of reliance; I can tell you, not one step would I have stirred out on the chance of meeting any other member of the choir on a day of this kind, but

I knew I might reckon on meeting *you* here.'

'Oh, I like coming to the practices,' said Pamela, wondering why Miss Mullen should specially want to see her. They were standing in the church porch waiting for Pamela's pony-cart, while the rain streamed off the roof in a white veil in front of them. 'You must let me drive you home,' she went on; 'but I don't think the trap will come till this downpour is over.'

Under the gallery stairs stood a bench, usually appropriated to the umbrellas and cloaks of the congregation; and after the rest of the choir had launched themselves forth upon the yellow torrent that took the place of the path through the churchyard, Pamela and Miss Mullen sat themselves down upon it to wait. Mrs Gascogne was practising her Sunday voluntary, and the stairs were trembling with the vibrations of the organ; it was a Largo of Bach's, and Pamela would infinitely have preferred to listen to it than to lend a polite ear to Charlotte's less tuneful but equally reverberating voice.

'I think I mentioned to you, Miss Dysart, that I have to go to Dublin next week for three or four days; teeth, you know, teeth – not that I suppose you have any experience of such miseries yet!'

Pamela did not remember, nor, beyond a sympathetic smile, did she at first respond. Her attention had been attracted by the dripping, deplorable countenance of Max, which was pleading to her round the corner of the church door for that sanctuary which he well knew to be eternally denied to him. There had been a time in Max's youth when he had gone regularly with Pamela to afternoon service, lying in a corner of the gallery in discreet slumber. But as he emerged from puppydom he had developed habits of snoring and scratching which had betrayed his presence to Mrs Gascogne, and the climax had come one Sunday morning when, in defiance of every regulation, he had flung himself from the drawing room window at Bruff, and followed the carriage to the church, at such speed as his crooked legs could compass. Finding the gallery door shut, he had made his way nervously up the aisle until, when nearing the chancel steps, he was so overcome with terror at the sight of the surpliced figure of the Archdeacon sternly fulminating the Commandments, that he had burst out into a loud fit of hysterical barking. Pamela and the culprit had made an abject visit to the Rectory next day, but the sentence of excommunication went forth, and Max's religious exercises were thenceforth limited to the churchyard. But on this unfriendly afternoon the sight of his long melancholy nose, and ears dripping with rain, was too much for even Pamela's rectitude.

'Oh, yes, teeth are horrible things,' she murmured, stealthily patting her waterproof in the manner known to all dogs as a signal of encouragement.

'Horrible things! Upon my word they are! Beaks, that's what we ought to have instead of them! I declare I don't know which is the worst, cutting your first set of teeth, or your last! But that's not what's distressing me most about going to Dublin.'

'Really,' said Pamela, who, conscious that Max was now securely hidden behind her petticoats, was able to give her whole attention to Miss Mullen; 'I hope it's nothing serious.'

'Well, Miss Dysart,' said Charlotte, with a sudden burst of candour, 'I'll tell you frankly what it is. I'm not easy in my mind about leaving that girl by herself – Francie, y' know – she's very young, and I suppose I may as well tell the truth, and say she's very pretty.' She paused for the confirmation that Pamela readily gave. 'So you'll understand now, Miss Dysart, that I feel anxious about leaving her in a house by herself, and the reason I wanted to see you so specially today was to ask if you'd do me a small favour, which, being your mother's daughter, I'm sure you'll not refuse.' She looked up at Pamela, showing all her teeth. 'I want you to be the good angel that you always are, and come in and look her up sometimes if you happen to be in town.'

The lengthened prelude to this modest request might have indicated to a more subtle soul than Pamela's that something weightier lay behind it; but her grey eyes met Miss Mullen's restless brown ones with nothing in them except kindly surprise that it was such a little thing that she had been asked to do.

'Of course I will,' she answered; 'mamma and I will have to come in about clearing away the rest of that awful bazaar rubbish, and I shall be only too glad to come and see her, and I hope she will come and lunch at Bruff some day while you are away.'

This was not quite what Charlotte was aiming at, but still it was something.

'You're a true friend, Miss Dysart,' she said gushingly, 'I knew you would be; it'll only be for a few days, at all events, that I'll bother you with me poor relation! I'm sure she'll be able to amuse herself in the evenings and mornings quite well, though indeed, poor child, I'm afraid she'll be lonely enough!'

Mrs Gascogne, putting on her gloves at the top of the stairs, thought to herself that Charlotte Mullen might be able to impose upon Pamela, but other people were not so easily imposed on. She leaned over the staircase railing, and said, 'Are you aware, Pamela, that your trap is waiting at the gate?' Pamela got up, and

Max, deprived of the comfortable shelter of her skirts, crawled forth from under the bench and sneaked out of the church door. 'I wouldn't have that dog's conscience for a good deal,' went on Mrs Gascogne as she came downstairs. 'In fact, I am beginning to think that the only people who get everything they want are the people who have no consciences at all.'

'There's a pretty sentiment for a clergyman's wife!' exclaimed Charlotte. 'Wait till I see the Archdeacon and ask him what sort of theology that is! Now wasn't that the very image of Mrs Gascogne?' she continued as Pamela and she drove away; 'the best and the most religious woman in the parish, but no one's able to say a sharper thing when she likes, and you never know what heterodoxy she'll let fly at you next!'

The rain was over, and the birds were singing loudly in the thick shrubs at Tally Ho as Pamela turned the roan pony in at the gate; the sun was already drawing a steamy warmth from the bepuddled road, and the blue of the afternoon sky was glowing freshly and purely behind a widening proscenium of clouds.

'Now you might just as well come in and have a cup of tea; it's going to be a lovely evening after all, and I happen to know there's a grand sponge cake in the house.' Thus spoke Charlotte, with hospitable warmth, and Pamela permitted herself to be persuaded. 'It was Francie made it herself; she'll be as proud as Punch at having you to – ' Charlotte stopped short with her hand on the drawing room door, and then opened it abruptly.

There was no one to be seen, but on the table were two half-empty cups of tea, and the new sponge cake, reduced by one-third, graced the centre of the board. Miss Mullen glared round the room. A stifled giggle broke from the corner behind the piano, and Francie's head appeared over the top, instantly followed by that of Mr Hawkins.

'We thought 'twas visitors when we heard the wheels,' said Miss Fitzpatrick, still laughing, but looking very much ashamed of herself, 'and we went to hide when they passed the window for fear we'd be seen.' She paused, not knowing what to say, and looked entreatingly at Pamela. 'I never thought it'd be you – '

It was borne in on her suddenly that this was not the manner in which Miss Dysart would have acted under similar circumstances, and for the first time a doubt as to the fitness of her social methods crossed her mind.

Pamela, as she drove home after tea, thought she understood why it was that Miss Mullen did not wish her cousin to be left to her own devices in Lismoyle.

18

There was no sound in the red gloom, except the steady trickle of running water, and the anxious breathing of the photographer. Christopher's long hands moved mysteriously in the crimson light, among phials, baths, and cases of negatives, while uncanny smells of various acids and compounds thickened the atmosphere. Piles of old trunks towered dimly in the corners, a superannuated sofa stood on its head by the wall, with its broken hind-legs in the air, three old ball skirts hung like ghosts of Bluebeard's wives upon the door, from which, to Christopher's developing tap, a narrow passage forced its angular way.

There was presently a step on the uncarpeted flight of attic stairs, accompanied by a pattering of broad paws, and Pamela, closely attended by the inevitable Max, slid with due caution into the room.

'Well, Christopher,' she began, sitting gingerly down in the darkness on an old imperial, a relic of the period when Sir Benjamin posted to Dublin in his own carriage, 'Mamma says she *is* to come!'

'Lawks!' said Christopher succinctly, after a pause occupied by the emptying of one photographic bath into another.

'Mamma said she "felt Charlotte Mullen's position so keenly in having to leave that girl by herself," ' pursued Pamela, ' "that it was only common charity to take her in here while she was away." '

'Well, my dear, and what are you going to do with her?' said Christopher cheerfully.

'Oh, I can't think,' replied Pamela despairingly; 'and I know that Evelyn does not care about her; only last night she said she dressed like a doll at a bazaar.'

Christopher busied himself with his chemicals and said nothing.

'The fact is, Christopher,' went on his sister decisively, '*you* will have to undertake her. Of course, I'll help you, but I really cannot face the idea of entertaining both her and Evelyn at the same time. Just imagine how they would hate it.'

'Let them hate it,' said Christopher, with the crossness of a good-natured person who feels that his good nature is going to make him do a disagreeable thing.

'Ah, Christopher, be good; it will only be for three days, and she's very easy to talk to; in fact,' ended Pamela apologetically, 'I think I rather like her!'

'Well, do you know,' said Christopher, 'the curious thing is, that though I can't talk to her and she can't talk to me, I rather like her, too – when I'm at the other end of the room.'

'That's all very fine,' returned Pamela dejectedly; 'it may amuse you to study her through a telescope, but it won't do any-one else much good; after all, you are the person who is really responsible for her being here. You saved her life.'

'I know I did,' replied her brother irritably, staring at the stumpy candle behind the red glass of the lantern, unaware of the portentous effect of its light upon his eyeglass, which shone like a ball of fire; 'that's much the worst feature of the case. It creates a dreadful bond of union. At that infernal bazaar, whenever I happened to come within hail of her, Miss Mullen collected a crowd and made a speech at us. I will say for her that she hid with Hawkins as much as she could, and did her best to keep out of my way. As I have said before, I have no personal objection to her, but I have no gift for competing with young women. Why not have Hawkins to dinner every night and to luncheon every day? It's much the simplest way of amusing her, and it will save me a great deal of wear and tear that I don't feel equal to.'

Pamela got up from the imperial.

'I hate you when you begin your nonsense of theorizing about yourself as if you were a mixture of Methuselah and Diogenes; I have seen you making yourself just as agreeable to young women as Mr Hawkins or anyone;' she paused at the door. 'She'll be here the day after tomorrow,' with a sudden collapse into pathos. 'Oh, Christopher, you *must* help me to amuse her.'

Two days afterwards Miss Mullen left for Dublin by the early train, and in the course of the morning her cousin got upon an outside car in company with her trunk, and embarked upon the preliminary stage of her visit to Bruff. She was dressed in the attire which in her own mind she specified as her 'Sunday clothes,' and as the car rattled through Lismoyle, she put on a pair of new yellow silk gloves with a confidence in their adequacy to the situation that was almost touching. She felt a great need

117

of their support. Never since she was grown up had she gone on a visit, except for a night or two to the Hemphills' summer lodgings at Kingstown, when such 'things' as she required were conveyed under her arm in a brown paper parcel, and she and the three Miss Hemphills had sociably slept in the back drawing room. She had been once at Bruff, a visit of ceremony, when Lady Dysart only had been at home, and she had sat and drunk her tea in unwonted silence, wishing that there were sugar in it, but afraid to ask for it, and respecting Charlotte for the ease with which she accepted her surroundings, and discoursed of high and difficult matters with her hostess. It was only the thought of writing to her Dublin friends to tell them of how she had stayed at Sir Benjamin Dysart's place that really upheld her during the drive; no matter how terrible her experiences might be, the fact would remain to her, sacred and unalterable.

Nevertheless, its consolations seemed very remote at the moment when the car pulled up at the broad steps of Bruff, and Gorman the butler came down them, and solemnly assisted her to alight, while the setter and spaniel, who had greeted her arrival with the usual official chorus of barking, smelt round her politely but with extreme firmness. She stood forlornly in the big cool hall, waiting till Gorman should be pleased to conduct her to the drawing room, uncertain as to whether she ought to take off her coat, uncertain what to do with her umbrella, uncertain of all things except of her own ignorance. A white stone double staircase rose overawingly at the end of the hall; the floor under her feet was dark and slippery, and when she did at length prepare to follow the butler, she felt that visiting at grand houses was not as pleasant as it sounded.

A door into the hall suddenly opened, and there issued from it the hobbling figure of an old man wearing a rusty tall hat down over his ears, and followed by a cadaverous attendant, who was holding an umbrella over the head of his master, like a Siamese courtier.

'D—n your eyes, James Canavan!' said Sir Benjamin Dysart, 'can't you keep the rain off my new hat, you blackguard!' Then spying Francie, who was crossing the hall, 'Ho-ho! That's a fine girl, begad! What's she doing in my hall?'

'Oh, hush, hush, Sir Benjamin!' said James Canavan, in tones of shocked propriety. 'That is a young lady visitor.'

'Then she's *my* visitor,' retorted Sir Benjamin, striking his ponderous stick on the ground, 'and a devilish pretty visitor, too! I'll drive her out in my carriage tomorrow.'

'You will, Sir Benjamin, you will,' answered his henchman, hurrying the master of the house along towards the hall door; while Francie, with a new and wholly unexpected terror added to those she had brought with her, followed the butler to the drawing room.

It was a large room. Francie felt it to be the largest she had ever been in, as she advanced round a screen, and saw Lady Dysart at an immeasurable distance working at a heap of dingy serge, and behind her, still further off, the well-curled head of Miss Hope-Drummond just topping the cushion of a low armchair.

'Oh, how do you do!' said Lady Dysart, getting up briskly, and dropping as she did so a large pair of scissors and the child's frock at which she had been working. 'You are very good to have come over so early.'

The geniality of Lady Dysart's manner might have assured anyone less alarmed than her visitor that there was no ill intention in this remark; but such discernment was beyond Francie.

'Miss Mullen told me to be over here by twelve, Lady Dysart,' she said abjectly, 'and as she had the car ordered for me I didn't like – '

Lady Dysart began to laugh, with the large and yet refined *bonhomie* that was with her the substitute for tact.

'Why shouldn't you come early, my dear child?' she said, looking approvingly at Francie's embarrassed countenance. 'I'll tell Pamela you are here. Evelyn, don't you know Miss Fitzpatrick?'

Miss Hope-Drummond, thus adjured, raised herself languidly from her chair, and shook hands with the newcomer, as Lady Dysart strode from the room with her customary business-like rapidity. Silence reigned for nearly a minute after the door closed; but at length Miss Hope-Drummond braced herself to the exertion of being agreeable.

'Very hot day, isn't it?' looking at Francie's flushed cheeks.

'It is indeed, roasting! I was nearly melting with the heat on the jaunting-car coming over,' replied Francie, with a desire to be as responsive as possible, 'but it's lovely and cool in here.'

She looked at Miss Hope-Drummond's spotless white gown, and wished she had not put on her Sunday terra-cotta.

'Oh, is it?'

Silence; during which Francie heard the wheels of her car grinding away down the avenue, and wished that she were on it.

'Have you been out on the lake much lately, Miss Hope-Drummond?'

Francie's wish was merely the laudable one of trying to keep the heavy ball of conversation rolling, but the question awoke a slumbering worm of discontent in her companion's well-ordered breast. Christopher was even now loosing from his moorings at the end of the park, without having so much as mentioned that he was going out; and Captain Cursiter, her own compatriot, attached – almost linked – to her by the bonds of mutual acquaintances, and her thorough knowledge of the Lincolnshire Cursiters, had not risen to the fly that she had only yesterday thrown over him on the subject of the steam launch.

'No; I had rather more than I cared for the last time we were out, the day of the picnic. I've had neuralgia in my face ever since that evening, we were all kept out so late.'

'Oh, my! That neuralgia's a horrid thing,' said Francie sympathetically. 'I didn't get any harm out of it with all the wetting and the knock on my head and everything. I thought it was lovely fun! But' – forgetting her shyness in the interest of the moment – 'Mr Hawkins told me that Cursiter said to him the world wouldn't get him to take out ladies in his boat again!'

Miss Hope-Drummond raised her dark eyebrows.

'Really? That is very crushing of Captain Cursiter.'

Francie felt in a moment an emphasis on the word Captain; but tried to ignore her own confusion.

'It doesn't crush *me*, I can tell you! I wouldn't give a pin to go in his old boat. I'd twice sooner go in a yacht, upsets and all!'

'Oh!'

Miss Hope-Drummond said no more than this, but her tone was sufficient. Her eyes strayed towards the book that lay in her lap, and the finger inserted in its pages showed, as if unconsciously, a tendency to open it again.

There was another silence, during which Francie studied the dark and unintelligible oil-paintings on the expanses of wall, the flowers, arranged with such easy and careless lavishness in strange and innumerable jars and vases; and lastly, Dinah, in a distant window, catching and eating flies with disgusting avidity. She felt as if her petticoats showed her boots more than was desirable, that her gloves were of too brilliant a tint, and that she ought to have left her umbrella in the hall. At this painful stage of her reflections she heard Lady Dysart's incautious voice outside:

'It's always the way with Christopher; he digs a hole and buries himself in it whenever he's wanted. Take her out and let her eat strawberries now; and then in the afternoon – ' the voice suddenly sank as if in response to an admonition, and Francie's already faint heart sank along with it. Oh, to be at the Hemphills', making toffee on the parlour fire, remote from the glories and sufferings of aristocratic houses! The next moment she was shaking hands with Pamela, and becoming gradually aware that she was in an atmosphere of ease and friendliness, much as the slow pleasure of a perfume makes itself slowly felt. The fact that Pamela had on a grass hat of sunburnt maturity, and a skirt which bore the imprint of dogs' paws was in itself reassuring, and as they went together down a shrubbery walk, and finally settled upon the strawberry beds in the wide, fragrant kitchen-garden, the first terrors began to subside in Francie's trembling soul, and she found herself breathing more naturally in this strange, rarefied condition of things. Even luncheon was less formidable than she had expected. Christopher was not there, the dreaded Sir Benjamin was not there, and Lady Dysart consulted her about the cutting-out of poor clothes, and accepted with an almost alarming enthusiasm the suggestions that Francie diffidently brought up from the depths of past experience of the Fitzpatrick wardrobe.

The long, unusual leisure of the afternoon passed by her like a pleasant dream, in which, as she sat in a basket-chair under the verandah outside the drawing-room windows, illustrated papers, American magazines, the snoring lethargy of the dogs, and the warm life and stillness of the air were about equally blended. Miss Hope-Drummond lay aloof in a hammock under a horse-chestnut tree at the end of the flower-garden, working at the strip of Russian embroidery that some day was to languish neglected on the stall of an English bazaar; Francie had seen her trail forth with her arms full of cushions, and dimly divined that her fellow guest was hardly tolerating the hours that were to her like fragments collected from all the holidays she had ever known. No wonder, she thought, that Pamela wore a brow of such serenity, when days like this were her ordinary portion. Five o'clock came, and with it, with the majestic punctuality of a heavenly body, came Gorman and the tea equipage, attended by his satellite, William, bearing the tea table. Francie had never heard the word idyllic, but the feeling that it generally conveys came to her as she lay back in her chair, and saw the roses swaying about the pillars of the verandah, and watched the clots of cream sliding into her cup over the broad lip of the cream jug, and thought how incredibly brilliant the silver was, and that Miss Dysart's hands looked awfully pretty while she was pouring out tea, and weren't a bit spoiled by being rather brown. It was consolatory that Miss Hope-Drummond had elected to have her tea conveyed to her in the hammock; it was too much trouble to get out of it, she called, in her shrill, languid voice, and no one had argued the matter with her. Lady Dysart, who had occupied herself during the afternoon in visiting the garden beds and giving a species of clinical lecture on each to the wholly unimpressed gardener, had subsided into a chair beside Francie, and began to discuss with her the evangelical preachers of Dublin, a mark of confidence and esteem which Pamela noticed with astonishment. Francie had got to her second cup of tea, and had evinced an edifying familiarity with Lady Dysart's most chosen divines, when the dogs, who had been seated opposite Pamela, following with lambent eyes the passage of each morsel to her lips, rushed from the verandah, and charged with furious barkings across the garden and down the lawn towards two figures, whom in their hearts they knew to be the sons of the house, but whom, for histrionic purposes, they affected to regard as dangerous strangers.

Miss Hope-Drummond sat up in her hammock and pinned her hat on straight.

'Mr Dysart,' she called, as Christopher and Garry neared her chestnut tree, 'you've just come in time to get me another cup of tea.'

Christopher dived under the chestnut branches, and presently, with what Miss Hope-Drummond felt to be unexampled stupidity, returned with it, but without his own. He had even the gaucherie to commend her choice of the hammock, and having done so, to turn and walk back to the verandah, and Miss Hope-Drummond asked herself for the hundredth time how the Castlemores *could* have put up with him.

'I met the soldiers out on the lake today,' Christopher remarked as he sat down; 'I told them to come and dine tomorrow.' He looked at Pamela with an eye that challenged her gratitude, but before she could reply, Garry interposed in tones muffled by cake.

'He did, the beast; and he might have remembered it was my birthday, and the charades and everything.'

'Oh, Garry, *must* we have charades?' said Pamela lamentably.

'Well, of course we must, you fool,' returned Garry with Scriptural directness; 'I've told all the men about the place, and Kitty Gascogne's coming to act, and James Canavan's going to put papa to bed early and help us – ' Garry's voice sank to the fluent complaining undertone that distinguishes a small boy with a grievance, and Christopher turned to his mother's guest.

'I suppose you've acted in charades, Miss Fitzpatrick?'

'Is it me act? Oh goodness, no, Mr Dysart! I never did such a thing but once, when I had to read Lady Macbeth's part at school, and I thought I'd died laughing the whole time.'

Pamela and Lady Dysart exchanged glances as they laughed at this reminiscence. Would Christopher ever talk to a girl with a voice like this? was the interpretation of Pamela's glance, while Lady Dysart's was a mere note of admiration for the way that the sunlight caught the curls on Francie's forehead as she sat up to speak to Christopher, and for the colour that had risen in her cheeks since his arrival, more especially since his announcement that Captain Cursiter and Mr Hawkins were coming to dinner. There are few women who can avoid some slight change of manner, and even of appearance, when a man is added to the company, and it may at once be said that Francie was far from trying to repress her increased interest on such an occasion.

'What made you think I could act, Mr Dysart?' she said, looking at him a little self-consciously; 'do you think I look like an actress?'

The question was interrupted by a cry from the chestnut tree, and Miss Hope-Drummond's voice was heard appealing to someone to come and help her out of the hammock.

'She can get out jolly well by herself,' remarked Garry, but Christopher got up and lounged across the grass in response to the summons, and Francie's question remained unanswered. Lady Dysart rose too, and watched her son helping Miss Hope-Drummond on to her feet, and strolling away with her in the direction of the shrubbery. Then she turned to Francie.

'Now, Miss Fitzpatrick, you shall come and explain that Dorcas Society sleeve to me, and I should not be surprised if you could help me with the acrostic.'

Lady Dysart considered herself to be, before all things, a diplomatist.

19

Dinner was over. Gorman was regaling his fellows in the servants hall with an account of how Miss Fitzpatrick had eaten her curry with a knife and fork, and her Scotch woodcock with a spoon, and how she had accepted every variety of wine that he had offered her, and taken only a mouthful of each, an eccentricity of which William was even now reaping the benefit in the pantry. Mrs Brady, the cook, dared say that by all accounts it was the first time the poor child had seen a bit served the way it would be fit to put into a Christian's mouth, and, indeed, it was little she'd learn of behaviour or dinners from Miss Mullen, except to make up messes for them dirty cats – a remark which obtained great acceptance from her audience. Mr Gorman then gave it as his opinion that Miss Fitzpatrick was as fine a girl as you'd meet between this and Dublin, and if he was Mr Christopher, he'd prefer her to Miss Hope-Drummond, even though the latter might be hung down with diamonds.

The object of this criticism was meantime congratulating herself that she had accomplished the last and most dreaded of the day's ceremonies, and, so far as she knew, had gone through it without disaster. She certainly felt as if she never had eaten so much in her life, and she thought to herself that, taking into consideration the mental anxiety and the loss of time involved in the consumption of one of these grand dinners, she infinitely preferred the tea and poached eggs which formed her ordinary repast. Pamela was at the piano, looking a long way off in the dim pink light of the shaded room, and was playing such strange music as Francie had never heard before, and secretly hoped never to hear again. She had always believed herself to be extremely fond of music, and was wont to feel very sentimental when she, and one of that tribe whom it is to be feared she spoke of as her 'fellows', sat on the rocks at the back of Kingstown pier and listened to the band playing 'Dorothy', or 'The Lost Chord', in the dark of the summer evening; but these minor murmurings, that seemed to pass by steep and painful chromatic paths from one woe to another, were to her merely exercises of varying difficulty and ugliness, in which Miss Dysart never seemed to get the chords quite right. She was too shy to get up and search for amusement among the books and papers upon a remote table, and accordingly she lay back in her chair and regarded Lady Dysart and Miss Hope-Drummond, both comfortably absorbed in conversation, and wondered whether she should ever have money enough to buy herself a tea-gown.

The door opened, and Christopher sauntered in; he looked round the room through his eye-glass, and then wandered towards the piano, where he sat down beside Pamela. Francie viewed this proceeding with less resentment than if he had been any other man in the world; she did not so much mind a neglect in which Miss Hope-Drummond was equally involved, and she was rather frightened than otherwise, when soon afterwards she saw him, in evident obedience to a hint from his sister, get up and come towards her with a large photograph book under his arm. He sat down beside her, and, with what Pamela, watching from the distant piano, felt to be touching docility, began to expound its contents to her. He had done this thing so often before, and he knew, or thought he knew so well what people were going to say, that nothing but the unfailing proprietary interest in his own handiwork supported him on these occasions. He had not, however, turned many pages before he found that Francie's comments were by no means of the ordinary tepid and perfunctory sort. The Oxford chapels were, it is true, surveyed by her in anxious silence; but a crowd of undergraduates leaning over a bridge to look at an eight – an instantaneous photograph of a bump-race, with its running accompaniment of maniacs on the bank – Christopher's room, with Dinah sitting in his armchair with a pipe in her mouth – were all examined and discussed with fervid interest, and a cry of unfeigned excitement greeted the page on which his own photography made its *début* with a deep-brown portrait of Pamela.

'Mercy on us! That's not Miss Dysart! What has she her face blackened for?'

'Oh, I did that when I didn't know much about it last winter, and it's rather over-exposed,' answered Christopher, regarding his work of art with a lenient parental eye.

'The poor thing! And was it the cold that turned her black that way?'

Christopher glanced at his companion's face to see whether

this ignorance was genuine, but before he had time to offer the scientific explanation, she had pounced on a group below.

'Why, isn't that the butler? Goodness! he's the dead image of the Roman Emperors in Mangnall's questions! And who are all the other people? I declare, one of them's that queer man I saw in the hall with the old gentleman –'. She stopped and stammered as she realized that she had touched on what must necessarily be a difficult subject.

'Yes, this is a photograph of the servants,' said Christopher, filling the pause with compassionate speed, 'and that's James Canavan. You'll see him tomorrow night taking a leading part in Garry's theatricals.'

'Why, d'ye tell me that man can act?'

'Act? I should think so!' he laughed, as if at some recollection or other. 'He can do anything he tries, or thinks he can. He began by being a sort of hedge-schoolmaster, but he was too mad to stick to it. Anyhow, my father took him up, and put him into the agency office, and now he's his valet, and teaches Garry arithmetic when he's at home, and writes poems and plays. I envy you your first sight of James Canavan on the boards,' he ended, laughing again.

'The boards!' Francie thought to herself. 'I wonder is it like a circus?'

The photographs progressed serenely after this. Francie began to learn something of the discreetness that must be observed in inspecting amateur portrait photography, and Christopher, on his side, found he was being better entertained by Miss Mullen's cousin than he could have believed possible. They turned page after page steadily and conversationally, until Christopher made a pause of unconscious pride and affection at a group of photographs of yachts in different positions.

'These are some of the best I have,' he said; 'that's my boat, and that is Mr Lambert's.'

'Oh, the nasty thing! I'm sure I don't want to see *her* again! and I shouldn't think you did either!' with an uncertain glance at him. It had seemed to her when, once or twice before, she had spoken of the accident to him, that it was a subject he did not care about. 'Mr Lambert says that the upsetting wasn't her fault a bit, and he likes going out in her just the same. I think he's a very brave man, don't you?'

'Oh, very,' replied Christopher perfunctorily; 'but he rather overdoes it, I think, sometimes, and you know you got the worst of that business.'

'I think *you* must have had the worst of it,' she said timidly. 'I never was able to half thank you – ' Even the equalizing glow from the pink lampshades could not conceal the deepening of the colour in her cheeks.

'Oh, please, don't try,' interrupted Christopher, surprised into a fellow-feeling of shyness, and hastily turning over the yachting page; 'it was nothing at all.'

'Indeed, I wanted to say it to you before,' persevered Francie, 'that time at the bazaar, but there always were people there. Charlotte told me that only for you the pike would be eating me at the bottom of the lake!' she ended with a nervous laugh.

'What a very unpleasant thing to say, and not strictly true,' said Christopher lightly. 'Do you recognize Miss Mullen in this?' he went on, hurrying from the subject.

'Oh, how pretty!' cried Francie, peering into a small and dark picture; 'but I don't see Charlotte. It's the waterfall in the grounds, isn't it?'

Pamela looked over from the piano again, amazed to hear her brother's voice raised in loud laughter. There was no denying that the picture was like a waterfall, and Francie at first rejected with scorn the explanation that it represented a Sunday-school feast.

'Ah, go on, Mr Dysart! Why, I see the white water, and the black rocks, and all!'

'That's the table cloth, and the black rocks are the children's faces, and that's Miss Mullen.'

'Well, I'm very glad you never took any Sunday-school feast ever *I* was at, if that's what you make them look like.'

'You don't mean to say you go to Sunday-school feasts?'

'Yes, why wouldn't I? I never missed one till this year; they're the grandest fun out!'

Christopher stared at her. He was not prepared for a religious aspect in Miss Mullen's remarkable young cousin.

'Do you teach in Sunday-schools?' He tried to keep the incredulity out of his voice, but Francie caught the tone.

'You're very polite! I suppose you think I know nothing at all, but I can tell you I could say down all the judges of Israel or the journeyings of St Paul this minute, and that's more than you could do!'

'By Jove, it is!' answered Christopher, with another laugh. 'And is that what you talk about at school feasts?'

Francie laid her head back on the cushion of her chair, and looked at him from under her lowered eyelashes. 'Wouldn't you like to know?' she said. She suddenly found that this evening she

127

was not in the least afraid of Mr Dysart. There were some, notably Roddy Lambert, who called him a prig, but she said to herself that she'd tell him as soon as she saw him that Mr Dysart was a very nice young man, and not a bit stuck-up.

'Very much,' Christopher replied, sticking his eye-glass into his eye, 'that was why I asked.' He really felt curious to know more of this unwonted young creature, with her ingenuous impudence and her lovely face. If anyone else had said the things that she had said, he would have been either bored or revolted, and it is possibly worth noting that, concurrently with a nascent interest in Francie, he was consciously surprised that he was neither bored nor revolted. Perhaps it was the influence of the half-civilized northern music that Pamela was playing, with its blood-stirring freshness, like the whistling wind of dawn, and its strange snatches of winding sweetness, that woke some slumbering part of him to a sense of her charm and youth. But Pamela guessed nothing of what Grieg's 'Peer Gynt' was doing for her brother, and only thought how gallantly he was fulfilling her behest.

Before he said good night to Francie, Christopher had learned a good deal that he did not know before. He had heard how she and Mr Whitty, paraphrased as 'a friend of mine', had got left behind on Bray Head, while the rest of the Sunday-school excursion was being bundled into the train, and how she and the friend had missed three trains, from causes not thoroughly explained, and how Mr Lambert, who had gone there with her, just for the fun of the thing, had come back to look for them, and had found them having tea in the station refreshment room, and had been mad. He had heard also of her stay at Kingstown, and of how a certain Miss Carrie Jemmison – sister, as was explained, of another 'friend' – was wont to wake her up early to go out bathing, by the simple expedient of pulling a string which hung out of the bedroom window over the hall door, and led thence to Miss Fitzpatrick's couch, where it was fastened to her foot; in fact, by half past ten o'clock, he had gathered a surprisingly accurate idea of Miss Fitzpatrick's manner of life, and had secretly been a good deal taken aback by it.

He said to himself, as he smoked a final cigarette, that she must be a nice girl somehow not to have been more vulgar than she was, and she really must have a soul to be saved. There was something about her – some limpid quality – that kept her transparent and fresh like a running stream, and cool, too, he thought, with a grin and with a great deal of reflective stroking of Dinah's apathetic head, as she lay on his uncomfortable lap trying to make the best of a bad business. He had not failed to notice the recurrence of Mr Lambert's name in these recitals, and was faintly surprised that he could not call to mind having heard Miss Fitzpatrick mentioned by that gentleman until just before her arrival in Lismoyle. Lambert was not usually reticent about the young ladies of his acquaintance, and from Francie's own showing he must have known her very well indeed. He wondered how she came to be such a friend of his; Lambert was a first-rate man of business and all that, but there was nothing else first rate about him that he could see. It showed the social poverty of the land that she should speak of him with confidence and even admiration; it was almost pathetic that she should know no better than to think Roddy Lambert a fine fellow. His thoughts wandered to the upset of the *Daphne*; what an ass Lambert had made of himself then. If she could know how remarkably near her friend, Mr Lambert, had come to drowning her on that occasion, she would not, perhaps, have quoted him so largely as a final opinion upon all matters. No one blamed a man for not being able to swim, but the fact that he was a bad swimmer was no excuse for his losing his head and coming cursing and swearing and doing his best to drown everyone else.

Christopher let Dinah slip on to the floor, and threw the end of his cigarette out of the open window of his room. He listened to the sleepy quacking of a wild-duck and the far-away barking of the gatehouse dog. The trees loomed darkly at the end of the garden; between them glimmered the pale ghost of the lake, streaked here and there with the long quivering reflections of the stars, and in and through the warm summer night, the darting flight of the bats wove a phantom net before his eyes. The Grieg music still throbbed an untiring measure in his head, and the thought of Lambert gave way to more accustomed meditations. He had leaned his elbows on the sill, and did not move till some time afterwards, when a bat brushed his face with her wings in an attempt to get into the lighted room. Then he got up and yawned a rather dreary yawn.

'Well, the world's a very pretty place,' he said to himself; 'it's a pity it doesn't seem to meet all the requirements of the situation.'

He was still young enough to forget at times the conventionality of cynicism.

20

Lieutenant Gerald Hawkins surveyed his pink and newly shaven face above his white tie and glistening shirt-front with a smile of commendation. His moustache was looking its best, and showing most conspicuously. There was, at least, that advantage in a complexion that burned red, he thought to himself, that it made a fair moustache tell. In his button-hole was a yellow rose, given him by Mrs Gascogne on condition, as she said (metaphorically, it is to be presumed), that he 'rubbed it well into Lady Dysart' that she had no blossom to equal it in shape and beauty. A gorgeous red silk sachet with his initials embroidered in gold upon it lay on the table, and as he took a handkerchief out of it his eye fell on an open letter that had lain partially hidden beneath one side of the sachet. His face fell perceptibly; taking it up he looked through it quickly, a petulant wrinkle appearing between his light eyebrows.

'Hang it! She ought to know I can't get any leave now before the Twelfth, and then I'm booked to Glencairn. It's all rot going on like this – ' He took the letter in both hands as if to tear it up, but changing his mind, stuffed it in among the pocket handkerchiefs, and hurried downstairs in response to a shout from below. His polo-cart was at the door, and in it sat Captain Cursiter, wearing an expression of dismal patience that scarcely warranted Mr Hawkins' first remark.

'Well, you seem to be in a good deal of a hurry, old chap. Is it your dinner or is it Hope-Drummond?'

'When I'm asked to dinner at eight, I like to get there before half past,' replied Cursiter sourly; 'and when you're old enough to have sense you will too.'

Mr Hawkins drove at full pace out of the barrack gates before he replied, 'It's all very fine for you to talk as if you were a thousand, Snipey, but, by George! we're all getting on a bit.' His ingenuous brow clouded under the peak of his cap, and his thoughts reverted to the letter that he had thrust into the sachet.

'I've been pretty young at times, I admit, but that's the sort of thing that makes you a lot older afterwards.'

'Good thing, too,' put in Cursiter unsympathetically.

'Yes, by Jove!' continued Mr Hawkins; 'I've often said I'd take a pull, and somehow it never came off, but I'm dashed if I'm not going to do it this time.'

Captain Cursiter held his peace, and waited for the confidence that experience had told him would inevitably follow. It did not come quite in the shape in which he had expected it.

'I suppose there isn't the remotest chance of my getting any leave now, is there?'

'No, not the faintest; especially as you want to go away for the Twelfth.'

'Yes, I'm bound to go then,' acknowledged Mr Hawkins with a sigh not unmixed with relief; 'I suppose I've just got to stay here.'

Cursiter turned round and looked up at his young friend. 'What are you up to now?'

'Don't be such an owl, Cursiter,' responded Mr Hawkins testily; 'why should there be anything up because I want all the leave I can get? It's a very common complaint.'

'Yes, it's a very common complaint,' replied Cursiter, with a certain acidity in his voice that was not lost upon Hawkins; 'but what gave it to you this time?'

'Oh, hang it all, Cursiter! I know what you're driving at well enough; but you're wrong. You always think you're the only man in the world who has any sense about women.'

'I didn't think I had said anything about women,' returned the imperturbable Cursiter, secretly much amused at the sensitiveness of Mr Hawkins' conscience.

'Perhaps you didn't; but you're always thinking about them and imagining other people are doing the same,' retorted Hawkins. 'And may I ask what my wanting leave has to say to the question?'

'You're in a funk,' said Cursiter, 'though mind you,' he added, 'I don't blame you for that.'

Mr Hawkins debated with himself for an instant, and a confession as to the perturbed condition of that overworked organ, his heart, trembled on his lips. He even turned round to speak, but found something so discouraging to confidence in the spare, brown face, with its uncompromisingly bitten moustache and observant eyes, that the impulse was checked.

'Since you seem to know so much about me and the reasons why I want leave, and all the rest of it, I need say no more.'

Captain Cursiter laughed. 'Oh! don't on my account.'

Hawkins subsided into a dignified silence, which Cursiter, as was his wont, did not attempt to break. He fell into meditation on the drift of what had been said to him, and thought that he would write to Greer (Greer was the adjutant) and see about getting Hawkins away from Lismoyle; and he was doing so well here, he grumbled mentally, and getting so handy in the launch. If only this infernal Fitzpatrick girl would have stayed with her cads in Dublin everything would have been as right as rain. There was no other woman here that signified except Miss Dysart, and it didn't seem likely she'd look at him, though you never could tell what a woman would or would not do.

Captain Cursiter was 'getting on', as captains go, and he was the less disposed to regard his junior's love affairs with an indulgent eye, in that he had himself served a long and difficult apprenticeship in such matters, and did not feel that he had profited much by his experiences. It had happened to him at an early age to enter ecstatically into the house of bondage, and in it he had remained with eyes gradually opening to its drawbacks, until, a few years before, the death of the only apparent obstacle to his happiness had brought him face to face with its realization. Strange to say, when this supreme moment arrived, Captain Cursiter was disposed for further delay; but it shows the contrariety of human nature, that when he found himself superseded by his own subaltern, an habitually inebriated viscount, instead of feeling grateful to his preserver, he committed the imbecility of horse-whipping him; and finding it subsequently advisable to leave his regiment, he exchanged into the infantry with a settled conviction that all women were liars.

The coach house at Bruff, though not apparently adapted for theatrical purposes, had been for many years compelled to that use by Garry Dysart, and when, at half past nine o'clock that night, Lady Dysart and her guests proceeded thither, they found that it had been arranged to the best possible advantage. The seats were few, and the carriages, ranging from an ancestral yellow chariot to Pamela's pony-trap, were drawn up for the use of the rest of the audience. A dozen or so of the workmen and farm labourers lined the walls in respectful silence; and the servants of the household were divided between the outside car and the chariot. In front of a door leading to the harness room, two clothes horses, draped with tablecloths, a long ottoman, once part of the furniture of a prehistoric yacht of Sir Benjamin's, two chairs, and a ladder, indicated the stage, and four stable-lanterns on the floor served as footlights. Lady Dysart, the Archdeacon, and Mrs Gascogne sat in three chairs of honour; the landau was occupied by the rest of the party, with the exception of Francie and Hawkins, who had followed the others from the drawing room at a little distance. When they appeared, the coach-box of the landau seemed their obvious destination; but at the same instant the wrangling voices of the actors in the harness room ceased, the play began, and when Pamela next looked round neither Francie nor Mr Hawkins was visible, and from the open window of an invalided brougham that had been pushed into the background came sounds of laughter that sufficiently indicated their whereabouts.

The most able and accustomed of dramatic critics would falter in the attempt to master the leading idea of one of Garry's entertainments; so far as this performance made itself intelligible, it consisted of nightmare snatches of 'Kenilworth', subordinated to the exigencies of stage properties, chiefest among these being Sir Benjamin's deputy-lieutenant's uniform. The sword and cocked hat found their obvious wearer in the Earl of Leicester, and the white plume had been yielded to Kitty Gascogne, whose small crimson face grinned consciously beneath the limp feathers. Lady Dysart's white bernouse was felt to confer an air of simplicity appropriate to the part of Amy Robsart, and its owner could not repress a groan as she realized that the heroine would inevitably be consigned to the grimy depths of the yacht ottoman, a receptacle long consecrated to the office of stage tomb. At present, however, it was employed as a sofa, on which sat Leicester and Amy, engaged in an exhausting conversation on State matters, the onus of which fell entirely upon the former, his companion's part in it consisting mainly of a sustained giggle. It presently became evident that even Garry was flagging, and glances towards the door of the harness room told that expected relief delayed its coming.

'He's getting a bit blown,' remarked Mr Hawkins from the window of the brougham. 'Go it, Leicester!'

Garry's only reply was to rise and stalk towards the door with a dignity somewhat impaired by the bagginess of the silver-laced trousers. The deserted countess remained facing the audience in an agony of embarrassment that might have softened the heart of anyone except her lord, whose direction, 'Talk about Queen Elizabeth, you ass!' was audible to everyone in the coach house.

Fortunately for Kitty Gascogne, her powers of soliloquy were not long tested. The door burst open, Garry hurried back to the ottoman, and had only time to seize Amy Robsart's hand and kneel at her feet when a tall figure took the stage with a mincing amble. James Canavan had from time immemorial been the leading lady in Garry's theatricals, and his appearance as Queen Elizabeth was such as to satisfy his oldest admirers. He wore a skirt which was instantly recognized by the household as belonging to Mrs Brady the cook, a crown made of gold paper inadequately restrained his iron-grey locks, a ham-frill ruff concealed his whiskers, and the deputy-lieutenant's red coat, with the old-fashioned long tails and silver epaulettes, completed his equipment.

His entrance brought down the house; even Lady Dysart forgot her anxiety to find out where Mr Hawkins' voice had come from, and collapsed into a state afterwards described by the under-housemaid as 'her ladyship in splits'.

'Oh fie, fie, fie!' said Queen Elizabeth in a piping falsetto, paying no heed to the demonstrations in her favour; 'Amy Robsart and Leicester! Oh, dear, dear, this will never do!'

Leicester still stooped over Amy's hand, but even the occupants of the brougham heard the whisper in which he said, 'You're not half angry enough! Go on again!'

Thus charged, Queen Elizabeth swept to the back of the stage, and, turning there, advanced again upon the lovers, stamping her feet and gesticulating with clenched fists. 'What! Amy Robsart and Leicester! Shocking! disgraceful!' she vociferated; then with a final burst, 'D—n it! I can't stand this!'

A roar of delight broke from the house; the delight always provoked in rural audiences by the expletive that age has been powerless to wither or custom to stale. Hawkins' amusement found vent in such a stentorian 'Bravo!' that Lady Dysart turned quickly at the sound, and saw his head and Francie's at the window of the brougham. Even in the indifferent light of the lamps, Francie discerned disapproval in her look. She sat back precipitately.

'Oh, Mr Hawkins!' she exclaimed, rashly admitting that she felt the position to be equivocal; 'I think I'd better get out.'

Now, if ever, was the time for Mr Hawkins to take that pull of which he had spoken so stoutly to Captain Cursiter, but in addition to other extenuating circumstances, it must be admitted that Sir Benjamin's burgundy had to some slight extent made summer in his veins, and caused him to forget most things except the fact that the prettiest girl he had ever seen was sitting beside him.

'No, you sha'n't,' he replied, leaning back out of the light, and taking her hand as if to prevent her from moving; 'you won't go, will you?'

He suddenly felt that he was very much in love, and threw such entreaty into the foregoing unremarkable words that Francie's heart beat foolishly, and her efforts to take away her hand were very feeble.

'You don't want to go away, do you? You like sitting here with me?'

The powers of repartee that Tommy Whitty had often found so baffling failed Francie unaccountably on this occasion. She murmured something that Hawkins chose to take for assent, and in a moment he had passed his arm round her waist, and possessed himself of the other hand.

'Now, you see, you can't get away,' he whispered, taking a wary look out of the window of the brougham. All the attention of the audience was engrossed upon the stage, where, at this moment, Queen Elizabeth having chased Amy and Leicester round the ottoman, was now doing her best not to catch them as they together scaled the clothes horse. The brougham was behind everyone; no one was even thinking of them, and Hawkins leaned towards Francie till his lips almost touched her cheek. She drew back from him, but the kiss came and went in a moment, and was followed by more, that she did not try to escape. The loud clapping of the audience on the exit of Queen Elizabeth brought Hawkins back to his senses; he heard the quick drawing of Francie's breath and felt her tremble as he pressed her to him, and he realized that so far from 'taking a pull', he had let himself get out of hand without a struggle. For this rash, enchanting evening, at all events, it was too late to try to recover lost ground. What could he do now but hold her hand more tightly than before, and ask her unrepentingly whether she forgave him. The reply met with an unlooked-for interruption.

The drama on the stage had proceeded to its climax. Amy Robsart was understood to have suffered a violent death in the harness room, and her entombment in the ottoman had followed as a matter of course. The process had been difficult; in fact, but for surreptitious aid from the corpse, the burial could scarcely have been accomplished; but the lid was at length closed, and the bereaved earl flung himself on his knees by the grave in an abandonment of grief. Suddenly from the harness room came

135

sounds of discordant triumph, and Queen Elizabeth bounded upon the stage, singing a war song, of which the refrain,

> With me long sword, saddle, bridle,
> Whack, fol de rol!

was alone intelligible. Amy Robsart's white plume was stuck in the queen's crown in token of victory, and its feathers rose on end as, with a flourish of the drawing-room poker which she carried as her sceptre, she leaped upon the grave, and continued her dance and song there. Clouds of dust and feathers rose from the cushions, and encouraged by the shouts of her audience, the queen's dance waxed more furious. There was a stagger, a crash, and a shrill scream rose from the corpse, as the lid gave way, and Queen Elizabeth stood knee-deep in Amy Robsart's tomb. An answering scream came from Mrs Gascogne and Lady Dysart, both of whom rushed from their places on to the stage, and dragged forth the unhappy Kitty, smothered in dust, redder in the face than ever, but unhurt, and still giggling.

Francie and Hawkins emerged from the brougham, and mingled quietly with the crowd in the general break-up that followed. The point at issue between them had not been settled, but arrangements had been made for the following day that ensured a renewal of the argument.

21

The crash of the prayer-gong was the first thing that Francie heard next morning. She had not gone to sleep easily the night before. It had been so much pleasanter to lie awake, that she had done so till she had gone past the stage when the process of going to sleep is voluntary, and she had nearly exhausted the pleasant aspect of things and got to their wrong side when the dawn stood at her window, a pallid reminder of the day that was before her, and she dropped into prosaic slumber. She came downstairs in a state of some anxiety as to whether the chill that she had perceived last night in Lady Dysart's demeanour would be still apparent. Breakfast was nearly over when she got into the room, and when she said good morning to Lady Dysart, she felt, though she was not eminently perceptive of the shades in a well-bred manner, that she had not been restored to favour.

She sat down at the table, with the feeling that was very familiar to her of being in disgrace, combating with the excitement and hurry of her nerves in a way that made her feel almost hysterical; and the fear that the strong revealing light of the long windows opposite to which she was sitting would show the dew of tears in her eyes, made her bend her head over her plate and scarcely raise it to respond to Pamela's good-natured efforts to put her at her ease. Miss Hope-Drummond presently looked up from her letters and took a quiet stare at the discomposed face opposite her. She had no particular dislike for Francie beyond the ordinary rooted distrust which she felt as a matter of course for those whom she regarded as fellow competitors, but on general principles she was pleased that discomfiture had come to Miss Fitzpatrick. It occurred to her that a deepening of the discomfiture would suit well with Lady Dysart's present mood, and might also be to her own personal advantage.

'I hope your dress did not suffer last night, Miss Fitzpatrick? Mine was ruined, but that was because Mr Dysart *would* make me climb on to the box for the last scene.'

'No, thank you, Miss Hope-Drummond – at least, it only got a little sign of dust.'

'Really? How nice! How lucky you were, weren't you?'

'She may have been lucky about her dress,' interrupted Garry, 'but I'm blowed if she could have seen much of the acting! Why on earth did you let Hawkins jam you into that old brougham, Miss Fitzpatrick?'

'Garry,' said Lady Dysart with unusual asperity, 'how often am I to tell you not to speak of grown-up gentlemen as if they were little boys like yourself? Run off to your lessons. If you have finished, Miss Fitzpatrick,' she continued, her voice chilling again, 'I think we will go into the drawing room.'

It is scarcely to be wondered at that Francie found the atmosphere of the drawing room rather oppressive. She was exceedingly afraid of her hostess; her sense of her misdoings was, like a dog's, entirely shaped upon other people's opinions, and depended in no way upon her own conscience; and she had now awakened to a belief that she had transgressed very badly indeed. 'And if she' ('she' was Lady Dysart, and for the moment Francie's standard of morality) 'was so angry about me sitting in the brougham with

137

him,' she thought to herself, as, having escaped from the house, she wandered alone under the oaks of the shady back avenue, 'what would she think if she knew the whole story?'

In Francie's society 'the whole story' would have been listened to with extreme leniency, if not admiration; in fact, some episodes of a similar kind had before now been confided by our young lady to Miss Fanny Hemphill, and had even given her a certain standing in the eyes of that arbiter of manners and morals. But on this, as on a previous occasion, she did not feel disposed to take Miss Hemphill into her confidence. For one thing, she was less distinct in her recollection of what had happened than was usual. It had seemed to her that she had lost her wonted clear and mocking remembrance of events from the moment when he had taken her hand, and what followed was blurred in her memory as a landscape is blurred by the quiver of heat in the air. For another, she felt it all to be so improbable, so uncertain, that she could not quite believe in it herself. Hawkins was so radically different from any other man she had ever known; so much more splendid in all ways, the very texture of his clothes, the scent on his handkerchief, breathed to her his high estate. That she should have any part in this greatness was still a little beyond belief, and as she walked softly in the deep grass under the trees, she kept saying to herself that he could not really care for her, that it was too good to be true.

It was almost pathetic that this girl, with her wild-rose freshness and vivid spring-like youth, should be humble enough to think that she was not worthy of Mr Hawkins, and sophisticated enough to take his lovemaking as a matter of common occurrence, that in no way involved anything more serious. Whatever he might think about it, however, she was certain that he would come here today, and being wholly without the power of self-analysis, she passed easily from such speculations to the simpler mental exercise of counting how many hours would have to crawl by before she could see him again. She had left the avenue, and she strolled aimlessly across a wide marshy place between the woods and the lake, that had once been covered by the water, but was now so far reclaimed that sedgy grass and bog-myrtle grew all over it, and creamy meadow-sweet and magenta loose-strife glorified the swampy patches and the edges of the drains. The pale azure of the lake lay on her right hand, with, in the distance, two or three white sails just tilted enough by the breeze to make them look like acute accents, gaily emphasizing the purpose of the lake and giving it its final expression. In front of

her spread a long, low wood, temptingly cool and green, with a
gate pillared by tall fir trees, from which, as she lifted the latch, a
bevy of wood-pigeons dashed out, startling her with the sudden
frantic clapping of their wings. It was a curious wood – very old,
judging by its scattered knots of hoary, weather-twisted pine
trees; very young, judging by the growth of ash saplings and
slender larches that made dense every inch of space except where
rides had been cut through them for the woodcock shooting.
Francie walked along the quiet path, thinking little of the
beauty that surrounded her, but unconsciously absorbing its rich
harmonious stillness. The little grey rabbits did not hear her
coming, and hopped languidly across the path, 'for all the world
like toys from Robinson's,' thought Francie; the honeysuckle
hung in delicious tangle from tree to tree; the wood-pigeons
crooned shrilly in the fir trees, and every now and then a bumble-
bee started from a clover blossom in the grass with a deep
resentful note, as when one plucks the lowest string of a violon-
cello. She had noticed a triple wheel-track over the moss and
primrose leaves of the path, and vaguely wondered what had
brought it there; but at a turn where the path took a long bend
to the lake she was no longer left in doubt. Drawn up under a
solemn pine tree near the water's edge was Sir Benjamin's bath-
chair, and in it the dreaded Sir Benjamin himself, vociferating at
the top of his cracked old voice, and shaking his oaken staff at
some person or persons not apparent.

Francie's first instinct was flight, but before she had time to
turn, her host had seen her, and changing his tone of fury to one
of hideous affability he called to her to come and speak to him.
Francie was too uncertain as to the exact extent of his intellect
to risk disobedience, and she advanced tremblingly.

'Come here, Miss,' said Sir Benjamin, goggling at her through
his gold spectacles. 'You're the pretty little visitor, and I promised I'd take you out driving in my carriage and pair. Come here
and shake hands with me, Miss. Where's your manners?'

This invitation was emphasized by a thump of his stick on the
floor of the chair, and Francie, with an almost prayerful glance
round for James Canavan, was reluctantly preparing to comply
with it, when she heard Garry's voice calling her.

'Miss Fitzpatrick! Hi! Come here!'

Miss Fitzpatrick took one look at the tremulous, irritable old
claw outstretched for her acceptance, and plunged incontinently
down a ride in the direction of the voice. In front of her stood a
sombre ring of immense pine trees, and in their shadow stood

Garry and James Canavan, apparently in committee upon some small object that lay on the thick mat of moss and pine needles.

'I heard the governor talking to you,' said Garry with a grin of intelligence, 'and I thought you'd sooner come and look at the rat that's just come out of this hole. Stinking Jemima's been in there for the last half hour after rabbits. She's my ferret, you know, a regular ripper,' he went on in excited narration, 'and I expect she's got the muzzle off and is having a high old time. She's just bolted this brute.'

The brute in question was a young rat that lay panting on its side, unable to move, with blood streaming from its face.

'Oh! the creature!' exclaimed Francie with compassionate disgust; 'what'll you do with it?'

'I'll take it home and try and tame it,' replied Garry; 'it's quite young enough. Isn't it, Canavan?'

James Canavan, funereal in his black coat and rusty tall hat, was regarding the rat meditatively, and at the question he picked up Garry's stick and balanced it in his hand.

> Voracious animals that we hate,
> Cats, rats, and bats deserve their fate,

he said pompously, and immediately brought the stick down on the rat's head with a determination that effectually disposed of all plans for its future, educational or otherwise.

Garry and Francie cried out together, but James Canavan turned his back unregardingly upon them and his victim, and stalked back to Sir Benjamin, whose imprecations, since Francie's escape, had been pleasantly audible.

'The old beast!' said Garry, looking resentfully after his late ally; 'you never know what he'll do next. I believe if mother hadn't been there last night, he'd have gone on jumping on Kitty Gascogne till he killed her. By the bye, Miss Fitzpatrick, Hawkins passed up the lake just now, and he shouted out to me to say that he'd be at the turf-boat pier at four o'clock, and he hoped none of you were going out.'

Then he had not forgotten her; he was going to keep his word, thought Francie, with a leap of the heart, but further thoughts were cut short by the sudden appearance of Pamela, Christopher, and Miss Hope-Drummond at the end of the ride. The treacherous slaughter of the rat was immediately recounted to Pamela at full length by Garry, and Miss Fitzpatrick addressed herself to Christopher.

'How sweet your woods are. Mr Dysart,' she began, feeling that some speech of the kind was suitable to the occasion. 'I declare, I'd never be tired walking in them!'

Christopher was standing a little behind the others, looking cool and lank in his flannels, and feeling a good deal less interested in things in general than he appeared. He had an agreeably craven habit of simulating enjoyment in the society of whoever fate threw him in contact with, not so much from a wish to please as from a politeness that had in it an unworthy fear of exciting displeasure; and so ably had he played the part expected of him that Miss Hope-Drummond had felt, as she strolled with him and his sister through the sunshiny wood, that he really was far more interested in her than she had given him credit for, and that if that goose Pamela were not so officious in always pursuing them about everywhere, they would have got on better still. She did not trouble her brothers in this way, and the idea that Mr Dysart would not have come at all without his sister did not occur to her. She was, therefore, by no means pleased when she heard him suggest to Miss Fitzpatrick that she should come and see the view from the point, and saw them walk away in that direction without any reference to the rest of the party.

Christopher himself could hardly have explained why he did it. It is possible that he felt Francie's ingenuous, unaffected vulgarity to be refreshing after the conversation in which Miss Hope-Drummond's own especial tastes and opinions had shed their philosophy upon a *réchauffé* of the society papers, and recollections of Ascot and Hurlingham. Perhaps also, after his discovery that Francie had a soul to be saved, he resented the absolute possession that Hawkins had taken of her the night before. Hawkins was a good little chap, but not the sort of person to develop a nascent intellectuality, thought this sage of seven-and-twenty.

'Why did you come out here by yourself?' he said to her, some little time after they had left the others.

'And why shouldn't I?' answered Francie, with the pertness that seldom failed her, even when, as on this morning, she felt a little uninterested in every subject except one.

'Because it gave us the trouble of coming out to look for you.'

'To see I didn't get into mischief, I suppose!'

'That hadn't occurred to me. Do you always get into mischief when you go out by yourself?'

'I would if I thought you were coming to stop me!'

141

'But why should I want to stop you?' asked Christopher, aware that this class of conversation was of a very undeveloping character, but feeling unable to better it.

'Oh, I don't know; I think everyone's always wanting to stop me,' replied Francie with a cheerful laugh; 'I declare I think it's impossible for me to do anything right.'

'Well, you don't seem to mind it very much,' said Christopher, the thought of how like she was to a typical 'June' in a Christmas Number striking him for the second time; 'but perhaps that's because you're used to it.'

'Oh, then, I can tell you I *am* used to it, but, indeed, I don't like it any better for that.'

There was a pause after this. They scrambled over the sharp loose rocks, and between the stunted fir trees of the lake shore, until they gained a comparatively level tongue of sandy gravel, on which the sinuous line of dead rushes showed how high the fretful waves had thrust themselves in winter. A glistening bay intervened between this point and the promontory of Bruff, a bay dotted with the humped backs of the rocks in the summer shallows, and striped with dark green beds of rushes, among which the bald coots dodged in and out with shrill metallic chirpings. Outside Bruff Point the lake spread broad and mild, turned to a translucent lavender grey by an idly drifting cloud; the slow curve of the shore was followed by the woods, till the hay fields of Lismoyle showed faintly beyond them, and, further on, the rival towers of church and chapel gave a finish to the landscape that not even conventionality could deprive of charm. Christopher knew every detail of it by heart. He had often solaced himself with it when, as now, he had led forth visitors to see the view, and had discerned their boredom with a keenness that was the next thing to sympathy; he had lain there on quiet autumn evenings, and tried to put into fitting words the rapture and the despair of the sunset, and had gone home wondering if his emotions were not mere selfconscious platitudes, rather more futile and contemptible than the unambitious adjectives, or even the honest want of interest, of the average sightseer. He waited rather curiously to see whether Miss Fitzpatrick's problematic soul would here utter itself. From his position a little behind her he could observe her without seeming to do so; she was looking down the lake with a more serious expression than he had yet seen on her face, and when she turned suddenly towards him, there was a wistfulness in her eyes that startled him.

'Mr Dysart,' she began, rather more shyly than usual; 'd'ye

know whose is that boat with the little sail, going away down the lake now?'

Christopher's mood received an unpleasant jar.

'That's Mr Hawkins' punt,' he replied shortly.

'Yes, I thought it was,' said Francie, too much preoccupied to notice the flatness of her companion's tone.

There was another pause, and then she spoke again.

'Mr Dysart, d'ye think – would you mind telling me, was Lady Dysart mad with me last night?' She blushed as she looked at him, and Christopher was much provoked to feel that he also became red.

'Last night?' he echoed in a tone of as lively perplexity as he could manage; 'what do you mean? Why should my mother be angry with you?' In his heart he knew well that Lady Dysart had been, as Francie expressed it, 'mad'.

'I know she was angry,' pursued Francie. 'I saw the look she gave me when I was getting out of the brougham, and then this morning she was angry too. I didn't think it was any harm to sit in the brougham.'

'No more it is. I've often seen her do it herself.'

'Ah! Mr Dysart, I didn't think you'd make fun of me,' she said with an accent on the 'you' that was flattering, but did not altogether please Christopher. 'You know,' she went on, 'I've never stayed in a house like this before. I mean – you're all so different –

'I think you must explain that remarkable statement,' said Christopher, becoming Johnsonian as was his wont when he found himself in a difficulty. 'It seems to me we're even depressingly like ordinary human beings.'

'You're different to me,' said Francie in a low voice, 'and you know it well.'

The tears came to her eyes, and Christopher, who could not know that this generality covered an aching thought of Hawkins, was smitten with horrified self-questioning as to whether anything he had said or done could have wounded this girl, who was so much more observant and sensitive than he could have believed.

'I can't let you say things like that,' he said clumsily. 'If we are different from you it is so much the worse for us.'

'You're trying to pay me a compliment now to get out of it,' said Francie, recovering herself. 'Isn't that just like a man!'

She felt, however, that she had given him pain, and the knowledge seemed to bring him more within her comprehension.

22

There are few things that so stimulate life, both social and vegetable, in a country neighbourhood, as the rivalry that exists, sometimes unconfessed, sometimes bursting into an open flame, among the garden owners of the district. The Bruff garden was a little exalted and removed from such competition, but the superiority had its depressing aspect for Lady Dysart in that it was counted no credit to her to excel her neighbours, although those neighbours took to themselves the highest credit when they succeeded in excelling her. Of all these Mr Lambert was the one she most feared and respected. He knew as well, if not better than she, the joints in the harness of Doolan the gardener, the weak battalions in his army of bedding-out plants, the failures in the ranks of his roses. Doolan himself, the despotic and self-confident, felt an inward qualm when he saw Mr Lambert strolling slowly through the garden with her ladyship, as he was doing this very afternoon, his observant eye taking in everything that Doolan would have preferred that it should not take in, while he paid a fitting attention to Lady Dysart's conversation.

'I cannot understand why these Victor Verdiers have not better hearts,' she was saying, with the dejection of a clergyman disappointed in his flock. 'Mrs Waller told me they were very greedy feeders, and so I gave them the cleanings of the scullery drain, but they don't seem to care for it. Doolan, of course, said Mrs Waller was wrong, but I should like to know what you thought about it.'

Mr Lambert delivered a diplomatic opinion, which sufficiently coincided with Lady Dysart's views, and yet kept her from feeling that she had been entirely right. He prided himself as much on his knowledge of women as of roses, and there were ultra feminine qualities in Lady Dysart, which made her act up to his calculations on almost every point. Pamela did not lend herself equally well to his theories; 'she hasn't half the go of her mother. She'd as soon talk to an old woman as to the smartest chap in Ireland,' was how he expressed the fine impalpable barrier that he always felt between himself and Miss Dysart. She was now exactly fulfilling this opinion by devoting herself to the entertainment of his wife, while the others were amusing themselves down at the launch; and being one of those few who can go through unpleasant social duties with 'all grace, and not with half disdain hid under grace', not even Lambert could guess that she desired anything more agreeable.

'Isn't it disastrous that young Hynes is determined upon going to America?' remarked Lady Dysart presently, as they left the garden; 'just when he had learned Doolan's ways, and Doolan *is* so hard to please.'

'America is the curse of this country,' responded Mr Lambert gloomily; 'the people are never easy till they get there and make a bit of money, and then they come swaggering back, saying Ireland's not fit to live in, and end by setting up a public house and drinking themselves to death. They're sharp enough to know the only way of making money in Ireland is by selling drink.' Lambert spoke with the conviction of one who is sure, not only of his facts, but of his hearer's sympathy. Then seeing his way to a discussion of the matter that had brought him to Bruff, he went on, 'I assure you, Lady Dysart, the amount of money that's spent in Lismoyle would frighten you. It's easy to know where the rent goes, and those that aren't drunken are thriftless, and there isn't one of them has the common honesty to give up their land when they've ruined it and themselves. Now, there's that nice farm, Gurthnamuckla, down by the lake-side, all going to moss from being grazed year after year, and the house falling to pieces for the want of looking after; and as for paying her rent – ' he broke off with a contemptuous laugh.

'Oh, but what can you expect from that wretched old Julia Duffy?' said Lady Dysart good-naturedly; 'she's too poor to keep the place in order.'

'I can expect one thing of her,' said Lambert, with possibly a little more indignation than he felt; 'that she'd pay up some of her arrears, or if she can't, that she'd go out of the farm. I could get a tenant for it tomorrow that would give me a good fine for it and put the house to rights into the bargain.'

'Of course, that would be an excellent thing, and I can quite see that she ought to go,' replied Lady Dysart, falling away from her first position; 'but what would happen to the poor old creature if she left Gurthnamuckla?'

'That's just what your son says,' replied Lambert with an

almost irrepressible impatience; 'he thinks she oughtn't to be disturbed because of some promise that she says Sir Benjamin made her, though there isn't a square inch of paper to prove it. But I think there can be no doubt that she'd be better and healthier out of that house; she keeps it like a pig-stye. Of course, as you say, the trouble is to find some place to put her.'

Lady Dysart turned upon him a face shining with the light of inspiration.

'The back-lodge!' she said, with Delphic finality. 'Let her go into the back-lodge when Hynes goes out of it!'

Mr Lambert received this suggestion with as much admiration as if he had not thought of it before.

'By Jove! Lady Dysart, I always say that you have a better head on your shoulders than any one of us! That's a regular happy thought.'

Any new scheme, no matter how revolutionary, was sure to be viewed with interest, if not with favour, by Lady Dysart, and if she happened to be its inventor, it was endowed with virtues that only flourished more strongly in the face of opposition. In a few minutes she had established Miss Duffy in the back-lodge, with, for occupation, the care of the incubator recently imported to Bruff, and hitherto a failure except as a cooking stove; and for support, the milk of a goat that should be chained to a laurel at the back of the lodge, and fed by hand. While these details were still being expanded, there broke upon the air a series of shrill, discordant whistles, coming from the direction of the lake.

'Good heavens!' ejaculated Lady Dysart. 'What can that be? Something must be happening to the steam launch; it sounds as if it were in danger!'

'It's more likely to be Hawkins playing the fool,' replied Lambert ill-temperedly. 'I saw him on the launch with Miss Fitzpatrick just after we left the pier.'

Lady Dysart said nothing, but her expression changed with such dramatic swiftness from vivid alarm to disapproval, that her mental attitude was as evident as if she had spoken.

'Hawkins is very popular in Lismoyle,' observed Lambert trepidly.

'That I can very well understand,' said Lady Dysart, opening her parasol with an abruptness that showed annoyance, 'since he takes so much trouble to make himself agreeable to the Lismoyle young ladies.'

Another outburst of jerky, amateur whistles from the steam launch gave emphasis to the remark.

'Oh, the trouble's a pleasure,' said Lambert acidly. 'I hope the pleasure won't be a trouble to the young ladies one of these days.'

'Why, what do you mean?' cried Lady Dysart, much interested.

'Oh, nothing,' said Lambert, with a laugh, 'except that he's been known to love and ride away before now.'

He had no particular object in lowering Hawkins in Lady Dysart's eyes, beyond the fact that it was an outlet for his indignation at Francie's behaviour in leaving him, her oldest friend, to go and make a common laughing stock of herself with that young puppy, which was the form in which the position shaped itself in his angry mind. He almost decided to tell Lady Dysart the episode of the Limerick tobacconist's daughter, when they saw Miss Hope-Drummond and Captain Cursiter coming up the shrubbery path towards them, and he was obliged to defer it to a better occasion.

'What was all that whistling about, Captain Cursiter?' asked Lady Dysart, with a certain vicarious severity.

Captain Cursiter seemed indisposed for discussion. 'Mr Hawkins was trying the whistle, I think,' he replied with equal severity.

'Oh, yes, Lady Dysart!' broke in Miss Hope-Drummond, apparently much amused; 'Mr Hawkins has nearly deafened us with that ridiculous whistle; they *would* go off down the lake, and when we called after them to ask where they were going, and told them they would be late for tea, they did nothing but whistle back at us in that absurd way.'

'Why? What? Who have gone? Whom do you mean by they?' Lady Dysart's handsome eyes shone like stars as they roved in wide consternation from one speaker to another.

'Miss Fitzpatrick and Mr Hawkins!' responded Miss Hope-Drummond with childlike gaiety; 'we were all talking on the pier, and we suddenly heard them calling out "good-bye!" And Mr Hawkins said he couldn't stop the boat, and off they went down the lake! I don't know when we shall see them again.'

Lady Dysart's feelings found vent in a long-drawn groan. 'Not able to stop the boat! Oh, Captain Cursiter, is there any danger? Shall I send a boat after them? Oh, how I wish this house was in the Desert of Sahara, or that that intolerable lake was at the bottom of the sea!'

This was not the first time that Captain Cursiter had been called upon to calm Lady Dysart's anxieties in connection with the lake, and he now unwillingly felt himself bound to assure her that Hawkins thoroughly understood the management of the *Serpolette*, that he would certainly be back in a few minutes, and that in any case, the lake was as calm as the conventional mill pond. Inwardly he was cursing himself for having yielded to Hawkins in putting in to Bruff; he was furious with Francie for the vulgar liberties taken by her with the steam whistle, an instrument employed by all true steam launchers in the most abstemious way; and lastly, he was indignant with Hawkins for taking his boat without his permission, and leaving him here, as isolated from all means of escape, and as unprotected, as if his clothes had been stolen while he was bathing.

The party proceeded moodily into the house, and, as moodily, proceeded to partake of tea. It was just about the time that Mrs Lambert was asking that nice, kind Miss Dysart for another cup of *very* weak tea – 'Hog-wash, indeed, as Mr Lambert calls it' – that the launch was sighted by her proprietor crossing the open space of water beyond Bruff Point and heading for Lismoyle. Almost immediately afterwards Mrs Lambert received the look from her husband which intimated that the time had arrived for her to take her departure, and some instinct told her that it would be advisable to relinquish the prospect of the second cup and to go at once.

If Mr Lambert's motive in hurrying back to Lismoyle was the hope of finding the steam launch there, his sending along our friend the black mare, till her sleek sides were in a lather of foam, was unavailing. As he drove on to the quay the *Serpolette* was already steaming back to Bruff round the first of the miniature headlands that jagged the shore, and the good turkey-hen's twitterings on the situation received even less attention than usual, as her lord pulled the mare's head round and drove home to Rosemount.

The afternoon dragged wearily on at Bruff; Lady Dysart's mood alternating between anger and fright as dinner-time came nearer and nearer and there was still no sign of the launch.

'What will Charlotte Mullen say to me?' she wailed, as she went for the twentieth time to the window and saw no sign of the runaways upon the lake vista that was visible from it. She found small consolation in the other two occupants of the drawing room. Christopher, reading the newspaper with every appearance of absorbed interest, treated the alternative theories of drowning or elopement with optimistic indifference; and Miss Hope-Drummond, while disclaiming any idea of either danger, dwelt on the social aspect of the affair so ably as almost to reduce her hostess to despair. Cursiter was down at the pier, seriously debating with himself as to the advisability of rowing the long four miles back to Lismoyle, and giving his opinion to Mr Hawkins in language that would, he hoped, surprise even that bland and self-satisfied young gentleman. There Pamela found him standing, as desolate as Sir Bedivere when the Three Queens had carried away King Arthur in their barge, and from thence she led him, acquiescing with sombre politeness in the prospect of dining out for the second time in one week, and wondering whether Providence would again condemn him to sit next Miss Hope-Drummond, and prattle to her about the Lincolnshire Cursiters. He felt as if talking to Pamela would make the situation more endurable. She knew how to let a man alone, and when she did talk she had something to say, and did not scream twaddle at you like a peacock. These unamiable reflections will serve to show the irritation of Captain Cursiter's mind, and as he stalked into dinner with Lady Dysart, and found that for her sake he had better make the best of his subaltern's iniquity, he was a man much to be pitied.

23

At about this very time it so happened that Mr Hawkins was also beginning to be sorry for himself. The run to Lismoyle had been capital fun, and though the steering and the management of the machinery took up more of his attention than he could have wished, he had found Francie's society more delightful than ever. The posting of a letter, which he had fortunately found in his pocket, had been the pretext for the expedition, and both he and Francie confidently believed that they would get back to Bruff at about six o'clock. It is true that Mr Hawkins received rather a shock when, on arriving at Lismoyle, he found that it was already six o'clock, but he kept this to himself, and lost no time in starting again for Bruff.

The excitement and hurry of the escapade had conspired, with the practical business of steering and attending to the various brass taps, to throw sentiment for a space into the background, and that question as to whether forgiveness should or should not be extended to him, hung enchantingly on the horizon, as delightful and as seductive as the blue islands that floated far away in the yellow haze of the lowered sun. There was not a breath of wind, and the launch slit her way through tranquil, oily spaces of sky that lay reflected deep in the water, and shaved the long rocky points so close that they could see the stones at the bottom looking like enormous cairngorms in the golden shallows.

'That was a near thing,' remarked Mr Hawkins complacently, as a slight grating sound told that they had grazed one of these smooth-backed monsters. 'Good business old Snipey wasn't on board!'

'Well, I'll tell old Snipey on you the very minute I get back!'

'Oh, you little horror!' said Mr Hawkins.

Both laughed at this brilliant retort, and Hawkins looked down at her, where she sat near him, with an expression of fondness that he did not take the least pains to conceal.

'Hang it! you know,' he said presently, 'I'm sick of holding this blooming wheel dead amidships; I'll just make it fast, and let her rip for a bit by herself.' He suited the action to the word, and came and sat down beside her.

'Now you're going to drown me again, I suppose, the way Mr Lambert did,' Francie said. She felt a sudden trembling that was in no way caused by the danger of which she had spoken; she knew quite well why he had left the wheel, and her heart stood still with the expectation of that explanation that she knew was to come.

'So you think I want to drown you, do you?' said Hawkins, getting very close to her, and trying to look under the wide brim of her hat. 'Turn round and look me in the face and say you're ashamed of yourself for thinking of such a thing.'

'Go on to your steering,' responded Francie, still looking down and wondering if he saw how her hands were trembling.

'But I'm not wanted to steer, and you do want me here, don't you?' replied Hawkins, his face flushing through the sunburn as he leaned nearer to her, 'and you know you never told me last night if you were angry with me or not.'

'Well, I was.'

'Ah, not very – ' A rather hot and nervous hand, burned to an unromantic scarlet, turned her face upwards against her will.

'Not very?' he said again, looking into her eyes, in which love lay helpless like a prisoner.

'Don't,' said Francie, yielding the position, powerless, indeed, to do otherwise.

Her delicate defeated face was drawn to his; her young soul rushed with it, and with passionate, innocent sincerity, thought it had found heaven itself. Hawkins could not tell how long it was before he heard again, as if in a dream, the click-clicking of the machinery, and wondered, in the dazed way of a person who is 'coming to' after an anaesthetic, how the boat was getting on.

'I must go back to the wheel, darling,' he whispered in the small ear that lay so close to his lips; 'I'm afraid we're a little bit off the course.'

As he spoke, his conscience reminded him that he himself had got a good deal off his course, but he put the thought aside. The launch was duly making for the headland that separated them from Bruff, but Hawkins had not reflected that in rounding the last point he had gone rather nearer to it than was usual, and that he was consequently inside the proper course. This, however, was an easy matter to rectify, and he turned the *Serpolette*'s head out towards the ordinary channel. A band of rushes lay between him and it, and he steered wide of them to avoid their parent shallow. Suddenly there was a dull shock, a quiver ran through the launch, and Hawkins found himself sitting abruptly on the india-rubber matting at Francie's feet. The launch had run at full speed upon the soft, muddy shallow that extended unconscionably far beyond the bed of rushes, and her sharp nose was now digging itself deeper and deeper into the mud. Hawkins lost no time in reversing the engine, but by the time they had gone full speed astern for five minutes, and had succeeded only in lashing the water into a thick, pea-soupy foam all round them, he began to feel exceedingly anxious as to their prospects of getting off again.

'Well, we've been and gone and done it this time,' he said, with a laugh that had considerably more discomfiture than mirth in it; 'I expect we've got to stay here till we're taken off.'

Francie looked all round the lake; not a boat was in sight, not even a cottage on the shore from which they might hope for help. She was standing up, pale, now that the tide of excitement had ebbed a little, and shaken by a giddy remembrance of that moment when the yacht heeled over and flung her into blackness.

'I told you you were going to drown me,' she said, shivering and laughing together; 'and oh! – what in the name of goodness will I say to Lady Dysart?'

'Oh, we'll tell her it was an accident, and she won't say a word,' said Hawkins with more confidence than he felt. 'If the worst comes to the worst I'll swim ashore and get a boat.'

'Oh don't, don't! you mustn't do that!' she cried, catching at his arm as if she already saw him jumping overboard; 'I'd be frightened – I couldn't bear to see you – don't go away from me!

Her voice failed pathetically, and, bared of all their wiles, her eyes besought him through the tears of a woman's terror and tenderness. Hawkins looked at her with a kind of ecstasy.

'Do you care so much as all that,' he said, 'you silly little thing!'

After this there was nothing to be done except sit down again, and with her head on his shoulder, allow that fatal anaesthetic to rob him of all considerations beyond Francie's kisses.

24

Dinner at Bruff was over. It had been delayed as long as possible in the belief that each moment would bring back the culprits, and it had dragged painfully through its eight courses, in spite of Lady Dysart's efforts to hasten Gorman and his satellite in their inexorable orbit. Everyone except Garry and Miss Hope-Drummond had been possessed by an anxiety which Lady Dysart alone had courage to express. She indeed, being a person who habitually said what other people were half afraid to think, had dilated on all possible calamities till Cursiter, whose temper was momently becoming worse, many times wished himself on the lake, rowing dinnerless and vengeful on the track of the fugitives.

The whole party was now out of doors, and on its way down to the landing place, in the dark twilight; Lady Dysart coming last of all, and driving before her the much incensed Gorman, whom she had armed with the gong, in the idea that its warlike roar would be at once a guide and a menace to the wanderers. So far it had only had the effect of drawing together in horrified questioning all the cattle in the lower part of the park, and causing them to rush, bellowing, along by the railings that separated

them from the siren who cried to them with a voice so commanding and so mysterious. Gorman was fully alive to the indignity
of his position, and to the fact that Master Garry, his ancient
enemy, was mocking at his humiliation; but any attempt to
moderate his attack upon the gong was detected by his mistress.

'Go on, Gorman! Beat it louder! The more they bellow the
better; it will guide them into the landing place.'

Christopher's affected misapprehension of his mother's pro-
nouns created a diversion for some time, as it was perhaps intended to do. He had set himself to treat the whole affair with
unsympathetic levity, but, in spite of himself, an insistent thorn
of anxiety made it difficult for him to make little of his mother's
vigorous panic. It was absurd, but her lamentations about the
dangers of the lake and of steam launches found a hollow echo
in his heart. He remembered, with a shudder that he had not felt
at the time, the white face rising and dipping in the trough of the
grey lake waves; and though his sense of humour, and of the
supreme inadequacy and staleness of swearing, usually deprived
him of that safety valve, he was conscious that in the background
of his mind the traditional adjective was monotonously coupling
itself with the name of Mr Hawkins. He was walking behind the
others down the path to the pier. Here and there great trees that
looked tired from their weight of foliage stood patiently spreading their arms to the dew, and in the intervals between Gorman's
fantasias on the gong, he could hear how the diffident airs from
the lake whispered confidentially to the sleeping leaves. There
was no moon; the sky was thickened with a light cloudiness, and
in the mystical twilight the pale broad blossoms of an elder-bush
looked like constellated stars in a nearer and darker firmament.
Christopher walked on, that cold memory of danger and disquiet
jarring the fragrance and peace of the rich summer night.

The searchers ranged themselves on the pier; the gong was
stilled, and except for the occasional stamping of a hoof, or low
booming complaint from the cattle, there was perfect silence. All
were listening for some sound from the lake before Christopher
and Cursiter carried out their intention of starting in a boat to
look for the launch. Suddenly in the misty darkness into which
all were staring, a vivid spark of light sprang out. It burned for a
few seconds only, a sharp distinct star, and then disappeared.

'There they are!' cried Lady Dysart. 'The gong, Gorman! The
gong!'

Gorman sounded with a will, and the harsh, brazen blare
spread and rolled over the lake, but there was no response.

153

'They *must* hear that,' said Cursiter to Christopher; 'why the devil don't he whistle?'

'How should I know?' answered Christopher, with a crossness which was in some irrational way the outcome of extreme relief; 'I suppose he fooled with it till it broke.'

'Perhaps they are not there after all,' suggested Miss Hope-Drummond cheerfully.

'How can you say such a thing, Evelyn!' exclaimed Lady Dysart indignantly; 'I know it was they, and the light was a signal of distress!'

'More likely to have been Hawkins lighting a cigarette,' said Christopher; 'if everyone would stop talking at the same time we might be able to hear something.'

A question ran like a ripple through Pamela's mind, 'What makes Christopher cross tonight?' but the next instant she forgot it. A distant shout, unmistakably uttered by Hawkins, came thinly to them across the water, and in another second or two the noise of oars could be distinctly heard. The sound advanced steadily.

'Show a light there on the pier!' called out a voice that was not Hawkins'.

Cursiter struck a match, a feeble illuminant that made everything around invisible except the faces of the group on the pier, and by the time it had been tossed, like a falling star, into the tarry blackness of the water, the boat was within conversational distance.

'Is Miss Fitzpatrick there?' demanded Lady Dysart.

'She is,' said Lambert's voice.

'What have you done with the launch?' shouted Cursiter, in a tone that made his subaltern quake.

'She's all right,' he made haste to reply. 'She's on that mud-shallow off Curragh Point, and Lambert's man is on board her now. Lambert saw us aground there from his window, and we were at her for an hour trying to get her off, and then it got so dark, we thought we'd better leave her and come on. She's all right, you know.'

'Oh,' said Captain Cursiter, in, as Hawkins thought to himself, a deuced disagreeable voice.

The boat came up alongside of the pier, and in the hubbub of inquiry that arose, Francie was conscious of a great sense of protection in Lambert's presence, angry though she knew he was. As he helped her out of the boat, she whispered tremulously:

154

'It was awfully good of you to come.'

He did not answer, and stepped at once into the boat again. In another minute the necessary farewells had been made, and he, Cursiter, and Hawkins were rowing back to the launch, leaving Francie to face her tribunal alone.

25

It was noon on the following day – a soaking, windy noon. Francie felt its fitness without being aware that she did so, as she knelt in front of her trunk, stuffing her few fineries into it with unscientific recklessness, and thinking with terror that it still remained for her to fee the elderly English upper housemaid with the half-crown that Charlotte had diplomatically given her for the purpose.

Everything had changed since yesterday, and changed for the worse. The broad window, out of which yesterday afternoon she had leaned in the burning sunshine to see the steam launch puffing her way up the lake, was now closed against the rain; the dirty flounces of her best white frock, that had been clean yesterday, now thrust themselves out from under the lid of her trunk in disreputable reminder of last night's escapade; and Lady Dysart, who had been at all events moderately friendly yesterday, now evidently considered that Francie had transgressed beyond forgiveness, and had acquiesced so readily in Francie's suggestion of going home for luncheon, that her guest felt sorry that she had not said breakfast. Even the padlock of her bonnet box refused to lock – was 'going bandy with her', as she put it in a phrase learnt from the Fitzpatrick cook – and she was still battling with it when the sound of wheels on the gravel warned her that the ordeal of farewell was at hand. The *blasé* calm with which Sarah helped her through the presentation of Charlotte's half-crown made her feel her social inferiority as keenly as the coldness of Lady Dysart's *adieux* made her realize that she was going away in disgrace, when she sought out her hostess and tried to stammer out the few words of orthodox gratitude that Charlotte had enjoined her not to forget.

155

Pamela, whose sympathies were always with the sinner, was kinder than ever, even anxiously kind, as Francie dimly perceived, and in some unexpected way her kindness brought a lump into the throat of the departing guest. Francie hurried mutely out on to the steps, where, in spite of the rain, the dogs and Christopher were waiting to bid her good-bye.

'You are very punctual,' he said. 'I don't know why you are in such a hurry to go away.'

'Oh, I think you've had quite enough of me,' Francie replied with a desperate attempt at gaiety. 'I'm sure you're all very glad to be shut of me.'

'That isn't a kind thing to say, and I think you ought to know that it is not true either.'

'Indeed then I know it *is* true,' answered Francie, preparing in her agitation to plunge into the recesses of the landau without any further ceremonies of farewell.

'Well, won't you even shake hands with me?'

She was already in the carriage; but at this reproach she thrust an impulsive hand out of the window. 'Oh, gracious –! I mean – I beg your pardon, Mr Dysart,' she cried incoherently, 'I – I'm awfully grateful for all your kindness, and to Miss Dysart –'

She hardly noticed how tightly he held her hand in his; but, as she was driven away, and, looking back, saw him and Pamela standing on the steps, the latter holding Max in her arms, and waving one of his crooked paws in token of farewell, she thought to herself that it must be only out of good nature they were so friendly to her; but anyhow they were fearfully nice.

'Thank goodness!' said Lady Dysart fervently, as she moved away from the open hall door – 'thank goodness that responsibility is off my hands. I began by liking the creature, but never, no, never, have I seen a girl so abominably brought up.'

'Not much notion of the *convenances*, has she?' observed Miss Hope-Drummond, who had descended from her morning task of writing many letters in a tall, square hand, just in time to enjoy the sight of Francie's departure, without having the trouble of saying good-bye to her.

'*Convenances!*' echoed Lady Dysart, lifting her dark eyes till nothing but the whites were visible; 'I don't suppose she could tell you the meaning of the word. "One master passion in the breast, like Aaron's serpent, swallows up the rest," and of all the man-eaters I have ever seen, she is the most cannibalistic!'

Miss Hope-Drummond laughed in polite appreciation, and rustled crisply away towards the drawing room. Lady Dysart looked approvingly after the tall, admirably neat figure, and thought, with inevitable comparison, of Francie's untidy hair and uncertainly draped skirts. She turned to Christopher and Pamela, and continued, with a lowered voice:

'Do you know, even the servants are all talking about her. Of course, they can't help noticing what goes on.'

Christopher looked at his mother with a singularly expressionless face.

'Gorman hasn't mentioned it to me yet, or William either.'

'If you had not interrupted me, Christopher,' said poor Lady Dysart, resentful of this irreproachably filial rebuke, 'I would have told you that none of the servants breathed a word on the subject to me. Evelyn was told it by her maid.'

'How Evelyn can discuss such things with her maid, I cannot imagine,' said Pamela, with unwonted heat; 'and Davis is such a particularly detestable woman.'

'I do not care in the least what sort of woman she is, she does hair beautifully, which is more than I can say for you,' replied Lady Dysart, with an Uhlan-like dash into the enemy's country.

'I suppose it was by Davis' advice that Evelyn made a point of ignoring Miss Fitzpatrick this whole morning,' continued Pamela, with the righteous wrath of a just person.

'It was quite unnecessary for her to trouble herself,' broke in Lady Dysart witheringly; 'Christopher atoned for all her deficiencies – taking advantage of Mr Hawkins' absence, I suppose.'

'If Hawkins had been there,' said Christopher, with the slowness that indicated that he was trying not to stammer, 'it would have saved me the trouble of making c – conversation for a person who did not care about it.'

'You may make your mind easy on that point, my dear!' Lady Dysart shot this parting shaft after her son as he turned away towards the smoking room. 'To do her justice, I don't think she is in the least particular, so long as she has a man to talk to!'

It is not to be wondered at that, as Francie drove through Lismoyle, she felt that the atmosphere was laden with reprobation of her and her conduct.

Her instinct told her that the accident to Captain Cursiter's launch, and her connection with it, would be a luscious topic of discourse for everyone, from Mrs Lambert downwards; and the thought kept her from deriving full satisfaction from the Bruff carriage and pair. Even when she saw Annie Beattie standing at her window with a duster in her hand, the triumph of her position was blighted by the reflection that if Charlotte did not know

157

everything before the afternoon was out, full details would be supplied to her at the party to which on this very evening they had been bidden by Mrs Beattie.

The prospect of the cross-examination which she would have to undergo grew in portentousness during the hour and a half of waiting at Tally Ho for her cousin's return, while, through and with her fears, the dirt and vulgarity of the house and the furniture, the sickly familiarities of Louisa, and the all-pervading smell of cats and cooking, impressed themselves on her mind with a new and repellent vigour. But Charlotte, when she arrived, was evidently still in happy ignorance of the events that would have interested her so profoundly. Her Dublin dentist had done his spiriting gently, her friends had been so hospitable that her lodging-house breakfasts had been her only expense in the way of meals, and the traditional battle with the Lismoyle car driver and his equally inevitable defeat, had raised her spirits so much that she accepted Francie's expurgated account of her sojourn at Bruff with almost boisterous approval. She even extended a jovial feeler in the direction of Christopher.

'Well, now, after all the chances you've had, Francie, I'll not give tuppence for you if you haven't Mr Dysart at your feet!'

It was not usually Francie's way to object to jests of this kind, but now she shrank from Charlotte's heavy hand.

'Oh, he was awfully kind,' she said hurriedly; 'but I don't think he'll ever want to marry anyone, not even Miss Hope-Drummond, for all as hard as she's trying!'

'Paugh! Let her try! *She*'ll not get him, not if she was to put her eyes on sticks! But believe you me, child, there never was a man yet that pretended he didn't want to marry that wasn't dying for a wife!'

This statement demanded no reply, and Miss Mullen departed to the kitchen to see the new kittens and to hold high inquisition into the doings of the servants during her absence.

Mrs Beattie gave but two parties in the year – one at Christmas, on account of the mistletoe; and one in July, on account of the raspberries, for which her garden was justly famous. This, it need scarcely be said, was the raspberry party, and accordingly when the afternoon had brought a cessation of the drizzling rain, Miss Ada and Miss Flossie Beattie might have been seen standing among the wet over-arching raspberry canes devoured by midges, scarlet from the steamy heat, and pestered by that most maddening of all created things, the common fly, but, nevertheless, filling basket after basket with fruit. Miss May and Miss Carrie spent a long and arduous day in the kitchen making tartlets, brewing syrupy lemonade, and decorating cakes with pink and white sugar devices and mottos archly stimulative of conversation. Upon Mrs Beattie and her two remaining daughters devolved the task of arranging the drawing-room chairs in a Christy minstrel circle, and borrowing extra teacups from their obliging neighbour, Mrs Lynch; while Mr Beattie absented himself judiciously until his normal five o'clock dinner hour, when he returned to snatch a perfunctory meal at a side table in the hall, his womenkind, after their wont, declining anything more substantial than nomadic cups of tea, brewed in the kitchen teapot, and drunk standing, like the Queen's health.

But by eight o'clock all preparations were completed, and the young ladies were in the drawing room, attired alike in white muslin and rose-coloured sashes, with faces pink and glossy from soap and water. In Lismoyle, punctuality was observed at all entertainments, not as a virtue but as a pleasure, and at half past eight the little glaring drawing room had rather more people in it than it could conveniently hold. Mrs Beattie had trawled Lismoyle and its environs with the purest impartiality; no one was invidiously omitted, not even young Mr Redmond the solicitor's clerk, who came in thick boots and a suit of dress clothes so much too big for him as to make his trousers look like twin concertinas, and also to suggest the more massive proportions of his employer, Mr Lynch. In this assemblage, Mrs Baker, in her celebrated maroon velvet, was a star of the first magnitude, only excelled by Miss Mullen, whose arrival with her cousin was, in a way, the event of the evening. Everyone knew that Miss Fitzpatrick had returned from Bruff that day, and trailing clouds of glory followed her in the mind's eye of the party as she came into the room. Most people, too, knew of the steam-launch adventure, so that when, later in the proceedings, Mr Hawkins made his appearance, poor Mrs Beattie was given small credit for having secured this prize.

'Are they engaged, do you think?' whispered Miss Corkran, the curate's sister, to Miss Baker.

'Engaged indeed!' echoed Miss Baker; 'no more than you are! If you knew him as well as I do you'd know that flirting's all he cares for!'

Miss Corkran, who had not the pleasure of Mr Hawkins' acquaintance, regarded him coldly through her spectacles, and said that for her own part she disapproved of flirting, but liked making gentlemen-friends.

'Well, I suppose I might as well confess,' said Miss Baker with a frivolous laugh, 'that there's nothing I care for like flirting, but p'pa's awful particular! Wasn't he for turning Dr M Call out of the house last summer because he cot me curling his moustache with my curling-tongs! "I don't care what you do with officers," says p'pa, "but I'll not have you going on with that Rathgar bounder of a fellow!" Ah, but that was when the poor "Foragers" were quartered here; they were the jolliest lot we ever had!'

Miss Corkran paid scant attention to these memories, being wholly occupied with observing the demeanour of Mr Hawkins, who was holding Miss Mullen in conversation. Charlotte's big, pale face had an intellectuality and power about it that would have made her conspicuous in a gathering more distinguished than the present, and even Mr Hawkins felt something like awe of her, and said to himself that she would know how to make it hot for him if she chose to cut up rough about the launch business.

As he reflected on that escapade he felt that he would have given a good round sum of money that it had not taken place. He had played the fool in his usual way, and now it didn't seem fair to back out of it. That, at all events, was the reason he gave to himself for coming to this blooming menagerie, as he inwardly termed Mrs Beattie's highest social effort; it wouldn't do to chuck the whole thing up all of a sudden, even though, of course, the little girl knew as well as he did that it was all nothing but a lark. This was pretty much the substance of the excuses that he had offered to Captain Cursiter; and they had seemed so successful at the time that he now soothed his guilty conscience with a *réchauffé* of them, while he slowly and conversationally made his way round the room towards the green rep sofa in the corner, whereon sat Miss Fitzpatrick, looking charming things at Mr Corkran, judging, at least, by the smile that displayed the reverend gentleman's prominent teeth to such advantage. Hawkins kept on looking at her over the shoulder of the Miss Beattie to whom he was talking, and with each glance he thought her looking more and more lovely. Prudence melted in a feverish longing to be near her again, and the direction of his wandering eye became at length so apparent that Miss Carrie afterwards told her sister that 'Mr Hawkins was *fear*fully gone about Francie Fitzpatrick – oh, the tender looks he cast at her!'

Mrs Beattie's entertainments always began with music, and the recognized musicians of Lismoyle were now contributing his or her share in accustomed succession. Hawkins waited until the time came for Mr Corkran to exhibit his wiry bass, and then definitely took up his position on the green sofa. When he had first come into the room their eyes had met with a thrilling sense of understanding, and since then Francie had felt rather than seen his steady and diplomatic advance in her direction. But somehow, now that he was beside her, they seemed to find little to say to each other.

'I suppose they're all talking about our running aground yesterday,' he said at last in a low voice. 'Does she know anything about it yet?' indicating Miss Mullen with a scarcely perceptible turn of his eye.

'No,' replied Francie in the same lowered voice; 'but she will before the evening's out. Everyone's quizzing me about it.' She looked at him anxiously as she spoke, and his light eyebrows met in a frown.

'Confound their cheek!' he said angrily; 'why don't you shut them up!'

'I don't know what to say to them. They only roar laughing at me, and say I'm not born to be drowned anyway.'

'Look here,' said Hawkins impatiently, 'what do they do at these shows? Have we got to sit here all the evening?'

'Hush! Look at Charlotte looking at you, and that's Carrie Beattie just in front of us.'

'I didn't come here to be wedged into a corner of this little beastly hole all the evening,' he answered rebelliously; 'can't we get out to the stairs or the garden or something?'

'Mercy on us!' exclaimed Francie, half frightened and half delighted at his temerity. 'Of course we can't! Why, they'll be going down to tea now in a minute – after that perhaps – '

'There won't be any perhaps about it,' said Hawkins, looking at her with an expression that made her blush and tremble, 'will there?'

'I don't know – not if you go away now,' she murmured, 'I'm so afraid of Charlotte.'

'I've nowhere to go; I only came here to see you.'

Captain Cursiter, at this moment refilling his second pipe, would not have studied the fascinating pages of the *Engineer* with such a careless rapture had he at all realized how Mr Hawkins was fulfilling his promises of amendment.

At this juncture, however, the ringing of a bell in the hall notified that tea was ready, and before Hawkins had time for individual action, he found himself swept forward by his hostess, and charged with the task of taking Mrs Rattray, the doctor's bride, down to the dining room. The supply of men did little more than yield a sufficiency for the matrons, and after these had gone forth with due state, Francie found herself in the midst of a throng of young ladies following in the wake of their seniors. As she came down the stairs she was aware of a tall man taking off his coat in a corner of the hall, and before she reached the dining room door Mr Lambert's hand was laid upon her arm.

26

Tea at Mrs Beattie's parties was a serious meal, and, as a considerable time had elapsed since any of the company, except Mr Hawkins, had dined, they did full justice to her hospitality. That young gentleman toyed with a plate of raspberries and cream and a cup of coffee, and spasmodically devoted himself to Mrs Rattray in a way that quite repaid her for occasional lapses of attention. Francie was sitting opposite to him, not at the table, where, indeed, there was no room for her, but on a window sill, where she was sharing a small table with Mr Lambert. They were partly screened by the window curtains, but it seemed to Hawkins that Lambert was talking a great deal and that she was eating nothing. Whatever was the subject of their conversation they were looking very serious over it, and, as it progressed, Francie seemed to get more and more behind her window curtain. The general clamour made it impossible for him to hear what they were talking about, and Mrs Rattray's demands upon his attention became more intolerable every moment, as he looked at Francie and saw how wholly another man was monopolizing her.

'And do you like being stationed here, Mr Hawkins?' said Mrs Rattray after a pause.

'Eh? what? Oh yes, of course I do – awfully! you're all such delightful people y'know!'

Mrs Rattray bridled with pleasure at this audacity.

'Oh, Mr Hawkins, I'm afraid you're a terrible flatterer! Do you know that one of the officers of the Foragers said he thought it was a beastly spawt!'

'Beastly what? Oh yes, I see. I don't agree with him at all; I think it's a capital good spot.' (Why did that old ass, Mrs Corkran, stick her great widow's cap just between him and the curtain? Francie had leaned forward and looked at him that very second, and that infernal white tow-row had got in his way.)

Mrs Rattray thought it was time to play her trump card.

'I suppose you read a great deal, Mr Hawkins? Dr Rattray takes the – a – the *Pink One* I think he calls it – I know, of course, it's only a paper for gentlemen,' she added hurriedly, 'but I believe it's very comical, and the doctor would be most happy to lend it to you.'

Mr Hawkins, whose Sunday mornings would have been a blank without the solace of the *Sporting Times*, explained that the loan was unnecessary, but Mrs Rattray felt that she had nevertheless made her point, and resolved that she would next Sunday study the *Pink One*'s inscrutable pages, so that she and Mr Hawkins might have, at least, one subject in common.

By this time the younger members of the company had finished their tea, and those nearest the door began to make a move. The first to leave the room were Francie and Lambert, and poor Hawkins, who had hoped that his time of release had at length come, found it difficult to behave as becomes a gentleman and a soldier, when Mrs Rattray, with the air of one who makes a concession, said she thought she could try another saucer of raspberries. Before they left the table the piano had begun again upstairs, and a muffled thumping, that shook flakes from the ceiling down on to the tea table, told that the realities of the evening had begun at last.

'I knew the young people would be at that before the evening was out,' said Mrs Beattie with an indulgent laugh, 'though the girls let on to me it was only a musical party they wanted.'

'Ah well, they'll never do it younger!' said Mrs Baker, leaning back with her third cup of tea in her hand. 'Girls will be girls, as I've just been saying to Miss Mullen.'

'Girls will be tom-fools!' said Miss Mullen with a brow of storm, thrusting her hands into her gloves, while her eyes followed Hawkins, who had at length detached Mrs Rattray from the pleasures of the table, and was hurrying her out of the room.

'Oh now, Miss Mullen, you mustn't be so cynical,' said Mrs Beattie from behind the tea-urn; 'we have six girls, and I declare now Mr Beattie and I wouldn't wish to have one less.'

'Well, they're a great responsibility,' said Mrs Corkran with a slow wag of her obtrusively widowed head, 'and no one knows that better than a mother. I shall never forget the anxiety I went through – it was just before we came to this parish – when my Bessy had an offer. Poor Mr Corkran and I disapproved of the young man, and we were both quite distracted about it. Indeed we had to make it a subject of prayer, and a fortnight afterwards the young man died. Oh, doesn't it show the wonderful force of prayer?'

'Well now, I think it's a pity you didn't let it alone,' said Mr Lynch, with something resembling a wink at Miss Mullen.

'I daresay Bessy's very much of your opinion,' said Charlotte, unable to refrain from a jibe at Miss Corkran, preoccupied though she was with her own wrath. She pushed her chair brusquely back from the table. 'I think, with your kind permissioir, Mrs Beattie, I'll go upstairs and see what's going on. Don't stn, Mr Lynch, I'm able to get that far by myself.'

When Miss Mullen arrived at the top of the steep flight of stairs, she paused on the landing amongst the exiled drawing-room chairs and tables, and looked in at seven or eight couples revolving in a space so limited as to make movement a difficulty, if not a danger, and in an atmosphere already thickened with dust from the carpet. She saw to her surprise that her cousin was dancing with Lambert, and, after a careful survey of the room, espied Mr Hawkins standing partnerless in one of the windows.

'I wonder what she's at now,' thought Charlotte to herself; 'is she trying to play Roddy off against him? The little cat, I wouldn't put it past her!'

As she looked at them wheeling slowly round in the cramped circle she could see that neither he nor Francie spoke to each other, and when, the dance being over, they sat down together in the corner of the room, they seemed scarcely more disposed to talk than they had been when dancing.

'Aha! Roddy's a good fellow,' she thought, 'he's doing his best to help me by keeping her away from that young scamp.'

At this point the young scamp in question crossed the room and asked Miss Fitzpatrick for the next dance in a manner that indicated just displeasure. The heat of the room and the exertion of dancing on a carpet had endued most of the dancers with the complexions of ripe plums, but Francie seemed to have been robbed of all colour. She did not look up at him as he proffered his request.

'I'm engaged for the next dance.'

Hawkins became very red. 'Well, the next after that,' he persisted, trying to catch her eye.

'There isn't any next,' said Francie, looking suddenly at him with defiant eyes; 'after the next we're going home.'

Hawkins stared for a brief instant at her with a sparkle of anger in his eyes. 'Oh, very well,' he said with exaggerated politeness of manner, 'I thought I was engaged to you for the first dance after supper, that was all.'

He turned away at once and walked out of the room, brushing past Charlotte at the door, and elbowed his way through the uproarious throng that crowded the staircase. Mrs Beattie, coming up from the tea table with her fellow matrons, had no idea of permitting her prize guest to escape so early. Hawkins was captured, his excuses were disregarded, and he was driven up the stairs again.

'Very well,' he said to himself, 'if she chooses to throw me over, I'll let her see that I can get on without her.' It did not occur to him that Francie was only acting in accordance with the theory of the affair that he had himself presented to Captain Cursiter. His mind was now wholly given to revenging the snub he had received, and, spurred by this desire, he advanced to Miss Lynch, who was reposing in an armchair in a corner of the landing, while her partner played upon her heated face with the drawing-room bellows, and secured her for the next dance.

When Mr Hawkins gave his mind to rollicking, there were few who could do it more thoroughly, and the ensuing polka was stamped through by him and Miss Lynch with a vigour that scattered all opposing couples like ninepins. Even his strapping partner appealed for mercy.

'Oh, Mr Hawkins,' she panted, 'wouldn't you chassy now please? if you twirl me any more, I think I'll die!'

But Mr Hawkins was deaf to entreaty; far from moderating his exertions, he even snatched the eldest Miss Beattie from her position as onlooker, and, compelling her to avail herself of the dubious protection of his other arm, whirled her and Miss Lynch round the room with him in a many-elbowing triangle. The progress of the other dancers was necessarily checked by this performance, but it was viewed with the highest favour by all the matrons, especially those whose daughters had been selected to take part in it. Francie looked on from the doorway, whither she

165

and her partner, the Reverend Corkran, had been driven for safety, with a tearing pain at her heart. Her lips were set in a fixed smile – a smile that barely kept their quivering in check – and her beautiful eyes shone upon the dazzled curate through a moisture that was the next thing to tears.

'I want to find Miss Mullen,' she said at last, dragging Mr Corkran towards the stairs, when a fresh burst of applause from the dancing room made them both look back. Hawkins' two partners had, at a critical turn, perfidiously let him go with such suddenness that he had fallen flat on the floor, and having pursued them as they polkaed round the room, he was now encircling both with one arm, and affecting to box their ears with his other hand, encouraged thereto by cries of 'Box them, Mr Hawkins!' from Mrs Beattie. 'Box them well!'

Charlotte was in the dining room, partaking of a gentlemanly glass of Marsala with Mr Beattie, and other heads of families.

'Great high jinks they're having upstairs!' she remarked, as the windows and tea cups rattled from the stamping overhead, and Mr Beattie cast many an anxious eye towards the ceiling. 'I suppose my young lady's in the thick of it, whatever it is!' She always assumed the attitude of the benevolently resigned chaperone when she talked about Francie, and Mr Lynch was on the point of replying in an appropriate tone of humorous condolence, when the young lady herself appeared on Mr Corkran's arm, with an expression that at once struck Charlotte as being very unlike high jinks.

'Why, child, what do you want down here?' she said. 'Are you tired dancing?'

'I am; awfully tired; would you mind going home, Charlotte?'

'What a question to ask before our good host here! Of course I mind going home!' eyeing Francie narrowly as she spoke; 'but I'll come if you like.'

'Why, what people you all are for going home!' protested Mr Beattie hospitably; 'there was Hawkins that we only stopped by main strength, and Lambert slipped away ten minutes ago, saying Mrs Lambert wasn't well, and he had to go and look after her! What's your reverence about letting her go away now, when they're having the fun of Cork upstairs?'

Francie smiled a pale smile, but held to her point, and a few minutes afterwards she and Charlotte had made their way through the knot of loafers at the garden gate, and were walking through the empty moonlit streets of Lismoyle towards Tally Ho. Charlotte did not speak till the last clanging of the *Bric-à-brac* polka had been left behind, and then she turned to Francie with a manner from which the affability had fallen like a garment.

'And now I'll thank you to tell me what's the truth of this I hear from everyone in the town about you and that young Hawkins being out till all hours of the night in the steam launch by yourselves?'

'It wasn't our fault. We were in by half past nine.' Francie had hardly spirit enough to defend herself, and the languor in her voice infuriated Charlotte.

'Don't give me any of your fine lady airs,' she said brutally; 'I can tell ye this, that if ye can't learn how to behave yourself decently I'll pack ye back to Dublin!'

The words passed over Francie like an angry wind, disturbing, but without much power to injure.

'All right, I'll go away when you like.'

Charlotte hardly heard her. 'I'll be ashamed to look me old friend, Lady Dysart, in the face!' She stormed on. 'Disgracing her house by such goings on with an unprincipled blackguard that has no more idea of marrying you than I have – not that that's anything to be regretted! An impudent little upstart without a halfpenny in his pocket, and as for family – ' her contempt stemmed her volubility for a mouthing moment. 'God only knows what gutter he sprang from; I don't suppose he has a drop of blood in his whole body!'

'I'm not thinking of marrying him no more than he is of marrying me,' answered Francie in the same lifeless voice, but this time faltering a little. 'You needn't bother me about him, Charlotte; he's engaged.'

'Engaged!' yelled Charlotte, squaring round at her cousin, and standing stock still in her amazement. 'Why didn't you tell me so before? When did you hear it?'

'I heard it some time ago from a person whose name I won't give you,' said Francie, walking on. 'They're to be married before Christmas.' The lump rose at last in her throat, and she trod hard on the ground as she walked, in the effort to keep the tears back.

Charlotte girded her velveteen skirt still higher, and hurried clumsily after the light, graceful figure.

'Wait, child! Can't ye wait for me? Are ye sure it's true?'

Francie nodded.

'The young reprobate! To be making you so remarkable, and to have the other one up his sleeve all the time! Didn't I say he had no notion of marrying ye?'

Francie made no reply, and Charlotte with some difficulty dis-

167

engaged her hand from her wrappings and patted her on the back.

'Well, never mind, me child,' she said with noisy cheerfulness; 'you're not trusting to the likes of that fellow! wait till ye're me Lady Dysart of Bruff, and it's little ye'll think of him then!'

They had reached the Tally Ho gate by this time; Francie opened it, and plunged into the pitch-dark tunnel of evergreens without a word.

27

The pre-eminently domestic smell of black currant jam pervaded Tally Ho next day. The morning had been spent by Charlotte and her retainers in stripping the straggling old bushes of the berries that resembled nothing so much as boot buttons in size, colour, and general consistency; the preserving pan had been borrowed, according to immemorial custom, from Miss Egan of the hotel, and at three o'clock of the afternoon the first relay was sluggishly seething and bubbling on the kitchen fire, and Charlotte, Norry, and Bid Sal were seated at the kitchen table snipping the brown tips of the shining fruit that still awaited its fate.

It was a bright, steamy day, when the hot sun and the wet earth turned the atmosphere into a Turkish bath, and the cats sat out of doors, but avoided the grass like the plague. Francie had docilely picked currants with the others. She was accustomed to making herself useful, and it did not occur to her to shut herself up in her room, or go for a walk, or, in fact, isolate herself with her troubles in any way. She had too little self-consciousness for these deliberate methods, and she moved among the currant bushes in her blue gown, and was merely uncomplainingly thankful that she was able to pull the broad leaf of her hat down so as to hide the eyes that were heavy from a sleepless night and red from the sting of tears. She went over again what Lambert had told her, as she mechanically dropped the currants into her tin can; the soldier servant had read the letters, and had told Michael, the Rosemount groom, and Michael had told Mr

Lambert. She wouldn't have cared a pin about his being engaged if he had only told her so at first. She had flirted with engaged men plenty of times, and it hadn't done anybody any harm, but this was quite different. She couldn't believe, after the way he went on, that he cared about another girl all the time, and yet Michael had said that the soldier had said that they were to be married at Christmas. Well, thank goodness, she thought, with a half sob, she knew about it now; he'd find it hard to make a fool of her again.

After the early dinner the practical part of the jam-making began, and for an hour Francie snipped at the currant tops as industriously as Charlotte herself. But by the time that the first brew was ready for the preserving pan, the heat of the kitchen, and the wearisomeness of Charlotte's endless discussions with Norry, made intolerable the headache that had all day hovered about her forehead, and she fetched her hat and a book and went out into the garden to look for coolness and distraction. She wandered up to the seat where she had sat on the day that Lambert gave her the bangle, and sitting down, opened her book, a railway novel, bought by Charlotte on her journey from Dublin. She read its stodgily sensational pages with hot tired eyes, and tried hard to forget her own unhappiness in the infinitely more terrific woes of its heroine; but now and then some chance expression, or one of those terms of endearment that were lavished throughout its pages, would leap up into borrowed life and sincerity, and she would shut her eyes and drift back into the golden haze on Lough Moyle, when his hand had pressed her head down on his shoulder, and his kisses had touched her soul. At such moments all the heated stillness of the lake was round her, with no creature nearer than the white cottages on the far hillsides; and when the inevitable present swam back to her, with carts rattling past on the road, and insects buzzing and blundering against her face, and Bid Sal's shrill summoning of the hens to their food, she would fling herself again into the book to hide from the pursuing pain and the undying, insane voice of hope.

Hope mastered pain, and reality mastered both, when, with the conventionality of situation to which life sometimes condescends, there came steps on the gravel, and looking up she saw that Hawkins was coming towards her. Her heart stopped and rushed on again like a startled horse, but all the rest of her remained still and almost impassive, and she leaned her head over her book to keep up the affectation of not having seen him.

'I saw your dress through the trees as I was coming up the drive,' he said after a moment of suffocating silence, 'and so – ' he held out his hand, 'aren't you going to shake hands with me?'

'How d'ye do, Mr Hawkins?' she gave him a limp hand and withdrew it instantly.

Hawkins sat down beside her, and looked hard at her half-averted face. He had solved the problem of her treatment of him last night in a way quite satisfactory to himself, and he thought that now that he had been sharp enough to have found her here, away from Miss Mullen's eye, things would be very different. He had quite forgiven her her share in the transgression; in fact, if the truth were known, he had enjoyed himself considerably after she had left Mrs Beattie's party, and had gone back to Captain Cursiter and disingenuously given him to understand that he had hardly spoken a word to Miss Fitzpatrick the whole evening.

'So you wouldn't dance with me last night,' he said, as if he were speaking to a child; 'wasn't that very unkind of you?'

'No, it was not,' she replied, without looking at him.

'Well *I* think it was,' he said, lightly touching the hand that held the novel.

Francie took her hand sharply away.

'I think you are being very unkind now,' he continued; 'aren't you even going to look at me?'

'Oh yes, I'll look at you if you like,' she said, turning upon him in a kind of desperation; 'it doesn't do me much harm, and I don't suppose it does you much good.'

The cool, indifferent manner that she had intended to assume was already too difficult for her, and she sought a momentary refuge in rudeness. He showed all the white teeth, that were his best point, in a smile that was patronizingly free from resentment.

'Why, what's the matter with her?' he said caressingly. 'I believe I know what it's all about. She's been catching it about that day in the launch! Isn't that it?'

'I don't know what you're talking about, Mr Hawkins,' said Francie, with an indifferent attempt at hauteur; 'but since you're so clever at guessing things I suppose there's no need of me telling you.'

Hawkins came closer to her, and forcibly took possession of her hands. 'What's the matter with you?' he said in a low voice; 'why are you angry with me? Don't you know I love you?' The unexpected element of uncertainty sharpened the edge of his feelings and gave his voice an earnestness that was foreign to it

Francie started visibly; 'No, I know you don't,' she said,

170

facing him suddenly, like some trapped creature; 'I know you're in love with somebody else!'

His eyes flinched as though a light had been flashed in them. 'What do you mean?' he said quickly, while a rush of blood darkened his face to the roots of his yellow hair, and made the veins stand out on his forehead; 'who told you that?'

'It doesn't matter who told me,' she said with a miserable satisfaction that her bolt had sped home; 'but I know it's true.'

'I give you my honour it's not!' he said passionately; 'you might have known better than to believe it.'

'Oh yes, I might,' she said with all the scorn she was master of; 'but I think 'twas as good for me I didn't.' Her voice collapsed at the end of the sentence, and the dry sob that rose in her throat almost choked her. She stood up and turned her face away to hide the angry tears that in spite of herself had sprung to her eyes.

Hawkins caught her hand again and held it tightly. 'I know what it is. I suppose they've been telling you of that time I was in Limerick; and that was all rot from beginning to end; anyone could tell you that.'

'It's not that; I heard all about that –'

Hawkins jumped up. 'I don't care what you heard,' he said violently. 'Don't turn your head away from me like that, I won't have it. I know that you care about me, and I know that I shouldn't care if everyone in the world was dead, so long as you were here.' His arm was around her, but she shook herself free.

'What about Miss Coppard?' she said; 'what about being married before Christmas?'

For a moment Hawkins could find no words to say. 'So you've got hold of that, have you?' he said, after some seconds of silence that seemed endless to Francie. 'And do you think that will come between us?'

'Of course it must come between us,' she said in a stifled voice; 'and you knew that all through.'

Mr Hawkins' engagement was a painful necessity about which he affaired himself as little as possible. He recognized it as a certain and not disagreeable road to paying his debts, which might with good luck be prolonged till he got his company, and, latterly, it had fallen more than ever into the background. That it should interfere with his amusements in any way made it an impertinence of a wholly intolerable kind.

'It shall *not* come between us!' he burst out; 'I don't care what happens, I won't give you up! I give you my honour I never cared twopence about her – I've never thought of her since I first saw you – I've thought of no one but you.'

His hot, stammering words were like music to her; but that staunchness of soul that was her redeeming quality still urged her to opposition.

'It's no good your going on like this. You know you're going to marry her. Let me go.'

But Mr Hawkins was not in the habit of being baulked of anything on which he had set his heart.

'No, I will not let you go,' he said, drawing her towards him with bullying tenderness. 'In the first place, you're not able to stand, and in the second place, I'm not going to marry anybody but you.'

He spoke with a certainty that convinced himself; the certainty of a character that does not count the cost either for itself or for others; and, in the space of a kiss, her distrust was left far behind her as a despicable thing.

28

Nearly three weeks had gone by since Mrs Beattie's party, and as Charlotte Mullen walked slowly along the road towards Rosemount one afternoon, her eyes fixed on the square toes of her boots, and her hands, as was her custom, in the pockets of her black jacket, she meditated agreeably upon recent events. Of these perhaps the pleasantest was Mr Hawkins' departure to Hythe, for a musketry course, which had taken place somewhat unexpectedly a fortnight ago. He was a good-for-nothing young limb, and engagement or no engagement it was a good job he was out of the place; and, after all, Francie had not seemed to mind. Almost equally satisfactory was the recollection of that facetious letter to Christopher Dysart in which she had so playfully reminded him of the ancient promise to photograph the Tally Ho cats, and hoped that she and her cousin would not come under that category. Its success had even been surprising, for not only had Christopher come and spent a long afternoon in that difficult enterprise, but had come again more than once, on pretexts that had appeared to Charlotte satisfactorily flimsy, and had apparently set aside what she knew to be his repugnance to herself. That he should lend Francie *John Inglesant* and Rossetti's *Poems* made Charlotte laugh in her sleeve. She had her own very sound opinion of her cousin's literary capacity, and had no sympathy for the scientific interest felt by a philosopher in the evolution of a nascent soul. Christopher's manner did not, it is true, coincide with her theory of a lover, which was crude, and founded on taste rather than experience, but she had imagination enough to recognize that Christopher, in lovemaking, as in most other things, would pursue methods unknown to her.

At this point in her reflections, congratulation began to wane. She thought she knew every twist and turn in Roddy Lambert, but lately she had not been able to explain him at all to her satisfaction. He was always coming to Tally Ho, and he always seemed in a bad temper when he was there; in fact she had never known him as ill-mannered as he was last week, one day when he and Christopher were there together, and she had tried, for various excellent reasons, to get him off into the dining room to talk business. She couldn't honestly say that Francie was running after him, though of course she had that nasty flirty way with every man, old or young, married or single; but all the same, there was something in it she didn't like. The girl was more trouble than she was worth; and if it wasn't for Christopher Dysart she'd have sent her packing back to Letitia Fitzpatrick, and told her that whether she could manage it or not she must keep her. But of course to have Sir Christopher Dysart of Bruff – she rolled the title on her tongue – as a cousin was worthy of patience.

As she walked up the trim Rosemount avenue she spied the owner of the house lying in a basket chair in the shade, with a pipe in his mouth, and in his hand that journal politely described by Mrs Rattray as 'the *Pink One*'.

'Hallo, Charlotte!' he said lazily, glancing up at her from under the peak of his cap, 'you look warm.'

'And you look what you are, and that's cool, in manners and body,' retorted Miss Mullen, coming and standing beside him, 'and if you had tramped on your four bones through the dust, maybe you'd be as hot as I am.'

'What do you wear that thick coat for?' he said, looking at it with a disfavour that he took no trouble to hide.

Charlotte became rather red. She had the Irish peasant

woman's love of heavy clothing and dislike of abating any item of it in summer.

'If you had my tendency to bronchitis, me fine fellow,' she said, seating herself on the uncomfortable garden bench beside which his chair had been placed, 'you'd think more of your health than your appearance.'

'Very likely,' said Mr Lambert, yawning and relapsing into silence.

'Well, Roddy,' resumed Charlotte more amicably, 'I didn't walk all the way here to discuss the fashions with you. Have y'any more news from the seat of war?'

'No; confound her, she won't stir, and I don't see what's going to make her unless I evict her.'

'Why don't ye writ her for the money?' said Charlotte, the spirit of her attorney grandfather gleaming in her eyes; 'that'd frighten her!'

'I don't want to do that if I can help it. I spoke to her about the lodge that Lady Dysart said she could have, and the old devil was fit to be tied; but we might get her to it before we've done with her.'

'If it was me I'd writ her now,' repeated Charlotte venomously; 'you'll find you'll have to come to it in the end.'

'It's a sin to see that lovely pasture going to waste,' said Lambert, leaning back and puffing at his pipe. 'Peter Joyce hasn't six head of cattle on it this minute.'

'If you and I had it, Roddy,' said Charlotte, eyeing him with a curious, guarded tenderness, 'it wouldn't be that way.'

Some vibration of the strong, incongruous tremor that passed through her as she spoke, reached Lambert's indolent perception and startled it. It reminded him of the nebulous understanding that taking her money seemed to have involved him in; he believed he knew why she had given it to him, and though he knew also that he held his advantage upon precarious terms, even his coarse-fibred nature found something repellent in the thought of having to diplomatize with such affections as Charlotte's.

'I was up at Murphy's yesterday,' he said, as if his train of ideas had not been interrupted. 'He has a grand filly there that I'd buy tomorrow if I had the money, or any place to put her. There's a pot of money in her.'

'Well, if you'll get me Gurthnamuckla,' said Charlotte with a laugh, in which nervousness was strangely apparent, 'you may buy up every young horse in the country and stable them in the parlour, so long as you'll leave the attics for me and the cats.'

Lambert turned his head upon its cushion, and looked at her.

'I think I'll leave you a little more space than that, Charlotte, if ever we stable our horses together.'

She glanced at him, as aware of the *double entendre*, and as stirred by it as he had intended her to be. Perhaps a little more than he had intended; at all events, he jerked himself into a sitting position, and, getting on to his feet, stretched himself with almost ostentatious ease.

'Where's Francie?' he asked, yawning.

'At home, dressmaking,' replied Miss Mullen. She was a little paler than usual. 'I think I'll go in now and have a cup of tea with Lucy,' she said, rising from the garden bench with something like an effort.

'Well, I daresay I'll take the mare down to Tally Ho, and make Francie go for a ride,' said Lambert; 'it's a pity for anyone to be stewing in the house on a day like this.'

'I wanted her to come here with me, but she wouldn't,' Charlotte called after him as he turned towards the path that led to the stables. 'Maybe she thought there might be metal more attractive for her at home!'

She grinned to herself as she went up the steps. 'Me gentleman may put that in his pipe and smoke it!' she thought; 'that little hussy would let him think it was for him she was sitting at home!'

Ever since Mrs Lambert's first entrance into Lismoyle society, she had found in Charlotte her most intimate and reliable ally. If Mr Lambert had been at all uneasy as to his bride's reception by Miss Mullen, he must have been agreeably surprised to find that after a month or so Charlotte had become as useful and pleasant to Mrs Lambert as in older days she had been to him. That Charlotte should have recognized the paramount necessity of his marrying money, had been to Lambert a proof of her eminent common sense. He had always been careful to impress his obvious destiny upon her, and he had always been grateful to that destiny for having harmlessly fulfilled itself, while yet old Mrs Mullen's money was in her own keeping, and her niece was, beyond all question, ineligible. That was Mr Lambert's view of the situation; whatever Charlotte's opinion was, she kept it to herself.

Mrs Lambert was more than usually delighted to see her ever sympathizing friend, on this hot afternoon. One of her chiefest merits in the turkey-hen's eyes was that she 'was as good as any doctor, and twice better than Dr Rattray, who would never believe the half she went through with palpitations, and buzzings in her eyes and roarings in her head,' and the first half hour or so of her visit was consumed in minute detail of her more recent symptoms. The fact that large numbers of women entertain their visitors with biographies, mainly abusive, of their servants, has been dwelt on to weariness by many writers; but, nevertheless, in no history of Mrs Lambert could this characteristic be conscientiously omitted.

'Oh, my dear,' she said, as her second cup of sweet weak tea was entered upon, 'you know that Eliza Hackett, that I got with the highest recommendations from the Honourable Miss Carrick, and thinking she'd be so steady, being a Protestant? Well, last Sunday she went to mass!' She paused, and Charlotte, one of whose most genuine feelings was a detestation of Roman Catholics, exclaimed:

'Goodness alive! what did you let her do that for?'

'How could I stop her?' answered Mrs Lambert plaintively, 'she never told one in the house she was going, and this morning, when I was looking at the meat with her in the larder, I took the opportunity to speak to her about it. "Oh," says she, turning round as cool as you please, "I consider the Irish Church hasn't the Apostolic succession!"'

'You don't tell me that fat-faced Eliza Hackett said that?' ejaculated Charlotte.

'She did, indeed,' replied Mrs Lambert deploringly; 'I was quite upset. "Eliza," says I, "I wonder you have the impudence to talk to me like that. You that was taught better by the Honourable Miss Carrick." "Ma'am," says she, up to my face, "Moses and Aaron was two holy Roman Catholic priests, and that's more than you can say of the archdeacon!" "Indeed, no," says I, "thank God he's not!" but I ask you, Charlotte, what could I say to a woman like that, that would wrest the Scriptures to her own purposes?'

Even Charlotte's strong brain reeled in the attempt to follow the arguments of Eliza the cook and Mrs Lambert.

'Well, upon my word, Lucy, it's little I'd have argued with her. I'd have just said to her, "Out of my house you march, if you don't go to your church!" I think that would have composed her religious scruples.'

'Oh! but, Charlotte,' pleaded the turkey-hen, 'I *couldn't* part with her; she knows just what gentlemen like, and Roderick's so particular about savouries. When I told him about her, he said he wouldn't care if she was a Mormon and had a dozen husbands, so long as she made good soup.'

Charlotte laughed out loud. Mr Lambert's turn of humour had a robustness about it that always roused a sympathetic chord in her.

'Well, that's a man all over! His stomach before anyone else's soul!'

'Oh, Charlotte, you shouldn't say such things! Indeed, Roderick will often take only the one cut of meat at his dinner these times, and if it isn't to his liking he'll take nothing; he's a great epicure. I don't know what's over him those last few weeks,' continued Mrs Lambert gloomily, 'unless it's the hot weather, and all the exercise he's taking, that's making him cross.'

'Well, from all I've ever seen of men,' said Charlotte, with a laugh, 'the hotter they get the better pleased they are. Take my word for it, there's no time a man's so proud of himself as when he's "larding the lean earth"!'

Mrs Lambert looked bewildered, but was too much affaired with her own thoughts to ask for an explanation of what seemed to her a strange term in cookery.

'Did he know Francie Fitzpatrick much in Dublin?' she said after a pause, in which she had given a saucerful of cream and sopped cake to her dog.

Charlotte looked at her hostess suddenly and searchingly as she stooped with difficulty to take up the saucer.

'He's known her since she was a child,' she replied, and waited for further developments.

'I thought it must be that way,' said Mrs Lambert with a dissatisfied sound in her voice; 'they're so very familiar-like talking to each other.'

Charlotte's heart paused for an instant in its strong, regular course. Was it possible, she thought, that wisdom was being perfected in the mouth of Lucy Lambert?

'I never noticed anything so wonderfully familiar,' she said, in a tone meant to provoke further confidence; 'I never knew Roddy yet that he wasn't civil to a pretty girl and as for Francie, any man comes handy to her! Upon my word, she'd dote on a tongs, as they say!'

Mrs Lambert fidgeted nervously with her long gold watch-chain. 'Well, Charlotte,' she said, a little defiantly, 'I've been married to him five years now, and I've never known him particular with any girl.'

'Then, my dear woman, what's this nonsense you're talking

about him and Francie?' said Charlotte, with Mephistophelian gaiety.

'Oh, Charlotte!' said Mrs Lambert, suddenly getting very red, and beginning to whimper, 'I never thought to speak of it – ' she broke off and began to root for her handkerchief, while her respectable midde-aged face began to wrinkle up like a child's, 'and, indeed, I don't want to say anything against the girl, for she's a nice girl, and so I've always found her, but I can't help noticing – ' she broke off again.

'What can't you help noticing?' demanded Charlotte roughly.

Mrs Lambert drew a long breath that was half suffocated by a sob. 'Oh, I don't know,' she cried helplessly; 'he's always going down to Tally Ho, by the way he'll take her out riding or boating or something, and though he doesn't say much, a little thing'll slip out now and again, and you can't say a word to him but he'll get cross.'

'Maybe he's in trouble about money unknown to you,' suggested Charlotte, who, for some reason or other, was not displaying her usual capacity for indictment, 'or maybe he finds "life not worth living because of the liver"!' she ended, with a mirthless laugh.

'Oh, no, no, Charlotte; indeed, it's no laughing joke at all – ' Mrs Lambert hesitated, then, with a little hysterical burst of sobs, 'he talks about her in his sleep!' she quavered out, and began to cry miserably.

Charlotte sat perfectly still, looking at Mrs Lambert with eyes that saw, but held no pity for, her abundant tears. How far more serious was this thing, if true, to her, than to that contemptible whining creature, whose snuffling gasps were exasperating her almost beyond the bounds of endurance. She waited till there was a lull.

'What did he say about her?' she asked in a hard, jeering voice.

'Oh, Charlotte, how can I tell you? all sorts of things he says, nonsense like, and springing up and saying she'll be drowned.'

'Well, if it's any comfort to you,' said Charlotte, 'she cares no more for him than the man in the moon! She has other fish to fry, I can tell you!'

'But what signifies that, Charlotte,' sighed Mrs Lambert, 'so long as he thinks about her?'

'Tell him he's a fool to waste his time over her,' suggested Charlotte scoffingly.

'Is it *me* tell him such a thing!' The turkey-hen lifted her wet red eyes from her saturated pocket handkerchief and began to laugh hysterically. 'Much regard he has for what *I* say to him! Oh, don't make me laugh, Charlotte – ' a frightened look came over her face, as if she had been struck, and she fell back in her chair. 'It's the palpitations,' she said faintly, with her hand on her heart. 'Oh, I'm going – I'm going – '

Charlotte ran to the chimney-piece, and took from it a bottle of smelling salts. She put it to Mrs Lambert's nose with one hand, and with the other unfastened the neck of her dress without any excitement or fuss. Her eyes were keen and quiet as she bent over the pale blotched face that lay on the antimacassar; and when Mrs Lambert began to realize again what was going on round her, she was conscious of a hand chafing her own, a hand that was both gentle and skilful.

29

'Metal more attractive!' Lambert thought there could not be a more offensive phrase in the English language than this, that had rung in his ears ever since Charlotte had flung it at him when he parted from her on his own avenue. He led the black mare straight to the dilapidated loose-box at Tally Ho Lodge, in which she had before now waited so often and so dismally, with nothing to do except nose about the broken manger for a stray oat or two, or make spiteful faces through the rails at her comrade, the chestnut, in the next stall. Lambert swung open the stable door, and was confronted by the pricked ears and interested countenance of a tall bay horse, whom he instantly recognized as being one of the Bruff carriage horses, looking out of the loose-box. Mr Lambert's irritation culminated at this point in appropriate profanity; he felt that all these things were against him, and the thought that he would go straight back to Rosemount made him stand still on the doorstep. But the next moment he had a vision of himself and the two horses turning in at the Rosemount gate, with the certain prospect of being laughed at by Charlotte and condoled with by his wife, and without so much as a sight of that maddening face that was every day thrusting itself more and more between him and his peace. It would be a confession of defeat at the hands of Christopher Dysart, which alone would be intolerable; besides, there wasn't a doubt but that, if Francie were given her choice, she would rather go out riding with him than anything.

Buoyed up by this reflection, he put the chestnut into the stable, and the mare into the cow-shed, and betook himself to the house. The hall door was open, and stepping over the cats on the door-mat, he knocked lightly at the drawing-room door, and walked in without waiting for an answer. Christopher was sitting with his back to him, holding one end of a folded piece of pink cambric, while Francie, standing up in front of him, was cutting along the fold towards him, with a formidable pair of scissors.

'Must I hold on to the end?' he was saying, as the scissors advanced in leaps towards his fingers.

'I'll kill you if you let go!' answered Francie, rather thickly, by reason of a pin between her front teeth. 'Goodness, Mr Lambert! you frightened the heels off me! I thought you were Louisa with the tea.'

'Good evening, Francie; good evening, Dysart,' said Lambert with solemn frigidity.

Christopher reddened a little as he looked round. 'I'm afraid I can't shake hands with you, Lambert,' he said with an un-avoidably foolish laugh, 'I'm dressmaking.'

'So I see,' replied Mr Lambert, with something as near a sneer as he dared. He always felt it a special unkindness of Providence to have placed this young man to reign over him, and the practical sentiment that it is well not to quarrel with your bread and butter had not unfrequently held him back from a much-desired jibe. 'I came, Francie,' he went on with the same portentous politeness, 'to see if you'd care to come for a ride with me.'

'When? Now?' said Francie, without much enthusiasm.

'Oh, not unless you like,' he replied, in a palpably offended tone.

'Well, how d'ye know I wouldn't like? Keep quiet now, Mr Dysart, I've another one for you to hold!'

'I'm afraid I must be going – ' began Christopher, looking helplessly at the billows of pink cambric which surrounded him on the floor. Lambert's arrival had suddenly made the situation seem vulgar.

'Ah, can't you sit still now?' said Francie, thrusting another length of material into his hand, and beginning to cut swiftly towards him. 'I declare you're very idle!'

Lambert stood silent while this went on, and then, with an angry look at Francie, he said, 'I understand, then, that you're not coming out riding today?'

'Do you?' asked Francie, pinning the seam together with marvellous rapidity; 'take care your understanding isn't wrong! Have you the horse down here?'

'Of course I have.'

'Well, I'll tell you what we'll do: we'll have tea first, and then we'll ride back with Mr Dysart; will that do you?'

'I wanted to ride in the opposite direction,' said Lambert; 'I had some business – '

'Oh, bother your old business!' interrupted Francie; 'anyway, I hear her bringing in the tea.'

'Oh, I hope you'll ride home with me,' said Christopher; 'I hate riding by myself.'

'Much I pity you!' said Francie, flashing a sidelong look at him as she went over to the tea table; 'I suppose you'd be frightened!'

'Quite so. Frightened and bored. That is what I feel like when I ride by myself,' said Christopher, trying to eliminate from his manner the constraint that Lambert's arrival had imparted to it, 'and my horse is just as bored; I feel apologetic all the time and wishing I could do something to amuse him that wouldn't be dangerous. Do come; I'm sure he'd like it.'

'Oh, how anxious you are about him!' said Francie, cutting bread and butter with a dexterous hand from the loaf that Louisa had placed on the table in frank confession of incapacity. 'I don't know what I'll do till I've had my tea. Here now, here's yours poured out for both of you; I suppose you'd like me to come and hand it to you!' with a propitiatory look at Lambert.

Thus adjured, the two men seated themselves at the table, on which Francie had prepared their tea and bread and butter with a propriety that reminded Christopher of his nursery days. It was a very agreeable feeling, he thought; and as he docilely drank his tea and laughed at Francie for the amount of sugar that she put into hers, the idealizing process to which he was unconsciously subjecting her advanced a stage. He was beginning to lose sight of her vulgarity, even to wonder at himself for ever having applied that crudely inappropriate word to her. She had some reflected vulgarities of course, thought the usually hypercritical Mr Christopher Dysart, and her literary progress along the lines he

181

had laid down for her was slow; but, lately, since his missionary resolve to let the light of culture illuminate her darkness, he had found out subtle depths of sweetness and sympathy that were, in their responsiveness, equivalent to intellect.

When Francie went up a few minutes later to put on her habit, Christopher did not seem disposed to continue the small talk in which his proficiency had been more surprising than pleasing to Mr Lambert.

He strolled over to the window, and looked meditatively out at Mrs Bruff and a great-grandchild or two embowered in a tangle of nasturtiums, and putting his hands in his pockets began to whistle *sotto voce*. Lambert looked him up and down, from his long thin legs to his small head, on which the light brown hair grew rather long, with a wave in it that was to Lambert the height of effeminacy. He began to drum with his fingers on the table to show that he too was quite undisturbed and at his ease.

'By the bye, Dysart,' he observed presently, 'have you heard anything of Hawkins since he left?'

Christopher turned round. 'No, I don't know anything about him except that he's gone to Hythe.'

'Gone to *hide*, d'ye say?' Lambert laughed noisily in support of his own joke.

'No, Hythe.'

'It seems to me it's more likely it's a case of hide,' Lambert went on with a wink; he paused, fiddled with his teaspoon, and smiled at his own hand as he did so. 'P'raps he thought it was time for him to get out of this.'

'Really?' said Christopher, with a lack of interest that was quite genuine.

Lambert's pulse bounded with the sudden desire to wake this supercilious young hound up for once, by telling him a few things that would surprise him.

'Well, you see it's a pretty strong order for a fellow to carry on as Hawkins did, when he happens to be engaged.'

The fact of Mr Hawkins' engagement had, it need scarcely be said, made its way through every highway and byway of Lismoyle; inscrutable as to its starting-point, impossible of verification, but all the more fascinating for its mystery. Lambert had no wish to claim its authorship; he had lived among gentlemen long eno'i_h to be aware that the second-hand confidences of a servant could not creditably be quoted by him. What he did not know, however, was whether the story had reached Bruff, or been believed there, and it was extremely provoking to him row that instead of being able to observe its effect on Christopher, whose back was to the light, his discoveries should be limited to the fact that his own face had become very red as he spoke.

'I suppose he knows his own affairs best,' said Christopher, after a silence that might have meant anything, or nothing.

'Well,' leaning back and putting his hands in his pockets, 'I don't tend to be straitlaced, but d—n it, you know, I think Hawkins went a bit too far.'

'I don't think I have heard who it is that he is engaged to,' said Christopher, who seemed remarkably unaffected by Mr Hawkins' misdemeanours.

'Oh, to a Yorkshire girl, a Miss – what's this her name is? – Coppard. Pots of money, but mighty plain about the head, I believe. He kept it pretty dark, didn't he?'

'Apparently it got out, for all that.'

Lambert thought he detected a tinge of ridicule in the voice, whether of him or of Hawkins he did not know; it gave just the necessary spur to that desire to open Christopher's eyes for him a bit.

'Oh, yes, it got out,' he said, putting his elbow on the table, and balancing his teaspoon on his forefinger, 'but I think there are very few that know for certain it's a fact – fortunately for our friend.'

'Why fortunately? I shouldn't think it made much difference to anyone.'

'Well, as a rule, girls don't care to flirt with an engaged man.'

'No, I suppose not,' said Christopher, yawning with a frank-ness that was a singular episode in his demeanour towards his agent.

Lambert felt his temper rising every instant. He was a man whose jealousy took the form of reviling the object of his affec-tions, if, by so doing, he could detach his rivals.

'Well, Francie Fitzpatrick knows it for one; but perhaps she's not one of the girls who object to flirting with an engaged man.'

Lambert got up and walked to the window; he felt that he could no longer endure seeing nothing of Christopher except a lank silhouette with an offensive repose of attitude. He propped his back against one of the shutters, and obviously waited for a comment.

'I should think it was an inexpensive amusement,' said Christopher, in his most impersonal and academic manner, 'but likely to pall.'

'Pall! Deuce a bit of it!' Lambert put a toothpick in his mouth, and began to chew it, to convey the effect of ease. 'I can tell you I've known that girl since she was the length of my stick, and I never saw her that she wasn't up to some game or other; and she wasn't over particular about engagements or anything else!'

Christopher slightly shifted his position, but did not speak, and Lambert went on:

'I'm very fond of the girl, and she's a good-hearted little thing; but, by Jove! I was sorry to see the way she went on with that fellow Hawkins. Here he was, morning, noon, and night, walking with her, and steam launching, and spooning, and setting all the old women in the place prating. I spoke to her about it, and much thanks I got, though there was a time she was ready enough to mind what I said to her.' During this recital Mr Lambert's voice had been deficient in the accent of gentlemanlike self-importance that in calmer moments he was careful to impart to it, and the raw Limerick brogue was on top as he said, 'Yes, by George! I remember the time when she wasn't above fancying your humble servant!'

He had almost forgotten his original idea; his own position, long brooded over, rose up out of all proportion, and confused his mental perspective, till Christopher Dysart's opinions were lost sight of. He was recalled to himself by a startling expression on the face of his confidant, an expression of almost unconcealed disgust, that checked effectively any further outpourings. Christopher did not look at him again, but turned from the window, and, taking up Miss Mullen's photograph book, proceeded to a minute inspection of its contents. Neither he nor Lambert quite knew what would happen next, each in his own way being angry enough for any emergency, and both felt an extreme relief when Francie's abrupt entrance closed the situation.

'Well, I wasn't long now, was I?' she said breathlessly; 'but what'll I do? I can't find my gloves!' She swept out of the corner of the sofa a cat that had been slumbering unseen behind a cushion. 'Here they are! and full of fleas, I'll be bound, after Clementina sleeping on them! Oh, goodness! Are both of you too angry to speak to me? I didn't think I was so long. Come on out to the yard; you can't say I'm keeping you now.'

She whirled out of the room, and by the time Lambert and Christopher got into the yard, she had somehow dragged the black mare out of the cowshed and was clambering on to her back with the aid of a wheelbarrow.

Riding has many charms, but none of its eulogists have pro-

184

perly dwelt on the advantages it offers to the unconversational. To ride in silence is the least marked form of unsociability, for something of the same reason that talking on horseback is one of the pleasantest modes of converse. The power of silence cuts both ways, and simplifies either confidence or its reverse amazingly. It so happened, however, that had Lambert had the inclination to make himself agreeable to his companions he could not have done so. Christopher's carriage horse trotted with the machine-like steadiness of its profession, and the black mare, roused to emulation, flew along beside him, ignoring the feebly expressed desire of her rider that she should moderate her pace. Christopher, indeed, seldom knew or cared at what pace his horse was going, and was now by no means sorry to find that the question of riding along with Lambert had been settled for him. The rough, young chestnut was filled with a vainglory that scorned to trot, and after a great deal of brilliant ramping and curveting he fell into a kind of heraldic action, half canter, half walk, that left him more and more hopelessly in the rear, and raised Lambert's temper to boiling point.

'We're going very fast, aren't we?' panted Francie, trying to push down her rebellious habit skirt with her whip, as they sped along the flat road between Lismoyle and Bruff. 'I'm afraid Mr Lambert can't keep up. That's a dreadfully wild horse he's riding.'

'Are we?' said Christopher vaguely. 'Shall we pull up? Here, woa, you brute!' He pulled the carriage horse into a walk, and looked at Francie with a laugh. 'I'm beginning to hope you're as bad a rider as I am,' he said sympathetically. 'Let me hold your reins, while you're pinning up that plait.'

'Oh, botheration take it! Is my hair down again? It always comes down if I trot fast,' bewailed Francie, putting up her hands to her dishevelled hair, that sparkled like gold in the sun.

'Do you know, the first time I ever saw you, your hair had come down out riding,' said Christopher, looking at her as he held her rein, and not giving a thought to the intimate appearance they presented to the third member of the party; 'if I were you I should start with it down my back.'

'Ah, nonsense, Mr Dysart; why would you have me make a Judy of myself that way?'

'Because it's the loveliest hair I've ever seen,' answered Christopher, the words coming to his lips almost without his volition, and in their utterance causing his heart to give one or two unexpected throbs.

'Oh!' There was as much astonishment as pleasure in the exclamation, and she became as red as fire. She turned her head away, and looked back to see where Lambert was.

She had heard from Hawkins only this morning, asking her for a piece of the hair that Christopher had called lovely. She had cut off a little curl from the place he had specified, near her temple, and had posted it to him this very afternoon after Charlotte went out; but all the things that Hawkins had said of her hair did not seem to her so wonderful as that Mr Dysart should pay her a compliment.

Lambert was quite silent after he joined them. In his heart he was cursing everything and everyone, the chestnut, Christopher, Francie, and most of all himself, for having said the things that he had said. All the good he had done was to leave no doubt in Christopher's mind that Hawkins was out of the running, and as for telling him that Francie was a flirt, an ass like that didn't so much as know the meaning of the word flirting. He knew now that he had made a fool of himself, and the remembrance of that disgusted expression on Christopher's face made his better judgement return as burningly as the blood into veins numbed with cold. At the crossroads next before Bruff, he broke in upon the exchange of experiences of the Dublin theatres that was going on very enjoyably beside him.

'I'm afraid we must part company here, Dysart,' he said in as civil a voice as he could muster; 'I want to speak to a farmer who lives down this way.'

Christopher made his farewells, and rode slowly down the hill towards Bruff. It was a hill that had been cut down in the Famine, so that the fields on either side rose high above its level, and the red poppies and yellowing corn nodded into the sky over his head. The bay horse was collecting himself for a final trot to the avenue gates, when he found himself stopped, and, after a moment of hesitation on the part of his rider, was sent up the hill again a good deal faster than he had come down. Christopher pulled up again on the top of the hill. He was higher now than the corn, and, looking across its multitudinous, rustling surface, he saw the figure that some errant impulse had made him come back to see. Francie's head was turned towards Lambert, and she was evidently talking to him. Christopher's eyes followed the pair till they were out of sight, and then he again turned his horse, and went home to Bruff.

30

One fine morning towards the end of August, Julia Duffy was sitting on a broken chair in her kitchen, with her hands in her lap, and her bloodshot eyes fixed on vacancy. She was so quiet that a party of ducks, which had hung uncertainly about the open door for some time, filed slowly in, and began to explore an empty pot or two with their long, dirty bills. The ducks knew well that Miss Duffy, though satisfied to accord the freedom of the kitchen to the hens and turkeys, had drawn the line at them and their cousins the geese, and they adventured themselves within the forbidden limits with the utmost caution, and with many side glances from their blinking, beady eyes at the motionless figure in the chair. They had made their way to a plate of potato skins and greasy cabbage on the floor by the table, and, forgetful of prudence, were clattering their bills on the delf as they gobbled, when an arm was stretched out above their heads, and they fled in cumbrous consternation.

The arm, however, was not stretched out in menace; Julia Duffy had merely extended it to take a paper from the table, and having done so, she looked at its contents in entire obliviousness of the ducks and their maraudings. Her misfortunes were converging. It was not a week since she had heard of the proclaimed insolvency of the man who had taken the grazing of Gurthnamuckla, and it was not half an hour since she had been struck by this last arrow of outrageous fortune, the letter threatening to process her for the long arrears of rent that she had felt lengthening hopelessly with every sunrise and sunset. She looked round the dreary kitchen that had about it all the added desolation of past respectability, at the rusty hooks from which she could remember the portly hams and flitches of bacon hanging; at the big fireplace where her grandfather's Sunday sirloin used to be roasted. Now cobwebs dangled from the hooks, and the old grate had fallen to pieces, so that the few sods of turf smouldered

187

on the hearthstone. Everything spoke of bygone plenty and present wretchedness.

Julia put the letter into its envelope again and groaned a long miserable groan. She got up and stood for a minute, staring out of the open door with her hands on her hips, and then went slowly and heavily up the stairs, groaning again to herself from the exertion and from the blinding headache that made her feel as though her brain were on fire. She went into her room and changed her filthy gown for the stained and faded black rep that hung on the door. From a bandbox of tanned antiquity she took a black bonnet that had first seen the light at her mother's funeral, and tied its clammy satin strings with shaking hands. Flashes of light came and went before her eyes, and her pallid face was flushed painfully as she went downstairs again, and finding, after long search, the remains of the bottle of blacking, laboriously cleaned her only pair of boots. She was going out of the house when her eye fell upon the plate from which the ducks had been eating; she came back for it, and, taking it out with her, scattered its contents to the turkeys, mechanically holding her dress up out of the dirt as she did so. She left the plate on the kitchen window-sill, and set slowly forth down the avenue.

Under the tree by the gate, Billy Grainy was sitting, engaged, as was his custom in moments of leisure, in counting the coppers in the bag that hung round his neck. He looked in amazement at the unexpected appearance of his patroness, and as she approached him he pushed the bag under his shirt.

'Where are ye goin'?' he asked.

Julia did not answer; she fumbled blindly with the bit of stick that fastened the gate, and, having opened it, went on without attempting to shut it.

'Where are ye goin' at all?' said Billy again, his bleared eyes following the unfamiliar outline of bonnet and gown.

Without turning, she said, 'Lismoyle,' and as she walked on along the sunny road, she put up her hand and tried to wipe away the tears that were running down her face. Perhaps it was the excitement with which every nerve was trembling that made the three miles to Rosemount seem as nothing to this woman, who, for the last six months, had been too ill to go beyond her own gate; and probably it was the same unnatural strength that prevented her from breaking down, when, with her mind full of ready-framed sentences that were to touch Mr Lambert's heart and appeal to his sense of justice, she heard from Mary Holloran at the gate that he was away for a couple of days to Limerick.

Without replying to Mary Holloran's exclamations of pious horror at the distance she had walked, and declining all offers of rest or food, she turned and walked on towards Lismoyle.

She had suddenly determined to herself that she would walk to Bruff and see her landlord, and this new idea took such possession of her that she did not realize at first the magnitude of the attempt. But by the time she had reached the gate of Tally Ho the physical power that her impulse gave her began to be conscious of its own limits. The flashes were darting like lightning before her eyes, and the nausea that was her constant companion robbed her of her energy. After a moment of hesitation she decided that she would go in and see her kinswoman, Norry the Boat, and get a glass of water from her before going farther. It wounded her pride somewhat to go round to the kitchen – she, whose grandfather had been on nearly the same social level as Miss Mullen's; but Charlotte was the last person she wished to meet just then. Norry opened the kitchen door, beginning, as she did so, her usual snarling maledictions on the supposed beggar, which, however, were lost in a loud invocation of her patron saint as she recognized her first cousin, Miss Duffy.

'And is it to leg it in from Gurthnamuckla ye done?' said Norry, when the first greetings had been exchanged, and Julia was seated in the kitchen, 'and you looking as white as the dhrivelling snow this minnit.'

'I did,' said Julia feebly, 'and I'd be thankful to you for a drink of water. The day's very close.'

'Faith ye'll get no wather in this house,' returned Norry in grim hospitality: 'I'll give ye a sup of milk, or would it be too much delay on ye to wait till I bile the kittle for a cup o' tay? Bad cess to Bid Sal! There isn't as much hot wather in the house this minute as'd write yer name!'

'I'm obliged to ye, Norry,' said Julia stiffly, her sick pride evolving a supposition that she could be in want of food; 'but I'm only after my breakfast myself. Indeed,' she added, assuming from old habit her usual attitude of medical adviser, 'you'd be the better yourself for taking less tea.'

'Is it me?' replied Norry indignantly. 'I take me cup o' tay morning and evening, and if 'twas throwing afther me I wouldn't take more.'

'Give me the cold wather, anyway,' said Julia wearily; 'I must go on out of this. It's to Bruff I'm going.'

'In the name o' God what's taking ye into Bruff, you that

189

should be in yer bed, in place of sthreelin' through the counthry this way?'

'I got a letter from Lambert today,' said Julia, putting her hand to her aching head, as if to collect herself, 'and I want to speak to Sir Benjamin about it.'

'Ah, God help yer foolish head!' said Norry impatiently; 'sure ye might as well be talking to the bird above there,' pointing to the cockatoo, who was looking down at them with ghostly solemnity. 'The owld fellow's light in his head this long while.'

'Then I'll see some of the family,' said Julia; 'they remember my fawther well, and the promise I had about the farm, and they'll not see me wronged.'

'Throth, then, that's true,' said Norry, with an unwonted burst of admiration; 'they was always and ever a fine family, and thim that they takes in their hands has the luck o' God! But what did Lambert say t'ye?' with a keen glance at her visitor from under her heavy eyebrows.

Julia hesitated for a moment.

'Norry Kelly,' she said, her voice shaking a little; 'if it wasn't that you're me own mother's sister's child, I would not reveal to you the disgrace that man is trying to put upon me. I got a letter from him this morning saying he'd process me if I didn't pay him at once the half of what's due. And Joyce that has the grazing is bankrupt, and owes me what I'll never get from him.'

'Blast his sowl!' interjected Norry, who was peeling onions with furious speed.

'I know there's manny would be thankful to take the grazing,' continued Julia, passing a dingy pocket handkerchief over her forehead; 'but who knows when I'd be paid for it, and Lambert will have me out on the road before that if I don't give him the rent.'

Norry looked to see whether both the kitchen doors were shut, and then, putting both her hands on the table, leaned across towards her cousin.

'Herself wants it,' she said in a whisper.

'Wants what? What are you saying?'

'Wants the farm, I tell ye, and it's her that's driving Lambert.'

'Is it Charlotte Mullen?' asked Julia, in a scarcely audible voice.

'Now ye have it,' said Norry, returning to her onions, and shutting her mouth tightly.

The cockatoo gave a sudden piercing screech, like a note of

190

admiration. Julia half got up, and then sank back into her chair.

'Are ye sure of that?'

'As sure as I have two feet,' replied Norry, 'and I'll tell ye what she's afther it for. It's to go live in it, and to let on she's as grand as the other ladies in the counthry.'

Julia clenched the bony, discoloured hand that lay on the table.

'Before I saw her in it I'd burn it over my head!'

'Not a word out o' ye about what I tell ye,' went on Norry in the same ominous whisper. 'Shure she have it all mapped this minnit, the same as a pairson'd be makin' a watch. She's sthriving to make a match with young Misther Dysart and Miss Francie, and b'leeve you me, 'twill be a quare thing if she'll let him go from her. Shure he's the gentlest crayture ever came into a house, and he's that innocent he wouldn't think how cute she was. If ye'd seen her, ere yesterday, follying him down to the gate, and she smilin' up at him as sweet as honey! The way it'll be, she'll sell Tally Ho house for a fortune for Miss Francie, though, indeed, it's little fortune himself'll ax!'

The words drove heavily through the pain of Julia's head, and their meaning followed at an interval.

'Why would she give a fortune to the likes of her?' she asked; 'isn't it what the people say, it's only for a charity she has her here?'

Norry gave her own peculiar laugh of derision, a laugh with a snort in it.

'Sharity! It's little sharity ye'll get from that one! Didn't I hear the old misthress tellin' her, and she sthretched for death – and Miss Charlotte knows well I heard her say it – "Charlotte," says she, and her knees, dhrawn up in the bed, "Francie must have her share." And that was the lasht word she spoke.' Norry's large wild eyes roved skywards out of the window as the scene rose before her. 'God rest her soul, 'tis she got the death aisy!'

'That Charlotte Mullen may get it hard!' said Julia savagely. She got up, feeling new strength in her tired limbs, though her head was reeling strangely, and she had to grasp at the kitchen table to keep herself steady. 'I'll go on now. If I die for it I'll go to Bruff this day.'

Norry dropped the onion she was peeling, and placed herself between Julia and the door.

'The divil a toe will ye put out of this kitchen,' she said, flourishing her knife; 'is it *you* walk to Bruff?'

'I must go to Bruff,' said Julia again, almost mechanically;

'but if you could give me a taste of sperrits, I think I'd be better able for the road.'

Norry pulled open a drawer, and took from the back of it a bottle containing a colourless liquid.

'Drink this to your health!' she said in Irish, giving some in a mug to Julia; 'it's potheen I got from friends of me own, back in Curraghduff.' She put her hand into the drawer again, and after a little search produced from the centre of a bundle of amorphous rags a cardboard box covered with shells. Julia heard, without heeding it, the clink of money, and then three shillings were slapped down on the table beside her. 'Ye'll go to Conolly's now, and get a car to dhrive ye,' said Norry defiantly; 'or howld on till I send Bid Sal to get it for ye. Not a word out o' ye now! Sure, don't I know well a pairson wouldn't think to put his money in his pocket whin he'd be hasting that way lavin' his house.'

She did not wait for an answer, but shuffled to the scullery door, and began to scream for Bid Sal in her usual tones of acrid ill-temper. As she returned to the kitchen, Julia met her at the door. Her yellow face, that Norry had likened by courtesy to the driven snow, was now very red, and her eyes had a hot stare in them.

'I'm obliged to you, Norry Kelly,' she said, 'but when I'm in need of charity I'll ask for it. Let me out, if you please.'

The blast of fury with which Norry was preparing to reply was checked by a rattle of wheels in the yard, and Bid Sal appeared with the intelligence that Jimmy Daly was come over with the Bruff cart, and Norry was to go out to speak to him. When she came back she had a basket of grapes in one hand and a brace of grouse in the other, and as she put them down on the table, she informed her cousin, with distant politeness, that Jimmy Daly would drive her to Bruff.

31

The drive in the spring-cart was the first moment of comparative ease from suffering that Julia had known that day. Her tormented brain was cooled by the soft steady rush of air in her face, and the mouthful of 'potheen' that she had drunk had at first the effect of dulling all her perceptions. The cart drove up the back avenue, and at the yard gate Julia asked the man to put her down. She clambered out of the cart with great difficulty, and going round to the hall door, went toilfully up the steps and rang the bell. Sir Benjamin was out, Lady Dysart was out, Mr Dysart was out; so Gorman told her, with a doubtful look at the black Sunday gown that seemed to him indicative of the bearer of a begging petition, and he did not know when they would be in. He shut the door, and Julia went slowly down the steps again.

She had begun to walk mechanically away from the house, when she saw Sir Benjamin in his chair coming up a side walk. His face, with its white hair, gold spectacles, and tall hat, looked so sane and dignified, that, in spite of what Norry had said, she determined to carry out her first intention of speaking to him. She shivered, though the sun blazed hotly down upon her, as she walked towards the chair, not from nervousness, but from the creeping sense of illness, and the ground rose up in front of her as if she were going uphill. She made a low bow to her landlord, and James Canavan, who knew her by sight, stopped the onward course of the chair.

'I wish to speak to you on an important matter, Sir Benjamin,' began Julia in her best voice; 'I was unable to see your agent, so I determined to come to yourself.'

The gold spectacles were turned upon her fixedly, and the expression of the eyes behind them was more intelligent than usual.

'Begad, that's one of the tenants, James,' said Sir Benjamin, looking up at his attendant.

'Certainly, Sir Benjamin, certainly; this lady is Miss Duffy, from Gurthnamuckla,' replied the courtly James Canavan. 'An old tenant, I might almost say an old friend of your honour's.'

'And what the devil brings her here?' inquired Sir Benjamin, glowering at her under the wide brim of his hat.

'Sir Benjamin,' began Julia again, 'I know your memory's failing you, but you might remember that after the death of my father, Hubert Duffy – ' Julia felt all the Protestant and aristocratic associations of the name as she said it – 'you made a promise to me in your office that I should never be disturbed in my holding of the land.'

'Devil so ugly a man as Hubert Duffy ever I saw,' said Sir Benjamin, with a startling flight of memory; 'and you're his daughter, are you? Begad, the dairymaid didn't distinguish herself!'

'Yes, I am his daughter, Sir Benjamin,' replied Julia, catching at this flattering recognition. 'I and my family have always lived on your estate, and my grandfather has often had the honour of entertaining you and the rest of the gentry, when they came foxhunting through Gurthnamuckla. I am certain that it is by no wish of yours, or of your kind and honourable son, Mr Christopher, that your agent is pairsecuting me to make me leave the farm – ' Her voice failed her, partly from the suffocating anger that rose in her at her own words, and partly from a dizziness that made the bathchair, Sir Benjamin, and James Canavan, float up and down in the air before her.

Sir Benjamin suddenly began to brandish his stick. 'What the devil is she saying about Christopher? What has Christopher to say to my tenants? D—n his insolence! He ought to be at school!'

The remarkable grimaces which James Canavan made at Julia from the back of the bathchair informed her that she had lighted upon the worst possible method of ingratiating herself with her landlord, but the information came too late.

'Send that woman away, James Canavan!' he screamed, making sweeps at her with his oak stick. 'She shall never put her d—d splay foot upon my avenue again. I'll thrash her and Christopher out of the place! Turn her out, I tell you, James Canavan!'

Julia stood motionless and aghast beyond the reach of the stick, until James Canavan motioned to her to move aside; she staggered back among the long arms of a *lignum vitae*, and the bathchair, with its still cursing, gesticulating occupant, went by her at a round pace. Then she came slowly and uncertainly out on to the path again, and looked after the chariot wheels of the Caesar to whom she had appealed.

James Canavan's coat tails were standing out behind him as he drove the bathchair round the corner of the path, and Sir Benjamin's imprecations came faintly back to her as she stood waiting till the throbbing giddiness should cease sufficiently for her to begin the homeward journey that stretched, horrible and impossible, before her. Her head ached wildly, and as she walked down the avenue she found herself stumbling against the edge of the grass, now on one side and now on the other. She said to herself that the people would say she was drunk, but she didn't care now what they said. It would be shortly till they saw her a disgraced woman, with the sheriff coming to put her out of her father's house on to the road. She gave a hard, short sob as this occurred to her, and she wondered if she would have the good luck to die, supposing she let herself fall down on the grass, and lay there in the burning sun and took no more trouble about anything. Her thoughts came to her slowly and with great difficulty, but, once come, they whirled and hammered in her brain with the reiteration of chiming bells. She walked on, out of the gate, and along the road to Lismoyle, mechanically going in the shade where there was any, and avoiding the patches of broken stones, as possibly a man might who was walking out to be shot, but apathetically unconscious of what was happening.

At about this time the person whose name Julia Duffy had so unfortunately selected to conjure with was sitting under a tree on the slope opposite the hall door at Tally Ho, reading aloud a poem of Rossetti's.

> Her eyes were like the wave within,
>   Like water reeds the poise
> Of her soft body, dainty thin;
>   And like the water's noise
>   Her plaintive voice.
>
> For him the stream had never welled
>   In desert tracks malign
> So sweet; nor had he ever felt
>   So faint in the sunshine
>   Of Palestine.

Francie's attention, which had revived at the description of the Queen, began to wander again. The sound in Christopher's voice told that the words were touching something deeper than his literary perception, and her sympathy answered to the tone, though the drift of the poem was dark to her. The music of the lines had just power enough upon her ear to predispose her to sentiment, and at present sentiment with Francie meant the tender repose of her soul upon the thought of Mr Gerald Hawkins.

A pause of turning over a leaf recalled her again to the fact of Christopher, with a transition not altogether unpleasant; she looked down at him as he lay on the grass, and began to wonder, as she had several times wondered before, if he really were in love with her. Nothing seemed more unlikely. Francie admitted it to herself as she watched his eyes following the lines in complete absorption, and knew that she had neither part nor lot in the things that touched him most nearly.

But the facts were surprising, there was no denying that. Even without Charlotte to tell her so she was aware that Christopher detested the practice of paying visits even more sincerely than most men, and was certainly not in the habit of visiting in Lismoyle. Except to see her, there was no reason that could bring him to Tally Ho. Surer than all fact, however, and rising superior to mere logic, was her instinctive comprehension of men and their ways, and sometimes she was almost sure that he came, not from kindness, or from that desire to improve her mind which she had discerned and compassionated, but because he could not help himself. She had arrived at one of these thrilling moments of certainty when Christopher's voice ceased upon the words, 'Thy jealous God,' and she knew that the time had come for her to say something appropriate.

'Oh thank you, Mr Dysart – that's – that's awfully pretty. It's a sort of religious thing, isn't it?'

'Yes, I suppose so,' answered Christopher, looking at her with a wavering smile, and feeling as if he had stepped suddenly to the ground out of a dream of flying; 'the hero's a pilgrim, and that's always something.'

'I know a lovely song called "The Pilgrim of Love",' said Francie timidly; 'of course it wasn't the same thing as what you were reading, but it was awfully nice too.'

Christopher looked up at her, and was almost convinced that she must have absorbed something of the sentiment if not the sense of what he had read, her face was so sympathetic and responsive. With that expression in her limpid eyes it gave him a peculiar sensation to hear her say the name of Love; it was even a delight, and fired his imagination with the picturing of what it would be like to hear her say it with all her awakened soul. He might have said something that would have suggested his feeling, in the fragmentary, inferential manner that Francie never knew what to make of, but that her eyes strayed away at a click of the latch of the avenue gate, and lost their unworldliness in the sharp and easy glance that is the unvalued privilege of the keen sighted.

'Who in the name of goodness is this?' she said, sitting up and gazing at a black figure in the avenue; 'it's some woman or other, but she looks very queer.'

'I can't see that it matters much who it is,' said Christopher irritably, 'so long as she doesn't come up here, and she probably will if you let her see you.'

'Mercy on us! she looks awful!' exclaimed Francie incautiously; 'why, it's Miss Duffy, and her face as red as I don't know what – oh, she's seen us!'

The voice had evidently reached Julia Duffy's ears; she came stumbling on, with her eyes fixed on the light blue dress under the beech tree, and when Christopher had turned, and got his eye-glass up, she was standing at the foot of the slope, looking at him with a blurred recognition.

'Mr Dysart,' she said in a hoarse voice, that, combined with her flushed face and staring eyes, made Christopher think she was drunk, 'Sir Benjamin has driven me out of his place like a beggar; me, whose family is as long on his estate as himself; and his agent wants to drive me out of my farm that was promised to me by your father I should never be disturbed in it.'

'You're Miss Duffy from Gurthnamuckla, are you not?' interrupted Christopher, eyeing her with natural disfavour, as he got up and came down the slope towards her.

'I am, Mr Dysart, I am,' she said defiantly, 'and you and your family have a right to know me, and I ask you to do me justice, that I shall not be turned out into the ditch for the sake of a lying double-faced schemer – ' Her voice failed as it had failed before when she spoke to Sir Benjamin, and the action of her hand that carried on her meaning had a rage in it that hid its despair.

'I think if you have anything to say you had better write it,' said Christopher, beginning to think that Lambert had some excuse for his opinion of Miss Duffy, but beginning also to pity what he thought was a spectacle of miserable middle-aged drunkenness; 'you may be sure that no injustice will be done to you – '

197

'Is it injustice?' broke in Julia, while the fever cloud seemed to roll its weight back for a moment from her brain; 'maybe you'd say there was injustice if you knew all I know. Where's Charlotte Mullen, till I tell her to her face that I know her plots and her thricks? 'Tis to say that to her I came here, and to tell her 'twas she lent money to Peter Joyce that was grazing my farm, and refused it to him secondly, the way he'd go bankrupt on me, and she's to have my farm and my house that my grandfather built, thinking to even herself with the rest of the gentry – '

Her voice had become wilder and louder, and Christopher, uncomfortably aware that Francie could hear this indictment of Miss Mullen as distinctly as he did, intervened again.

'Look here, Miss Duffy,' he said in a lower voice, 'it's no use talking like this. If I can help you I will, but it would be a good deal better if you went home now. You – you seem ill, and it's a great mistake to stay here exciting yourself and making a noise. Write to me, and I'll see that you get fair play.'

Julia threw back her head and laughed, with a venom that seemed too concentrated for drunkenness.

'Ye'd better see ye get fair play yerself before you talk so grand about it!' She pointed up at Francie. 'Mrs Dysart indeed!' – she bowed with a sarcastic exaggeration, that in saner moments she would not have been capable of – 'Lady Dysart of Bruff, one of these days, I suppose!' – she bowed again. 'That's what Miss Charlotte Mullen has laid out for ye,' addressing herself to Christopher, 'and ye'll not get away from that one till ye're under her foot!'

She laughed again; her face became vacant and yet full of pain, and she staggered away down the avenue, talking violently and gesticulating with her hands.

32

Mrs Lambert gathered up her purse, her list, her bag, and her parasol from the table in Miss Greely's ware-room, and turned to give her final directions.

'Now, Miss Greely, before Sunday for certain; and you'll be careful about the set of the skirt, that it doesn't firk up at the side, the way the black one did – '

'*We* understand the set of a skirt, Mrs Lambert,' interposed the elder Miss Greely in her most aristocratic voice; 'I think you may leave that to us.'

Mrs Lambert retreated, feeling as snubbed as it was intended that she should feel, and with a last injunction to the girl in the shop to be sure not to let the Rosemount messenger leave town on Saturday night without the parcel that he'd get from upstairs, she addressed herself to the task of walking home. She was in very good spirits, and the thought of a new dress for church next Sunday was exhilarating; it was a pleasant fact also that Charlotte Mullen was coming to tea, and she and Muffy, the Maltese terrier, turned into Barrett's to buy a teacake in honour of the event. Mrs Beattie was also there, and the two ladies and Mrs Barrett had a most enjoyable discussion on tea; Mrs Beattie advocating 'the one and threepenny from the Stores', while Mrs Barrett and her other patroness agreed in upholding the Lismoyle three-and-sixpenny against all others. Mrs Lambert set forth again with her teacake in her hand, and with such a prosperous expression of countenance that Nance the Fool pursued her down the street with a confidence that was not unrewarded.

'That the hob of heaven may be yer scratching post!' she screamed, in the midst of one of her most effective fits of coughing, as Mrs Lambert's round little dolmaned figure passed complacently onward, 'that Pether and Paul may wait on ye, and that the saints may be surprised at yer success! She's sharitable the craythur,' she ended in a lower voice, as she rejoined the rival confederate who had yielded to her the right of plundering the last passer-by, 'and sign's on it, it thrives with her; she's got very gross!'

'Faith it wasn't crackin' blind nuts made her that fat,' said the confidante unamiably, 'and with all her riches she didn't give ye the price of a dhrink itself!'

Mrs Lambert entered her house by the kitchen, so as to give directions to Eliza Hackett about the teacake, and when she got upstairs she found Charlotte already awaiting her in the dining room, occupied in reading a pamphlet on stall feeding, with apparently as complete a zest as if it had been one of those yellow paper-covered volumes whose appearance aroused such a respectful horror in Lismoyle.

'Well, Lucy, is this the way you receive your visitors?' she began jocularly, as she rose and kissed her hostess's florid cheek; 'I needn't ask how you are, as you're looking blooming.'

'I declare I think this hot summer suits me. I feel stronger than I've done this good while back, thank God. Roddy was saying this morning he'd have to put me and Muffy on banting, we'd both put up so much flesh.'

The turkey-hen looked so pleased as she recalled this conjugal endearment that Charlotte could not resist the pleasure of taking her down a peg or two.

'I think he's quite right,' she said with a laugh; 'nothing ages ye like fat, and no man likes to see his wife turning into an old woman.'

Poor Mrs Lambert took the snub meekly, as was her wont. 'Well, anyway, it's a comfort to feel a little stronger, Charlotte; isn't it they say, "laugh and grow fat".' She took off her dolman and rang the bell for tea. 'Tell me, Charlotte,' she went on, 'did you hear anything about that poor Miss Duffy?'

'I was up at the infirmary this morhing asking the Sister about her. It was Rattray himself found her lying on the road, and brought her in; he says it's inflammation of the brain, and if she pulls through she'll not be good for anything afterwards.'

'Oh, my, my!' said Mrs Lambert sympathetically. 'And to think of her being at our gate lodge that very day! Mary Holloran said she had that dying look in her face you couldn't mistake.'

'And no wonder, when you think of the way she lived,' said Charlotte angrily; 'starving there in Gurthnamuckla like a rat that'd rather die in his hole than come out of it.'

'Well, she's out of it now, poor thing,' ventured Mrs Lambert.

'She is! and I think she'll stay out of it. She'll never be right in her head again, and her things'll have to be sold to support her and pay someone to look after her, and if they don't fetch that much she'll have to go into the county asylum. I wanted to talk to Roddy about that very thing,' went on Charlotte, irritation showing itself in her voice; 'but I suppose he's going riding or boating or amusing himself somehow, as usual.'

'No, he's not!' replied Mrs Lambert, with just a shade of triumph. 'He's taken a long walk by himself. He thought perhaps he'd better look after his figure as well as me and Muffy, and he wanted to see a horse he's thinking of buying. He says he'd like to be able to leave me the mare to draw me in the phaeton.'

'Where will he get the money to buy it?' asked Charlotte sharply.

'Oh! I leave all the money matters to him,' said Mrs Lambert,

200

with that expression of serene satisfaction in her husband that had already had a malign effect on Miss Mullen's temper. 'I know I can trust him.'

'You've a very different story today to what you had the last time I was here,' said Charlotte with a sneer. 'Are all your doubts of him composed?'

The entrance of the tea tray precluded all possibility of answer; but Charlotte knew that her javelin was quivering in the wound. The moment the door closed behind the servant, Mrs Lambert turned upon her assailant with the whimper in her voice that Charlotte knew so well.

'I greatly regretted, Charlotte,' she said, with as much dignity as she could muster, 'speaking to you the way I did, for I believe now I was totally mistaken.'

It might be imagined that Charlotte would have taken pleasure in Mrs Lambert's security, inasmuch as it implied her own; but, so far from this being the case, it was intolerable to her that her friend should be blind to the fact that tortured her night and day.

'And what's changed your mind, might I ask?'

'His conduct has changed my mind, Charlotte,' replied Mrs Lambert severely; 'and that's enough for me.'

'Well, I'm glad you're pleased with his conduct, Lucy; but if he was *my* husband I'd find out what he was doing at Tally Ho every day in the week before I was so rejoiced about him.'

Charlotte's face had flushed in the heat of argument, and Mrs Lambert felt secretly a little frightened.

'Begging your pardon, Charlotte,' she said, still striving after dignity, 'he's not there every day, and when he does go it's to talk business with you he goes, about Gurthnamuckla and money and things like that.'

Charlotte sat up with a dangerous look about her jaw. She could hardly believe that Lambert could have babbled her secrets to this despised creature in order to save himself. 'He appears to tell you a good deal about his business affairs,' she said, her eyes quelling the feeble resistance in Mrs Lambert's; 'but he doesn't seem to tell you the truth about other matters. He's telling ye lies about what takes him to Tally Ho; it isn't to talk business – ' the colour deepened in her face. 'I tell ye once for all, that as sure as God's in heaven he's fascinated with that girl! This isn't the beginning of it – ye needn't think it! She flirted with him in Dublin, and though she doesn't care two snaps of her fingers for him she's flirting with him now!'

The real Charlotte had seldom been nearer the surface than

at this moment; and Mrs Lambert cowered before the manifestation.

'You're very unkind to me, Charlotte,' she said in a voice that was tremulous with fright and anger; 'I wonder at you, that you could say such things to me about my own husband.'

'Well, perhaps you'd rather I said it to you now in confidence than that every soul in Lismoyle should be prating and talking about it, as they will be if ye don't put down yer foot, and tell Roddy he's making a fool of himself!'

Mrs Lambert remained stunned for a few seconds at the bare idea of putting down her foot where Roderick was concerned, or of even insinuating that that supreme being could make a fool of himself, and then her eyes filled with tears of mortification.

'He is *not* making a fool of himself, Charlotte,' she said, endeavouring to pluck up spirit, 'and you've no right to say anything of the kind. You might have more respect for your family than to be trying to raise scandal this way and upsetting me, and I not able for it!'

Charlotte looked at her, and kept back with an effort the torrent of bullying fury that was seething in her. She had no objection to upsetting Mrs Lambert, but she preferred that hysterics should be deferred until she had established her point. Why she wished to establish it she did not explain to herself, but her restless jealousy, combined with her intolerance of the Fool's Paradise in which Mrs Lambert had entrenched herself, made it impossible for her to leave the subject alone.

'I think ye know it's not my habit to raise scandal, Lucy, and I'm not one to make an assertion without adequate grounds for it,' she said in her strong, acrid voice; 'as I said before, this flirtation is an old story. I have my own reasons for knowing that there was more going on than anyone suspected, from the time she was in short frocks till she came down here, and now, if she hadn't another affair on hand, she'd have the whole country in a blaze about it. Why, d'ye know that habit she wears? It was your husband paid for that!'

She emphasized each word between her closed teeth, and her large face was so close to Mrs Lambert's, by the time she had finished speaking, that the latter shrank back.

'I don't believe you, Charlotte,' she said with trembling lips; 'how do you know it?'

Charlotte had no intention of telling that her source of information had been the contents of a writing case of Francie's, an absurd receptacle for photographs and letters that bore the

202

word 'Papeterie' on its greasy covers, and had a lock bearing a family resemblance to the lock of Miss Mullen's workbox. But a cross-examination by the turkey-hen was easily evaded.

'Never you mind how I know it. It's true.' Then, with a connection of ideas that she would have taken more pains to conceal in dealing with anyone else, 'Did ye ever see any of the letters she wrote to him when she was in Dublin?'

'No, Charlotte; I'm not in the habit of looking at my husband's letters. I think the tea is drawn,' she continued, making a last struggle to maintain her position, 'and I'd be glad to hear no more on the subject.' She took the cosy off the teapot, and began to pour out the tea, but her hands were shaking, and Charlotte's eye made her nervous. 'Oh, I'm very tired – I'm too long without my tea. Oh, Charlotte, why do you annoy me this way when you know it's so bad for me?' She put down the teapot, and covered her face with her hands. 'Is it me own dear husband that you say such things of? Oh, it couldn't be true, and he always so kind to me; indeed, it isn't true, Charlotte,' she protested piteously between her sobs.

'Me dear Lucy,' said Charlotte, laying her broad hand on Mrs Lambert's knee, 'I wish I could say it wasn't, though of course the wisest of us is liable to error. Come now!' she said, as if struck by a new idea. 'I'll tell ye how we could settle the matter! It's a way you won't like, and it's a way I don't like either, but I solemnly think you owe it to yourself, and to your position as a wife. Will you let me say it to you?'

'Oh, you may, Charlotte, you may,' said Mrs Lambert tearfully.

'Well, my advice to you is this, to see what old letters of hers he has, and ye'll be able to judge for yourself what the truth of the case is. If there's no harm in them I'll be only too ready to congratulate ye on proving me in the wrong, and if there is, why, ye'll know what course to pursue.'

'Is it look at Roddy's letters?' cried Mrs Lambert, emerging from her handkerchief with a stare of horror; 'he'd kill me if he thought I looked at them!'

'Ah, nonsense, woman, he'll never know you looked at them,' said Charlotte, scanning the room quickly; 'is it in his study he keeps his private letters?'

'No, I think it's in his old despatch box up on the shelf there,' answered Mrs Lambert, a little taken with the idea, in spite of her scruples.

'Then ye're done,' said Charlotte, looking up at the despatch box in its absolute security of Bramah lock; 'of course he has his keys with him always.'

'Well then, d'ye know,' said Mrs Lambert hesitatingly, 'I think I heard his keys jingling in the pocket of the coat he took off before he went out, and I didn't notice him taking them out of it – but, oh, my dear, I wouldn't dare to open any of his things. I might as well quit the house if he found it out.'

'I tell you it's your privilege as a wife, and your plain duty besides, to see those letters,' urged Charlotte. 'I'd recommend you to go up and get those keys now, this minute; it's like the hand of Providence that he should leave them behind him.'

The force of her will had its effect. Mrs Lambert got up, and, after another declaration that Roderick would kill her, went out of the room and up the stairs at a pace that Charlotte did not think her capable of. She heard her step hurrying into the room overhead, and in a surprisingly short time she was back again, uttering pants of exhaustion and alarm, but holding the keys in her hand.

'Oh,' she said, 'I thought every minute I heard him coming to the door! Here they are for you, Charlotte, take them! I'll not have anything more to say to them.'

She flung the keys into Miss Mullen's lap, and prepared to sink into her chair again. Charlotte jumped up, and the keys rattled on to the floor.

'And d'ye think I'd lay a finger on them?' she said, in such a voice that Mrs Lambert checked herself in the action of sitting down, and Muffy fled under his mistress's chair and barked in angry alarm. 'Pick them up yourself! It's no affair of mine!' She pointed with a fateful finger at the keys, and Mrs Lambert obediently stooped for them. 'Now, there's the desk, ye'd better not lose any more time, but get it down.'

The shelf on which the desk stood was the highest one of a small bookcase, and was just above the level of Mrs Lambert's head, so that when, after many a frightened look out of the window, she stretched up her short arms to take it down, she found the task almost beyond her.

'Come and help me, Charlotte,' she cried; 'I'm afraid it'll fall on me!'

'I'll not put a hand to it,' said Charlotte, without moving, while her ugly, mobile face twitched with excitement; 'it's you have tne right and no one else, and I'd recommend ye to hurry!'

The word hurry acted electrically on Mrs Lambert; she put forth all her feeble strength, and lifting the heavy despatch box from the shelf, she staggered with it to the dinner table.

'Oh, it's the weight of the house!' she gasped, collapsing on to a chair beside it.

'Here, open it now quickly, and we'll talk about the weight of it afterwards,' said Charlotte so imperiously that Mrs Lambert, moved by a power that was scarcely her own, fumbled through the bunch for the key.

'There it is! Don't you see the Bramah key?' exclaimed Charlotte, hardly repressing the inclination to call her friend a fool and to snatch the bunch from her; 'press it in hard now, or ye'll not get it to turn.'

If the lock had not been an easy one, it is probable that Mrs Lambert's helpless fingers would never have turned the key, but it yielded to the first touch, and she lifted the lid. Charlotte craned over her shoulder with eyes that ravened on the contents of the box.

'No, there's nothing there,' she said, taking in with one look the papers that lay in the tray; 'lift up the tray!'

Mrs Lambert, now past remonstrance, did as she was bid, and some bundles of letters and a few photographs were brought to light.

'Show the photographs!' said Charlotte in one fierce breath.

But here Mrs Lambert's courage failed. 'Oh, I can't, don't ask me!' she wailed, clasping her hands on her bosom, with a terror of some irrevocable truth that might await her adding itself to the fear of discovery.

Charlotte caught one of her hands, and, with a guttural sound of contempt, forced it down on to the photographs.

'Show it to me!'

Her victim took up the photographs, and turning them round, revealed two old pictures of Lambert in riding clothes, with Francie beside him in a very badly made habit, with her hair down her back.

'What d'ye think of that?' said Charlotte. She was gripping Mrs Lambert's sloping shoulder, and her breath was coming hard and short. 'Now, get out her letters. There they are in the corner!'

'Ah, she's only a child in that picture,' said Mrs Lambert in a tone of relief, as she hurriedly put the photographs back.

'Open the letters and ye'll see what sort of a child she was.'

Mrs Lambert made no further demur. She took out the bundle that Charlotte pointed to, and drew the top one from its retaining

205

india-rubber strap. Even in affairs of the heart Mr Lambert was a tidy man.

'My dear Mr Lambert,' she read aloud, in a deprecating, tearful voice that was more than ever like the quivering chirrup of a turkey-hen, 'the cake was scrumptious, all the girls were after me for a bit of it, and asking where I got it, but I wouldn't tell. I put it under my pillow three nights, but all I dreamt of was Uncle Robert walking round and round Stephen's Green in his nightcap. You must have had a grand wedding. Why didn't you ask me there to dance at it? So now no more from your affectionate friend, F. Fitzpatrick.'

Mrs Lambert leaned back, and her hands fell into her lap.

'Well, thank God there's no harm in that, Charlotte,' she said, closing her eyes with a sigh that might have been relief, though her voice sounded a little dreamy and bewildered.

'Ah, you began at the wrong end,' said Charlotte, little attentive to either sigh or tone, 'that was written five years ago. Here, what's in this?' She indicated the one lowest in the packet.

Mrs Lambert opened her eyes.

'The drops!' she said with sudden energy, 'on the sideboard – oh, save me –!'

Her voice fainted away, her eyes closed, and her head fell limply on to her shoulder. Charlotte sprang instinctively towards the sideboard, but suddenly stopped and looked from Mrs Lambert to the bundle of letters. She caught it up, and plucking out a couple of the most recent, read them through with astonishing speed. She was going to take out another when a slight movement from her companion made her throw them down.

Mrs Lambert was slipping off the high dining-room chair on which she was sitting, and there was a look about her mouth that Charlotte had never seen there before. Charlotte had her arm under her in a moment, and, letting her slip quietly down, laid her flat on the floor. Through the keen and crowding contingencies of the moment came a sound from outside, a well-known voice calling and whistling to a dog, and in the same instant Charlotte had left Mrs Lambert and was deftly and swiftly replacing letters and photographs in the despatch box. She closed the lid noiselessly, put it back on its shelf with scarcely an effort, and after a moment of uncertainty, slipped the keys into Mrs Lambert's pocket. She knew that Lambert would never guess at his wife's one breach of faith. Then, with a quickness almost incredible in a woman of her build, she got the drops from the sideboard, poured them out, and, on her way back to the inert figure on the floor, rang the bell violently. Muffy had crept from under the table to snuff with uncanny curiosity at his mistress's livid face, and as Charlotte approached, he put his tail between his legs and yapped shrilly at her.

'Get out, ye damned cur!' she exclaimed, the coarse, superstitious side of her nature coming uppermost now that the absorbing stress of those acts of self-preservation was over. Her big boot lifted the dog and sent him flying across the room, and she dropped on her knees beside the motionless, tumbled figure on the floor. 'She's dead! she's dead!' she cried out, and as if in protest against her own words she flung water upon the unresisting face, and tried to force the drops between the closed teeth. But the face never altered; it only acquired momentarily the immovable placidity of death, that asserted itself in silence, and gave the feeble features a supreme dignity, in spite of the thin dabbled fringe and the gold ear-rings and brooch, that were instinct with the vulgarities of life.

33

Few possessed of any degree of imagination can turn their backs on a churchyard, after having witnessed there the shovelling upon and stamping down of the last poor refuge of that which all feel to be superfluous, a mere fragment of the inevitable *débris* of life, without a clinging hope that in some way or other the process may be avoided for themselves. In spite of philosophy, the body will not picture its surrender to the sordid thraldom of the undertaker and the mastery of the spade, and preferably sees itself falling through cold miles of water to some vague resting-place below the tides, or wedged beyond search in the grip of an ice crack, or swept as grey ash into a cinerary urn; anything rather than the prisoning coffin and blind weight of earth. So Christopher thought impatiently, as he drove back to Bruff from Mrs Lambert's funeral, in the dismal solemnity of black clothes and a brougham, while the distant rattle of a reaping machine was like a voice full of the health and energy of life, that talked on of harvest and would not hear of graves.

207

That the commonplace gloom of a funeral should have plunged his general ideas into despondency is, however, too much to believe of even such a super-sensitive mind as Christopher's. It gave a darker wash of colour to what was already clouded, and probably it was its trite, terrific sneer at human desire and human convention that deadened his heart from time to time with fatalistic suggestion; but it was with lesser facts than these that he strove. Miss Mullen depositing hysterically a wreath upon her friend's coffin, in the acute moment of lowering it into the grave; Miss Mullen sitting hysterically beside him in the carriage as he drove her back to Tally Ho in the eyes of all men; Miss Mullen lying, still hysterical, on her drawing-room sofa, holding in her black-gloved hand a tumbler of sal volatile and water, and eventually commanding her emotion sufficiently to ask him to bring her, that afternoon, a few books and papers, to quiet her nerves, and to rob of its weariness the bad night that would inevitably be her portion.

It was opposite these views, which, as far as tears went, might well be called dissolving, that his mind chiefly took its stand, in unutterable repugnance, and faint endeavour to be blind to his own convictions. He was being chased. Now that he knew it he wondered how he could ever have been unaware of it; it was palpable to anyone, and he felt in advance what it would be like to hear the exultant winding of the huntsman's horn, if the quarry were overtaken. The position was intolerable from every rational point of view; Christopher with his lethargic scorn of social tyrannies and stale maxims of class, could hardly have believed that he was sensible of so many of these points, and despised himself accordingly. Julia Duffy's hoarse voice still tormented his ear in involuntary spasms of recollection, keeping constantly before him the thought of the afternoon of four days ago, when he and Francie had been informed of the destiny allotted to them. The formless and unquestioned dream through which he had glided had then been broken up, like some sleeping stretch of river when the jaws of the dredger are dashed into it, and the mud is dragged to light, and the soiled waves carry the outrage onward in ceaseless escape. Nothing now could place him where he had been before, nor could he wish to regain that purposeless content. It was better to look things in the face at last and see where they were going to end. It was better to know himself to be Charlotte's prize than to give up Francie.

This was what it meant, he said to himself, while he changed his funeral garb, and tried to get into step with the interrupted march of the morning. The alternative had been with him for four days, and now, while he wrote his letters, and sat at luncheon, and collected the books that were to interpose between Miss Mullen and her grief, the choice became more despotic than ever, in spite of the antagonism that met it in every surrounding. All the chivalry that smouldered under the modern malady of exhausted enthusiasm ranged itself on Francie's side; all the poetry in which he had steeped his mind, all his own poetic fancy, combined to blind him to many things that he would otherwise have seen. He acquitted her of any share in her cousin's coarse scheming with a passionateness that in itself testified to the terror lest it might be true. He had idealized her to the pitch that might have been expected, and clothed her with his own refinement, as with a garment, so that it was her position that hurt him most, her embarrassment that shamed him beyond his own.

Christopher's character is easier to feel than to describe; so conscious of its own weakness as to be almost incapable of confident effort, and with a soul so humble and straightforward that it did not know its own strength and simplicity. Some dim understanding of him must have reached Francie, with her ignorant sentimentalities and her Dublin brogue; and as a seaweed stretches vague arms up towards the light through the conflict of the tides, her pliant soul rose through its inherited vulgarities, and gained some vision of higher things. Christopher could not know how unparalleled a person he was in her existence, of how wholly unknown a type. Hawkins and he had been stars of unimagined magnitude; but though she had attained to the former's sphere with scarcely an effort, Christopher remained infinitely remote. She could scarcely have believed that as he drove from Bruff in the quiet sunshine of the afternoon, and surmounted the hill near its gate, the magic that she herself had newly learned about was working its will with him.

The corn that had stood high between him and Francie that day when he had ridden back to look after her, was bound in sheaves on the yellow upland, and the foolish omen set his pulses going. If she were now passing along that other road there would be nothing between him and her. He had got past the stage of reason, even his power of mocking at himself was dead, or perhaps it was that there seemed no longer anything that could be mocked at. In spite of his knowledge of the world the position had an aspect that was so serious and beautiful as to overpower the others, and to become one of the mysteries of life into which he had thought himself too cheap and shallow to enter. A few weeks ago a visit to Tally Ho would have been a penance and a weariness of the flesh, a thing to be groaned over with Pamela, and endured only for the sake of collecting some new pearl of rhetoric from Miss Mullen. Now each thought of it brought again the enervating thrill, the almost sickening feeling of subdued excitement and expectation.

It was the Lismoyle market day, and Christopher made his way slowly along the street, squeezing between carts and barrels, separating groups locked together in the extremity of bargaining, and doing what in him lay to avoid running over the old women, who, blinded by their overhanging hoods and deaf by nature, paraded the centre of the thoroughfare with a fine obliviousness of dog-carts and their drivers. Most of the better class of shops had their shutters up in recognition of the fact that Mrs Lambert, a customer whom neither cooperative stores nor eighteenpenny teas had been able to turn from her allegiance, had this morning passed their doors for the last time, in slow, incongruous pomp, her silver-mounted coffin commanding all eyes as the glass-sided hearse moved along with its quivering bunches of black plumes. The funeral was still a succulent topic in the gabble of the market; Christopher heard here and there such snatches of it as:

'Rest her sowl, the crayture! 'Tis she was the good wife, and more than all, she was the beautiful housekeeper!'

'Is it *he* lonesome afther her? No, nor if he berrid ten like her.'

'She was a spent little woman always, and 'tis she that doted down on him.'

'And ne'er a child left afther her! Well, she must be exshcused.'

'Musha, I'd love her bones!' shouted Nance the Fool, well aware of the auditor in the dog-cart, 'there wasn't one like her in the nation, nor in the world, no, nor in the town o' Galway!'

Towards the end of the street, at the corner of a lane leading to the quay, something like a fight was going on, and, as he approached, Christopher saw, over the heads of an admiring audience, the infuriated countenance of a Lismoyle beggar woman, one of the many who occasionally legalized their existence by selling fish, between long bouts of mendicancy and drunkenness. Mary Norris was apparently giving what she would call the length and breadth of her tongue to some customer who had cast doubts upon the character of her fish, a customer who was for the moment quiescent, and hidden behind the tall figure of her adversary.

'Whoever says thim throuts isn't leppin' fresh out o' the lake he's a dom liar, and it's little I think of tellin' it t'ye up to yer nose! There's not one in the counthry but knows yer thricks and yer chat, and ye may go home out o' that, with yer bag sthrapped round ye, and ye can take the tay-leaves and the dhrippin' from the servants, and huxther thim to feed yer cats, but thanks be to God ye'll take nothing out o' my basket this day!'

There was a titter of horrified delight from the crowd.

'Ye never spoke a truer word than that, Mary Norris,' replied a voice that sent a chill down Christopher's back; 'when I come into Lismoyle, it's not to buy rotten fish from a drunken fish fag, that'll be begging for crusts at my hall door tomorrow. If I hear another word out of yer mouth I'll give you and your fish to the police, and the streets'll be rid of you and yer infernal tongue for a week, at all events, and the prison'll have a treat that it's pretty well used to!'

Another titter rewarded this sally, and Charlotte, well pleased, turned to walk away. As she did so, she caught sight of Christopher, looking at her with an expression from which he had not time to remove his emotions, and for a moment she wished that the earth would open and swallow her up. She reddened visibly, but recovered herself, and at once made her way out into the street towards him.

'How are you again, Mr Dysart? You just came in time to get a specimen of the *res angusta domi*,' she said, in a voice that contrasted almost ludicrously with her last utterances. 'People like David, who talk about the advantages of poverty, have probably never tried buying fish in Lismoyle. It's always the way with these drunken old hags. They repay your charity by impudence and bad language, and one has to speak pretty strongly to them to make one's meaning penetrate to their minds.'

Her eyes were still red and swollen from her violent crying at the funeral. But for them, Christopher could hardly have believed that this was the same being whom he had last seen on the sofa at Tally Ho, with the black gloves and the sal volatile.

'Oh yes, of course,' he said vaguely; 'everyone has to undergo Mary Norris some time or other. If you are going back to Tally Ho now, I can drive you there.'

The invitation was lukewarm as it well could be, but had it been the most fervent in the world Charlotte had no intention of accepting it.

'No thank you, Mr Dysart. I'm not done my marketing yet, but Francie's at home and she'll give you tea. Don't wait for me. I've no appetite for anything today. I only came out to get a

mouthful of fresh air, in hopes it might give me a better night,
though, indeed, I've small chance of it after what I've gone
through.'

Christopher drove on, and tried not to think of Miss Mullen
or of his mother or Pamela, while his too palpably discreet
hostess elbowed her way through the crowd in the opposite
direction.

Francie was sitting in the drawing room awaiting her visitor.
She had been up very early making the wreath of white asters
that Charlotte had laid on Mrs Lambert's coffin, and had shed
some tears over the making of it, for the sake of the kindly little
woman who had never been anything but good to her. She had
spent a trying morning in ministering to Charlotte; after her
early dinner she had dusted the drawing room, and refilled the
vases in a manner copied as nearly as possible from Pamela's
arrangement of flowers; and she was now feeling as tired as
might reasonably have been expected. About Christopher she
felt thoroughly disconcerted and out of conceit with herself. It
was strange that she, like him, should least consider her own
position when she thought about the things that Julia Duffy
had said to them; her motive was very different, but it touched
the same point. It was the effect upon Christopher that she
ceaselessly pictured, that she longed to understand: whether or
not he believed what he had heard, and whether, if he believed,
he would ever be the same to her. His desertion would have been
much less surprising than his allegiance, but she would have
felt it very keenly, with the same aching resignation with which
we bear one of nature's acts of violence. When she met him this
morning her embarrassment had taken the simple form of
distance and avoidance, and a feeling that she could never show
him plainly enough that she, at least, had no designs upon him;
yet, through it all, she clung to the belief that he would not
change towards her. It was burning humiliation to see Charlotte
spread her nets in sight of the bird, but it did not prevent her
from dressing herself as becomingly as she could when the
afternoon came, nor, so ample are the domains of sentiment,
did some nervous expectancy in the spare minutes before
Christopher arrived deter her from taking out of her pocket a
letter worn by long sojourn there, and reading it with delaying
and softened eyes.

Her correspondence with Hawkins had been fraught with
difficulties; in fact, it had been only by the aid of a judicious
shilling and an old pair of boots bestowed on Louisa, that she

212

had ensured to herself a first sight of the contents of the postbag, before it was conveyed, according to custom, to Miss Mullen's bedroom. Somehow since Mr Hawkins had left Hythe and gone to Yorkshire the quantity and quality of his letters had dwindled surprisingly. The three thick weekly budgets of sanguine anticipation and profuse endearments had languished into a sheet or two every ten days of affectionate retrospect in which less and less reference was made to breaking off his engagement with Miss Coppard, that trifling and summary act which was his ostensible mission in going to his *fiancée*'s house; and this, the last letter from him, had been merely a few lines of excuse for not having written before, ending with regret that his leave would be up in a fortnight, as he had had a ripping time on old Coppard's moor, and the cubbing was just beginning, a remark which puzzled Francie a good deal, though its application was possibly clearer to her than the writer had meant it to be. Inside the letter was a photograph of himself, that had been done at Hythe, and was transferred by Francie from letter to letter, in order that it might never leave her personal keeping; and, turning from the barren trivialities over which she had been poring, Francie fell to studying the cheerful, unintellectual face therein portrayed above the trim glories of a mess jacket.

She was still looking at it when she heard the expected wheels; she stuffed the letter back into her pocket, then, remembering the photograph, pulled the letter out again and put it into it. She was putting the letter away for the second time when Christopher came in, and in her guilty self-conciousness she felt that he must have noticed the action.

'How did you get in so quickly?' she said, with a confusion that heightened the general effect of discovery.

'Donovan was there and took the trap,' said Christopher, 'and the hall door was open, so I came in.'

He sat down, and neither seemed certain for a moment as to what to say next.

'I didn't really expect you to come, Mr Dysart,' began Francie, the colour that the difficulty with the photograph had given her ebbing slowly away; 'you have a right to be tired as well as us, and Charlotte being upset that way and all, made it awfully late before you got home, I'm afraid.'

'I met her a few minutes ago, and was glad to see that she was all right again,' said Christopher perfunctorily; 'but certainly if I had been she, and had had any option in the matter, I should have stayed at home this morning.'

Both felt the awkwardness of discussing Miss Mullen, but it seemed a shade less than the awkwardness of ignoring her.

'She was such a friend of poor Mrs Lambert's,' said Francie; 'and I declare,' she added, glad of even this trivial chance of showing herself antagonistic to Charlotte, 'I think she delights in funerals.'

'She has a peculiar way of showing her delight,' replied Christopher, with just enough ill-nature to make Francie feel that her antagonism was understood and sympathized with.

Francie gave an irrepressible laugh. 'I don't think she minds crying before people. I wish everyone minded crying as little as she does.'

Christopher looked at her, and thought he saw something about her eyes that told of tears.

'Do you mind crying?' he said, lowering his voice, while more feeling escaped into his glance than he had intended; 'it doesn't seem natural that you should ever cry.'

'You're very inquisitive!' said Francie, the sparkle coming back to her eye in a moment; 'why shouldn't I cry if I choose?'

'I should not like to think that you had anything to make you cry.'

She looked quickly at him to see if his face were as sincere as his voice; her perceptions were fine enough to suggest that it would be typical of Christopher to show her by a special deference and friendliness that he was sorry for her, but now, as ever, she was unable to classify those delicate shades of manner and meaning that might have told her where his liking melted into love. She had been accustomed to see men as trees walking, beings about whose individuality of character she did not trouble herself; generally they made love to her, and, if they did not, she presumed that they did not care about her, and gave them no further attention. But this test did not seem satisfactory in Christopher's case.

'I know what everyone thinks of me,' she said, a heart truth welling to the surface as she felt herself pitied and comprehended; 'no one believes I ever have any trouble about anything.'

Christopher's heart throbbed at the bitterness in a voice that he had always known so wholly careless and undisturbed; it increased his pity for her a thousandfold, but it stirred him with a strange and selfish pleasure to think that she had suffered. Whatever it was that was in her mind, it had given him a glimpse of that deeper part of her nature, so passionately guessed at, so long unfindable. He did not for an instant think of Hawkins, having explained away that episode to himself some time before in the light of his new reading of Francie's character; it was Charlotte's face as she confronted Mary Norris in the market that came to him, and the thought of what it must be to be under her roof and dependent on her. He saw now the full pain that Francie bore in hearing herself proclaimed as the lure by which he was to be captured, and that he should have brought her thus low roused a tenderness in him that would not be gainsaid.

'*I* don't think it,' he said, stammering; 'you might believe that I think more about you than other people do. I know you feel things more than you let anyone see, and that makes it all the worse for anyone who – who is sorry for you, and wants to tell you so – '

This halting statement, so remarkably different in diction from the leisurely sentences in which Christopher usually expressed himself, did not tend to put Francie more at her ease. She reddened slowly and painfully as his shortsighted, grey eyes rested upon her. Hawkins filled so prominent a place in her mind that Christopher's ambiguous allusions seemed to be directed absolutely at him, and her hand instinctively slipped into her pocket and clasped the letter that was there, as if in that way she could hold her secret fast.

'Ah, well,' – she tried to say it lightly – 'I don't want so very much pity yet awhile; when I do, I'll ask you for it!'

She disarmed the words of her flippancy by the look with which she lifted her dark-lashed eyes to him, and Christopher's last shred of common sense sank in their tender depths and was lost there.

'Is that true?' he said, without taking his eyes from her face. 'Do you really trust me? would you promise always to trust me?'

'Yes, I'm sure I'd always trust you,' answered Francie, beginning in some inexplicable way to feel frightened; 'I think you're awfully kind.'

'No, I am not kind,' he said, turning suddenly very white, and feeling his blood beating down to his fingertips; 'you must not say that when you know it's – ' Something seemed to catch in his throat and take his voice away. 'It gives me the greatest pleasure to do anything for you,' he ended lamely.

The clear crimson deepened in Francie's cheeks. She knew in one startling instant what Christopher meant, and her fingers twined and untwined themselves in the crochet sofa cover as she sat, not daring to look at him, and not knowing in the least what to say.

215

'How can I be kind to you?' went on Christopher, his vacillation swept away by the look in her downcast face that told him she understood him; 'it's just the other way, it's you who are kind to me. If you only knew what happiness it is to me– to – to be with you – to do anything on earth for you – you know what I mean – I see you know what I mean.'

A vision rose up before Francie of her past self, loitering about the Dublin streets, and another of an incredible and yet possible future self, dwelling at Bruff in purple and fine linen, and then she looked up and met Christopher's eyes. She saw the look of tortured uncertainty and avowed purpose that there was no mistaking; Bruff and its glories melted away before it, and in their stead came Hawkins' laughing face, his voice, his touch, his kiss, in overpowering contrast to the face opposite to her, with its uncomprehended intellect and refinement, and its pale anxiety.

'Don't say things like that to me, Mr Dysart,' she said tremulously; 'I know how good you are to me, twice, twice too good, and if I was in trouble, you'd be the first I'd come to. But I'm all right,' with an attempted gaiety and unconcern that went near bringing the tears to her eyes; 'I can paddle my own canoe for a while yet!'

Her instinct told her that Christopher would be quicker than most men to understand that she was putting up a line of defence, and to respect it; and with the unfailing recoil of her mind upon Hawkins, she thought how little such a method would have prevailed with him.

'Then you don't want me?' said Christopher, almost in a whisper.

'Why should I want you or anybody?' she answered, determined to misunderstand him, and to be like her usual self in spite of the distress and excitement that she felt; 'I'm well able to look after myself, though you mightn't think it, and I don't want anything this minute, only my tea, and Norry's as cross as the cats, and I know she won't have the cake made!' She tried to laugh, but the laugh faltered away into tears. She turned her head aside, and putting one hand to her eyes, felt with the other in her pocket for her handkerchief. It was underneath Hawkins' letter, and as she snatched it out, it carried the letter along with it.

Christopher had started up, unable to bear the sight of her tears, and as he stood there, hesitating on the verge of catching her in his arms, he saw the envelope slip down on to the floor. As it fell, the photograph slid out of its worn covering, and lay face uppermost at his feet. He picked it up, and having placed it with the letter on the sofa beside Francie, he walked to the window and looked sightlessly out into the garden. A heavily-laden tray bumped against the door, the handle turned, and Louisa, having pushed the door open with her knee, staggered in with the tea tray. She had placed it on the table and was back again in the kitchen, talking over the situation with Bid Sal, before Christopher spoke.

'I'm afraid I can't stay any longer,' he said, in a voice that was at once quieter and rougher than its wont; 'you must forgive me if anything that I said has – has hurt you – I didn't mean it to hurt you.' He stopped short and walked towards the door. As he opened it, he looked back at her for an instant, but he did not speak again.

34

The kitchen at Tally Ho generally looked its best at ten o'clock in the morning. Its best is, in this case, a relative term, implying the temporary concealment of the plates, loaves of bread, dirty rubbers, and jam pots full of congealed dripping that usually adorned the tables, and the sweeping of outlying potato skins and cinders into a chasm beneath the disused hothearth. When these things had been done, and Bid Sal and her bare feet had been effaced into some outer purlieu, Norry felt that she was ready to receive the Queen of England if necessary, and awaited the ordering of dinner with her dress let down to its full length, a passably clean apron, and an expression of severe and exalted resignation. On the morning now in question Charlotte was standing in her usual position, with her back to the fire and her hands spread behind her to the warmth, scanning with a general's eye the routed remnants of yesterday's dinner, and debating with herself as to the banner under which they should next be rallied.

'A curry, I think, Norry,' she called out; 'plenty of onions and apples in it, and that's all ye want.'

'Oh, musha! God knows ye have her sickened with yer curries,' replied Norry's voice from the larder; "twas ere yestherday ye had the remains of th' Irish stew in curry, an' she didn't ate what'd blind your eye of it. Wasn't Louisa tellin' me!'

'And so I'm to order me dinners to please Miss Francie!' said Charlotte, in tones of surprising toleration; 'well, ye can make a haricot of it if ye like. Perhaps her ladyship will eat that.'

'Faith, 'tis aiqual to me what she ates – ' here came a clatter of crockery, and a cat shot like a comet from the larder door, followed by Norry's foot and Norry's blasphemy – 'or if she never ate another bit. And where's the carrots to make a haricot? Bid Sal's afther tellin' me there's ne'er a one in the garden; but sure, if ye sent Bid Sal to look for salt wather in the say she wouldn't find it!'

Miss Mullen laughed approvingly. 'There's carrots in plenty; and see here, Norry, you might give her a jam dumpling – use the gooseberry jam that's going bad. I've noticed meself that the child isn't eating, and it won't do to have the people saying we're starving her.'

'Whoever'll say that, he wasn't looking at me yestherday, and I makin' the cake for herself and Misther Dysart! Eight eggs, an' a cupful of sugar and a cupful of butther, and God knows what more went in it, an' the half of me day gone bating it, and afther all they left it afther them!'

'And whose fault was that but your own for not sending it up in time?' rejoined Charlotte, her voice sharpening at once to vociferative argument: 'Miss Francie told me that Mr Dysart was forced to go without his tea.'

'Late or early I'm thinkin' thim didn't ax it nor want it,' replied Norry, issuing from the larder with a basketful of crumpled linen in her arms, and a visage of the utmost sourness; 'there's your clothes for ye now, that was waitin' on me yestherday to iron them, in place of makin' cakes.'

She got a bowl of water and began to sprinkle the clothes and roll them up tightly, preparatory to ironing them, her ill-temper imparting to the process the air of whipping a legion of children and putting them to bed. Charlotte came over to the table, and, resting her hands on it, watched Norry for a few seconds in silence.

'What makes you say they didn't want anything to eat?' she asked; 'was Miss Francie ill, or was anything the matter with her?'

'How do I know what ailed her?' replied Norry, pounding a

pillow-case with her fist before putting it away; 'I have somethin' to do besides followin' her or mindin' her.'

'Then what are ye talking about?'

'Ye'd betther ax thim that knows. 'Twas Louisa seen her within in the dhrawn' room, an' whatever was on her she was cryin'; but, sure, Louisa tells lies as fast as a pig'd gallop.'

'What did she say?' Charlotte darted the question at Norry as a dog snaps at a piece of meat.

'Then she said plinty, an' 'tis she that's able. If ye told that one a thing and locked the doore on her the way she couldn't tell it agin, she'd bawl it up the chimbley.'

'Where's Louisa?' interrupted Charlotte impatiently.

'Meself can tell ye as good as Louisa,' said Norry instantly taking offence; 'she landed into the dhrawn' room with the tay, and there was Miss Francie sittin' on the sofa and her handkerchief in her eyes, and Misther Dysart beyond in the windy and not a word nor a stir out of him, only with his eyes shtuck out in the garden, an' she cryin' always.'

'Psha! Louisa's a fool! How does she know Miss Francie was crying? I'll bet a shilling 'twas only blowing her nose she was.'

Norry had by this time spread a ragged blanket on the table, and, snatching up the tongs, she picked out of the heart of the fire a red-hot heater and thrust it into a box iron with unnecessary violence.

'An' why wouldn't she cry? Wasn't I listenin' to her cryin' in her room lasht night an' I goin' up to bed?' She banged the iron down on the table and began to rub it to and fro on the blanket. 'But what use is it to cry, even if ye dhragged the hair out of yer head? Ye might as well be singin' and dancin'.'

She flung up her head, and stared across the kitchen under the wisps of hair that hung over her unseeing eyes with such an expression as Deborah the Prophetess might have worn. Charlotte gave a grunt of contempt, and picking Susan up from the bar of the table, she put him on her shoulder and walked out of the kitchen.

Francie had been since breakfast sitting by the window of the dining room, engaged in the cheerless task of darning a stocking on a soda-water bottle. Mending stockings was not an art that she excelled in; she could trim a hat or cut out a dress, but the dark, unremunerative toil of mending stockings was as distasteful to her as stone-breaking to a tramp, and the simile might easily be carried out by comparing the results of the process to macadamizing. It was a still, foggy morning; the boughs of the scarlet-blossomed fuchsia were greyed with moisture, and shining drops studded the sash of the open window like sea anemones. It was a day that was both close and chilly, and intolerable as the atmosphere of the Tally Ho dining room would have been with the window shut, the breakfast things still on the table, and the all-pervading aroma of cats, the damp, lifeless air seemed only a shade better to Francie as she raised her tired eyes from time to time and looked out upon the discouraging prospect. Everything stood in the same trance of stillness in which it had been when she had got up at five o'clock and looked out at the sluggish dawn broadening in blank silence upon the fields. She had leaned out of her window till she had become cold through and through, and after that had unlocked her trunk, taken out Hawkins' letters, and going back to bed had read and re-read them there. The old glamour was about them; the convincing sincerity and assurance that was as certain of her devotion as of his own, and the unfettered lavishness of expression that made her turn hot and cold as she read them. She had time to go through many phases of feeling before the chapel bell began to ring for eight o'clock Mass, and she stole down to the kitchen to see if the post had come in. The letters were lying on the table; three or four for Charlotte, the local paper, a circular about peat litter addressed to the Stud groom, Tally Ho, and, underneath all, the thick rough envelope with the ugly boyish writing that had hardly changed since Mr Hawkins had written his first letters home from Cheltenham College. Francie caught it up, and was back in her own room in the twinkling of an eye. It contained only a few words.

'Dearest Francie, only time for a line today to say that I am staying on here for another week, but I hope ten days will see me back at the old mill. I want you like a good girl to keep things as dark as possible. I don't see my way out of this game yet. No more today. Just off to play golf; the girls here are nailers at it. Thine ever, Gerald.'

This was the ration that had been served out to her hungry heart, the word that she had wearied for for a week; that once more he had contrived to postpone his return, and that the promise he had made to her under the tree in the garden was as far from being fulfilled as ever. Christopher Dysart would not have treated her this way, she thought to herself, as she stooped over her darning and bit her lip to keep it from quivering, but then she would not have minded much whether he wrote to her or not – that was the worst of it. Francie had always confidently announced to her Dublin circle of friends her intention of marrying a rich man, good looking, and a lord if possible, but certainly rich. But here she was, on the morning after what had been a proposal, or what had amounted to one, from a rich young man who was also nice looking, and almost the next thing to a lord, and instead of sitting down triumphantly to write the letter that should thrill the North Side down to its very grocers' shops, she was darning stockings, red-eyed and dejected, and pondering over how best to keep from her cousin any glimmering of what had happened. All her old self posed and struck attitudes before the well-imagined mirror of her friends' minds, and the vanity that was flattered by success cried out petulantly against the newer soul that enforced silence upon it. She felt quite impartially how unfortunate it was that she should have given her heart to Gerald in this irrecoverable way, and then with a headlong change of ideas she said to herself that there was no one like him, and she would always, *always* care for him, and nobody else.

This point having been emphasized by a tug at her needle that snapped the darning cotton, Miss Fitzpatrick was embarking upon a more pleasurable train of possibilities when she heard Charlotte's foot in the hall, and fell all of a sudden down to the level of the present. Charlotte came in and shut the door with her usual decisive slam; she went over to the sideboard and locked up the sugar and jam with a sharp glance to see if Louisa had tampered with either, and then sat down at her davenport near Francie and began to look over her account books.

'Well, I declare,' she said after a minute or two, 'it's a funny thing that I have to buy eggs, with my yard full of hens! This is a state of things unheard of till you came into the house, my young lady!'

Francie looked up and saw that this was meant as a pleasantry.

'Is it me? I wouldn't touch an egg to save my life!'

'Maybe you wouldn't,' replied Charlotte with the same excessive jocularity, 'but you can give tea-parties, and treat your friends to sponge cakes that are made with nothing but eggs!'

Francie scented danger in the air, and having laughed nervously to show appreciation of the jest, tried to change the conversation.

'How do you feel today, Charlotte?' she asked, working away at her stocking with righteous industry; 'is your headache gone? I forgot to ask after it at breakfast.'

'Headache? I'd forgotten I'd ever had one. Three tabloids of antipyrin and a good night's rest; that was all *I* wanted to put me

221

on my pegs again. But if it comes to that, me dear child, I'd trouble you to tell me what makes you the colour of blay calico last night and this morning? It certainly wasn't all the cake you had at afternoon tea. I declare I was quite vexed when I saw that lovely cake in the larder, and not a bit gone from it.'

Francie coloured. 'I was up very early yesterday making that cross, and I daresay that tired me. Tell me, did Mr Lambert say anything about it? Did he like it?'

Charlotte looked at her, but could discern no special expression in the piquant profile that was silhouetted against the light.

'He had other things to think of besides your wreath,' she said coarsely; 'when a man's wife isn't cold in her coffin, he has something to think of besides young ladies' wreaths!'

There was silence after this, and Francie wondered what had made Charlotte suddenly get so cross for nothing; she had been so good-natured for the last week. The thought passed through her mind that possibly Mr Lambert had taken as little notice of Charlotte as of the wreath; she was just sufficiently aware of the state of affairs to know that such a cause might have such an effect, and she wished she had tried any other topic of conversation. Darning is, however, an occupation that does not tend to unloose the strings of the tongue, and even when carried out according to the unexacting methods of Macadam, it demands a certain degree of concentration, and Francie left to Charlotte the task of finding a more congenial subject. It was chosen with unexpected directness.

'What was the matter with you yesterday afternoon when Louisa brought in the tea?'

Francie felt as though a pistol had been let off at her ear; the blood surged in a great wave from her heart to her head, her heart gave a shattering thump against her side, and then went on beating again in a way that made her hands shake.

'Yesterday afternoon, Charlotte?' she said, while her brain sought madly for a means of escape and found none; 'there – there was nothing the matter with me.'

'Look here now, Francie;' Charlotte turned away from her davenport, and faced her cousin with her fists clenched on her knees; 'I'm *in loco parentis* to you for the time being – your guardian, if you understand that better – and there's no good in your beating about the bush with me. What happened between you and Christopher Dysart yesterday afternoon?'

'Nothing happened at all,' said Francie in a low voice that gave the lie to her words.

222

'You're telling me a falsehood! How have you the face to tell me there was nothing happened when even that fool Louisa could see that something had been going on to make you cry, and to send him packing out of the house not a quarter of an hour after he came into it!'

'I told you before he couldn't wait,' said Francie, trying to keep the tremble out of her voice. She held the conventional belief that Charlotte was queer, but very kind and jolly, but she had a fear of her that she could hardly have given a reason for. It must have been by that measuring and crossing of weapons that takes place unwittingly and yet surely in the consciousness of everyone who lives in intimate connection with another, that she had learned, like her great-aunt before her, the weight of the real Charlotte's will, and the terror of her personality.

'Stuff and nonsense!' broke out Miss Mullen, her eyes beginning to sparkle ominously; 'thank God I'm not such an ass as the people you've taken in before now; ye'll not find it so easy to make a fool of me as ye think! Did he make ye an offer or did he not?' She leaned forward with her mouth half open, and Francie felt her breath strike on her face, and shrank back.

'He – he did not.'

Charlotte dragged her chair a pace nearer so that her knees touched Francie.

'Ye needn't tell me any lies, Miss; if he didn't propose, he said something that was equivalent to a proposal. Isn't that the case?'

Francie had withdrawn herself as far into the corner of the window as was possible, and the dark folds of the maroon rep curtain made a not unworthy background for her fairness. Her head was turned childishly over her shoulder in the attempt to get as far as she could from her tormentor, and her eyes travelled desperately and yet unconsciously over the dingy lines of the curtain.

'I told you already, Charlotte, that he didn't propose to me,' she answered; 'he just paid a visit here like anyone else, and then he had to go away early.'

'Don't talk such balderdash to me! I know what he comes here for as well as you do, and as well as every soul in Lismoyle knows it, and I'll trouble ye to answer one question – do ye mean to marry him?' She paused, and gave the slight and shapely arm a compelling squeeze.

Francie wrenched her arm away. 'No, I don't!' she said, sitting up and facing Charlotte with eyes that had a dawning light of battle in them.

Charlotte pushed back her chair, and with the same action was on her feet.

'Oh, my God!' she bawled, flinging up both her arms with the fists clenched; 'd'ye hear that? She dares to tell me that to me face after all I've done for her!' Her hands dropped down, and she stared at Francie with her thick lips working in a dumb transport of rage. 'And who are ye waiting for? Will ye tell me that! You, that aren't fit to lick the dirt off Christopher Dysart's boots!' she went on, with the uncontrolled sound in her voice that told that rage was bringing her to the verge of tears; 'for the Prince of Wales' son, I suppose? Or are ye cherishing hopes that your friend Mr Hawkins would condescend to take a fancy to you again?' She laughed repulsively, waiting with a heaving chest for the reply, and Francie felt as if the knife had been turned in the wound.

'Leave me alone! What is it to you who I marry?' she cried passionately; 'I'll marry who I like, and no thanks to you!'

'Oh, indeed,' said Charlotte, breathing hard and loud between the words; 'it's nothing to me, I suppose, that I've kept the roof over your head and put the bit into your mouth, while ye're carrying on with every man that ye can get to look at ye!'

'I'm not asking you to keep me,' said Francie, starting up in her turn and standing in the window facing her cousin; 'I'm able to keep myself, and to wait as long as I choose till I get married; *I'm* not afraid of being an old maid!'

They glared at each other, the fire of anger smiting on both their faces, lighting Francie's cheek with a malign brilliance, and burning in ugly purple-red on Charlotte's leathery skin. The girl's aggressive beauty was to Charlotte a keener taunt than the rudimentary insult of her words; it brought with it a swarm of thoughts that buzzed and stung in her soul like poisonous flies.

'And might one be permitted to ask how long you're going to wait?' she said, with quivering lips drawn back; 'will six months be enough for you, or do you consider the orthodox widower's year too long to wait? I daresay you'll have found out what spending there is in twenty-five pounds before that, and ye'll go whimpering to Roddy Lambert, and asking him to make ye Number Two, and to pay your debts and patch up your character!'

'Roddy Lambert!' cried Francie, bursting out into shrill unpleasant laughter; 'I think I'll try and do better than that,

thank ye, though you're so kind in making him a present to me!'
Then, firing a random shot, 'I'll not deprive you of him, Charlotte; you may keep him all to yourself!'

It is quite within the bounds of possibility that Charlotte might at this juncture have struck Francie, and thereby have put herself for ever into a false position, but her guardian angel, in the shape of Susan, the grey tomcat, intervened. He had jumped in at the window during the discussion, and having rubbed himself unnoticed against Charlotte's legs with stiff, twitching tail, and cold eyes fixed on her face, he, at this critical instant, sprang upwards at her, and clawed on to the bosom of her dress, hanging there in expectation of the hand that should help him to the accustomed perch on his mistress's shoulder. The blow that was so near being Francie's descended upon the cat's broad confident face and hurled him to the ground. He bolted out of the window again, and when he was safely on the gravel walk, turned and looked back with an expression of human anger and astonishment.

When Charlotte spoke her voice was caught away from her as Christopher Dysart's had been the day before. All the passions have but one instrument to play on when they wish to make themselves heard, and it will yield but a broken sound when it is too hardly pressed.

'Dare to open your mouth to me again, and I'll throw you out of the window after the cat!' was what she said in that choking whisper. 'Ye can go out of this house tomorrow and see which of your lovers will keep ye the longest, and by the time that they're tired of ye, maybe ye'll regret that your impudence got ye turned out of a respectable house!' She turned at the last word, and, like a madman who is just sane enough to fear his own madness, flung out of the room without another glance at her cousin.

Susan sat on the gravel path, and in the intervals of licking his paws in every crevice and cranny, surveyed his mistress's guest with a stony watchfulness as she leaned her head against the window sash and shook in a paroxysm of sobs.

225

35

More than the half of September had gone by.
A gale or two had browned the woods, and the sky was beginning
to show through the trees a good deal. Miss Greely removed the
sunburned straw hats from her window, and people lighted their
fires at afternoon tea time, and daily said to each other, with
sapient gloom, that the evenings were closing in very much. The
summer visitors had gone, and the proprietors of lodgings had
moved down from the attics to the front parlours, and were
restoring to them their usual odour of old clothes, sour bread,
and apples. All the Dysarts, with the exception of Sir Benjamin,
were away; the Bakers had gone to drink the waters at Lisdoon-
varna; the Beatties were having their yearly outing at the Sea
Road in Galway; the Archdeacon had exchanged duties with an
English cleric, who was married, middle-aged, and altogether
unadvantageous, and Miss Mullen played the organ, and
screamed the highest and most ornate tunes in company with
the attenuated choir.

The barracks kept up an outward seeming of life and cheerfulness, imparted by the adventitious aid of red coats and bugle
blowing, but their gaiety was superficial, and even upon Cursiter,
steam launching to nowhere in particular and back again, had
begun to pall. He looked forward to his subaltern's return with
an eagerness quite out of proportion to Mr Hawkins' gifts of
conversation or companionship; solitude and steam launching
were all very well in moderation, but he could not get the steam
launch in after dinner to smoke a pipe, and solitude tended to
unsettling reflections on the vanity of his present walk of life.
Hawkins, when he came, was certainly a variant in the monotony,
but Cursiter presently discovered that he would have to add to
the task of amusing himself the still more arduous one of amusing
his companion. Hawkins dawdled, moped, and grumbled, and
either spent the evenings in moody silence, or in endless harangues
on the stone-broken nature of his finances, and the contrariness

of things in general. He admitted his engagement to Miss Coppard with about as ill a grace as was possible, and when rallied about it, became sulky and snappish, but of Francie he never spoke, and Cursiter augured no good from these indications. Captain Cursiter knew as little as the rest of Lismoyle as to the reasons for Miss Fitzpatrick's abrupt disappearance from Tally Ho, but, unlike the generality of Francie's acquaintances, had accepted the fact unquestioningly, and with a simple gratitude to Providence for its interposition in the matter. If only partridge shooting did not begin in Ireland three weeks later than in any civilized country, thought this much harassed child's guide, it would give them both something better to do than loafing about the lake in the *Serpolette*. Well, anyhow, the 20th was only three days off now, and Dysart had given them leave to shoot as much as they liked over Bruff, and, thank the Lord, Hawkins was fond of shooting, and there would be no more of this talk of running up to Dublin for two or three days to have his teeth overhauled, or to get a new saddle, or some nonsense of that kind. Neither Captain Cursiter nor Mr Hawkins paid visits to anyone at this time; in fact, were never seen except when, attired in all his glory, one or the other took the soldiers to church, and marched them back again with as little delay as possible; so that the remnant of Lismoyle society pronounced them very stuck-up and unsociable, and mourned for the days of the Tipperary Foragers.

It was on the first day of the partridge-shooting that Mr Lambert came back to Rosemount. The far-away banging of the guns down on the farms by the lake was the first thing he heard as he drove up from the station; and the thought that occurred to him as he turned in at his own gate was that public opinion would scarcely allow him to shoot this season. He had gone away as soon after his wife's funeral as was practicable, and having honeymooned with his grief in the approved fashion (combining with this observance the settling of business matters with his wife's trustees in Limerick), the stress of his new position might be supposed to be relaxed. He was perfectly aware that the neighbourhood would demand no extravagance of sorrow from him; no one could expect him to be more than decently regretful for poor Lucy. He had always been a kind husband to her, he reflected, with excusable satisfaction; that is to say, he had praised her housekeeping, and generally bought her whatever she asked for, out of her own money. He was glad now that he had had the good sense to marry her; it had made her very happy, poor thing, and he was certainly now in a better position than he could ever have hoped to be if he had not done so. All these soothing and comfortable facts, however, did not prevent his finding the dining room very dreary and silent when he came downstairs next morning in his new black clothes. His tea tasted as if the water had not been boiled, and the urn got in his way when he tried to prop up the newspaper in his accustomed manner; the bacon dish had been so much more convenient, and the knowledge that his wife was there, ready to receive gratefully any crumb of news that he might feel disposed to let fall, had given a zest to the reading of his paper that was absent now. Even Muffy's basket was empty, for Muffy, since his mistress's death, had relinquished all pretence at gentility, and after a day of miserable wandering about the house, had entered into a league with the cook and residence in the kitchen.

Lambert surveyed all his surroundings with a loneliness that surprised himself: the egg-cosy that his wife had crocheted for him, the half-empty medicine bottle on the chimney-piece, the chair in which she used to sit, and felt that he did not look forward to the task before him of sorting her papers and going through her affairs generally. He got to work at eleven o'clock, taking first the letters and papers that were locked up in a work-table, a walnut-topped and silken-fluted piece of furniture that had been given to Mrs Lambert by a Limerick friend, and, having been considered too handsome for everyday use, had been consecrated by her to the conservation of letters and of certain valued designs for Berlin wool work and receipts for crochet stitches. Lambert lighted a fire in the drawing room, and worked his way down through the contents of the green silk pouch, finding there every letter, every note even, that he had ever written to his wife, and committing them to the flames with a curious sentimental regret. He had not remembered that he had written her so many letters, and he said to himself that he wished those old devils of women in Lismoyle, who, he knew, had always been so keen to pity Lucy, could know what a good husband he had been to her. Inside the envelope of one of his own letters was one from Francie Fitzpatrick, evidently accident-ally thrust there; a few crooked lines to say that she had got the lodgings for Mrs Lambert in Charles Street, but the landlady wouldn't be satisfied without she got two and sixpence extra for the kitchen fire. Lambert put the note into his pocket, where there was already another document in the same handwriting, bearing the Bray postmark with the date of September 18, and when all was finished, and the grate full of flaky spectral black heaps, he went upstairs and unlocked the door of what had been his wife's room. The shutters were shut, and the air of the room had a fortnight's closeness in it. When he opened the shutters there was a furious buzzing of flies, and although he had the indifference about fresh air common to his class, he flung up the window, and drew a long breath of the brilliant morning before he went back to his dismal work of sorting and destroying. What was he to do with such things as the old photographs of her father and mother, her work basket, her salts bottle, the handbag that she used to carry into Lismoyle with her? He was not an imaginative man, but he was touched by the smallness, the familiarity of these only relics of a trivial life, and he stood and regarded the sheeted furniture, and the hundred odds and ends that lay about the room, with an acute awakening to her absence that, for the time, almost obliterated his own figure, posing to the world as an interesting young man, who, while anxious to observe the decencies of bereavement, could not be expected to be inconsolable for a woman so obviously beneath his level.

A voice downstairs called his name, a woman's voice, saying, 'Roderick!' and for a moment a superstitious thrill ran through him. Then he heard a footstep in the passage, and the voice called him again, 'Are you there, Roderick?'

This time he recognized Charlotte Mullen's voice, and went out on to the landing to meet her. The first thing that he noticed was that she was dressed in new clothes, black and glossy and well made. He took them in with the glance that had to be responsive as well as observant, as Charlotte advanced upon him, and, taking his hand in both hers, shook it long and silently.

'Well, Roderick,' she said at length, 'I'm glad to see you back again, though it's a sad homecoming for you and for us all.'

Lambert pressed her large well-known hand, while his eyes rested solemnly upon her face. 'Thank you, Charlotte, I'm very much obliged to you for coming over to see me this way, but it's no more than what I'd have expected of you.'

He had an ancient confidence in Charlotte and an ease in her society – after all, there are very few men who will not find some saving grace in a woman whose affections they believe to be given to them – and he was truly glad to see her at this juncture. She was exactly the person that he wanted to help him in the direful task that he had yet to perform; her capable hands should undertake all the necessary ransacking of boxes and wardrobes, while he sat and looked on at what was really much more a woman's work than a man's. These thoughts passed through his mind while he and Charlotte exchanged conventionalities suitable to the occasion, and spoke of Mrs Lambert as 'she', without mentioning her name.

'Would you like to come downstairs, Charlotte, and sit in the drawing room?' he said presently; 'if it wasn't that I'm afraid you might be tired after your walk, I'd ask you to help me with a very painful bit of work that I was just at when you came.'

They had been standing in the passage, and Charlotte's eyes darted towards the half-open door of Mrs Lambert's room.

'You're settling her things, I suppose?' she said, her voice treading eagerly upon the heels of his; 'is it *that* you want me to help you with?'

He led the way into the room without answering, and indicated its contents with a comprehensive sweep of his hand.

'I turned the key in this door myself when I came back from the funeral, and not a thing in it has been touched since. Now I must set to work to try and get the things sorted, to see what I should give away, and what I should keep, and what should be destroyed,' he said, his voice resuming its usual business tone, tinged with just enough gloom to mark his sense of the situation.

Charlotte peeled off her black gloves and stuffed them into her pocket. 'Sit down, my poor fellow, sit down, and I'll do it all,' she said, stripping an armchair of its sheet and dragging it to the window; 'this is no fit work for you.'

There was no need to press this view upon Lambert; he dropped easily into the chair provided for him, and in a couple of minutes the work was under way.

'Light your pipe now and be comfortable,' said Charlotte, issuing from the wardrobe with an armful of clothes and laying them on the bed; 'there's work here for the rest of the morning.' She took up a black satin skirt and held it out in front of her; it had been Mrs Lambert's 'Sunday best', and it seemed to Lambert as though he could hear his wife's voice asking anxiously if he thought the day was fine enough for her to wear it. 'Now what would you wish done with this?' said Charlotte, looking at it fondly, and holding the band against her own waist to see the length. 'It's too good to give to a servant.'

Lambert turned his head away. There was a crudeness about this way of dealing that was a little jarring at first.

'I don't know what's to be done with it,' he said, with all a man's helpless dislike of such details.

230

'Well, there's this, and her sealskin, and a lot of other things that are too good to be given to servants,' went on Charlotte, rapidly bringing forth more of the treasures of the poor turkey-hen's wardrobe, and proceeding to sort them into two heaps on the floor. 'What would you think of making up the best of the things and sending them up to one of those dealers in Dublin? It's a sin to let them go to loss.'

'Oh, damn it, Charlotte! I can't sell her clothes!' said Lambert hastily. He pretended to no sentiment about his wife, but some masculine instinct of chivalry gave him a shock at the thought of making money out of the conventional sanctities of a woman's apparel.

'Well, what else do you propose to do with them?' said Charlotte, who had already got out a pencil and paper and was making a list.

'Upon my soul, I don't know,' said Lambert, beginning to realize that there was but one way out of the difficulty, and perceiving with irritated amusement that Charlotte had driven him towards it like a sheep, 'unless you'd like them yourself?'

'And do you think I'd accept them from you?' demanded Charlotte, with an indignation so vivid that even the friend of her youth was momentarily deceived and almost frightened by it; 'I, that was poor Lucy's oldest friend! Do you think I could bear – '

Lambert saw the opportunity that had been made for him.

'It's only because you were her oldest friend that I'd offer them to you,' he struck in; 'and if you won't have them yourself, I thought you might know of someone that would.'

Charlotte swallowed her wrath with a magnanimous effort. 'Well, Roddy, if you put it in that way, I don't like to refuse,' she said, wiping a ready tear away with a black-edged pocket handkerchief; 'it's quite true, I know plenty would be glad of a help. There's that unfortunate Letitia Fitzpatrick, that I'll be bound hasn't more than two gowns to her back; I might send her a bundle.'

'Send them to whom you like,' said Lambert, ignoring the topic of the Fitzpatricks as intentionally as it had been introduced; 'but I'd be glad if you could find some things for Julia Duffy; I suppose she'll be coming out of the infirmary soon. What we're to do about that business I don't know,' he continued, filling another pipe. 'Dysart said he wouldn't have her put out if she could hold on anyway at all – '

'Heavenly powers!' exclaimed Charlotte, letting fall a collection of rolled-up kid gloves, 'd'ye mean to say you didn't hear she's in the Ballinasloe Asylum? She was sent there three days ago.'

'Great Scott! Is she gone mad? I was thinking all this time what I was to do with her!'

'Well, you needn't trouble your head about her any more. Her wits went as her body mended, and a board of J.P.'s and M.D.'s sat upon her, and as one of them was old Fatty Ffolliott, you won't be surprised to hear that that was the end of Julia Duffy.'

Both laughed, and both felt suddenly the incongruity of laughter in that room. Charlotte went back to the chest of drawers whose contents she was ransacking, and continued:

'They say she sits all day counting her fingers and toes and calling them chickens and turkeys, and saying that she has the key of Gurthnamuckla in her pocket, and not a one can get into it without her leave.'

'And are you still on for it?' said Lambert, half reluctantly, as it seemed to Charlotte's acute ear, 'for if you are, now's your time. I might have put her out of it two years ago for non-payment of rent, and I'll just take possession and sell off what she has left behind her towards the arrears.'

'On for it? Of course I am. You might know I'm not one to change my mind about a thing I'm set upon. But you'll have to let me down easy with the fine, Roddy. There isn't much left in the stocking these times, and one or two of my poor little dabblings in the money market have rather "gone agin me".'

Lambert thought in a moment of those hundreds that had been lent to him, and stirred uneasily in his chair. 'By the way, Charlotte,' he said, trying to speak like a man to whom such things were trifles, 'about that money you lent me – I'm afraid I can't let you have it back for a couple of months or so. Of course, I needn't tell you, poor Lucy's money was only settled on me for my life, and now there's some infernal delay before they can hand even the interest over to me; but, if you don't mind waiting a bit, I can make it all square for you about the farm, I know.'

He inwardly used a stronger word than infernal as he reflected that if Charlotte had not got that promise about the farm out of him when he was in a hole about money, he might have been able, somehow, to get it himself now.

'Don't mention that – don't mention that,' said Charlotte, absolutely blushing a little, 'it was a pleasure to me to lend it to you, Roddy; if I never saw it again I'd rather that than that you should put yourself out to pay me before it was convenient to you.' She caught up a dress and shook its folds out with unnecessary vehemence. 'I won't be done all night if I delay this way. Ah! how well I remember this dress! Poor dear Lucy got it for Fanny Waller's wedding. Who'd ever think she'd have kept it for all those years! Roddy, what stock would you put on Gurthnamuckla?'

'Dry stock,' answered Lambert briefly.

'And how about the young horses? You don't forget the plan we had about them? You don't mean to give it up, I hope?'

'Oh, that's as you please,' replied Lambert. He was very much interested in the project, but he had no intention of letting Charlotte think so.

She looked at him, reading his thoughts more clearly than he would have liked, and they made her the more resolved upon her own line of action. She saw herself settled at Gurthnamuckla, with Roddy riding over three or four times a week to see his young horses, that should graze her grass and fill her renovated stables, while she, the bland lady of the manor, should show what a really intelligent woman could do at the head of affairs; and the three hundred pound debt should never be spoken of, but should remain, like a brake, in readiness to descend and grip at the discretion of the driver. There was no fear of his paying it of his own accord. He was not the man she took him for if he paid a debt without due provocation; he had a fine crop of them to be settled as it was, and that would take the edge off his punctilious scruples with regard to keeping her out of her money.

The different heaps on the floor increased materially while these reflections passed through Miss Mullen's brain. It was characteristic of her that a distinct section of it had never ceased from appraising and apportioning dresses, dolmans and bonnets, with a nice regard to the rival claims of herself, Eliza Hackett the cook, and the rest of the establishment, and still deeper in its busy convolutions – though this simile is probably unscientific – lurked and grew the consciousness that Francie's name had not yet been mentioned. The wardrobe was cleared at last, a scarlet flannel dressing gown topping the heap that was destined for Tally Ho, and Charlotte had already settled the question as to whether she should bestow her old one upon Norry or make it into a bed for a cat. Lambert finished his second pipe, and stretching himself, yawned drearily, as though, which was indeed the case, the solemnity of the occasion had worn off and its tediousness had become pronounced. He looked at his watch.

233

'Half-past twelve, by Jove! Look here, Charlotte, let's come down and have a glass of sherry.'

Charlotte got up from her knees with alacrity, though the tone in which she accepted the invitation was fittingly lugubrious. She was just as glad to leave something unfinished for the afternoon, and there was something very intimate and confidential about a friendly glass of sherry in the middle of a joint day's work. It was not until Lambert had helped himself a second time from the decanter of brown sherry that Miss Mullen saw her opportunity to approach a subject that was becoming conspicuous by its absence. She had seated herself, not without consciousness, in what had been Mrs Lambert's chair; she was feeling happier than she had been since the time when Lambert was a lanky young clerk in her father's office, with a precocious moustache and an affectionately free-and-easy manner, before Rosemount had been built, or Lucy Galvin thought of. She could think of Lucy now without resentment, even with equanimity, and that last interview, when her friend had died on the very spot where the sunlight was now resting at her feet, recurred to her without any unpleasantness. She had fought a losing battle against fate all her life, and she could not be expected to regret having accepted its first overture of friendship, any more than she need be expected to refuse another half glass of that excellent brown sherry that Lambert had just poured out for her. 'Charlotte could take her whack,' he was wont to say to their mutual friends in that tone of humorous appreciation that is used in connection with a gentlemanlike capacity for liquor.

'Well, how are you all getting on at Tally Ho?' he said presently, and not all the self-confidence induced by the sherry could make his voice as easy as he wished it to be; 'I hear you've lost your young lady?'

Charlotte was provoked to feel the blood mount slowly to her face and remain like a hot straddle across her cheeks and nose.

'Oh yes,' she said carelessly, inwardly cursing the strength of Lambert's liquor, 'she took herself off in a huff, and I only hope she's not repenting of it now.'

'What was the row about? Did you smack her for pulling the cats' tails?' Lambert had risen from the table and was trimming his nails with a pocket knife, but out of the tail of his eye he was observing his visitor very closely.

'I gave her some good advice, and I got the usual amount of gratitude for it,' said Charlotte, in the voice of a person who has been deeply wounded, but is not going to make a fuss about it. She had no idea how much Lambert knew, but she had, at all events, one line of defence that was obvious and secure.

Lambert, as it happened, knew nothing except that there had been what the letter in his pocket described as 'a real awful row', and his mordant curiosity forced him to the question that he knew Charlotte was longing for him to ask.

'What did you give her advice about?'

'I may have been wrong,' replied Miss Mullen, with the liberality that implies the certainty of having been right, 'but when I found that she was carrying on with that good-for-nothing Hawkins, I thought it my duty to give her my opinion, and upon me word, as long as he's here she's well out of the place.'

'How did you find out she was carrying on with Hawkins?' asked Lambert, with a hoarseness in his voice that belied its indifference.

'I knew that they were corresponding, and when I taxed her with carrying on with him she didn't attempt to deny it, and told me up to my face that she could mind her own affairs without my interference. "Very well, Miss," says I, "you'll march out of my house!" and off she took herself next morning, and has never had the decency to send me a line since.'

'Is she in Dublin now?' asked Lambert with the carelessness that was so much more remarkable than an avowed interest.

'No; she's with those starving rats of Fitzpatricks; they were glad enough to get hold of her to squeeze what they could out of her twenty-five pounds a year, and I wish them joy of their bargain!'

Charlotte pushed back her chair violently, and her hot face looked its ugliest as some of the hidden hatred showed itself. But Lambert felt that she did well to be angry. In the greater affairs of life he believed in Charlotte, and he admitted to himself that she had done especially well in sending Francie to Bray.

36

The house that the Fitzpatricks had taken in Bray for the winter was not situated in what is known as the fashionable part of the town. It commanded no view either of the Esplanade or of Bray Head; it had, in fact, little view of any kind except the backs of other people's houses, and an oblique glimpse of a railway bridge at the end of the road. It was just saved from the artisan level by a tiny bow window on either side of the hall door, and the name, Albatross Villa, painted on the gateposts; and its crowning claim to distinction was the fact that by standing just outside the gate it was possible to descry, under the railway bridge, a small square of esplanade and sea that was Mrs Fitzpatrick's justification when she said gallantly to her Dublin friends that she'd never have come to Bray for the winter only for being able to look out at the waves all day long.

Poor Mrs Fitzpatrick did not tell her friends that she had, nowadays, things to occupy herself with that scarcely left her time for taking full advantage of this privilege. From the hour of the awakening of her brood to that midnight moment when, with fingers roughened and face flushed from the darning of stockings, she toiled up to bed, she was scarcely conscious that the sea existed, except when Dottie came in with her boots worn into holes by the pebbles of the beach, or Georgie's Sunday trousers were found to be smeared with tar from riding astride the upturned boats. There were no longer for her the afternoon naps that were so pleasantly composing after four o'clock dinner; it was now her part to clear away and wash the dishes and plates, so as to leave Bridget, the 'general', free to affair herself with the clothes-lines in the back garden, whereon the family linen streamed and ballooned in the east wind that is the winter prerogative of Bray. She had grown perceptibly thinner under this discipline, and her eyes had dark swellings beneath them that seemed pathetically unbecoming to anyone who, like Francie, had last seen her when the rubicund prosperity of Mountjoy

Square had not yet worn away. Probably an Englishwoman of her class would have kept her household in comparative comfort with less effort and more success, but Aunt Tish was very far from being an Englishwoman; her eyes were not formed to perceive dirt, nor her nose to apprehend smells, and her idea of domestic economy was to indulge in no extras of soap or scrubbing brushes, and to feed her family on strong tea and indifferent bread and butter, in order that Ida's and Mabel's hats might be no whit less ornate than those of their neighbours.

Francie had plunged into the heart of this squalor with characteristic recklessness; and the effusion of welcome with which she had been received, and the comprehensive abuse lavished by Aunt Tish upon Charlotte, were at first sufficient to make her forget the frowziness of the dining room, and the fact that she had to share a bedroom with her cousins, the two Misses Fitzpatrick. Francie had kept the particulars of her fight with Charlotte to herself. Perhaps she felt that it would not be easy to make the position clear to Aunt Tish's comprehension, which was of a rudimentary sort in such matters, and apt to jump to crude conclusions. Perhaps she had become aware that even the ordinary atmosphere of her three months at Lismoyle was as far beyond Aunt Tish's imagination as the air of Paradise, but she certainly was not inclined to enlarge on her sentimental experiences to her aunt and cousins; all that they knew was, that she had 'moved in high society', and that she had fought with Charlotte Mullen on general and laudable grounds. It was difficult at times to parry the direct questions of Ida, who, at sixteen, had already, with the horrible precocity prevalent in her grade of society, passed through several flirtations of an outdoor and illicit kind; but if Ida's curiosity could not be parried it could be easily misled, and the family belief in Francie's power of breaking, impartially, the hearts of all the young men whom she met, was a shield to her when she was pressed too nearly about 'young Mr Dysart,' or 'th' officers'. Loud, of course, and facetious were the lamentations that Francie had not returned 'promised' to one or other of these heroes of romance, but not even Ida's cultured capacity could determine which had been the more probable victim. The family said to each other in private that Francie had 'got very close'; even the boys were conscious of a certain strangeness about her, and did not feel inclined to show her, as of yore, the newest subtlety in catapults, or the latest holes in their coats.

She herself was far more conscious of strangeness and remoteness; though, when she had first arrived at Albatross Villa, the crowded, carpetless house and the hourly conflict of living were reviving and almost amusing after the thunderous gloom of her exit from Tally Ho. Almost the first thing she had done had been to write to Hawkins to tell him of what had happened; a letter that her tears had dropped on, and that her pen had flown in the writing of, telling how she had been turned out because she had refused – or as good as refused – Mr Dysart for his – Gerald's – sake, and how she hoped he hadn't written to Tally Ho, 'for it's little chance there'd be Charlotte would send on the letter'. Francie had intended to break off at this point, and leave to Gerald's own conscience the application of the hint; but an unused half sheet at the end of her letter tempted her on, and before she well knew what she was saying, all the jealousy and hurt tenderness and helpless craving of the past month were uttered without a thought of diplomacy or pride. Then a long time had gone by, and there had been no answer from Hawkins. The outflung emotion that had left her spent and humbled, came back in bitterness to her, as the tide gives back in a salt flood the fresh waters of a river, and her heart closed upon it, and bore the pain as best it might.

It was not till the middle of October that Hawkins answered her letter. She knew before she opened the envelope that she was going to be disappointed; how could anyone explain away a silence of two months on one sheet of small notepaper, one side of which, as she well knew, was mainly occupied by the regimental crest, much less reply in the smallest degree to that letter that had cost so much in the writing, and so much more in the repenting of its length and abandonment? Mr Hawkins had wisely steered clear of both difficulties by saying no more than that he had been awfully glad to hear from her, and he would have written before if he could, but somehow he never could find a minute to do so. He would have given a good deal to have seen that row with Miss Mullen, and as far as Dysart was concerned, he thought Miss Mullen had the rights of it; he was going away on first leave now, and wouldn't be back at Lismoyle till the end of the year, when he hoped he would find her and old Charlotte as good friends as ever. He, Mr Hawkins, was really not worth fighting about; he was stonier broke than he had ever been, and, in conclusion, he was hers (with an illegible hieroglyphic to express the exact amount), Gerald Hawkins.

Like the last letter she had had from him, this had come early in the morning, but on this occasion she could not go up to her room to read it in peace. The apartment that she shared with Ida and Mabel offered few facilities for repose, and none for seclusion, and, besides, there was too much to be done in the way of helping to lay the table and get the breakfast. She hurried about the kitchen in her shabby gown, putting the kettle on to a hotter corner of the range, pouring treacle into a jampot, and filling the sugar basin from a paper bag with quick, trembling fingers; her breath came pantingly, and the letter that she had hidden inside the front of her dress crackled with the angry rise and fall of her breast. That he should advise her to go and make friends with Charlotte, and tell her she had made a mistake in refusing Mr Dysart, and never say a word about all that she had said to him in her letter –!

'Francie's got a letter from her sweetheart!' said Mabel, skipping round the kitchen, and singing the words in a kind of chant. 'Ask her for the lovely crest for your album, Bobby!'

Evidently the ubiquitous Mabel had studied the contents of the letterbox.

'Ah, it's well to be her,' said Bridget, joining in the conversation with her accustomed ease; 'it's long before *my* fella would write me a letter!'

'And it's little you want letters from him,' remarked Bobby, in his slow, hideous, Dublin brogue, 'when you're out in the lane talking to another fella every night.'

'Ye lie!' said Bridget, with a flattered giggle, while Bobby ran up the kitchen stairs after Francie, and took advantage of her having the teapot in one hand and the milk jug in the other to thrust his treacly fingers into her pocket in search of the letter.

'Ah, have done!' said Francie angrily; 'look, you're after making me spill the milk!'

But Bobby, who had been joined by Mabel, continued his persecutions, till his cousin, freeing herself of her burdens, turned upon him and boxed his ears with a vigour that sent him howling upstairs to complain to his mother.

After this incident, Francie's life at Albatross Villa went on, as it seemed to her, in a squalid monotony of hopelessness. The days became darker and colder, and the food and firing more perceptibly insufficient, and strong tea a more prominent feature of each meal, and even Aunt Tish lifted her head from the round of unending, dingy cares, and saw some change in Francie. She said to Uncle Robert, with an excusable thought of Francie's ungrudging help in the household, and her contribution to it of five shillings a week, that it would be a pity if the sea air didn't suit the girl; and Uncle Robert, arranging a greasy satin tie under his beard at the looking glass, preparatory to catching the 8.30 train for Dublin, had replied that it wasn't his fault if it didn't, and if she chose to be fool enough to fight with Charlotte Mullen she'd have to put up with it. Uncle Robert was a saturnine little man of small abilities, whose reverses had not improved his temper, and he felt that things were coming to a pretty pass if his wife was going to make him responsible for the sea air, as well as the smoky kitchen chimney, and the scullery sink that Bobby had choked with a dead jelly fish, and everything else.

The only events that Francie felt to be at all noteworthy were her letters from Mr Lambert. He was not a brilliant letter-writer, having neither originality, nor the gift which is sometimes bestowed on unoriginal people, of conveying news in a simple and satisfying manner; but his awkward and sterile sentences were as cold waters to the thirsty soul that was always straining back towards its time of abundance. She could scarcely say the word Lismoyle now without a hesitation, it was so shrined in dear and miserable remembrance, with all the fragrance of the summer embalming it in her mind, that, unselfconscious as she was, the word seemed sometimes too difficult to pronounce. Lambert himself had become a personage of a greater world, and had acquired an importance that he would have resented had he known how wholly impersonal it was. In some ways she did not like him quite as much as in the Dublin days, when he had had the advantage of being the nearest thing to a gentleman that she had met with; perhaps her glimpses of his home life and the fact of his friendship with Charlotte had been disillusioning, or perhaps the comparison of him with other and newer figures upon her horizon had not been to his advantage; certainly it was more by virtue of his position in that other world that he was great.

It was strange that in these comparisons it was to Christopher that she turned for a standard. For her there was no flaw in Hawkins; her angry heart could name no fault in him except that he had wounded it; but she illogically felt Christopher's superiority without being aware of deficiency in the other. She did not understand Christopher, she had hardly understood him at that moment to which she now looked back with a gratified vanity that was tempered by uncertainty and not unmingled with awe; but she knew him just well enough, and had just enough perception to respect him. Fanny Hemphill and Delia Whitty would have regarded him with a terror that would have kept them dumb in his presence, but for which they would have compensated themselves at other times by explosive gigglings at his lack of all that they admired most in young men. Some errant streak of finer sense made her feel his difference from the men she knew, without wanting to laugh at it; as has already been said, she respected him, an emotion not hitherto awakened by a varied experience of 'gentlemen friends'.

There were times when the domestic affairs of Albatross Villa touched their highest possibility of discomfort, when Bridget had gone to the christening of a friend's child at Enniskerry, and returned next day only partially recovered from the potations that had celebrated the event; or when Dottie, unfailing purveyor of diseases to the family, had imported German measles from her school. At these times Francie, as she made fires, or beds, or hot drinks, would think of Bruff and its servants with a regret that was none the less burning for its ignobleness. Several times when she lay awake at night, staring at the blank of her own future, while the stabs of misery were sharp and unescapable, she had thought that she would write to Christopher, and tell him what had happened, and where she was. In those hours when nothing is impossible and nothing is unnatural, his face and his words, when she saw him last, took on their fullest meaning, and she felt as if she had only to put her hand out to open that which she had closed. The diplomatic letter, about nothing in particular, that should make Christopher understand that she would like to see him again, was often half composed, had indeed often lulled her sore heart and hot eyes to sleep with visions of the divers luxuries and glories that this single stepping-stone should lead to. But in the morning, when the children had gone to school, and she had come in from marketing, it was not such an easy thing to sit down and write a letter about nothing in particular to Mr Dysart. Her defeat at the hands of Hawkins had taken away her belief in herself. She could not even hint to Christopher the true version of her fight with Charlotte, sure though she was that an untrue one had already found its way to Bruff; she could not tell him that Bridget had got drunk, and that butter was so dear they had to do without it; such emergencies did not somehow come within the scope of her promise to trust him, and, besides, there was the serious possibility of his volunteering to see her. She would have given a good deal to see him, but not at Albatross Villa. She pictured him to herself, seated in the midst of the Fitzpatrick family, with Ida making eyes at him from under her fringe, and Bridget scuffling audibly with Bobby outside the door. Tally Ho was a palace compared with this, and yet she remembered what she had felt when she came back to Tally Ho from Bruff. When she thought of it all, she wondered whether she could bring herself to write to Charlotte, and try to make friends with her again. It would be dreadful to do, but her life at Albatross Villa was dreadful, and the dream of another visit to Lismoyle, when she could revenge herself on Hawkins by showing him his unimportance to her, was almost too strong for her pride. How much of it was due to her thirst to see him again at any price, and how much to a pitiful hankering after the fleshpots of Egypt, it is hard to say; but November and December dragged by, and she did not write to Christopher or Charlotte, and Lambert remained her only correspondent at Lismoyle.

It was a damp, dark December, with rain and wind nearly every day. Bray Head was rarely without a cap of grey cloud, and a restless pack of waves mouthing and leaping at its foot. The Esplanade was a mile-long vista of soaked grass and glistening asphalt, whereon the foot of man apparently never trod; once or twice a storm had charged it from the south-east, and had hurled sheets of spray and big stones on to it, and pounded holes in the concrete of its sea wall. There had been such a storm the week before Christmas. The breakers had rushed upon the long beach with a 'broad-flung, shipwrecking roar', and the windows of the houses along the Esplanade were dimmed with salt and sand. The rain had come in under the hall door at Albatross Villa, the cowl was blown off the kitchen chimney, causing the smoke to make its exit through the house by various routes, and, worst of all, Dottie and the boys had not been out of the house for two days. Christmas morning was signalized by the heaviest downpour of the week. It was hopeless to think of going to church, least of all for a person whose most presentable boots were relics of the past summer, and bore the cuts of lake rocks on their dulled patent leather. The post came late, after its wont, but it did not bring the letter that Francie had not been able to help expecting. There had been a few Christmas cards, and one letter which did indeed bear the Lismoyle postmark, but was only a bill from the Misses Greely, forwarded by Charlotte, for the hat that she had bought to replace the one that was lost on the day of the capsize of the *Daphne*.

The Christmas mid-day feast of tough roast beef and pallid plum pudding was eaten, and then, unexpectedly, the day brightened, a thin sunlight began to fall on the wet roads and the dirty, tossing sea, and Francie and her younger cousins went forth to take the air on the Esplanade. They were the only human beings upon it when they first got there; in any other weather Francie might have expected to meet a friend or two from Dublin there, as had occurred on previous Sundays, when the still enamoured Tommy Whitty had ridden down on his bicycle, or Fanny Hemphill and her two medical student brothers had asked her to join them in a walk round Bray Head. The society of the Hemphills and Mr Whitty had lost, for her, much of its pristine charm, but it was better than nothing at all; in fact, those who saw the glances that Miss Fitzpatrick, from mere force of habit, levelled at Mr Whitty, or were witnesses of a pebble-throwing encounter with the Messrs Hemphill, would not have guessed that she desired anything better than these amusements.

'Such a Christmas Day!' she thought to herself, 'without a soul to see or talk to! I declare, I think I'll turn nurse in a hospital, the way Susie Brennan did. They say those nurses have grand fun, and 'twould be better than this awful old place anyhow!' She had walked almost to the squat Martello tower, and while she looked discontentedly up at Bray Head, the last ray of sun struck on its dark shoulder as if to challenge her with the magnificence of its outline and the untruthfulness of her indictment. 'Oh, you may shine away!' she exclaimed, turning her back upon both sunlight and mountain and beginning to walk back to where Bobby and Dottie were searching for jellyfish among the seaweed cast up by the storm, 'the day's done for now, it's as good for me to go up to the four o'clock service as be streeling about in the cold here.'

Almost at the same moment the chimes from the church on the hill behind the town struck out upon the wind with beautiful severity, and obeying them listlessly, she left the children and turned up the steep suburban road that was her shortest way to Christ Church.

It was a long and stiffish pull; the wind blew her hair about till it looked like a mist of golden threads, the colour glowed dazzlingly in her cheeks, and the few men whom she passed bestowed upon her a stare of whose purport she was well aware. This was a class of compliment which she neither resented nor was surprised at, and it is quite possible that some months before she might have allowed her sense of it to be expressed in her face. But she felt now as if the approval of a man in the street was not worth what it used to be. It was, of course, agreeable in its way, but on this Christmas afternoon, with all its inevitable reminders of the past and the future, it brought with it the thought of how soon her face had been forgotten by the men who had praised it most.

The gas was lighted in the church, and the service was just beginning as she passed the decorated font and went uncertainly up a side aisle till she was beckoned into a pew by a benevolent old lady. She knelt down in a corner, beside a pillar that was wreathed with a thick serpent of evergreens, and the old lady looked up from her admission of sin to wonder that such a pretty girl was allowed to walk through the streets by herself. The heat of the church had brought out the aromatic smell of all the green things, the yellow gas flared from its glittering standards, and the glimmering colours of the east window were dying into darkness with the dying daylight. When she stood up for the psalms she looked round the church to see if there were anyone there whom she knew; there were several familiar faces, but no one with whom she had ever exchanged a word, and turning round again she devoted herself to the hopeless task of finding out the special psalms that the choir were singing. Having failed in this, she felt her religious duties to be for the time suspended, and her thoughts strayed afield over things in general, settling down finally on a subject that had become more pressing than was pleasant.

It is a truism of ancient standing that money brings no cure for heartache, but it is also true that if the money were not there the heartache would be harder to bear. Probably if Francie had returned from Lismoyle to a smart house in Merrion Square, with a carriage to drive in, and a rich relative ready to pay for new winter dresses, she would have been less miserable over Mr Hawkins' desertion than she was at Albatross Villa; she certainly would not have felt as unhappy as she did now, standing up with the shrill singing clamouring in her ears, while she tried in different ways to answer the question of how she was to pay for the dresses that she had bought to take to Lismoyle. Twenty-five pounds a year does not go far when more than half of it is expended upon board and lodging, and a whole quarter has been anticipated to pay for a summer visit, and Lambert's prophecy that she would find herself in the county court some day seemed not unlikely to come true. In her pocket was a letter from a Dublin shop, containing more than a hint of legal proceedings; and even if she were able to pay them a temporizing two pounds in a month, there still would remain five pounds due, and she would not have a farthing left to go on with. Everything was at its darkest for her. Her hardy, supple nature was dispirited beyond its power of reaction, and now and then the remembrance of the Sundays of last summer caught her, till the pain came in her throat, and the gaslight spread into shaking stars.

The service went on, and Francie rose and knelt mechanically with the rest of the congregation. She was not irreligious, and even the name of scepticism was scarcely understood by her, but she did not consider that religion was applicable to love affairs and bills; her mind was too young and shapeless for anything but a healthy, negligent belief in what she had been taught, and it did not enter into her head to utilise religion as a last resource, when everything else had turned out a failure. She regarded it with respect, and believed that most people grew good when they grew old, and the service passed over her head with a vaguely pleasing effect of music and light. As she came out into the dark lofty porch a man stepped forward to meet her. Francie started violently.

'Oh, goodness gracious!' she cried, 'you frightened my life out!'

But for all that, she was glad to see Mr Lambert.

37

That evening when Mrs Fitzpatrick was putting on her best cap and her long cameo ear-rings she said to her husband:

'Well now, Robert, you mark my words, he's after her.'

'Tchah!' replied Mr Fitzpatrick, who was not in a humour to admit that any woman could be attractive, owing to the postponement of his tea by his wife so that cakes might be baked in Mr Lambert's honour; 'you can't see a man without thinking he's in love with someone or other.'

'I suppose you think it's to see yourself he's come all the way from Lismoyle,' rejoined Mrs Fitzpatrick with becoming spirit, 'and says he's going to stop at Breslin's Hotel for a week?'

'Oh, very well, have it your own way,' said Mr Fitzpatrick acrimoniously. 'I suppose you have it all settled, and he'll be married to her by special licence before the week's out.'

'Well, I don't care, Robert, you wouldn't think to look at him that he'd only buried his wife four months and a half ago – though I will say he's in deep mourning – but for all that no one'd blame him that he didn't think much of that poor creature, and 'twould be a fine match for Francie if she'd take him.'

'Would she take him!' echoed Mr Fitzpatrick scornfully; 'would a duck swim? I never saw the woman yet that wouldn't half hang herself to get married!'

'Ah, have done being so cross, Robert, Christmas day and all; I wonder you married at all since you think so little of women.'

Finding the argument not easy to answer, Mr Fitzpatrick said nothing, and his wife, too much interested to linger over side issues, continued,

'The girls say they heard him asking her to drive to the Dargle with him tomorrow, and he's brought a grand box of sweets for the children as a Christmas box, and six lovely pair of gloves for Francie! 'Pon me word, I call her a very lucky girl!'

'Well, if I was a woman it isn't that fellow I'd fancy,' said Mr Fitzpatrick, unexpectedly changing his ground, 'but as, thank God, I'm not, it's no affair of mine.' Having delivered himself of this sentiment, Mr Fitzpatrick went downstairs. The smell of hot cakes rose deliciously upon the air, and, as his niece emerged from the kitchen with a plateful of them in her hand, and called to him to hurry before they got cold, he thought to himself that Lambert would have the best of the bargain if he married her.

Francie found the evening surprisingly pleasant. She was, as she had always been, entirely at her ease with Mr Lambert, and did not endure, on his account, any vicarious suffering because the tablecloth was far from clean, and the fact that Bridget put on the coal with her fingers was recorded on the edges of the plates. If he chose to come and eat hot cakes in the bosom of the Fitzpatrick family instead of dining at his hotel, he was just as well able to do without a butter knife as she was, and, at all events, he need not have stayed unless he liked, she thought, with a little flash of amusement and pride that her power over him, at least, was not lost. There had been times during the last month or two when she had believed that he, like everyone else, had forgotten her, and it was agreeable to find that she had been mistaken.

The next day proved to be one of the softest and sunniest of the winter, and, as they flew along the wet road towards the Dargle, on the smartest of the Bray outside cars, a great revival took place in Francie's spirits. They left their car at the gate of the glen to which the Dargle river has given its name, and strolled together along the private road that runs from end to end of it. A few holidaymakers had been tempted down from Dublin by the fine day, but there was nothing that even suggested the noisy pleasure parties that vulgarize the winding beauty of the ravine on summer bank holidays.

'Doesn't it look fearful lonely today?' said Francie, who had made her last visit there as a member of one of these same pleasure parties, and had enjoyed herself highly. 'You can't hear a thing but the running of the water.'

They were sitting on the low parapet of the road, looking down the brown slope of the treetops to the river, that was running a foaming race among the rocks at the bottom of the cleft.

'I don't call it lonely,' said Lambert, casting a discontented sidelong glance at a couple walking past arm-in-arm, evidently in the silently blissful stage of courtship; 'how many more would you like?'

'Oh, lots,' replied Francie, 'but I'm not going to tell you who they are!'

'I know one, anyhow,' said Lambert, deliberately leading up to a topic that up to this had been only slightly touched on. When he had walked home from the church with Francie the evening before, he had somehow not been able to talk to her consecutively; he had felt a nervous awkwardness that he had not believed himself capable of, and the fact that he was holding an umbrella over her head and that she had taken his arm had seemed the only thing that he could give his mind to.

'Who do you know?'

Francie had plucked a ribbon of hart's tongue from the edge of the wall, and was drawing its cold satiny length across her lips.

'Wouldn't you like it now if you saw – ' he paused and looked at Francie – 'who shall we say – Charlotte Mullen coming up the road?'

'I wouldn't care.'

'Wouldn't you though! You'd run for your life, the way you

did before out of Lismoyle,' said Lambert, looking hard at her and laughing not quite genuinely.

The strip of hart's tongue could not conceal a rising glow in the face behind it, but Francie's voice was as undaunted as ever as she replied,

'Who told you I ran for my life?'

'You told me so yourself.'

'I didn't. I only told you I'd had a row with her.'

'Well, that's as good as saying you had to run. You don't suppose I thought you'd get the better of Charlotte?'

'I daresay you didn't, because you're afraid of her yourself!'

There was a degree of truth in this that made Mr Lambert suddenly realize Francie's improper levity about serious things.

'I'll tell you one thing I'm afraid of,' he said severely, 'and that is that you made a mistake in fighting with Charlotte. If you'd chosen to – to do as she wished, she's easy enough to get on with.'

Francie flung her fern over the parapet and made no answer.

'I suppose you know she's moved into Gurthnamuckla?' he went on.

'I know nothing about anything,' interrupted Francie; 'I don't know how long it isn't since you wrote to me, and when you do you never tell me anything. You might be all dead and buried down there for all I know or care!'

The smallest possible glance under her eyelids tempered this statement and confused Mr Lambert's grasp of his subject.

'Do you mean that, about not caring if I was dead or no? I daresay you do. No one cares now what happens to me.'

He almost meant what he said, her elusiveness was so exasperating, and his voice told his sincerity. Last summer she would have laughed pitilessly at his pathos, and made it up with him afterwards. But she was changed since last summer, and now as she looked at him she felt a forlorn kinship with him.

'Ah, what nonsense!' she said caressingly. 'I'd be awfully sorry if anything happened you.' As if he could not help himself he took her hand, but before he could speak she had drawn it away. 'Indeed, you might have been dead,' she went on hurriedly, 'for all you told me in your letters. Begin now and tell me the Lismoyle news. I think you said the Dysarts were away from Bruff still, didn't you?'

Lambert felt as if a hot and cold spray of water had been turned on him alternately. 'The Dysarts? Oh, yes, they've been

248

away for some time,' he said, recovering himself; 'they've been in London, I believe, staying with her people, since you're so anxious to know about them.'

'Why wouldn't I want to know about them?' said Francie, getting off the wall. 'Come on and walk a bit; it's cold sitting here.'

Lambert walked on by her side rather sulkily; he was angry with himself for having let his feelings run away with him, and he was angry with Francie for pulling him up so quickly.

'Christopher Dysart's off again,' he said abruptly; 'he's got another of these diplomatic billets.' He believed that Francie would find the information unpleasant, and he was in some contradictory way disappointed that she seemed quite unaffected by it. 'He's unpaid *attaché* to old Lord Castlemore at Copenhagen,' he went on; 'he started last week.'

So Christopher was gone from her too, and never wrote her a line before he went. They're all the same, she thought, all they want is to spoon a girl for a bit, and if she lets them do it they get sick of her, and whatever she does they forget her the next minute. And there was Roddy Lambert trying to squeeze her hand just now, and poor Mrs Lambert, that was worth a dozen of him, not dead six months. She walked on, and forced herself to talk to him, and to make enquiries about the Bakers, Dr Rattray, Mr Corkran, and other lights of Lismoyle society. It was absurd, but it was none the less true that the news that Mr Corkran was engaged to Carrie Beattie gave her an additional pang. The enamoured glances of the curate were fresh in her memory, and the thought that they were being now bestowed upon Carrie Beattie's freckles and watering eyes was, though ludicrous, not altogether pleasing. She burst out laughing suddenly.

'I'm thinking of what all the Beatties will look like dressed as bridesmaids,' she explained; 'four of them, and every one of them roaring, crying, and their noses bright red!'

The day was clouding over a little, and a damp wind began to stir among the leaves that still hung red on the beech trees. Lambert insisted with paternal determination that Francie should put on the extra coat that he was carrying for her, and the couple who had recently passed them, and whom they had now overtaken, looked at them sympathetically, and were certain that they also were engaged. It took some time to reach the far gate of the Dargle, sauntering as they did from bend to bend of the road, and stopping occasionally to look down at the river, or up at the wooded height opposite, with conventional expressions of admiration; and by the time they had passed down between the high evergreens at the lodge, to where the car was waiting for them, Francie had heard all that Lambert could tell her of Lismoyle news. She had also been told what a miserable life Mr Lambert's was, and how lonely he was at Rosemount since poor Lucy's death, and she knew how many young horses he had at grass on Gurthnamuckla, but neither mentioned the name of Mr Hawkins.

The day of the Dargle expedition was Tuesday, and during the remainder of the week Mr Lambert became so familiar a visitor at Albatross Villa, that Bridget learned to know his knock, and did not trouble herself to pull down her sleeves, or finish the mouthful of bread and tea with which she had left the kitchen, before she opened the door. Aunt Tish did not attempt to disguise her satisfaction when he was present, and rallied Francie freely in his absence; the children were quite aware of the state of affairs, having indeed discussed the matter daily with Bridget; and Uncle Robert, going gloomily up to his office in Dublin, had to admit to himself that Lambert was certainly paying her great attention, and that after all, all things considered, it would be a good thing for the girl to get a rich husband for herself when she had the chance. It was rather soon after his wife's death for a man to come courting, but of course the wedding wouldn't come off till the twelve months were up, and at the back of these reflections was the remembrance that he, Uncle Robert, was Francie's trustee, and that the security in which he had invested her five hundred pounds was becoming less sound than he could have wished.

As is proverbially the case, the principal persons concerned were not as aware as the lookers-on of the state of the game. Francie, to whom flirtation was as ordinary and indispensable as the breath of her nostrils, did not feel that anything much out of the common was going on, though she knew quite well that Mr Lambert was very fond of her; and Mr Lambert had so firmly resolved on allowing a proper interval to elapse between his wife's death and that election of her successor upon which he was determined, that he looked upon the present episode as of small importance, and merely a permissible relaxation to a man whose hunting had been stopped, and who had, in a general way, been having the devil of a dull time. He was to go back to Lismoyle on Monday, the first of the year; and it was settled that he was to take Francie on Sunday afternoon to walk on Kingstown pier. The social laws of Mrs Fitzpatrick's world were not rigorous, still less was her interpretation of them; an un-chaperoned expedition to Kingstown pier would not, under any circumstances, have scandalized her, and considering that Lambert was an old friend and had been married, the proceeding became almost prudishly correct. As she stood at her window and saw them turn the corner of the road on their way to the station, she observed to Mabel that there wouldn't be a hand-somer couple going the pier than what they were. Francie had that stylish way with her that she always gave a nice set to a skirt, and it was wonderful the way she could trim up an old hat the same as new.

It was a very bright clear afternoon, and a touch of frost in the air gave the snap and brilliancy that are often lacking in an Irish winter day. On such a Sunday Kingstown pier assumes a fair semblance of its spring and summer gaiety; the Kingstown people walk there because there is nothing else to be done at Kingstown, and the Dublin people come down to snatch what they can of sea air before the short afternoon darkens, and the hour arrives when they look out for members of the St George's Yacht Club to take them in to tea. There was a fair sprinkling of people on the long arm of granite that curves for a mile into Dublin Bay, and as Mr Lambert paced along it he was as agree-ably conscious as his companion of the glances that met and followed their progress. It satisfied his highest ambition that the girl of his choice should be thus openly admired by men whom, year after year, he had looked up at with envious respect as they stood in the bow window of Kildare Street Club, with figures that time was slowly shaping to its circular form, on the principle of correspondence with environment. He was a man who had always valued his possessions according to other people's estimation of them, and this afternoon Francie gained new distinction in his eyes.

Abstract admiration, however, was one thing, but the very concrete attentions of Mr Thomas Whitty were quite another affair. Before they had been a quarter of an hour on the pier, Francie was hailed by her Christian name, and this friend of her youth, looking more unmistakably than ever a solicitor's clerk, joined them, flushed with the effort of overtaking them, and evidently determined not to leave them again.

I spotted you by your hair, Francie,' Mr Whitty was pleased to observe, after the first greetings; 'you must have been getting a new dye for it; I could see it a mile off!'

'Oh, yes,' responded Francie, 'I tried a new bottle the other day, the same you use for your moustache, y'know! I thought I'd like people to be able to see it without a spyglass.'

As Mr Whitty's moustache was represented by three sickly hairs and a pimple, the sarcasm was sufficiently biting to yield Lambert a short-lived gratification.

'Mr Lambert dyes his black,' continued Francie, without a change of countenance. She had the Irish love of a scrimmage in her, and she thought it would be great fun to make Mr Lambert cross.

'D'ye find the colour comes off?' murmured Tommy Whitty, eager for revenge, but too much afraid of Lambert to speak out loud.

Even Francie, though she favoured the repartee with a giggle, was glad that Lambert had not heard.

'D'ye find you want your ears boxed?' she returned in the same tone of voice; 'I won't walk with you if you don't behave.' Inwardly, however, she decided that Tommy Whitty was turning into an awful cad, and felt that she would have given a good deal to have wiped out some lively passages in her previous acquaintance with him.

At the end of half an hour Mr Whitty was still with them, irrepressibly intimate and full of reminiscence. Lambert, after determined efforts to talk to Francie, as if unaware of the presence of a third person, had sunk into dangerous silence, and Francie had ceased to see the amusing side of the situation, and was beginning to be exhausted by much walking to and fro. The sun set in smoky crimson behind the town, the sun-set gun banged its official recognition of the fact, followed by the wild, clear notes of a bugle, and a frosty afterglow lit up the sky, and coloured the motionless water of the harbour. A big bell boomed a monotonous summons to afternoon service, and people began to leave the pier. Those who had secured the entrée of the St George's Yacht Club proceeded comfortably thither for tea, and Lambert felt that he would have given untold sums for the right to take Francie in under the pillared portico, leaving Tommy Whitty and his seedy black coat in outer darkness. The party was gloomily tending towards the station, when the happy idea occurred to Mr Lambert of having tea at the Marine Hotel; it might not have the distinction of the club, but it would at all events give him the power of shaking off that damned presuming counter-jumper, as in his own mind he furiously designated Mr Whitty.

'I'm going to take you up to the hotel for tea, Francie,' he said

252

decisively, and turned at once towards the gate of the Marine gardens. 'Good evening, Whitty.'

The look that accompanied this valedictory remark was so conclusive that the discarded Tommy could do no more than accept the position. Francie would not come to his help, being indeed thankful to get rid of him, and he could only stand and look after the two figures, and detest Mr Lambert with every fibre of his little heart. The coffee room at the hotel was warm and quiet, and Francie sank thankfully into an armchair by the fire.

'I declare this is the nicest thing I've done today,' she said, with a sigh of tired ease; 'I was dead sick of walking up and down that old pier.'

This piece of truckling was almost too flagrant, and Lambert would not even look at her as he answered:

'I thought you seemed to be enjoying yourself, or I'd have come away sooner.'

Francie felt none of the amusement that she would once have derived from seeing Mr Lambert in a bad temper; he had stepped into the foreground of her life and was becoming a large and serious object there, too important and powerful to be teased with any degree of pertinacity.

'Enjoy myself!' she exclaimed, 'I was thinking all the time that my boots would be cut to pieces with the horrid gravel; and,' she continued, laying her head on the plush-covered back of her chair, and directing a laughing, propitiatory glance at her companion, 'you know I had to talk twice as much to poor Tommy because you wouldn't say a word to him. Besides, I knew him long before I knew you.'

'Oh, of course, if you don't mind being seen with a fellow that looks like a tailor's apprentice, I have nothing to say against it,' replied Lambert, looking down on her, as he stood fingering his moustache, with one elbow on the chimney piece. His eyes could not remain implacable when they dwelt on the face that was upturned to him, especially now, when he felt both in face and manner something of pathos and gentleness that was as new as it was intoxicating.

If he had known what it was that had changed her he might have been differently affected by it; as it was, he put it down to the wretchedness of life at Albatross Villa, and was glad of the adversity that was making things so much easier for him. His sulkiness melted away in spite of him; it was hard to be sulky, with Francie all to himself, pouring out his tea and talking to him with an intimateness that was just tipped with flirtation; in fact, as the moments slipped by, and the thought gripped him that the next day would find him alone at Rosemount, every instant of this last afternoon in her society became unspeakably precious. The *tête-à-tête* across the tea table prolonged itself so engrossingly that Lambert forgot his wonted punctuality, and their attempt to catch the five o'clock train for Bray resulted in bringing them breathless to the station as their train steamed out of it.

38

The Irish mailboat was well up to time on that frosty thirty-first of December. She had crossed from Holyhead on an even keel, and when the Bailey light on the end of Howth had been sighted, the passengers began to think that they might risk congratulations on the clemency of the weather, and some of the hardier had ordered tea in the saloon, and were drinking it with incredulous enjoyment.

'I shall go mad, Pamela, perfectly mad, if you cannot think of any word for that tenth light. C and H – can't you think of *any*thing with C and H? I found out all the others in the train, and the least you might do is to think of this one for me. That dreadful woman snoring on the sofa just outside my berth put everything else out of my head.'

This plaint, uttered in a deep and lamentable contralto, naturally drew some attention towards Lady Dysart, as she swept down the saloon towards the end of the table, and Pamela, becoming aware that the lady referred to was among the audience, trod upon her mother's dress and thus temporarily turned the conversation.

'C and H,' she repeated, 'I'm afraid I can't think of anything; the only word I can think of beginning with C is Christopher.'

'Christopher!' cried Lady Dysart, 'why, Christopher ends with an R.'

As Lady Dysart for the second time pronounced her son's

254

name the young man who had just come below, and was having a whisky and soda at the bar at the end of the saloon, turned quickly round and put down his glass. Lady Dysart and her daughter were sitting with their backs to him, but Mr Hawkins did not require a second glance, and made his way to them at once.

'And so you've been seeing poor Christopher off to the North Pole,' he said, after the first surprise and explanations had been got over. 'I can't say I envy him. They make it quite cold enough in Yorkshire to suit me.'

'Don't they ever make it hot for you there?' asked Lady Dysart, unable to resist the chance of poking fun at Mr Hawkins, even though in so doing she violated her own cherished regulations on the subject of slang. All her old partiality for him had revived since Francie's departure from Lismoyle, and she found the idea of his engagement far more amusing than he did.

'No, Lady Dysart, they never do,' said Hawkins, getting very red, and feebly trying to rise to the occasion; 'they're always very nice and kind to me.'

'Oh, I daresay they are!' replied Lady Dysart archly, with a glance at Pamela like that of a naughty child who glories in its naughtiness. 'And is it fair to ask when the wedding is to come off? *We* heard something about the spring!'

'Who gave you that interesting piece of news?' said Hawkins, trying not to look foolish.

'A bridesmaid,' said Lady Dysart, closing her lips tightly, and leaning back with an irrepressible gleam in her eye.

'Well, she knows more than I do. All I know about it is, that I believe the regiment goes to Aldershot in May, and I suppose it will be some time after that.' Mr Hawkins spoke with a singularly bad grace, and before further comment could be made he turned to Pamela. 'I saw a good deal of Miss Hope-Drummond in the north,' he said, with an effort so obvious and so futile at turning the conversation that Lady Dysart began to laugh.

'Why, she was the bridesmaid – ' she began incautiously, when the slackening of the engines set her thoughts flying from the subject in hand to settle in agony upon the certainty that Doyle would forget to put her scent bottle into her dressing bag, and then the whole party went up on deck.

It was dark, and the revolving light on the end of the east pier swung its red eye upon the steamer as she passed within a few yards of it, churning a curving road towards the double line of lamps that marked the jetty. The lights of Kingstown mounted

255

row upon row, like an embattled army of stars, the great sweep of Dublin Bay was pricked out in lessening yellow points, and a new moon that looked pale green by contrast sent an immature shaft along the sea in meek assertion of her presence. The paddles dropped their blades more and more languidly into the water, then they ceased, and the vessel slid silently alongside the jetty, with the sentient ease of a living thing. The warps were flung ashore, the gangways thrust on board, and in an instant the sailors were running ashore with the mail bags on their backs, like a string of ants with their eggs. The usual crowd of loafers and people who had come to meet their friends formed round the passengers' gangway, and the passengers filed down it in the brief uncoveted distinction that the exit from a steamer affords.

Lady Dysart headed her party as they left the steamer, and her imposing figure in her fur-lined cloak so filled the gangway that Pamela could not, at first, see who it was that met her mother as she stepped on to the platform. The next moment she found herself shaking hands with Mr Lambert, and then, to her un-bounded astonishment, with Miss Fitzpatrick. The lamps were throwing strong light and shadow upon Francie's face, and Pamela's first thought was how much thinner she had become.

'Mr Lambert and I missed our train back to Bray,' Francie began at once in a hurried deprecating voice, 'and we came down to see the boat come in just to pass the time – ' Her voice stopped as if she had suddenly gasped for breath, and Pamela heard Hawkins' voice say behind her:

'How de do, Miss Fitzpatrick? Who'd have thought of meetin' you here?' in a tone of cheerfully casual acquaintanceship.

Even Pamela, with all her imaginative sympathy, did not guess what Francie felt in that sick and flinching moment, when everything rung and tingled round her as if she had been struck; the red had deserted her cheek like a cowardly defender, and the ground felt uneven under her feet, but the instinct of self-control that is born of habit and convention in the feeblest of us came mechanically to her help.

'And I never thought I'd see you either,' she answered, in the same tone; 'I suppose you're all going to Lismoyle together, Miss Dysart?'

'No, we stay in Dublin tonight,' said Pamela, with sufficient consciousness of the situation to wish to shorten it. 'Oh, thank you, Mr Hawkins, I should be very glad if you would put these rugs in the carriage.'

Hawkins disappeared with the rugs in the wake of Lady

256

Dysart, and Lambert and Pamela and Francie followed slowly together in the same direction. Pamela was in the difficult position of a person who is full of a sympathy that it is wholly out of the question to express.

'I am so glad that we chanced to meet you here,' she said, 'we have not heard anything of you for such a long time.'

The kindness in her voice had the effect of conveying to Francie how much in need of kindness she was, and the creeping smart of tears gathered under her eyelids.

'It's awfully kind of you to say so, Miss Dysart,' she said, with something in her voice that made even the Dublin brogue pathetic; 'I didn't think anyone at Lismoyle remembered me now.'

'Oh, we don't forget people quite so quickly as that,' said Pamela, thinking that Mr Hawkins must have behaved worse than she had believed; 'I see this is our carriage. Mamma, did you know that Miss Fitzpatrick was here?'

Lady Dysart was already sitting in the carriage, her face fully expressing the perturbation that she felt, as she counted the parcels that Mr Hawkins was bestowing in the netting.

'Oh yes,' she said, with a visible effort to be polite, 'I saw her just now; do get in, my dear, the thing may start at any moment.'

If her mind had room for anything beside the anxieties of travelling, it was disapprobation of Francie and of the fact that she was going about alone with Mr Lambert, and the result was an absence of geniality that added to Francie's longing to get away as soon as possible. Lambert was now talking to Pamela, blocking up the doorway of the carriage as he stood on the step, and over his shoulder she could see Hawkins, still with his back to her, and still apparently very busy with the disposal of the dressing bags and rugs. He was not going to speak to her again, she thought, as she stood a little back from the open door with the frosty air nipping her through her thin jacket; she was no more to him than a stranger, she, who knew every turn of his head, and the feeling of his yellow hair that the carriage lamp was shining upon. The very look of the first-class carriage seemed to her, who had seldom, if ever, been in one, to emphasize the distance that there was between them. The romance that always clung to him even in her angriest thoughts was slaughtered by this glimpse of him, like some helpless atom of animal life by the passing heel of a schoolboy. There was no scaffold, with its final stupendous moment, and incentive to heroism; there was nothing but an ignoble end in commonplace neglect.

The ticket collector slammed the door of the next carriage, and

Francie stepped back still further to make way for Lambert as he got off the step. She had turned her back on the train, and was looking vacantly at the dark outlines of the steamer when she became aware that Hawkins was beside her.

'Er – good-bye – ' he said awkwardly, 'the train's just off.'

'Good-bye,' replied Francie, in a voice that sounded strangely to her, it was so everyday and conventional.

'Look here,' he said, looking very uncomfortable, and speaking quickly, 'I know you're angry with me. I couldn't help it. I tried to get out of it, but it – it couldn't be done. I'm awfully sorry about it – '

If Francie had intended to reply to this address, it was placed beyond her power to do so. The engine, which had been hissing furiously for some minutes, now set up the continuous ear-piercing shriek that precedes the departure of the boat train, and the guard, hurrying along the platform, signified to Hawkins in dumb show that he was to take his seat. The whistle continued unrelentingly; Hawkins put out his hand, and Francie laid hers in it. She looked straight at him for a second, and then, as she felt his fingers close hard round her hand in dastardly assurance of friendship if not affection, she pulled it away, and turned to Lambert, laughing and putting her hands up to her ears to show that she could hear nothing in the din. Hawkins jumped into the carriage again, Pamela waved her hand at the window, and Francie was left with Lambert on the platform, looking at the red light on the back of the guard's van, as the train wound out of sight into the tunnel.

39

It was a cold east-windy morning near the middle of March, when the roads were white and dusty, and the clouds were grey, and Miss Mullen, seated in her new dining room at Gurthnamuckla, was finishing her Saturday balancing of accounts. Now that she had become a landed proprietor, the process was more complicated than it used to be. A dairy, pigs, and poultry cannot be managed and made to pay without thought and trouble, and, as Charlotte had every intention of making Gurthna-muckla pay, she spared neither time nor account books, and was beginning to be well satisfied with the result. She had laid out a good deal of money on the house and farm, but she was going to get a good return for it, or know the reason why; and as no tub of skim milk was given to the pigs, or barrow of turnips to the cows, without her knowledge, the chances of success seemed on her side.

She had just entered, on the page headed Receipts, the sale of two pigs at the fair, and surveyed the growing amount in its neat figures with complacency; then, laying down her pen, she went to the window, and directed a sharp eye at the two men who were spreading gravel on the reclaimed avenue, and straightening the edges of the grass.

"Pon my word, it's beginning to look like a gentleman's avenue,' she said to herself, eyeing approvingly the arch of the elm tree branches, and the clumps of yellow daffodils, the only spots of light in the colourless landscape, while the cawing of the building rooks had a pleasant manorial sound in her ears. A young horse came galloping across the lawn, with floating mane and tail, and an intention to jump the new wooden railings that only failed him at the last moment, and resulted in two soapy slides in the grass, that Charlotte viewed from her window with wonderful equanimity. 'I'll give Roddy a fine blowing up when he comes over,' she thought, as she watched the colt cutting capers among the daffodils; 'I'll ask him if he'd like me to have his four precious colts in to tea. He's as bad about them as I am about the cats!' Miss Mullen's expression denoted that the re-proof would not be of the character to which Louisa was accus-tomed, and Mrs Bruff, who had followed her mistress into the window, sprang on a chair, and, arching her back, leaned against the well-known black alpaca apron with a feeling that the occasion was exceptionally propitious. The movements of Charlotte's character, for it cannot be said to possess the power of development, were akin to those of some amphibious thing, whose strong, darting course under the water is only marked by a bubble or two, and it required almost an animal instinct to note them. Every bubble betrayed the creature below, as well as the limitations of its power of hiding itself, but people never thought of looking out for these indications in Charlotte, or even suspected that she had anything to conceal. There was an almost blatant simplicity about her, a humorous rough and readiness which, joined with her literary culture, proved business capacity. and

259

dreaded temper, seemed to leave no room for any further aspect, least of all of a romantic kind.

Having opened the window for a minute to scream abusive directions to the men who were spreading gravel, she went back to the table, and, gathering her account books together, she locked them up in her davenport. The room that, in Julia Duffy's time, had been devoted to the storage of potatoes, was now beginning life again, dressed in the faded attire of the Tally Ho dining room. Charlotte's books lined one of its newly-papered walls; the foxhunting prints that dated from old Mr Butler's reign at Tally Ho hung above the chimney-piece, and the maroon rep curtains were those at which Francie had stared during her last and most terrific encounter with their owner. The air of occupation was completed by a basket on the rug in front of the fire with four squeaking kittens in it, and by the Bible and the grey manual of devotion out of which Charlotte read daily prayers to Louisa the orphan and the cats. It was an ugly room, and nothing could ever make it anything else, but with the aid of the brass-mounted grate, a few bits of Mrs Mullen's silver on the sideboard, and the deep-set windows, it had an air of respectability and even dignity that appealed very strongly to Charlotte. She enjoyed every detail of her new possessions, and, unlike Norry and the cats, felt no regret for the urban charms and old associations of Tally Ho. Indeed, since her aunt's death, she had never liked Tally Ho. There was a strain of superstition in her that, like her love of land, showed how strongly the blood of the Irish peasant ran in her veins; since she had turned Francie out of the house she had not liked to think of the empty room facing her own, in which Mrs Mullen's feeble voice had laid upon her the charge that she had not kept; her dealings with table-turning and spirit-writing had expanded for her the bound-aries of the possible, and made her the more accessible to terror of the supernatural. Here, at Gurthnamuckla, there was nothing to harbour these suggestions; no brooding evergreens rustling outside her bedroom window, no rooms alive with the little incidents of a past life, no doors whose opening and shutting were like familiar voices reminding her of the footsteps that they had once heralded. This new house was peopled only by the pleasant phantoms of a future that she had fashioned for herself out of the slightest and vulgarest materials, and her wakeful nights were spent in schemings in which the romantic and the practical were logically blended.

Norry the Boat did not, as has been hinted, share her mistress's satisfaction in Gurthnamuckla. For four months she had reigned in its kitchen, and it found no more favour in her eyes than on the day when she, with her roasting-jack in one hand and the cockatoo's cage in the other, had made her official entry into it. It was not so much the new range, or the barren tidiness of the freshly-painted cupboards; these things had doubtless been at first very distressing, but time had stored the cupboards with the miscellanies that Norry loved to hoard, and Bid Sal had imparted a home-like feeling to the range by wrenching the hinge of the oven door so that it had to be kept closed with the poker. Even the unpleasantly dazzling whitewash was now turning a comfortable yellow brown, and the cobwebs were growing about the hooks in the ceiling. But none of these things thoroughly consoled Norry. Her complaints, it is true, did not seem adequate to account for her general aspect of discontent. Miss Mullen heard daily lamentations over the ravages committed by Mr Lambert's young horses on the clothes bleaching on the furze bushes, the loss of 'the clever little shcullery that we had in Tally Ho,' and the fact that 'if a pairson was on his dying bed for the want of a grain o' tay itself, he should thravel three miles before he'd get it,' but the true grievance remained locked in Norry's bosom. Not to save her life would she have admitted that what was really lacking in Gurthnamuckla was society. The messengers from the shops, the pedlar women; above all, the beggars; of these she had been deprived at a blow, and life had become a lean ill-nurtured thing without the news with which they had daily provided her. Billy Grainy and Nance the Fool were all that remained to her of this choice company, the former having been retained in his offices of milk-seller, messenger, and post-boy, and the latter, like Abdiel, faithful among the faithless, was undeterred by the distance that had discouraged the others of her craft, and limped once a week to Gurthnamuckla for the sake of old times and a mug of dripping.

By these inadequate channels a tardy rill of news made its way to Miss Mullen's country seat, but it came poisoned by the feeling that everyone else in Lismoyle had known it for at least a week, and Norry felt herself as much aggrieved as if she had been charged 'pence apiece' for stale eggs.

It was therefore the more agreeable that, on this same raw, grey Saturday morning, when Norry's temper had been unusually tried by a search for the nest of an outlaying hen, Mary Holloran, the Rosemount lodgewoman, should have walked into the kitchen.

'God save all here!' she said, sinking on to a chair, and wiping away with her apron the tears that the east wind had brought to her eyes; 'I'm as tired as if I was afther walking from Galway with a bag o' male!'

'Musha, then, *cead failthe*, Mary,' replied Norry with unusual geniality; 'is it from Judy Lee's wake ye're comin'?'

'I am, in throth; Lord ha' mercy on her!' Mary Holloran raised her eyes to the ceiling and crossed herself, and Norry and Bid Sal followed her example. Norry was sitting by the fire singeing the yellow carcase of a hen, and the brand of burning paper in her hand heightened the effect of the gesture in an almost startling way. 'Well now,' resumed Mary Holloran, 'she was as nice a woman as ever threw a tub of clothes on the hill, and an honest poor craythure through all. She battled it out well, as owld as she was.'

'Faith thin, an' if she did die itself she was in the want of it,' said Norry sardonically; 'sure there isn't a winther since her daughter wint to America that she wasn't anointed a couple of times. I'm thinkin' the people th' other side o' death will be throuncin' her for keepin' them waitin' on her this way!'

Mary Holloran laughed a little and then wiped her face with the corner of her apron, and sighed so as to restore a fitting tone to the conversation.

'The neighbours was all gethered in it last night,' she observed; 'they had the two rooms full in it, an' a half gallon of whisky, and porther and all sorts. Indeed, her sisther's two daughthers showed her every respect; there wasn't one comin' in it, big nor little, but they'd fill them out a glass o' punch before they'd sit down. God bless ye, Bid Sal,' she went on, as if made thirsty by the recollection; 'have ye a sup o' tay in that taypot that's on th' oven? I'd drink the lough this minute!'

'Is it the like o' that ye'd give the woman?' vociferated Norry in furious hospitality, as Bid Sal moved forward to obey this behest; 'make down the fire and bile a dhrop o' wather the way she'll get what'll not give her a sick shtummuck. Sure, what's in that pot's the lavin's afther Miss Charlotte's breakfast for Billy Grainy when he comes with the post; and good enough for the likes of him.'

'There was a good manny axing for ye last night,' began Mary Holloran again, while Bid Sal broke up a box with the kitchen cleaver, and revived the fire with its fragments and a little paraffin oil. 'And you a near cousin o' the corp'. Was it herself wouldn't let you in it?'

262

'Whether she'd let me in it or no I have plenty to do besides running to every corp'-house in the counthry,' returned Norry with an acerbity that showed how accurate Mary Holloran's surmise had been; 'if thim that was in the wake seen me last night goin' out to the cow that's afther calvin' with the quilt off me bed to put over her, maybe they'd have less chat about me.'

Mary Holloran was of a pacific turn, and she tried another topic. 'Did ye hear that John Kenealy was afther summonsing me mother before the Binch?' she said, unfastening her heavy blue cloak and putting her feet up on the fender of the range.

'Ah, God help ye, how would I hear annything?' grumbled Norry; 'it'd be as good for me to be in heaven as to be here, with ne'er a one but Nance the Fool comin' next or nigh me.'

'Oh, indeed, that's the thruth,' said Mary Holloran with polite but transient sympathy. 'Well, whether or no, he summonsed her, and all the raison he had for putting that scandal on her was thim few little hins and ducks she have, that he seen different times on his land, themselves and an owld goat thravellin' the fields, and not a bit nor a bite before them in it that they'd stoop their heads to, only what sign of grass was left afther the winther, and faith! that's little. 'Twas last Tuesday, Lady-Day an' all, me mother was bringin' in a goaleen o' turf, an' he came thundherin' round the house, and every big rock of English he had he called it to her, and every soort of liar and blagyard – oh, indeed, his conduck was not fit to tell to a jackass – an' he summonsed her secondly afther that. Ye'd think me mother'd lose her life when she seen the summons, an' away she legged it into Rosemount to meself, the way I'd spake to the masther to lane heavy on Kenealy the day he'd bring her into coort. "An' indeed," says I to the masther, "is it to bring me mother into coort!" says I;· "sure she's hardly able to lave the bed," says I, "an owld little woman that's not four stone weight! She's not that size," says I –' Mary Holloran measured accurately off the upper joints of her first two fingers – ' "Sure ye'd blow her off yer hand! And Kenealy sayin' she pelted the pavement afther him, and left a backward sthroke on him with the shovel!" says I. But in any case the masther gave no satisfaction to Kenealy, and he arbith-rated him the way he wouldn't be let bring me mother into coort, an' two shillin' she paid for thresspass, and thank God she's able to do that same, for as desolate as Kenealy thinks her.'

'Lambert's a fine arbithrator,' said Norry, dispassionately. 'Here, Bid Sal, run away out to the lardher and lave this within it,' handing over the singed hen, 'and afther that, go on out and cut cabbages for the pigs. Divil's cure to ye! Can't ye make haste! I suppose ye think it's to be standin' looking' at the people that ye get four pounds a year an' yer dite! Thim gerrls is able to put annyone that'd be with them into decay,' she ended, as Bid Sal reluctantly withdrew, 'and there's not a word ye'll say but they'll gallop through the counthry tellin' it.' Then, dropping into a conversational tone, 'Nance was sayin' Lambert was gone to Dublin agin, but what signifies what the likes of her'd say; it couldn't be he'd be goin' in it agin and he not home a week from it.'

Mary Holloran pursed up her mouth portentously.

'Faith he *could* go in it, and it's in it he's gone,' she said, beginning upon a new cup of tea, as dark and sweet as treacle, that Norry had prepared for her. 'Ah, musha! Lord have mercy on thim that's gone; 'tis short till they're forgotten!'

Norry contented herself with an acquiescing sound, devoid of interrogation, but dreary enough to be encouraging. Mrs Holloran's saucer had received half the contents of her cup, and was now delicately poised aloft on the outspread fingers of her right hand, while her right elbow rested on the table according to the etiquette of her class, and Norry knew that the string of her friend's tongue would loosen of its own accord.

'Seven months last Monday,' began Mary Holloran in the voice of a professional reciter; 'seven months since he berrid her, an' if he gives three more in the widda ye may call me a liar.'

'Tell the truth!' exclaimed Norry, startled out of her self-repression and stopping short in the act of poking the fire. 'D'ye tell me it's to marry again he'd go, an' the first wife's clothes on his cook this minit?'

Mary Holloran did not reveal by look or word the gratification that she felt. 'God forbid I'd rise talk or dhraw scandal,' she continued with the same pregnant calm, 'but the thruth it is an' no slandher, for the last month there's not a week – arrah what week – no, but there's hardly the day, but a letther goes to the post for – for one you know well, an' little boxeens and re*jes*tered envelopes an' all sorts. An' letthers coming from that one to him to further ordhers! Sure I know the writin'. Haven't she her name written the size of I don't know what on her likeness that he have shtuck out on the table.'

Mary Holloran broke off like a number of a serial story, with a carefully interrupted situation, and sipped her tea assiduously. Norry advanced slowly from the fireplace with the poker still clutched in her hand, and her glowing eyes fixed upon her friend, as if she were stalking her.

'For the love o' God, woman!' she whispered, 'is it Miss Francie?'

'Now ye have it,' said Mary Holloran.

Norry clasped her hands, poker and all, and raised them in front of her face, while her eyes apparently communed with a familiar spirit at the other end of the kitchen. They puzzled Mary Holloran, who fancied she discerned in them a wild and quite irrelevant amusement, but before further opinions could be interchanged, a dragging step was heard at the back door, a fumbling hand lifted the latch, and Billy Grainy came in with the postbag over his shoulder and an empty milk can in his hand.

'Musha, more power to ye, Billy!' said Mary Holloran, concealing her disgust at the interruption with laudable good breeding, and making a grimace of lightning quickness at Norry, expressive of the secrecy that was to be observed; ''tis you're the grand post boy!'

'Och thin I am,' mumbled Billy sarcastically, as he let the postbag slip from his shoulders to the table, 'divil a boot nor a leg is left on me with the thravelling!' He hobbled over to the fireplace, and, taking the teapot off the range, looked into it suspiciously. 'This is a quare time o' day for a man to be atin' his breakfast! Divil dom the bit I'd ate in this house agin if it wasn't for the nathure I have for the place –'

Norry banged open a cupboard, and took from it a mug with some milk in it, and a yellow pie dish, in which were several stale ends of loaves.

'Take it or lave it afther ye!' she said, putting them down on the table. 'If ye had nathure for risin' airly out o' yer bed the tay wouldn't be waitin' on ye this way, an' if ourselves can't plaze ye, ye can go look for thim that will. "Thim that's onaisy let thim quit!"' Norry cared little whether Billy Grainy was too deaf to take in this retort or no. Mary Holloran and her own self-respect were alike gratified, and taking up the postbag she proceeded with it to the dining room.

'Well, Norry,' said Charlotte jocularly, looking round from the bookshelf that she was tidying, 'is it only now that old thief's brought the post? or have ye been flirting with him in the kitchen all this time?'

Norry retired from the room with a snarl of indescribable scorn, and Charlotte unlocked the bag and drew forth its contents. There were three letters for her, and she laid one of them aside at once while she read the other two. One was from a resident in Ferry Lane, an epistle that began startlingly, 'Honored Madman,' and slanted over two sides of the notepaper in lamentable entreaties for a reduction of the rent and a little more time to pay it in. The other was an invitation from Mrs Corkran to meet a missionary, and tossing both down with an equal contempt, she addressed herself to the remaining one. She was in the act of opening it when she caught sight of the printed name of a hotel upon its flap, and she suddenly became motionless, her eyes staring at the name, and her face slowly reddening all over.

'Bray!' she said between her teeth, 'what takes him to Bray, when he told me to write to him to the Shelbourne?'

She opened the letter, a long and very neatly written one, so neat, in fact, as to give to a person who knew Mr Lambert's handwriting in all its phases the idea of very unusual care and a rough copy.

'My dear Charlotte,' it began, 'I know you will be surprised at the news I have to tell you in this letter, and so will many others; indeed I am almost surprised at it myself.' Charlotte's left hand groped backwards till it caught the back of a chair and held on to it, but her eyes still flew along the lines. 'You are my oldest and best friend, and so you are the first I would like to tell about it, and I would value your good wishes far beyond any others that might be offered to me, especially as I hope you will soon be my relation as well as my friend. I am engaged to Francie Fitzpatrick, and we are to be married as soon as possible.'

The reader sat heavily down upon the chair behind her, her colour fading from red to a dirty yellow as she read on. 'I am aware that many will say that I am not showing proper respect towards poor dear Lucy in doing this, but you, or any one that knew her well, will support me in saying that I never was wanting in that to her when she was alive, and that she would be the last to wish I should live a lonely and miserable life now that she is gone. It is a great pleasure to me to think that she always had such a liking for Francie, for her own sake as well as because she was your cousin. It was my intention to have put off the marriage for a year, but I heard a couple of days ago from Robert Fitzpatrick that the investment that Francie's little fortune had been put into was in a very shaky state, and that there is no present chance of dividends from it. He offered to let her live with them as usual, but they have not enough to support themselves. Francie was half starved there, and it is no place for her to be, and so we have arranged to be married very quietly down here at Bray, on the twentieth – just a week from today. I will take her to London, or perhaps a little further for a week or so, and about the first or second week in April I hope to be back in Rosemount. I know, my dear Charlotte, my dear old friend, that this must appear a sudden and hasty step, but I have considered it well and thoroughly. I know too that when Francie left your house there was some trifling little quarrel between you, but I trust you will forget all about that, and that you will be the first to welcome her when she returns to her new home. She begs me to say that she is sorry for anything she said to annoy you, and would write to you if she thought you would like to hear from her. I hope you will be as good a friend to her as you have always been to me, and will be ready to help and advise her in her new position. I would be greatly obliged to you if you would let the Lismoyle people know of my marriage, and of the reasons that I have told you for hurrying it on this way; you know yourself how glad they always are to get hold of the wrong end of a story. I am going to write to Lady Dysart myself. Now, my dear Charlotte, I must close this letter. The above will be my address for a week, and I will be very anxious to hear from you. With much love from Francie and myself, I remain your attached friend,

'RODERICK LAMBERT.'

A human soul, when it has broken away from its diviner part and is left to the anarchy of the lower passions, is a poor and humiliating spectacle, and it is unfortunate that in its animal want of self-control it is seldom without a ludicrous aspect. The weak side of Charlotte's nature was her ready abandonment of herself to fury that was, as often as not, wholly incompatible with its cause, and now that she had been dealt the hardest blow that life could give her, there were a few minutes in which rage, and hatred, and thwarted passion took her in their fierce hands, and made her for the time a wild beast. When she came to herself she was standing by the chimney-piece, panting and trembling; the letter lay in pieces on the rug, torn by her teeth, and stamped here and there with the semicircle of her heel; a chair was lying on its side on the floor, and Mrs Bruff was crouching aghast under the sideboard, looking out at her mistress with terrified inquiry.

Charlotte raised her hand and drew it across her mouth with

the unsteadiness of a person in physical pain, then, grasping the edge of the chimney-piece, she laid her forehead upon it and drew a few long shuddering breaths. It is probable that if anyone had then come into the room, the human presence, with its mysterious electric quality, would have drawn the storm outwards in a burst of hysterics; but solitude seems to be a non-conductor, and a parched sob, that was strangled in its birth by an imprecation, was the only sound that escaped from her. As she lifted her head again her eyes met those of a large cabinet photograph of Lambert that stared brilliantly at her with the handsome fatuity conferred by an over-touched negative. It was a recent one, taken during one of those visits to Dublin whose object had been always so plausibly explained to her, and as she looked at it, the biting thought of how she had been hoodwinked and fooled, by a man to whom she had all her life laid down the law, drove her half mad again. She plucked it out of its frame with her strong fingers, and thrust it hard down into the smouldering fire.

'If it was hell I'd do the same for you!' she said, with a moan like some furious feline creature, as she watched the picture writhe in the heat, 'and for her too!' She took up the poker, and with it drove and battered the photograph into the heart of the fire, and then, flinging down the poker with a crash that made Louisa jump as she crossed the hall, she sat down at the dinner table and made her first effort at self-control.

'His old friend!' she said, gasping and choking over the words; 'the cur, the double-dyed cur! Lying and cringing to me, and borrowing my money, and – and – ' even to herself she could not now admit that he had gulled her into believing that he would eventually marry her – 'and sneaking after her behind my back all the time! And now he sends me her love – her love! Oh, my God Almighty – ' she tried to laugh, but instead of laughter came tears as she saw herself helpless, and broken, and aimless for the rest of her life – 'I won't break down – I won't break down – ' she said, grinding her teeth together with the effort to repress her sobs. She staggered blindly to the sideboard, and, unlocking it, took out a bottle of brandy. She put the bottle to her mouth and took a long gulp from it, while the tears ran down her face.

40

Sometimes there comes in Paris towards the beginning of April a week or two of such weather as is rarely seen in England before the end of May. The horse-chestnut buds break in vivid green against the sober blue of the sky, there is a warmth about the pavements that suggests the coming blaze of summer, the gutter rivulets and the fountains sparkle with an equal gaiety, and people begin to have their coffee out of doors again. The spring, that on the day Francie was married at Bray was still mainly indicated by east wind and fresh mackerel, was burgeoning in the woods at Versailles with a hundred delicate surprises of blossom and leaf and thick white storm of buds, and tourists were being forced, like asparagus, by the fine weather, and began to appear in occasional twos and threes on the wide square in front of the palace. A remnant of the winter quiet still hung over everything, and a score or two of human beings, dispersed through the endless rooms and gardens, only made more emphatic the greatness of the extent and of the solitude. They certainly did not bring much custom to the little woman who had been beguiled by the fine weather to set up her table of cakes and oranges in a sunny angle of the palace wall, and sat by it all day picturesque and patient in her white cap, while her strip of embroidery lengthened apace in the almost unbroken leisure. Even the first Sunday of April, from which she had hoped great things, brought her, during many bland and dazzling hours, nothing except the purchase of a few sous worth of sweets, and the afternoon was well advanced before she effected a sale of any importance. A tall gentleman, evidently a Monsieur Anglais, was wandering about, and she called to him to tell him of the excellence of her *brioches* and the beauty of her oranges. Ordinarily she had not found that English gentlemen were attracted by her wares, but there was something helpless about this one that gave her confidence. He came up to her table and inspected its dainties with bewildered disfavour, while a comfortable clink of silver came from the pocket in which one hand was fumbling.

'Pain d'épices! Des gâteaux! Ver' goot, ver' sveet!' she said encouragingly, bringing forth her entire English vocabulary with her most winning smile.

'I wish to goodness I knew what the beastly things are made of,' the Englishman murmured to himself. 'I can't go wrong with oranges anyhow. Er – cela, et cela s'il vous plaît,' producing in his turn his whole stock of French, 'combieng.' He had only indicated two oranges, but the little woman had caught the anxious glance at her cakes, and without more ado chose out six of the most highly glazed *brioches*, and by force of will and volubility made her customer not only take them but pay her two francs for them and the oranges.

The tall Englishman strode away round the corner of the palace with these provisions, and along the great terrace towards a solitary figure sitting forlornly at the top of one of the flights of steps that drop in noble succession down to the expanses of artificial water that seem to stretch away into the heart of France.

'I couldn't find anywhere to get tea,' he said as soon as he was within speaking distance; 'I couldn't find anything but an old woman selling oranges, and I got you some of those, and she made me get some cakes as well – I don't know if they're fit to eat.'

Mr Lambert spoke with a very unusual timorousness, as he placed his sticky purchases in Francie's lap, and sat down on the step beside her.

'Oh, thank you awfully, Roddy, I'm sure they're lovely,' she answered, looking at her husband with a smile that was less spontaneous than it used to be, and looking away again immediately.

There was something ineffably wearying to her in the adoring, proprietary gaze that she found so unfailingly fixed upon her whenever she turned her eyes towards him; it seemed to isolate her from other people and set her upon a ridiculous pedestal, with one foolish worshipper declaiming his devotion with the fervour and fatuity of those who for two hours shouted the praises of Diana of the Ephesians. The supernatural mist that blurs the irksome and the ludicrous till it seems like a glory was not before her eyes; every outline was clear to her, with the painful distinctness of a caricature.

'I don't think you could eat the oranges here,' he said, 'they'd be down on us for throwing the skins about. Are you too tired to come down into the gardens where they wouldn't spot us?' He laid his hand on hers, 'You *are* tired. What fools we were to go walking round all those infernal rooms! Why didn't you say you had enough of it?'

270

Francie was aching with fatigue from walking slowly over leagues of polished floor, with her head thrown back in perpetual perfunctory admiration of gilded ceilings and battle pictures, but she got up at once, as much to escape from the heavy warmth of his hand as from the mental languor that made discussion an effort. They went together down the steps, too much jaded by uncomprehended sightseeing to take heed of the supreme expression of art in nature that stretched out before them in mirrors of Triton- and dolphin-guarded water and ordered masses of woodland, and walked slowly along a terrace till they came to another flight of steps that fell suddenly from the stately splendours of the terraces down to the simplicities of a path leading into a grove of trees.

The path wound temptingly on into the wood, with primroses and celandine growing cool and fresh in the young grass on either side of it; the shady greenness was like the music of stringed instruments after the brazen heroics of a military band. They loitered along, and Francie slipped her hand into Lambert's arm, feeling, unconsciously, a little more in sympathy with him, and more at ease with life. She had never pretended either to him or to herself that she was in love with him; her engagement had been the inevitable result of poverty, and aimlessness, and bitterness of soul, but her instinctive leniency towards any man who liked her, joined with her old friendliness for Mr Lambert, made it as easy a way out of her difficulties as any she could have chosen. There was something flattering in the knowledge of her power over a man whom she had been accustomed to look up to, and something, too, that appealed incessantly to her good nature; besides which there is to nearly every human being some comfort in being the first object of another creature's life. She was almost fond of him as she walked beside him, glad to rest her weight on his arm, and to feel how big and reliable he was. There was nothing in the least romantic about having married him, but it was eminently creditable. Her friends in the north side of Dublin had been immensely impressed by it, and she knew enough of Lismoyle society to be aware that there also she would be regarded with gratifying envy. She quite looked forward to meeting Hawkins again, that she might treat him with the cool and assured patronage proper to the heights of her new position; he had himself seared the wound that he had given her, and now she felt that she was thankful to him.

'Hang this path! it has as many turns as a corkscrew,' remarked Mr Lambert, bending his head to avoid a down-stretched branch of hawthorn, covered with baby leaves and giant thorns. 'I thought we'd have come to a seat long before this; if it was Stephen's Green there'd have been twenty by this time.'

'There would, and twenty old men sitting on each of them!' retorted Francie. 'Mercy! who's that hiding behind the tree? Oh, I declare, it's only one of those everlasting old statues, and look at a lot more of them! I wonder if it was that they hadn't room enough for them up in the house that they put them out here in the woods?'

They had come to an enclosed green space in the wood, a daisy-starred oval of grass, holding the spring sunshine in serene remoteness from all the outer world of terraces and gardens, and made mysterious and poetical as a vale in Ida by the strange pale presences that peopled every nook of an ivy-green crag at its further side. A clear pool reflected them, but waveringly, because of the ripples caused by a light drip from the overhanging rock; the trees towered on the encircling high ground and made a wall of silence round the intenser silences of the statues as they leaned and postured in a trance of suspended activity; the only sound was the monotone of the falling water, dropping with a cloistered gravity in the melodious hollow of the cave.

'I'm not going to walk another foot,' said Francie, sitting down on the grass by the water's edge; 'here, give me the oranges, Roddy, no one'll catch us eating them here, and we can peg the skins at that old thing with its clothes dropping off and the harp in its hand.'

It was thus that Mrs Lambert described an Apollo with a lyre who was regarding them from the opposite rock with classic preoccupation. Lambert lighted a cigar, and leaning back on his elbow in the grass, watched Francie's progress through her inelegant meal with the pride of the provider. He looked at her half wonderingly, she was so lovely in his eyes, and she was so incredibly his own; he felt a sudden insanity of tenderness for her that made his heart throb and his cheek redden, and would have ennobled him to the pitch of dying for her on the spot, had such an extravagance been demanded of him. He longed to put his arms round her, and tell her how dear, how adorable, how entirely delightful she was, but he knew that she would probably only laugh at him in that maddening way of hers. or at all events make him feel that she was far less interested in the declaration than he was. He gave a quick sigh, and stretching out his hand laid it on her shoulder as if to assure himself of his ownership of her.

'That dress fits you awfully well. I like you better in that than. in anything.'

'Then I'd better take care and not get the juice on it,' Francie replied, with her mouth full of orange; 'lend me a loan of your handkerchief.'

Lambert removed a bundle of letters and a guide book from his pocket, and finally produced the handkerchief.

'Why, you've a letter there from Charlotte, haven't you?' said Francie, with more interest than she had yet shown, 'I didn't know you had heard again from her.'

'Yes, I did,' said Lambert, putting the letters back in his pocket, 'I wish to goodness we hadn't left our address at the Charing Cross Hotel. People might let a man alone when he's on his honeymoon.'

'What did she say?' inquired Francie lightly. 'Is she cross? The other one she wrote was as sweet as syrup, and "Love to dear Francie" and all.'

'Oh, no, not a bit,' said Mr Lambert, who had been secretly surprised and even slightly wounded by the fortitude with which Miss Mullen had borne the intelligence of his second marriage, 'but she's complaining that my colts have eaten her best white petticoat.'

'You may give her one of my new ones,' suggested Francie.

'Oh yes, she'd like that, wouldn't she?' said Lambert with a chuckle; 'she's so fond of you, y'know!'

'Oh, she's quite friendly with me now, though I know you're dying to make out that she'll not forgive me for marrying you,' said Francie, flinging her last bit of orange-peel at the Apollo; 'you're as proud as Punch about it. I believe you'd have married her, only she wouldn't take you!'

'Is that your opinion!' said Mr Lambert with a smile that conveyed a magnanimous reticence as to the facts of the case; 'you're beginning to be jealous, are you? I think I'd better leave you at home the day I go over to talk the old girl into good humour about her petticoat!'

In his heart Mr Lambert was less comfortable than the tone of his voice might have implied; there had been in the letter, in spite of its friendliness and singular absence of feminine pique, an allusion to that three hundred pounds that circumstances had forced him to accept from her. His honeymoon, and those new clothes that Francie had bought in London, had run away with no end of money, and it would be infernally inconvenient if Charlotte was going, just at this time of all others, to come down on him for money that he had never asked her for. He turned these things over uncomfortably in his mind as he lay back on the grass, looking up at Francie's profile, dark against the soft blue of the sky; and even while he took one of her hands and drew it down to his lips he was saying to himself that he had never yet failed to come round Charlotte when he tried, and it would not be for want of trying if he failed now.

The shadows of the trees began to stretch long fingers across the grass of the Bosquet d'Apollon, and Lambert looked at his watch and began to think of *table d'hôte* at the Louvre Hotel. Pleasant, paradisaically pleasant as it was here in the sun, with Francie's hand in his, and one of his best cigars in his mouth, he had come to the age at which not even Paradise would be enjoyable without a regular dinner hour.

Francie felt chilly and exhausted as they walked back and climbed the innumerable flights of steps that lay between them and the Palace; she privately thought that Versailles would be a horrible place to live in, and not to be compared in any way to Bruff, but, at all events, it would be a great thing to say she had been there, and she could read up all the history part of it in the guide-book when she got back to the hotel. They were to go up the Eiffel tower the next day; that would be some fun, any-how, and to the Hippodrome in the evening, and, though that wouldn't be as good as Hengler's circus, the elephants and horses and things wouldn't be talking French and expecting her to answer them, like the housemaids and shopmen. It was a rest to lean back in the narrow carriage, with the pair of starveling ponies, that rattled along with as much whip-cracking and general pomp as if it were doing ten miles an hour instead of four, and to watch the poplars and villas pass by in placid succession, delightfully devoid of historical interest.

It was getting dark when they reached Paris, and the breeze had become rough and cold. The lamps were shining among the trees on the Boulevards, and the red and green eyes of the cabs and trams crossed and recrossed each other like a tangle of fire-flies. The electric lights of the Place du Louvre were at length in sight, lofty and pale, like globes of imprisoned daylight above the mundane flare of the gas, and Francie's eyes turned towards them with a languid relief. Her old gift of living every moment of her day seemed gone, and here, in this wonderful Paris, that had so suddenly acquired a real instead of a merely geographical existence for her, the stream of foreign life was passing by her, and leaving her face as uninterested and wearied as it ever had

274

been when she looked out of the window at Albatross Villa at the messenger boys and bakers' carts. The street was crowded, and the carriage made slower and slower way through it, till it became finally wedged in the centre of a block. Lambert stood up, and entered upon a one-sided argument with the driver as to how to get out, while Francie remained silent, and indifferent to the situation. A piano-organ at a little distance from them was playing the Boulanger March, with the brilliancy of its tribe, its unfaltering vigour dominating all other sounds. It was a piece of music in which Francie had herself a certain proficiency, and, shutting her eyes with a pang of remembrance, she was back in the Tally Ho drawing room, strumming it on Charlotte's piano, while Mr Hawkins, holding the indignant Mrs Bruff on his lap, forced her unwilling paws to thump a bass. Now the difficult part, in which she always broke down, was being played; he had pretended there that he was her music teacher, and had counted out loud, and rapped her over the knuckles with a tea-spoon, and gone on with all kinds of nonsense. The carriage started forward again with a jerk, and Lambert dropped back into his place beside her.

'Of all the asses unhung these French fellows are the biggest,' he said fervently, 'and that infernal organ banging away the whole time till I couldn't hear my own voice, much less his jabber. Here we are at last, anyhow, and you've got to get out before me.'

The tears had sprung overwhelmingly to her eyes, and she could not answer a word. She turned her back on her husband, and stepping out of the carriage she walked unsteadily across the courtyard in the white glare of the electric light, leaving the hotel servant, who had offered his arm at the carriage door, to draw what conclusions seemed good to him from the spectacle of her wet cheeks and trembling lips. She made for the broad flight of steps, and went blindly up them under the drooping fans of the palms, into the reading room on the first floor. The piano-organ was still audible outside, reiterating to madness the tune that had torn open her past, and she made a hard effort to forget its associations and recover herself, catching up an illustrated paper to hide her face from the people in the room. It was a minute or two before Lambert followed her.

'Here's a go!' he said, coming towards her with a green envelope in his hand, 'here's a wire to say that Sir Benjamin's dead, and they want me back at once.'

41

The morning after Lambert received the tele-
gram announcing Sir Benjamin's death, he dispatched one to Miss
Charlotte Mullen at Gurthnamuckla, in which he asked her to
notify his immediate return to his household at Rosemount. He
had always been in the habit of relying on her help in small as well
as great occasions, and now that he had had that unexpectedly civil
letter from her, he had turned to her at once without giving the
matter much consideration. It was never safe to trust to a servant's
interpretation of the cramped language of a telegram, and moreover, in his self-sufficient belief in his own knowledge of women,
he thought that it would flatter her and keep her in good humour
if he asked her to give directions to his household. He would have
been less confident of his own sagacity had he seen the set of
Miss Mullen's jaw as she read the message, and heard the laugh
which she permitted to herself as soon as Louisa had left the
room.

'It's a pity he didn't hire me to be his major-domo as well as
his steward and stud groom!' she said to herself, 'and his finan-
cier into the bargain! I declare I don't know what he'd do without
me!'

The higher and more subtle side of Miss Mullen's nature had
exacted of the quivering savage that had been awakened by
Lambert's second marriage that the answer to his letter should
be of a conventional and non-committing kind; and so, when
her brain was still on fire with hatred and invective, her facile
pen glided pleasantly over the paper in stale felicitations and
stereotyped badinage. It is hard to ask pity for Charlotte, whose
many evil qualities have without pity been set down, but the seal
of ignoble tragedy had been set on her life; she had not asked
for love, but it had come to her, twisted to burlesque by the
malign hand of fate. There is pathos as well as humiliation in
the thought that such a thing as a soul can be stunted by the
trivialities of personal appearance, and it is a fact not beyond the
reach of sympathy that each time Charlotte stood before her

glass her ugliness spoke to her of failure, and goaded her to revenge.

It was a wet morning, but at half-past eleven o'clock the black horse was put into the phaeton, and Miss Mullen, attired in a shabby mackintosh, set out on her mission to Rosemount. A cold north wind drove the rain in her face as she flogged the old horse along through the shelterless desolation of rock and scrub, and in spite of her mackintosh she felt wet and chilled by the time she reached Rosemount yard. She went into the kitchen by the back door, and delivered her message to Eliza Hackett, whom she found sitting in elegant leisure, retrimming a bonnet that had belonged to the late Mrs Lambert.

'And is it the day after tomorrow, Miss, please?' demanded Eliza Hackett with cold resignation.

'It is, me poor woman, it is,' replied Charlotte, in the tone of facetious intimacy that she reserved for other people's servants. 'You'll have to stir your stumps to get the house ready for them.'

'The house is cleaned down and ready for them as soon as they like to walk into it,' replied Eliza Hackett with dignity, 'and if the new lady faults the drawing-room chimbley for not being swep, the master will know it's not me that's to blame for it, but the sweep that's gone dhrilling with the Mileetia.'

'Oh, she's not the one to find fault with a man for being a soldier any more than yourself, Eliza!' said Charlotte, who had pulled off her wet gloves and was warming her hands. 'Ugh! How cold it is! Is there any place upstairs where I could sit while you were drying my things for me?'

The thought had occurred to her that it would not be un-interesting to look round the house, and as it transpired that fires were burning in the dining room and in Mr Lambert's study she left her wet cloak and hat in the kitchen and ascended to the upper regions. She glanced into the drawing room as she passed its open door, and saw the blue rep chairs ranged in a solemn circle, gazing with all their button eyes at a three-legged table in the centre of the room; the blinds were drawn down, and the piano was covered with a sheet; it was altogether as inexpressive of everything, except bad taste, as was possible. Charlotte passed on to the dining room and stationed herself in front of an in-different fire there, standing with her back to the chimney-piece and her eyes roving about in search of entertainment. Nothing was changed, except that the poor turkey-hen's medicine bottles and pill boxes no longer lurked behind the chimney-piece ornaments; the bare dinner table suggested only how soon Francie

277

would be seated at its head, and Charlotte presently prowled on to Mr Lambert's study at the end of the passage, to look for a better fire, and a room less barren of incident.

The study grate did not fail of its reputation of being the best in the house, and Mr Lambert's chair stood by the hearthrug in wide-armed invitation to the visitor. Charlotte sat down in it and slowly warmed one foot after the other, while the pain rose hot and unconquerable in her heart. The whole room was so gallingly familiar, so inseparably connected with the time when she had still a future, vague and improbable as it was, and could live in sufficient content on its slight sustenance. Another future had now to be constructed, she had already traced out some lines of it, and in the perfecting of these she would henceforward find the cure for what she was now suffering. She roused herself, and glancing towards the table saw that on it lay a heap of unopened newspapers and letters; she got up with alacrity and addressed herself to the congenial task of examining each letter in succession.

'H'm! They're of a very bilious complexion,' she said to herself. 'There's one from Langford,' turning it over and looking at the name on the back. 'I wonder if he's ordering a Victoria for her ladyship? I wouldn't put it past him. Perhaps he'd like me to tell her whose money it was paid Langford's bill last year!'

She fingered the letter longingly, then, taking a hairpin from the heavy coils of her hair, she inserted it under the flap of the envelope. Under her skilful manipulation it opened easily, and without tearing, and she took out its contents. They consisted of a short but severe letter from the head of the firm, asking for 'a speedy settlement of this account, now so long overdue,' and of the account in question. It was a bill of formidable amount, from which Charlotte soon gathered the fact that twenty pounds only of the money she had lent Lambert last May had found its way into the pockets of the coachbuilder. She replaced the bill and letter in the envelope, and, after a minute of consideration, took up for the second time two large and heavy letters that she had thrown aside when first looking through the heap. They had the stamp of the Lismoyle bank upon them, and obviously contained bank books. Charlotte saw at a glance that the hairpin would be of no avail with these envelopes, and after another pause for deliberation she replaced all the letters in their original position, and went down the passage to the top of the kitchen stairs.

'Eliza,' she called out, 'have ye a kettle boiling down there?

Ah, that's right –' as Eliza answered in the affirmative. 'I never knew a well kept kitchen yet without boiling water in it! I'm chilled to me bones, Eliza,' she continued. 'I wonder could you put your hand on a drop of spirits anywhere, and I'd ask ye for a drop of hot grog to keep the life in me, and' – as Eliza started with hospitable speed in search of the materials, – 'let me mix it meself, like a good woman; I know very well I'd be in the lock-up before night if I drank what *you'd* brew for me!'

Retiring on this jest, Miss Mullen returned to the study, and was sitting over the fire with a newspaper when the refreshment she had asked for was brought in.

'I cut ye a sandwich to eat with it, Miss,' said Eliza Hackett, on whom Charlotte's generosity in the matter of Mrs Lambert's clothing had not been thrown away; 'I know meself that as much as the smell o' sperrits would curdle under me nose, takin' them on an empty stomach. Though, indeed, if ye walked Lismoyle's ye'd get no better brandy than what's in that little bottle. 'Tis out o' the poor mistress's medicine chest I got it. Well, well, she's where she won't want brandy now!'

Eliza withdrew with a well-ordered sigh, that, as Charlotte knew, was expressive of future as well as past regret, and Mr Lambert's 'oldest friend' was left in sole possession of his study. She first proceeded to mix herself a tumbler of brandy and water, and then she lifted the lid of the brass punch kettle, and taking one of the envelopes that contained the bank books, she held it in the steam till the gum of the flap melted. The book in it was Lambert's private banking account, and Charlotte studied it for some time with greedy interest, comparing the amounts of the drafts and cash payments with the dates against each. Then she opened the other envelope, keeping a newspaper ready at hand to throw over the books in case of interruption, and found, as she had anticipated, that it was the bank book of the Dysart estate. After this she settled down to hard work for half an hour, comparing one book with another, making lists of figures, sipping her brandy and water meanwhile, and munching Eliza Hackett's sandwiches. Having learned what she could of the bank books, she fastened them up in their envelopes, and, again having recourse to the kettle that was simmering on the hob, she made, with slow, unslaked avidity, an examination of some of the other letters on the table. When everything was tidy again she leaned back in the chair, and remained in deep meditation over her paper of figures, until the dining-room clock sent a muffled reminder through the wall that it was two o'clock.

Ferry Row had, since Charlotte's change of residence, breathed a freer air. Even her heavy washing was now done at home, and her visits to her tenantry might be looked forward to only when rents were known to be due. There was nothing that they expected less than that, on this wet afternoon, so soon, too, after a satisfactory quarter-day, they should hear the well-known rattle of the old phaeton, and see Miss Mullen, in her equally well-known hat and waterproof, driving slowly past house after house, until she arrived at the disreputable abode of Dinny Lydon the tailor. Having turned the cushions of the phaeton upside down to keep them dry, Miss Mullen knocked at the door, and was admitted by Mrs Lydon, a very dirty woman, with a half-finished waistcoat over her arm.

'Oh, ye're welcome, Miss Mullen, ye're welcome! Come in out o' the rain, asthore,' she said, with a manner as greasy as her face. 'Himself have the coat waitin' on ye these three days to thry on.'

'Then I'm afraid the change for death must be on Dinny if he's beginning to keep his promises,' replied Charlotte, adventuring herself fearlessly into the dark interior. 'I'd be thrown out in all my calculations, Dinny, if ye give up telling me lies.'

This was addressed through a reeking fog of tobacco smoke to a half-deformed figure seated on a table by the window.

'Oh, with the help o' God I'll tell yer honour a few lies yet before I die,' replied Dinny Lydon, removing his pipe and the hat which, for reasons best known to himself, he wore while at work, and turning on Charlotte a face that, no less than his name, told of Spanish, if not Jewish blood.

'Well, that's the truth, anyway,' said Charlotte, with a friendly laugh; 'but I won't believe in the coat being ready till I see it. Didn't ye lose your apprentice since I saw ye?'

'Is it that young gobsther?' rejoined Mrs Lydon acridly, as she tendered her unsavoury assistance to Charlotte in the removal of her waterproof; 'if that one was in the house yer coat wouldn't be finished in a twelvemonth with all the time Dinny lost cursing him. Faith! it was last week he hysted his sails and away with him. Mind ye, 'twas he was the first-class puppy!'

'Was it the trade he didn't like?' asked Charlotte; 'or was it the skelpings he got from Dinny?'

'Throth, it was not, but two plates in the sate of his breeches was what he faulted, and the divil mend him!'

'Two plates!' exclaimed Charlotte, in not unnatural bewilderment; 'what in the name of furtune was he doing with them?'

'Well, indeed, Miss Mullen, with respex t'ye, when he came here he hadn't as much rags on him as'd wipe a candlestick,' replied Mrs Lydon, with fluent spitefulness; 'yerself knows that ourselves has to be losing with puttin' clothes on thim apprentices, an' feedin' them as lavish and as natty as ye'd feed a young bonnuf, an' afther all they'd turn about an' say they never got so much as the wettin' of their mouths of male nor tay nor praties –' Mrs Lydon replenished her lungs with a long breath, – 'and this lad the biggest dandy of them all, that wouldn't be contint without Dinny'd cut the brea'th of two fingers out of a lovely throusers that was a little sign bulky on him and was gethered into nate plates –'

'Oh, it's well known beggars can't bear heat,' said Charlotte, interrupting for purposes of her own a story that threatened to expand unprofitably, 'and that was always the way with all the M'Donaghs. Didn't I meet that lad's cousin, Shamus Bawn, driving a new side-car this morning, and his father only dead a week. I suppose now he's got the money he thinks he'll never get to the end of it, though indeed it isn't so long since I heard he was looking for money, and found it hard enough to get it.'

Mrs Lydon gave a laugh of polite acquiescence, and wondered inwardly whether Miss Mullen had as intimate a knowledge of everyone's affairs as she seemed to have of Shamus Bawn's.

'Oh, they say a manny a thing –' she observed with well simulated sanity. 'Arrah! *dheen dheffeth*, Dinny! *thurrum cussoge um'na.*'

'Yes, hurry on and give me the coat, Dinny,' said Charlotte, displaying that knowledge of Irish that always came as a shock to those who were uncertain as to its limitations.

The tailor untwisted his short legs and descended stiffly to the floor, and having helped Charlotte into the coat, pushed her into the light of the open door, and surveyed his handiwork with his large head on one side, and the bitten ends of thread still hanging on his lower lip.

'It turned well,' he said, passing his hand approvingly over Miss Mullen's thick shoulder; 'afther all, the good stuff's the best; that's fine honest stuff that'll wear forty of them other thrash. That's the soort that'll shtand.'

'To the death!' interjected Mrs Lydon fervently.

'How many wrinkles are there in the back?' said Charlotte; 'tell me the truth now, Dinny; remember 'twas only last week you were "making your sowl" at the mission.'

'Tchah!' said Dinny Lydon contemptuously, 'it's little I regard the mission, but I wouldn't be bothered tellin' ye lies about the likes o' this,' surreptitiously smoothing as he spoke a series of ridges above the hips; 'that's a grand clane back as ever I see.'

'How independent he is about his missions!' said Charlotte jibingly. 'Ha! Dinny, me man, if you were sick you'd be the first to be roaring for the priest!'

'Faith, divil a roar,' returned the atheistical Dinny; 'if I couldn't knock the stone out of the gap for meself, the priest couldn't do it for me.'

'Oh, Gaad! Dinny, have conduct before Miss Mullen!' cried Mrs Lydon.

'He may say what he likes, if he wouldn't drop candle grease on my jacket,' said Charlotte, who had taken off the coat and was critically examining every seam; 'or, indeed, Mrs Lydon, I believe it was yourself did it!' she exclaimed, suddenly intercepting an indescribable glance of admonition from Mrs Dinny to her husband; 'that's wax candle grease! I believe you wore it yourself at Michael M'Donagh's wake, and that's why it was finished four days ago.'

Mrs Lydon uttered a shriek of merriment at the absurdity of the suggestion, and then fell to disclaimers so voluble as at once to convince Miss Mullen of her guilt. The accusation was not pressed home, and Dinny's undertaking to remove the grease with a hot iron was accepted with surprising amiability. Charlotte sat down on a chair whose shattered frame bore testimony to the renowned violence of Mrs Lydon when under the influence of liquor, and encouraging the singed and half-starved cat on to her lap, she addressed herself to conversation.

'Wasn't Michael M'Donagh husband to your mother's cousin?' she said to the tailor; 'I'm told he had a very large funeral.'

'He had that,' answered Dinny; pushing the black hair back from his high forehead, and looking more than ever like a Jewish rabbi; 'three priests, an' five an' twenty cars, an' fifteen pounds of althar money.'

'Well, the three priests have a right to pray their big best for him, with five pounds apiece in their pockets,' remarked Charlotte; 'I suppose it was the M'Donagh side gave the most of the altar. Those brothers of old Michael's are all stinking of money.'

'Oh, they're middlin' snug,' said Dinny, who had just enough family feeling for the M'Donaghs to make him chary of admitting their wealth; 'annyway, they're able to slap down their five shillin's or their ten shillin' bit upon the althar as well as another.'

'Who got the land?' asked Charlotte, stroking the cat's filthy head, and thereby perfuming her fingers with salt fish.

'Oh, how do I know what turning and twisting of keys there was in it afther himself dyin'?' said the tailor, with the caution which his hearers understood to be a fatiguing but inevitable convention; 'they say the daughter got the biggest half, an' Shamus Bawn got the other. There's where the battle'll be between them.' He laughed sardonically, as he held up the hot iron and spat upon it to ascertain its heat.

'He'd better let his sister alone,' said Charlotte. 'Shamus Bawn has more land this minute than he has money enough to stock, with that farm he got from Mr Lambert the other day, without trying to get more.'

'Oh, Jim's not so poor altogether that he couldn't bring the law on her if he'd like,' said Dinny, immediately resenting the slighting tone; 'he got a good lump of a fortune with the wife.'

'Ah, what's fifty pounds!' said Charlotte scornfully. 'I daresay he wanted every penny of it to pay the fine on Knocklara.'

'Arrah, fifty pounds! God help ye!' exclaimed Dinny Lydon with superior scorn. 'No, but a hundhred an' eighty was what he put down on the table to Lambert for it, and it's little but he had to give the two hundhred itself.'

Mrs Lydon looked up from the hearth where she was squatted, fanning the fire with her red petticoat to heat another iron for her husband. 'Sure I know Dinny's safe tellin' it to a lady,' she said, rolling her dissolute cunning eye from her husband to Miss Mullen; 'but ye'll not spake of it, asthore. Jimmy had some dhrink taken when he shown Dinny the docket, because Lambert said he wouldn't give the farm so chape to e'er a one but Jimmy, an' indeed Jimmy'd break every bone in our body if he got the wind of a word that 'twas through us the neighbours had it to say he had that much money with him. Jimmy's very close in himself that way.'

Charlotte laughed good-humouredly. 'Oh, there's no fear of me, Mrs. Lydon. It's no affair of mine either way,' she said reassuringly. 'Here, hurry with me jacket, Dinny; I'll be glad enough to have it on me going home.'

42

Sir Benjamin Dysart's funeral was an event of the past. It was a full three weeks since the family vault in Lismoyle Churchyard had closed its door upon that ornament of county society; Lady Dysart's friends were beginning to recover from the strain of writing letters of condolence to her on her bereavement, and Christopher, after sacrificing to his departed parent's memory a week of perfect sailing weather, had had his boat painted, and had relapsed into his normal habit of spending as much of his time as was convenient on the lake.

There was still thè mingled collapse and stir in the air that comes between the end of an old régime and the beginning of a new. Christopher had resigned his appointment at Copenhagen, feeling that his life would, for the future, be vaguely filled with new duties and occupations, but he had not yet discovered anything very novel to do beyond signing his name a good many times, and trying to become accustomed to hearing himself called Sir Christopher; occupations that seemed rather elementary in the construction of a career. His want of initiative energy in everyday matters kept him motionless and apathetic, waiting for his new atmosphere to make itself palpable to him, and prepared to resign himself to its conditions. He even, in his unquenchable self-consciousness, knew that it would be wholesome for him if these were such as he least liked; but in the meantime he remained passively unsettled, and a letter from Lord Castlemore, in which his tact and conscientiousness as a secretary were fully set forth, roused no outside ambition in him. He re-read it on a shimmering May morning, with one arm hanging over the tiller of his boat, as she crept with scarcely breathing sails through the pale streaks of calm that lay like dreams upon the lake. He was close under the woods of Bruff, close enough to feel how still and busy they were in the industry of spring. It seemed to him that the sound of the insects was like the humming of her loom, and almost mechanically he turned over the envelope of Lord

Castlemore's letter, and began in the old familiar way to scrawl a line or two on the back of it.

The well-known crest, however, disconcerted his fancy, and he fell again to ruminating upon the letter itself. If this expressed the sum of his abilities, diplomatic life was certainly not worth living. Tact and conscientiousness were qualities that would grace the discharge of a doctor's butler, and might be expected from anyone of the most ordinary intelligence. He could not think that his services to his country, as concentrated in Lord Castlemore, were at all remarkable; they had given him far less trouble than the most worthless of those efforts in prose and verse that, as he thought contemptuously, were like the skeletons that mark the desert course of a caravan; he did not feel the difficulty, and he, therefore, thought the achievement small. A toying breeze fluttered the letter in his hand, and the boat tilted languidly in recognition of it. The water began to murmur about the keel, and Christopher presently found himself gliding smoothly towards the middle of the lake.

He looked across at Lismoyle, spreading placidly along the margin of the water, and as he felt the heat of the sun and the half-forgotten largeness of summer in the air, he could have believed himself back in the August of last year, and he turned his eyes to the trees of Rosemount as if the sight of them would bring disillusionment. It was some time now since he had first been made ashamed of the discovery that disillusionment also meant relief. For some months he had clung to his dream; at first helplessly, with a sore heart, afterwards with a more conscious taking hold, as of something gained, that made life darker, but for ever richer. It had been torture of the most simple, unbearable kind, to drive away from Tally Ho, with the knowledge that Hawkins was preferred to him; but sentiment had deftly usurped the place of his blind suffering, and that stage came that is almost inevitable with poetic natures, when the artistic sense can analyse sorrow, and sees the beauty of defeat. Then he had heard that Francie was going to marry Lambert, and the news had done more in one moment to disillusion him than common sense could do in years. The thought stung him with a kind of horror for her that she could tolerate such a fate as marrying Roddy Lambert. He knew nothing of the tyrannies of circumstance. To prosperous young men like Christopher, poverty, except barefooted and in rags, is a name, and unpaid bills a joke. That Albatross Villa could have driven her to the tremendous surrender of marriage was a thing incredible. All that was left for him to believe was that he had been mistaken, and that the lucent quality that he thought he had found in her soul had existed only in his imagination. Now when he thought of her face it was with a curious half regret that so beautiful a thing should no longer have any power to move him. Some sense of loss remained, but it was charged with self pity for the loss of an ideal. Another man in Christopher's position would not probably have troubled himself about ideals, but Christopher, fortunately, or unfortunately for him, was not like other men.

The fact must even be faced that he had probably never been in love with her, according to the common acceptation of the term. His intellect exhausted his emotions and killed them with solicitude, as a child digs up a flower to see if it is growing, and his emotions themselves had a feminine refinement, but lacked the feminine quality of unreasoning pertinacity. From self-pity for the loss of an ideal to gratitude for an escape is not far to go, and all that now remained to him of bitterness was a gentle self-contempt for his own inadequacy in falling in love, as in everything else.

It may be imagined that in Lismoyle Francie was a valued and almost invariable topic of conversation. Each visitor to Rosemount went there in the character of a scout, and a detailed account of her interview was published on every possible occasion.

'Well, I took my time about calling on her,' observed Mrs Baker; 'I thought I'd let her see I was in no hurry.'

Mrs Corkran, with whom Mrs Baker was having tea, felt guiltily conscious of having called on Mrs Lambert two days after her arrival, and hastened to remind the company of the pastoral nature of the attention.

'Oh, of course we know clergymen's families can't pick their company,' went on Mrs Baker, dismissing the interruption not without a secret satisfaction that Carrie Beattie, who, in the absence of Miss Corkran, was pouring out tea for her future mother-in-law, should see that other people did not consider the Rev. Joseph such a catch as she did. 'Only that Lambert's such a friend of Mr Baker's and always banked with him, I declare I don't know that I'd have gone at all. I assure you it gave me quite a turn to see her stuck up there in poor Lucy Lambert's chair, talking about the grand hotels that she was in, in London and Paris, as if she never swept out a room or cleaned a saucepan in her life.'

286

'She had all the walls done round with those penny fans,' struck in Miss Kathleen Baker, 'and a box of French bongbongs out on the table; and oh, mamma! did you notice the big photograph of him and her together on the chimney-piece?'

'I could notice nothing, Kathleen, and I didn't want to notice them,' replied Mrs Baker; 'I could think of nothing but of what poor Lucy Lambert would say to see her husband dancing attendance on that young hussy without so much as a mourning ring on him, and her best tea-service thrashed about as if it was kitchen delf.'

'Was he very devoted, Mrs Baker?' asked Miss Beattie with a simper.

'Oh, I suppose he was,' answered Mrs Baker, as if in contempt for any sentiment inspired by Francie, 'but I can't say I observed anything very particular.'

'Oh, then, *I* did!' said Miss Baker with a nod of superior intelligence; 'I was watching them all the time; every word she uttered he was listening to it, and when she asked for the tea cosy he *flew* for it!'

'Eliza Hackett told my Maria there was shocking waste going on in the house now; fires in the drawing room from eight o'clock in the morning, and this the month of May!' said Mrs Corkran with an approving eye at the cascade of cut paper that decked her own grate, 'and the cold meat given to the boy that cleans the boots!'

'Roddy Lambert'll be sorry for it some day when it's too late,' said Mrs Baker darkly, 'but men are all alike; it's out of sight out of mind with them!'

'Oh, Mrs Baker,' wheezed Mrs Corkran with asthmatic fervour, 'I think you're altogether too cynical; I'm sure that's not your opinion of Mr Baker.'

'I don't know what he might do if I was dead,' replied Mrs Baker, 'but I'll answer for it he'll not be carrying on with Number Two while *I'm* alive, like other people I know!'

'Oh, don't say such things before these young ladies,' said Mrs Corkran; 'I wish them no greater blessing of Providence than a good husband, and I think I may say that dear Carrie will find one in my Joseph.'

The almost death-bed solemnity of this address paralysed the conversation for a moment, and Miss Beattie concealed her blushes by going to the window to see whose was the vehicle that had just driven by.

287

'Oh, it's Mr Hawkins!' she exclaimed, feeling the importance of the information.

Kathleen Baker sprang from her seat and ran to the window. 'So it is!' she cried, 'and I bet you sixpence he's going to Rosemount! My goodness, I wish it was today we had gone there!'

43

Hawkins had, like Mrs Baker, been in no hurry to call upon the bride. He had seen her twice in church, he had once met her out driving with her husband, and, lastly, he had come upon her face to face in the principal street of Lismoyle, and had received a greeting of aristocratic hauteur, as remarkable as the newly acquired English accent in which it was delivered. After these things a visit to her was unavoidable, and, in spite of a bad conscience, he felt, when he at last set out for Rosemount, an excitement that was agreeable after the calm of life at Lismoyle.

There was no one in the drawing room when he was shown into it, and as the maid closed the door behind him he heard a quick step run through the hall and up the stairs. 'Gone to put on her best bib and tucker,' he said to himself with an increase of confidence; 'I'll bet she saw me coming.' The large photograph alluded to by Miss Baker was on the chimney-piece, and he walked over and examined it with great interest. It obeyed the traditions of honeymoon portraits, and had the inevitable vulgarity of such; Lambert, sitting down, turned the leaves of a book, and Francie, standing behind him, rested one hand on his shoulder, while the other held a basket of flowers. In spite of its fatuity as a composition, both portraits were good, and they had moreover an air of prosperity and new clothes that Mr Hawkins found to be almost repulsive. He studied the photograph with deepening distaste until he was aware of a footstep at the door, and braced himself for the encounter, with his heart beating uncomfortably and unexpectedly.

They shook hands with the politeness of slight acquaintance, and sat down, Hawkins thinking he had never seen her look so pretty or so smart, and wondering what he was going to talk to her about. It was evidently going to be war to the knife, he thought, as he embarked haltingly upon the weather, and found that he was far less at his ease than he had expected to be.

'Yes, it's warmer here than it was in England,' said Francie, looking languidly at the rings on her left hand; 'we were perished there after Paris.'

She felt that the familiar mention of such names must of necessity place her in a superior position, and she was so stimulated by their associations with her present grandeur that she raised her eyes, and looked at him. Their eyes met with as keen a sense of contact as if their hands had suddenly touched, and each, with a perceptible jerk, looked away.

'You say that Paris was hot, was it?' said Hawkins, with something of an effort. 'I haven't been there since I went with some people the year before last, and it was as hot then as they make it. I thought it rather a hole.'

'Oh, indeed?' said Francie, chillingly; 'Mr Lambert and I enjoyed it greatly. You've been here all the spring, I suppose?'

'Yes; I haven't been out of this place except for Punchestown, since I came back from leave;' then with a reckless feeling that he would break up this frozen sea of platitudes, 'since that time that I met you on the pier at Kingstown.'

'Oh yes,' said Francie, as if trying to recall some unimportant incident; 'you were there with the Dysarts, weren't you?'

Hawkins became rather red. She was palpably overdoing it, but that did not diminish the fact that he was being snubbed, and though he might, in a general and guarded way, have admitted that he deserved it, he realized that he bitterly resented being snubbed by Francie.

'Yes,' he said, with an indifference as deliberately exaggerated as her own, 'I travelled over with them. I remember how surprised we were to see you and Mr Lambert there.'

She felt the intention on his part to say something disagreeable, and it stung her more than the words.

'Why were you surprised?' she asked coolly.

'Well – er – I don't exactly know,' stammered Mr Hawkins, a good deal taken aback by the directness of the inquiry; 'we didn't exactly know where you were – thought Lambert was at Lismoyle, you know.' He began to wish he had brought Cursiter with him; no one could have guessed that she would have turned into such a cat and given herself such airs; her ultra-refinement, and her

289

affected accent, and her exceeding prettiness, exasperated him in a way that he could not have explained, and though the visit did not fail of excitement, he could not flatter himself that he was taking quite the part in it that he had expected. Certainly Mrs Lambert was not maintaining the rôle that he had allotted her; huffiness was one thing, but infernal swagger was quite another. It is painful for a young man of Mr Hawkins' type to realize that an affection that he has inspired can wane and even die, and Francie's self-possession was fast robbing him of his own.

'I hear that your regiment is after being ordered to India?' she said cheerfully, when it became apparent that Hawkins could find no more to say.

'Yes, so they say; next trooping season will about see us, I expect, and they're safe to send us to Aldershot first, so we may be out of this at any minute.' He glanced at her as he spoke, to see how she took it.

'Oh, that'll be very nice for you,' answered Francie, still more cheerfully. 'I suppose,' she went on with her most aristocratic drawl, 'that you'll be married before you go out?'

She had arranged the delivery of this thrust before she came downstairs, and it glided from her tongue as easily as she could have wished.

'Yes, I daresay I shall,' he answered defiantly, though the provokingly ready blush of a fair man leaped to his face. He looked at her, angry with himself for reddening, and angrier with her for blazoning her indifference, by means of a question that seemed to him the height of bad taste and spitefulness. As he looked, the colour that burned in his own face repeated itself in hers with slow relentlessness; at the sight of it a sudden revulsion of feeling brought him dangerously near to calling her by her name, with reproaches for her heartlessness, but before the word took form she had risen quickly, and, saying something incoherent about ordering tea, moved towards the bell, her head turned from him with the helpless action of a shy child.

Hawkins, hardly knowing what he was doing, started forward, and as he did so the door opened, and a well-known voice announced:

'Miss Charlotte Mullen!'

The owner of the voice advanced into the room, and saw, as anyone must have seen, the flushed faces of its two occupants, and felt that nameless quality in the air that tells of interruption.

'I took the liberty of announcing myself,' she said, with her most affable smile; 'I knew you were at home, as I saw Mr Hawkins' trap at the door, and I just walked in.'

As she shook hands and sat down she expanded easily into a facetious description of the difficulties of getting her old horse along the road from Gurthnamuckla, and by the time she had finished her story Hawkins' complexion had regained its ordinary tone, and Francie had resumed the air of elegant nonchalance appropriate to the importance of the married state. Nothing, in fact, could have been more admirable than Miss Mullen's manner. She praised Francie's new chair covers and Indian tea; she complimented Mr Hawkins on his new pony; even going so far as to reproach him for not having been out to Gurthnamuckla to see her, till Francie felt some pricks of conscience about the sceptical way that she and Lambert had laughed together over Charlotte's amiability when she paid her first visit to them. She found inexpressible ease in the presence of a third person as capable as Charlotte of carrying on a conversation with the smallest possible assistance; sheltered by it she slowly recovered from her mental overthrow, and, furious as she was with Hawkins for his part in it, she was beginning to be able to patronize him again by the time that he got up to go away.

'Well, Francie, my dear child,' began Charlotte, as soon as the door had closed behind him, 'I've scarcely had a word with you since you came home. You had such a reception the last day I was here that I had to content myself with talking to Mrs Beattie, and hearing all about the price of underclothes. Indeed I had a good mind to tell her that only for your magnanimity she wouldn't be having so much to say about Carrie's trousseau!'

'Indeed she was welcome to him!' said Francie, putting her chin in the air, 'that little wretch, indeed!'

It was one of the moments when she touched the extreme of satisfaction in being married, and in order to cover, for her own and Charlotte's sake, the remembrance of that idiotic blush, she assumed a little extra bravado.

'Talking of your late admirers – ' went on Charlotte, 'for I hope for poor Roddy's sake they're not present ones – I never saw a young fellow so improved in his manners as Mr Hawkins. There was a time I didn't fancy him – as you may remember, though we've agreed to say nothing more about our old squabbles – but I think he's chastened by adversity. That engagement, you know – ' she paused, and cast a side-long, unobtrusive glance at Francie. 'He's not the first young man that's been whipped in before marriage as well as after it, and I think the more he looks at it the less he likes it.'

'He's been looking at it a long time now,' said Francie with a laugh that was intended to be careless, but into which a sneer made its way. 'I wonder Roddy isn't in,' she continued, changing the subject to one in which no pitfalls lurked; 'I wouldn't be surprised if he's gone to Gurthnamuckla to see you, Charlotte; he's been saying ever since we came back he wanted to have a talk with you, but he's been so busy he hadn't a minute.'

'If I'm not greatly mistaken,' said Charlotte, standing up so as to be able to see out of the window, 'here's the man of the house himself. What horse is that he's on?' her eyes taking in with unwilling admiration the swaggering ease of seat and square-ness of shoulder that had so often captivated her taste, as Lambert, not unaware of spectators at the window, overcame much callow remonstrance on the part of the young horse he was riding, at being asked to stand at the door till a boy came round to take him.

'Oh, that's the new four-year-old that Roddy had taken in off Gurthnamuckla while we were away,' said Francie, leaning her elbow against the shutter and looking out too. 'He's an awful wild young brat of a thing! Look at the way he's hoisting now! Roddy says he'll have me up on him before the summer's out, but I tell him that if he does I won't be on him long.' Her eyes met her husband's, and she laughed and tapped on the glass, beckoning imperiously to him to come in.

Charlotte turned away from the window, and when, a few minutes afterwards, Mr Lambert came into the room, the visitor had put her gloves on, and was making her farewells to her hostess.

'No, Roddy,' she said, 'I must be off now. I'm like the beggars, "tay and turn out" is my motto. But supposing now that you bring this young lady over to lunch with me tomorrow – no, not tomorrow, that's Sunday – come on Monday. How would that suit your book?'

Lambert assented with a good grace that struck Francie as being wonderfully well assumed, and followed Miss Mullen out to put her in her phaeton.

Francie closed the door behind them, and sat down. She was glad she had met Hawkins and got it over, and as she re-viewed the incidents of his visit, she thought that on the whole she had come very near her own ideal behaviour. Cool, sarcastic, and dignified, even though she had, for one moment, got a little

292

red, he could not but feel that she had acted as became a married lady, and shown him his place once for all. As for him, he had been horrible, she thought bitterly; sitting up and talking to her as if he had never seen her before, and going on as if he had never – she got up hastily as if to escape from the hateful memories of last year that thrust themselves suddenly into her thoughts. How thankful she was that she had shown him she was not inconsolable; she wished that Roddy had come in while he was there, and had stood over him, and overshadowed him with his long legs and broad shoulders, and his air of master of the house. Why on earth had Charlotte praised him? Gurthnamuckla must have had the most extraordinarily sweetening effect upon her, for she seemed to have a good word for everybody now, and Roddy's notion that she would want to be coaxed into a good temper was all nonsense, and conceited nonsense too, and so she would tell him. It was not in Francie's light, wholesome nature to bear malice; the least flutter of the olive branch, the faintest glimmer of the flag of truce, was enough to make her forgive an injury and forget an insult.

When her husband came back she turned towards him with a sparkle in her eye.

'Well, Roddy, I hope you squeezed her hand when you were saying good-bye? I daresay now you'll want me to believe that it's all in honour of you that she's asked us over to lunch tomorrow, and I suppose that's what she was telling you out in the hall? Aren't you sorry you didn't marry her instead of me?'

Lambert did not answer, but came over to where she was standing, and putting his arm round her, drew her towards him and kissed her with a passion that seemed too serious an answer to her question. She could not know, as she laughed and hid her face from him, that he was saying to himself, 'Of course he was bound to come and call, he'd have had to do that, no matter who she was!'

44

Spring, that year, came delicately in among the Galway hills; in primroses, in wild bursts of gorse, and in the later snow of hawthorn, unbeaten by the rain or the wet west wind of rougher seasons. A cuckoo had dropped out of space into the copse at the back of Gurthnamuckla, and kept calling there with a lusty sweetness; a mist of green breathed upon the trees, and in the meadows by the lake a corncrake was adding a diffident guttural or two to the chirruping chorus of coots and moorhens. Mr Lambert's three-year-olds grew and flourished on the young rich grass, and, in the turbulence of their *joie de vivre*, hunted the lambs, and bit the calves, and jumped every barrier that the ingenuity of Miss Mullen's herdsmen could devise. 'Those brutes must be put into the Stone Field,' the lady of the house had said, regarding their gambols with a sour eye; 'I don't care whether the grass is good or bad, they'll have to do with it;' and when she and her guests went forth after their lunch to inspect the farm in general and the young horses in particular, it was to the Stone Field that they first bent their steps.

No one who has the idea of a green-embowered English lane can hope to realize the fortified alley that wound through the heart of the pastures of Gurthnamuckla, and was known as the Farm Lane. It was scarcely wide enough for two people to walk abreast; loose stone walls, of four or five feet in thickness, towered on either side of it as high as the head of a tall man; to meet a cow in it involved either retreat or the perilous ascent of one of the walls. It embodied the simple expedient of bygone farmers for clearing their fields of stones, and contained raw material enough to build a church. Charlotte, Mr Lambert, and Francie advanced in single file along its meaningless windings, until it finished its career at the gate of the Stone Field, a long tongue of pasture that had the lake for a boundary on three of its sides, and was cut off from the mainland by a wall not inferior in height and solidity to those of the lane.

'There, Roddy,' said Miss Mullen, as she opened the gate,

'there's where I had to banish them, and I don't think they're too badly off.'

The young horses were feeding at the farthest point of the field, fetlock deep in the flowery grass, with the sparkling blue of the lake making a background to their slender shapes.

'They look like money, Charlotte, I think. That brown filly ought to bring a hundred at least next Ballinasloe fair, when she knows how to jump,' said Lambert, as he and Charlotte walked across the field, leaving Francie, who saw no reason for pretending an interest that was not expected of her, to amuse herself by picking cowslips near the gate.

'I'm glad to hear you say that, Roddy,' replied Charlotte. 'It's a comfort to think anything looks like money these bad times; I've never known prices so low.'

'They're lower than I ever thought they'd go, by Jove,' Lambert answered gloomily. 'I'm going up to Mayo, collecting, next week, and if I don't do better there than I've done here, I daresay Dysart won't think so much of his father's shoes after all.'

He was striding along, taking no trouble to suit his pace to Charlotte's, and perhaps the indifference to her companionship that it showed, as well as the effort involved in keeping beside him, had the effect of irritating her.

'Maybe he might think them good enough to kick people out with,' she said with a disagreeable laugh; 'I remember, in the good old times, when my father and Sir Benjamin ruled the roost, we heard very little about bad collections.'

It struck Lambert that though this was the obvious moment for that business talk that he had come over for, it was not a propitious one. 'I wonder if the macaroni cheese disagreed with her?' he thought; 'it was beastly enough to do it, anyhow.' 'You may remember,' he said aloud, 'that in the good old times the property was worth just about double what it is now, and a matter of three or four hundred pounds either way made no difference to signify.'

'D'ye think ye'll be that much short this time?'

She darted the question at him with such keenness that Lambert inwardly recoiled before it, though it was the point to which he had wished to bring her.

'Oh, of course one can't be sure,' he said, retreating from his position; 'but I've just got a sort of general idea that I'll be a bit under the mark this time.'

He was instinctively afraid of Charlotte, but in this moment he knew, perhaps for the first time, how much afraid. In theory he believed in his old power over her, and clung to the belief with the fatuity of a vain man, but he had always been uncomfortably aware that she was intellectually his master, and though he thought he could still sway her heart with a caress, he knew he could never outwit her.

'Oh, no one knows better than I do what a thankless business it is, these times,' said Charlotte with a reassuring carelessness; 'it's a case of "pull devil, pull baker," though indeed I don't know under which head poor Christopher Dysart comes. And as we've got on to the sordid topic of money, Roddy, I'm not going to ask yer honour for a reduction of the rint, ye needn't be afraid – but I've been rather pinched by the expense I've been put to in doing up the house and stocking the farm, and it would be mighty convaynient to *me*, if it would be convaynient to *you*, to let me have a hundred pounds or so of that money I lent you last year.'

'Well – Charlotte – ' began Lambert, clearing his throat, and striking with his stick at the heads of the buttercups, 'that's the very thing I've been anxious to talk to you about. The fact is, I've had an awful lot of expense myself this last twelve months, and, as I told you, I can't lay a finger on anything except the interest of what poor Lucy left me – and – er – I'd give you any percentage you like, you know –?' He broke off for an instant, and then began again. 'You can see for yourself what a sin it would be to sell those things now,' he pointed at the three young horses, 'when they'll just bring three times the money this time next year.'

'Oh yes,' said Charlotte, 'but my creditors might say it was more of a sin for me not to pay my debts.'

Lambert stood still, and dug his stick into the ground, and Charlotte, watching him, knew that she had put in her sickle and reaped her first sheaf.

'All right,' he said, biting his lip, 'if your creditors can manage to hold out till after the fair next week, I daresay by selling every horse I've got I could let you have your money then.' As he made the offer, he trusted that its quixotic heroism would make Charlotte ashamed of herself; no woman could possibly expect such a sacrifice as that from a man, and the event proved that he was right.

This was not the sacrifice that Miss Mullen wished for.

'Oh, pooh, pooh, Roddy! you needn't take me up in such earnest as that,' she said in her most friendly voice, and Lambert congratulated himself upon his astuteness; 'I only meant that if you could let me have a hundred or so in the course of the next month, it would be a help to my finances.'

Lambert could not bring himself to admit that he was as little able to pay her one hundred as three; at all events, a month would give him time to look about him, and if he made a good collection he could easily borrow it from the estate account.

'Oh, if that's all,' he answered, affecting more relief than he felt, ' I can let you have it in a fortnight or so.'

They were near the lake by this time, and the young horses feeding by its margin flung up their heads and stared in statuesque surprise at their visitors.

'They'll not let you near them,' said Charlotte, as Lambert walked slowly towards them; 'they're as wild as hawks. And, goodness me! that girl's gone out of the field and left the gate open! Wait a minute till I go back and shut it.'

Lambert stood and looked after her as she hastened cumbrously back towards the gate, and wondered how he had ever liked her, or brought himself to have any dealings with her, and his eye left her quickly to follow the red parasol that, moving slowly along above the grey wall, marked Francie's progress along the lane. Charlotte hurried on towards the g tc, well satisfied with the result of her conversation, and she was w t in some fifty yards of it when a loud and excited shout from Lambert, combined with the thud of galloping hoofs, made her start round. The young horses had been frightened by Lambert's approach, and after one or two circling swoops, had seen the open gate, and, headed by the brown filly, were careering towards it.

'The gate! Charlotte!' roared Lambert, rushing futilely after the horses, 'shut the gate!'

Charlotte was off in an instant, realizing as quickly as Lambert what might happen if Francie were charged in the narrow lane by this living avalanche; even in the first instant of comprehension another idea had presented itself. Should she stumble and so not reach the gate in time? It was fascinatingly simple, but it was too simple, and it was by no means certain.

Charlotte ran her hardest, and, at some slight personal risk, succeeded in slamming the gate in the face of the brown filly, as she and her attendant squires dashed up to it. There was a great deal of slipping about and snorting, before the trio recovered themselves, and retired to pass off their discomfiture in a series of dislocating bucks and squealing snaps at each other, and then

Charlotte, purple from her exertions, advanced to meet Lambert with the smile of the benefactor broad upon her face. His was blotched white and red with fright and running; without a breath left to thank her, he took her hand, and wrung it with a more genuine emotion than he had ever before felt for her.

Francie, meanwhile, strolled slowly up the lane towards the house, with her red parasol on her shoulder and her bunch of cowslips in her hand. She knew that the visit to the Stone Field was only the preliminary to a crawling inspection of every cow, sheep, and potato ridge on the farm, and she remembered that she had seen a novel of attractive aspect on the table in the drawing room. She felt singularly uninterested in everything; Gurthnamuckla was nothing but Tally Ho over again on a larger and rather cleaner scale; the same servants, the same cats, the same cockatoo, the same leathery pastry and tough mutton. Last summer these things had mingled themselves easily into her every-day enjoyment of life, as amusing and not unpleasant elements; now she promised herself that, no matter what Roddy said, this was the last time she would come to lunch with Charlotte.

Roddy was very good to her and all that, but there was nothing new about him either, and marriage was an awful humdrum thing after all. She looked back with something of regret to the crowded drudging household at Albatross Villa; she had at least had something to do there, and she had not been lonely; she often found herself very lonely at Rosemount. Before she reached the house she decided that she would ask Ida Fitzpatrick down to stay with her next month, and give her her return ticket, and a summer dress, and a new –. Her thoughts came to a startling full stop as, round the corner of the house, she found herself face to face with Mr Hawkins.

She had quite made up her mind that when she next saw him she would merely bow to him, but she had not reckoned on the necessities of such an encounter as this, and before she had time to collect herself she was shaking hands with him and listening to his explanation of what had brought him there.

'I met Miss Mullen after church yesterday,' he said awkwardly, 'and she asked me to come over this afternoon. I was just going out to look for her.'

'Oh, really,' said Francie, moving on towards the hall door; 'she and Mr Lambert are off in those fields there.'

Hawkins stood looking irresolutely at her as she walked up to the open door that in Miss Duffy's time had been barricaded

298

against all comers. She went in as unswervingly as if she had already forgotten his existence, and then yielding, according to his custom, to impulse, he followed her.

She had already taken up a book, and was seated in a chair by the window when he came in, and she did not even lift her eyes at his entrance. He went over to the polished centre table, and, opening a photograph book, turned over a few of the leaves noisily. There was a pause, tense on both sides as silence and self-consciousness could make it, and broken only by the happy, persistent call of the cuckoo and the infant caws of the young rooks in the elms by the gate. The photograph book was shut with a bang, and Hawkins, taking his resolution in both hands, came across the room, and stood in front of Francie.

'Look here!' he said, with a strange mixture of anger and entreaty in his voice; 'how much longer is this sort of thing to go on? Are you always going to treat me in this sort of way?'

'I don't know what you mean,' answered Francie, looking up at him with eyes of icy blue, and then down at her book again. Her heart was beating in leaps, but of this Hawkins was naturally not aware.

'You can't pretend not to know what I mean – this sort of rot of not speaking to me, and looking as if you had never seen me before. I told you I was sorry and all that. I don't know what more you want!'

'I don't want ever to speak to you again.' She turned over a page of her book, and forced her eyes to follow its lines.

'You know that's impossible; you know you've got to speak to me again, unless you want to cut me and kick up a regular row. I don't know why you're going on like this. It's awfully unfair, and it's awfully hard lines.' Since his visit to Rosemount, the conviction had been growing on him that in marrying another man she had treated him heartlessly, and he spoke with the fervour of righteous resentment.

'Oh, that comes well from you!' exclaimed Francie, dropping the book, and sitting up with all her pent-in wrath ablaze at last; 'you that behaved in a way anyone else would be ashamed to think of! Telling me lies from first to last, and trying to make a fool of me – It was a good thing I didn't believe more than the half you said!'

'I told you no lie,' said Hawkins, trying to stand his ground. 'All I did was that I didn't answer your letters because I couldn't get out of that accursed engagement, and I didn't know what to say to you, and then the next thing I knew was that you were engaged, without a word of explanation to me or anything.'

'And will you tell me what call there was for me to explain anything to you?' burst out Francie, looking, with the hot flash in her eyes, more lovely than he had ever seen her; 'for all I knew of you, you were married already to your English heiress – Miss Coppers, or whatever her name is – I wonder at your impudence in daring to say things like that to me!' The lift of her head, and the splendid colour in her cheeks would have befitted an angry goddess, and it is not surprising that Hawkins did not take offence at the crudity of the expression, and thought less of the brogue in which it was uttered than of the quiver of the young voice that accused him.

'Look here,' he said, for the second time, but with a new and very different inflection, 'don't let us abuse each other any more. I couldn't answer your letters. I didn't know what to say, except to tell you that I was a cad and a beast, and I didn't see much good in doing that. Evidently,' he added, with a bitterness that was at least half genuine, 'it didn't make much difference to you whether I did nor not.'

She did not reply, except by a glance that was intended to express more than words could convey of her contempt for him, but somewhere in it, in spite of her, he felt a touch of reproach, and it was it that he answered as he said:

'Of course if you won't believe me you won't, and it don't make much odds now whether you do or no; but I think if you knew how – ' he stammered, and then went on with a rush – 'how infernally I've suffered over the whole thing, you'd be rather sorry for me.'

Francie shaped her lips to a thin and tremulous smile of disdain, but her hands clutched each other under the book in her lap with the effort necessary to answer him. 'Oh, yes, I *am* sorry for you; I'd be sorry for anyone that would behave the way you did,' she said, with a laugh that would have been more effective had it been steadier; 'but I can't say you look as if you wanted my pity.'

Hawkins turned abruptly away and walked towards the door, and then, as quickly, came back to her side.

'They're coming across the lawn now,' he said; 'before they come, don't you think you could forgive me – or just say you do, anyhow. I did behave like a brute, but I never thought you'd have cared. You may say the worst things about me you can

300

think of, if you'll only tell me you forgive me.' His voice broke in the last words in a way that gave them irresistible conviction.

Francie glanced out of the window, and saw her husband and Charlotte slowly approaching the house. 'Oh, very well,' she said proudly, without turning her head; 'after all there's nothing to forgive.'

45

Lambert and Francie were both very silent as they drove away from Gurthnamuckla. He was the first to speak.

'I've asked Charlotte to come over and stay with you while I'm away next week. I find I can't get through the work in less than a fortnight, and I may be kept even longer than that, because I've got to go to Dublin.'

'Asked Charlotte!' said Francie, in a tone of equal surprise and horror. 'What on earth made you do that?'

'Because I didn't wish you should be left by yourself all that time.'

'I think you might have spoken to me first,' said Francie, with deepening resentment. 'I'd twice sooner be left by myself than be bothered with that old cat.'

Lambert looked quickly at her. He had come back to the house with his nerves still strained from his fright about the open gate, and his temper shaken by his financial difficulties, and the unexpected discovery of Hawkins in the drawing room with his wife had not been soothing.

'I don't choose that you should be left by yourself,' he said, in the masterful voice that had always, since her childhood, roused Francie's opposition. 'You're a deal too young to be left alone, and – ' with an involuntary softening of his voice – 'and a deal too pretty, confound you!' He cut viciously with his whip at a long-legged greyhound of a pig that was rooting by the side of the road.

'D'ye mean me or the pig?' said Francie, with a laugh that was still edged with defiance.

'I mean that I'm not going to have the whole country prating about you, and they would if I left you here by yourself.'

'Very well, then, if you make me have Charlotte to stay with me I'll give tea parties every day, and dinners and balls every night. I'll make the country prate, I can tell you, and the money fly too!'

Her eyes were brighter than usual, and there was a fitfulness about her that stirred and jarred him, though he could hardly tell why.

'I think I'll take you with me,' he said, with the impotent wrath of a lover who knows that the pain of farewell will be all on his side. 'I won't trust you out of my sight.'

'All right! I'll go with you,' she said, becoming half serious. 'I'd like to go.'

They were going slowly up hill, and the country lay bare and desolate in the afternoon sun, without a human being in sight. Lambert took the reins in his right hand, and put his arm round her.

'I don't believe you. I know you wouldn't care a hang if I never came back – kiss me!' She lifted her face obediently, and as her eyes met his she wondered at the unhappiness in them. 'I can't take you, my darling,' he whispered; 'I wish to God I could. I'm going to places you couldn't stay at, and – and it would cost too much.'

'Very well; never say I didn't make you a good offer,' she answered, her unconquerable eyes giving him a look that told she could still flirt with her husband.

'Put my cloak on me, Roddy; the evening's getting cold.'

They drove on quickly, and Lambert felt the gloom settling down upon him again. He hated going away and leaving Francie; he hated his financial difficulties, and their tortuous, uncertain issues; and, above all, he hated Hawkins. He would have given the whole world to know how things had been between him and Francie last year; anything would be less intolerable than suspicion.

The strip of grass by the roadside widened as they left the rocky country, and the deep dints of galloping hoofs became apparent on it. Lambert pointed to them with his whip, and laughed contemptuously.

'If I had a thick-winded pony like your friend Mr Hawkins, I wouldn't bucket her up hill in that sort of way. She'd do well enough if he had the sense to take her easy; but in all my knowledge of soldiers – and I've seen a good few of them here now – I've never seen a more self-sufficient jackass in the matter of horses than Hawkins. I wouldn't trust him with a donkey.'

'You'd better tell him so,' said Francie indifferently. Lambert chose to suspect a sneer in the reply.

'Tell him so!' he said hotly. 'I'd tell him so pretty smart, if I thought there was a chance of his getting outside a horse of mine. But I think it'll be a long day before that happens!'

'Maybe he wouldn't thank you for one of your horses.'

'No, I'll bet he wouldn't say thank you,' said Lambert, a thrill of anger darting to his brain. 'He's a lad that'll take all he can get, and say nothing about it, and chuck it away to the devil when he's done with it.'

'I'm sure I don't care what he does!' exclaimed Francie, with excusable impatience. 'I wonder if he's able to get into a passion about nothing, the way you're doing now!'

'It didn't look this afternoon as if you cared so little about what he does!' said Lambert, his breath coming short. 'May I ask if you knew he was coming, that you were in such a hurry back to the house to meet him? I suppose you settled it when he came to see you on Saturday.'

'Since you know all about it, there's no need for me to contradict you!' Francie flashed back.

One part of Lambert knew that he was making a fool of himself, but the other part, which was unfortunately a hundred times the stronger, drove him on.

'Oh, I daresay you found it very pleasant, talking over old times,' he retorted, releasing the thought at last like a long-caged beast; 'or was he explaining how it was he got tired of you?'

Francie sat still and dumb; the light surface anger startled out of her in a moment, and its place taken by a suffocating sense of outrage and cruelty. She did not know enough of love to recognize it in this hideous disguise of jealousy; she only discerned the cowardly spitefulness, and it cut down to that deep place in her soul where, since childhood, had lain her trust in him. She did not say a word, and Lambert went on:

'Oh, I see you are too grand to answer me; I suppose it's because I'm only your husband that you think I'm not worth talking to.' He gave the horse a lash of the whip, and then chucked up its head as it sprang forward, making the trap rock and jerk. The hateful satisfaction of taunting her about Hawkins was beginning to die in him like drunkenness, and he dimly saw what it was going to cost him. 'You make me say these sort of things to you,' he broke out, seeing that she would not speak 'How can I help it, when you treat me like the dirt under your feet, and fight with me if I say a word to you that you don't like? I'd like to see the man that would stand it!'

He looked down at her, and saw her head drooping forward, and her hand up to her face. He could not say more, as at that moment Mary Holloran was holding the gate open for him to drive in; and as he lifted his wife out of the trap at the hall door, and saw the tears that she could no longer hide from him, he knew that his punishment had begun, and the iron entered into his soul.

46

A few days afterwards Lambert started on his rent-collecting tour. Peace of a certain sort was restored, complete in outward seeming, but with a hidden flaw that both knew and pretended to ignore. When Lambert sat by himself in the smoking carriage of the morning train from Lismoyle, with the cold comfort of a farewell kiss still present with him, he was as miserable and anxious a man as could easily have been found. Charlotte had arrived the night before, and with all her agreeability had contrived to remind him that she expected a couple of hundred pounds on his return. He could never have believed that she would have dunned him in this way, and the idea occurred to him for the first time that she was perhaps taking this method of paying him out for what, in her ridiculous vanity, she might have imagined to be his bad treatment of her. But none the less, it was a comfort to him to think that she was at his house. He did not say so to himself, but he knew that he could not have found a better spy.

Dislike, as has been said, was a sentiment that Francie found great difficulty in cultivating. She conducted a feud in the most slipshod way, with intervals of illogical friendship, of which anyone with proper self-respect would have been ashamed, and she consequently accepted, without reservation, the fact that Charlotte was making herself pleasant with a pleasantness that a more suspicious person would have felt to be unwholesome.

Charlotte, upon whose birth so many bad fairies had shed their malign influence, had had at all events one attraction bestowed upon her, the gift of appreciation, and of being able to express her appreciation – a faculty that has been denied to many good and Christian people. The evil spirit may have torn her at sight of Francie enthroned at the head of Roddy Lambert's table, but it did not come out of her in any palpable form, nor did it prevent her from enjoying to the utmost the change from the grease and smoke of Norry's cooking, and the slothful stupidity of the Protestant orphan. Charlotte was one of the few women for whom a good cook will exert herself to make a savoury; and Eliza Hackett felt rewarded when the parlour-maid returned to the kitchen with the intelligence that Miss Mullen had taken two helpings of cheese soufflé, and had sent her special compliments to its constructor. Another of the undoubted advantages of Rosemount was the chance it afforded Charlotte of paying off with dignity and ease the long arrears of visits that the growing infirmities of the black horse were heaping up against her. It was supremely bitter to hear Francie ordering out the waggonette as if she had owned horses and carriages all her life, but she could gulp it down for the sake of the compensating comfort and economy. In the long *tête-à-têtes* that these drives involved, Charlotte made herself surprisingly pleasant to her hostess. She knew every scandal about every family in the neighbourhood, and imparted them with a humour and an easy acquaintance with the aristocracy that was both awe-inspiring and encouraging to poor Francie, whose heart beat fast with shyness and conscious inferiority, as, card case in hand, she preceded Miss Mullen to Mrs Ffolliott's or Mrs Flood's drawing room. It modified the terror of Mrs Flood's hooked nose to remember that her mother had been a Hebrew barmaid, and it was some consolation to reflect that General Ffolliott's second son had had to leave his regiment for cheating at cards, when she became aware that she alone, among a number of afternoon callers at Castle Ffolliott, had kept on her gloves during tea.

In every conversation with Charlotte it seemed to Francie that she discovered, as if by accident, some small but disagreeable fact about her husband. He had been refused by such and such a girl; he had stuck so and so with a spavined horse; he had taken a drop too much at the hunt ball; and, in a general way, he owed the agency and his present position in society solely to the efforts of Miss Mullen and her father.

Francie accepted these things, adding them to her previous store of disappointment in Roddy, with the philosophy that she had begun to learn at Albatross Villa, and that life was daily teaching her more of. They unconsciously made themselves into a background calculated to give the greatest effect to a figure that now occupied a great deal of her thoughts.

It was at Mrs Waller's house that she first met Hawkins after her encounter with him at Gurthnamuckla. He came into the room when it was almost time for her to face the dreadful ordeal of leave-taking, and she presently found herself talking to him with considerably less agitation than she had felt in talking about Paris to Miss Waller. The memory of their last meeting kept her eyes from his, but it made the ground firm under her feet, and in the five minutes before she went away she felt that she had effectually shown him the place she intended him to occupy, and that he thoroughly understood that conversation with her was a grace, and not a right. The touch of deference and anxiety in his self-assured manner were as sweet to her as the flowers strewed before a conqueror, and laid themselves like balm on the wound of her husband's taunt. Some day Roddy would see for himself the sort of way things were between her and Mr Hawkins, she thought, as she drove down the avenue, and unconsciously held her head so high and looked so brilliant, that Charlotte, with that new-born amiability that Francie was becoming accustomed to, complimented her upon her colour, and declared that, after Major Waller's attentions, she would have to write to Roderick and decline further responsibility as a chaperone.

They drove to Bruff two or three days afterwards, to return the state visit paid by Pamela on her mother's behalf, and, during some preliminary marketing in Lismoyle, they came upon Hawkins walking through the town in the Rosemount direction, with an air of smartness and purpose about him that bespoke an afternoon call.

'I was just going to see you,' he said, looking rather blank.

'We're on our way to Bruff,' replied Francie, too resolved on upholding her dignity to condescend to any conventional regrets.

Mr Hawkins looked more cheerful, and, observing that as he also owed a visit at Bruff this would be a good day to pay it, was turning back to the barracks for his trap, when Miss Mullen intervened with almost childlike impulsiveness.

'I declare now, it vexes my righteous soul to think of your getting out a horse and trap, with two seats going a-begging here. It's not my carriage, Mr Hawkins, or I promise you you should have one of them.'

Hawkins looked gratefully at her, and then uncertainly at Francie.

'He's welcome to come if he likes,' said Francie frigidly, thinking with a mixture of alarm and satisfaction of what Roddy would say if he heard of it.

Hawkins waited for no further invitation, and got into the waggonette. A trait of character as old as humanity was at this time asserting itself, with singular freshness and force, in the bosom of Mr Gerald Hawkins. He had lightly taken Francie's heart in his hand, and as lightly thrown it away, without plot or premeditation; but now that another man had picked it up and kept it for his own, he began to see it as a thing of surpassing value. He could have borne with a not uninteresting regret the idea of Francie languishing somewhere in the suburbs of Dublin, and would even, had the chance come in his way, have flirted with her in a kind and consolatory manner. But to see her here, prosperous, prettier than ever, and possessing the supreme attraction of having found favour in someone else's eyes, was a very different affair. The old glamour took him again, but with tenfold force, and, while he sat in the waggonette and talked to his ancient foe, Miss Mullen, with a novel friendliness, he gnawed the ends of his moustache in the bitterness of his soul because of the coldness of the eyes that were fascinating him.

It was a bright and blowy afternoon, with dazzling masses of white cloud moving fast across the blue, and there was a shifting glimmer of young leaves in the Bruff avenue, and a gusty warmth of fragrance from lilacs and laurel blossoms on either side. As this strangely compounded party of visitors drove up to the hall door they caught sight of Christopher going down the lawn towards the boathouse, and in answer to a call from Mr Hawkins, he turned and came back to meet them. He was only on his way to the boathouse to meet Cursiter, he explained, and he was the only person at home, but he hoped that they would, none the less, come in and see him. Hawkins helped Francie out of the carriage, giving her a hand no less formal than that which she gave him. She recognized the formality, and was not displeased to think that it was assumed in obedience to her wish.

They all strolled slowly on towards the boathouse, Hawkins walking behind with Miss Mullen, Francie in front with her host.

307

It was not her first meeting with him since her return to Lismoyle, and she found it quite easy to talk with him of her travels, and of those small things that make up the sum of ordinary afternoon conversation. She had come to believe now that she must have been mistaken on that afternoon when he had stood over her in the Tally Ho drawing room and said those unexpected things to her – things that, at the time, seemed neither ambiguous nor Platonic. He was now telling her, in the quietly hesitating voice that had always seemed to her the very height of good breeding, that the weather was perfect, and that the lake was lower than he had ever known it at that time of year, with other like commonplaces, and though there was something wanting in his manner that she had been accustomed to, she discerned none of the awkwardness that her experience had made her find inseparable from the rejected state.

There was no sign of Captain Cursiter or his launch when they reached the pier, and, after a fruitless five minutes of waiting, they went on, at Christopher's suggestion, to see the bluebells in the wood that girdled the little bay of Bruff. Before they reached the gate of the wood, Miss Mullen had attached herself to Christopher, having remarked, with engaging frankness, that Mr Hawkins could only talk to her about Lismoyle, and she wanted Sir Christopher to tell her of the doings of the great world; and Francie found herself following them with Hawkins by her side. The walk turned inwards and upwards from the lake, climbing, by means of a narrow flight of moss-grown stone steps, till it gained the height of about fifty feet above the water. Walking there, the glitter of the lake came up brokenly to the eye, through the beech-tree branches, that lay like sprays of maidenhair beneath them; and over the hill and down to the water's edge and far away among the grey beech stems, the bluebells ran like a blue mist through all the wood. Their perfume rose like incense about Francie and her companion as they walked slowly, and ever more slowly, along the path. The spirit of the wood stole into their veins, and a pleasure that they could not have explained held them in silence that they were afraid to break.

Hawkins was the first to make a different comment.

'They're ripping, aren't they? They're a great deal better than they were last year.'

'I didn't see them last year.'

'No, I know you didn't,' he said quickly; 'you didn't come to Lismoyle till the second week in June.'

'You seem to remember more about it than I do,' said Francie, still maintaining her attitude of superiority.

'I don't think I'm likely to forget it,' he said, turning and looking at her.

She looked down at the ground with a heightening colour and a curl of the lip that did not come easily. If she found it hard to nurse her anger against Charlotte, it was thrice more difficult to harden herself to the voice to which one vibrating string in her heart answered in spite of her.

'Oh, there's nothing people can't forget if they try!' she said, with a laugh. 'I always find it much harder to remember!'

'But people sometimes succeed in doing things they don't like,' said Hawkins pertinaciously.

'Not if they don't want to,' replied Francie, holding her own, with something of her habitual readiness.

Hawkins' powers of repartee weakened a little before this retort. 'No, I suppose not,' he said, trying to make up by bitterness of tone for want of argument.

Francie was silent, triumphantly silent, it seemed to him, as he walked beside her and switched off the drooping heads of the bluebells with his stick. He had experiences that might have taught him that this appetite for combat, this determination to trample on him, was a more measurable thing than the contempt that will not draw a sword; but he was able to think of nothing except that she was unkind to him, and that she was prettier now than he had ever seen her. He was so thoroughly put out that he was not aware of any awkwardness in the silence that had progressed, unbroken, for a minute or two. It was Francie to whom it was apparently most trying, as, at length, with an obvious effort at small talk, she said:

'I suppose that's Captain Cursiter coming up the lake?' indicating, through an opening in the branches, a glimpse of a white funnel and its thong of thinly streaming vapour; 'he seems as fond of boating as ever.'

'Yes, I daresay he is,' said Hawkins, without pretending any interest, real or polite, in the topic. He was in the frame of mind that lies near extravagance of some kind, whether of temper or sentiment, and, being of a disposition not versed in self-repression, he did not attempt diplomacy. He looked sulkily at the launch, and then, with a shock of association, he thought of the afternoon that he and Francie had spent on the lake, and the touch of unworthiness that there was in him made him long to remind her of her subjugation.

'Are *you* as fond of boating as – as you were when we ran aground last year?' he said, and looked at her daringly.

He was rewarded by seeing her start perceptibly and turn her head away, and he had the grace to feel a little ashamed of himself. Francie looked down the bluebell slope till her eyes almost ached with the soft glow of colour, conscious that every moment of delay in answering told against her, but unable to find the answer. The freedom and impertinence of the question did not strike her at all; she only felt that he was heartlessly trying to humiliate her.

'I'd be obliged to you, Mr Hawkins,' she said, her panting breath making her speak with extreme difficulty, 'if you'd leave me to walk by myself.'

Before she spoke he knew that he had made a tremendous mistake, and, as she moved on at a quickened pace, he felt he must make peace with her at any price.

'Mrs Lambert,' he said, with a gravity and deference which he had never shown to her before, 'is it any use to beg your pardon? I didn't know what I was saying – I hardly know now what I did say – but if it made you angry or – or offended you, I can only say I'm awfully sorry.'

'Thank you, I don't want you to say anything,' she answered, still walking stiffly on.

'If it would give you any pleasure, I swear I'll promise never to speak to you again!' Hawkins continued; 'shall I go away now?' His instinct told him to risk the question.

'Please yourself. It's nothing to me what you do.'

'Then I'll stay – '

Following on what he said, like an eldritch note of exclamation, there broke in the shrill whistle of the *Serpolette* as she turned into the bay of Bruff, and an answering hail from Christopher rose to them, apparently from the lower path by the shore of the lake.

'That's Cursiter,' said Hawkins irritably; 'I suppose we shall have to go back now.'

She turned, as if mechanically accepting the suggestion, and, in the action, her eyes passed by him with a look that was intended to have as little reference to him as the gaze of a planet in its orbit, but which, even in that instant, was humanized by avoidance. In the space of that glance, he knew that his pardon was attainable, if not attained, but he had cleverness enough to retain his expression of gloomy compunction.

It was quite true that Francie's anger, always pitiably short-lived, had yielded to the flattery of his respect. Every inner, unformed impulse was urging her to accept his apology, when three impatient notes from the whistle of the steam launch came up through the trees, and seemed to open a way for her to outside matters from the narrow stress of the moment.

'Captain Cursiter seems in a great hurry about something,' she said, her voice and manner conveying sufficiently well that she intended to pass on with dignity from the late dispute. 'I wonder what he wants.'

'Perhaps we've got the route,' said Hawkins, not sorry to be able to remind her of the impending calamity of his departure; 'I shouldn't be a bit surprised.'

They walked down the flight of stone steps, and reached the gate of the wood in silence. Hawkins paused with his hand on the latch.

'Look here, when am I going to see you again?' he said.

'I really don't know,' said Francie, with recovered ease. She felt the wind blowing in on her across the silver scales of the lake, and saw the sunshine flashing on Captain Cursiter's oars as he paddled himself ashore from the launch, and her spirits leaped up in 'the inescapable joy of spring.' 'I should think anyone that goes to church tomorrow will see me there.'

Her glance veered towards his cloudy downcast face, and an undignified desire to laugh came suddenly upon her. He had always looked so babyish when he was cross, and it had always made her feel inclined to laugh. Now that she was palpably and entirely the conqueror, the wish for further severity had died out, and the spark of amusement in her eye was recklessly apparent when Hawkins looked at her.

His whole expression changed in a moment. 'Then we're friends?' he said eagerly.

Before any answer could be given, Christopher and Charlotte came round a bend in the lower path, and even in this moment Francie wondered what it was that should cause Charlotte to drop her voice cautiously as she neared them.

47

It was very still inside the shelter of the old turf quay at Bruff. The stems of the lilies that curved up through its brown-golden depths were visible almost down to the black mud out of which their mystery of silver and gold was born; and, while the water outside moved piquantly to the breeze, nothing stirred it within except the water spiders, who were darting about, pushing a little ripple in front of them, and finding themselves seriously inconvenienced by the pieces of broken rush and the sodden fragments of turf that perpetually stopped their way. It had rained and blown very hard all the day before, and the innermost corners of the tiny harbour held a motionless curve of foam, yellowish brown, and flecked with the feathers of a desolated moorhen's nest.

Civilization at Bruff had marched away from the turf quay. The ruts of the cart track were green from long disuse and the willows had been allowed to grow across it, as a last sign of superannuation. In old days every fire at Bruff had been landed at the turf quay from the bogs at the other side of the lake; but now, since the railway had come to Lismoyle, coal had taken its place. It was in vain that Thady the turf cutter had urged that turf was a far handsomer thing about a gentleman's place than coal. The last voyage of the turf boat had been made, and she now lay, grey from rottenness and want of paint, in the corner of the miniature dock that had once been roofed over and formed a boathouse. Tall, jointed reeds, with their spiky leaves and stiff stems, stood out in the shallow water, leaning aslant over their own reflections, and, further outside, green rushes grew thickly in long beds, the homes of dabchicks, coots, and such like water people. Standing on the brown rock that formed the end of the quay, the spacious sky was so utterly reproduced in the lake, cloud for cloud, deep for deep, that it only required a little imagination to believe oneself floating high between two atmospheres. The young herons, in the fir trees on Curragh Point, were

312

giving utterance to their meditations on things in general in raucous monosyllables, and Charlotte Mullen, her feet planted firmly on two of the least rickety stones of the quay, was continuing a conversation that had gone on one-sidedly for some time.

'Yes, Sir Christopher, my feeling for your estate is like the feeling of a child for the place where he was reared; it is the affection of a woman whose happiest days were passed with her father in your estate office!'

The accurate balance of the sentence and its nasal cadence showed that Charlotte was delivering herself of a well-studied peroration. Her voice clashed with the stillness as dissonantly as the clamour of the young herons. Her face was warm and shiny, and Christopher looked away from it, and said to himself that she was intolerable.

'Of course – yes – I understand – ' he answered stammeringly, her pause compelling him to speak; 'but these are very serious things to say – '

'Serious!' Charlotte dived her hand into her pocket to make sure that her handkerchief was within hail. 'D'ye think, Sir Christopher, I don't know that well! I that have lain awake crying every night since I heard of it, not knowing how to decide between me affection for me friend and my duty to the son of my dear father's old employer!'

'I think anyone who makes charges of this kind,' interrupted Christopher coldly, 'is bound to bring forward something more definite than mere suspicion.'

Charlotte took her hand out of her pocket without the handkerchief, and laid it for a moment on Christopher's arm.

'My dear Sir Christopher, I entirely agree with you,' she said in her most temperate, ladylike manner, 'and I am prepared to place certain facts before you, on whose accuracy you may perfectly rely, although circumstances prevent my telling you how I learned them.'

The whole situation was infinitely repugnant to Christopher. He would himself have said that he had not nerve enough to deal with Miss Mullen; and joined with this, and his innate and overstrained dislike of having his affairs discussed, was the unendurable position of conniving with her at a treachery. Little as he liked Lambert, he sided with him now with something more than a man's ordinary resentment against feminine espionage upon another man. He was quite aware of the subdued eagerness

313

in Charlotte's manner, and it mystified while it disgusted him; but he was also aware that nothing short of absolute flight would check her disclosures. He could do nothing now but permit himself the single pleasure of staring over her head with a countenance barren of response to her histrionic display of expression.

'You ask me for something more definite than mere suspicion,' continued Charlotte, approaching one of the supremest gratifications of her life with full and luxurious recognition. 'I can give you two facts, and if, on investigation, you find they are not correct, you may go to Roderick Lambert, and tell him to take an action for libel against me! I daresay you know that a tenant of yours, named James M'Donagh – commonly called Shamus Bawn – recently got the goodwill of Knocklara, and now holds it in addition to his father's farm, which he came in for last month.' Christopher assented. 'Jim M'Donagh paid one hundred and eighty pounds fine on getting Knocklara. I ask you to examine your estate account, and you will see that the sum credited to you on that transaction is no more than seventy.'

'May I ask how you know this?' Christopher turned his face towards her for a moment as he asked the question, and encountered, with even more aversion than he had expected, her triumphing eyes.

'I'm not at liberty to tell you. All I say is, go to Jim M'Donagh, and ask him the amount of his fine, and see if he won't tell you just the same sum that I'm telling you now.'

Captain Cursiter, at this moment steering the *Serpolette* daintily among the shadows of Bruff Bay, saw the two incongruous figures on the turf quay, one short, black, and powerful, the other tall, white, and passive, and wondered, through the preoccupation of crawling to his anchorage, what it was that Miss Mullen was holding forth to Dysart about, in a voice that came to him across the water like the gruff barking of a dog. He thought, too, that there was an almost shipwrecked welcome in the shout with which Christopher answered his whistle, and was therefore surprised to see him remain where he was, apparently enthralled by Miss Mullen's conversation, instead of walking round to meet him at the boat-house pier.

Charlotte had, in fact, by this time, compelled Christopher to give her his whole attention. As he turned towards her again, he admitted to himself that the thing looked rather serious, though he determined, with the assistance of a good deal of antagonistic irritability, to keep his opinion to himself. This feeling was uppermost as he said: 'I have never had the least reason to feel a want of confidence in Mr Lambert, Miss Mullen, and I certainly could not discredit him by going privately to M'Donagh to ask him about the fine.'

'It's a pity all unfaithful stewards haven't as confiding a master as you, Sir Christopher,' said Charlotte, with a laugh. She felt Christopher's attitude towards her as a man in armour may have felt the arrows strike him, and no more, and it came easily to her to laugh. 'However,' she went on, correcting her manner quickly, as she saw a very slight increase of colour in Christopher's face, 'the burden of proof does not lie with James M'Donagh. Last November, as you may possibly remember, my name made its first appearance on your rent roll, as the tenant of Gurthnamuckla, and in recognition of that honour,' – Charlotte felt that there was an academic polish about her sentences that must appeal to a University man – 'I wrote your agent a cheque for one hundred pounds, which was duly cashed some days afterwards.' She altered her position, so that she could see his face better, and said deliberately: 'Not one penny of that has been credited to the estate! This I know for a fact.'

'Yes,' said Christopher, after an uncomfortable pause, 'that's very – very curious, but, of course – until I know a little more, I can't give any opinion on the matter. I think, perhaps, we had better go round to meet Captain Cursiter – '

Charlotte interrupted him with more violence than she had as yet permitted to escape.

'If you want to know more, I can tell you more, and plenty more! For the last year and more, Roddy Lambert's been lashing out large sums of ready money beyond his income, and I know his income to the penny and the farthing! Where did he get that money from? I ask you. What paid for his young horses, and his new dog-cart, and his new carpets, yes! and his honeymoon trip to Paris? I ask you what paid for all that? It wasn't his first wife's money paid for it, I know that for a fact, and it certainly wasn't the second wife's!'

She was losing hold of herself; her gestures were of the sort that she usually reserved for her inferiors, and the corners of her mouth bubbled like a snail. Christopher looked at her and began to walk away. Charlotte followed him, walking unsteadily on the loose stones, and inwardly cursing his insolence as well as her own forgetfulness of the method she had laid down for the interview. He turned and waited for her when he reached the path, and had time to despise himself for not being able to conceal his feelings from a woman so abhorrent and so contemptible.

'I am – er – obliged for your information,' he said stiffly. In spite of his scorn for his own prejudice, he would not gratify her by saying more.

'You will forgive me, Sir Christopher,' replied Charlotte with an astonishing resumption of dignity, 'if I say that that is a point that is quite immaterial to me. I require no thanks. I felt it to be my duty to tell you these painful facts, and what I suffer in doing it concerns only myself.'

They walked on in silence between the lake and the wood, with the bluebells creeping outwards to their feet through the white beech stems, and as the last turn of the path brought them in sight of Francie and Hawkins, Charlotte spoke again:

'You'll remember that all this is in strict confidence, Sir Christopher.'

'I shall remember,' said Christopher curtly.

An hour later, Pamela, driving home with her mother, congratulated herself, as even the best people are prone to do, when she saw on the gravel-sweep the fresh double wheel tracks that indicated that visitors had come and gone. She felt that she had talked enough for one afternoon during the visit to old Lady Eyrecourt, whose deaf sister had fallen to her share, and she did not echo her mother's regret at missing Miss Mullen and her cousin. She threw down the handful of cards on the hall table again, and went with a tired step to look for Christopher in the smoking room, where she found him with Captain Cursiter, the latter in the act of taking his departure. The manner of her greeting showed that he was an accustomed sight there, and, as a matter of fact, since Christopher's return Captain Cursiter had found himself at Bruff very often. He had discovered that it was, as he expressed it, the only house in the country where the women let him alone. Lady Dysart had expressed the position from another point of view, when she had deplored to Mrs Gascogne Pamela's 'hopeless friendliness' towards men, and Mrs Gascogne had admitted that there might be something discouraging to a man in being treated as if he were a younger sister.

This unsuitable friendliness was candidly apparent in Pamela's regret when she heard that Cursiter had come to Bruff with the news that his regiment was to leave Ireland for Aldershot in a fortnight.

'Here's Captain Cursiter trying to stick me with the launch

at an alarming reduction, as the property of an officer going abroad,' said Christopher. 'He wants to take advantage of my grief, and he won't stay and dine here and let me haggle the thing out comfortably.'

'I'm afraid I haven't time to stay,' said Cursiter rather cheerlessly. 'I've got to go up to Dublin tomorrow, and I'm very busy. I'll come over again – if I may – when I get back.' He felt all the awkwardness of a self-conscious man in the prominence of making a farewell that he is beginning to find more unpleasant than he had expected.

'Oh yes! indeed, you must come over again,' said Pamela, in the soft voice that was just Irish enough for Saxons of the more ignorant sort to fail to distinguish, save in degree, between it and Mrs Lambert's Dublin brogue.

It remained on Captain Cursiter's ear as he stalked down through the shrubberies to the boat-house, and, as he steamed round Curragh Point, and caught the sweet, turfy whiff of the Irish air, he thought drearily of the arid glare of Aldershot, and, without any apparent connection of ideas, he wondered if the Dysarts were really coming to town next month.

Not long after his departure Lady Dysart rustled into the smoking room in her solemnly sumptuous widow's dress.

'Is he gone?' she breathed in a stage whisper, pausing on the threshold for a reply.

'No; he's hiding behind the door,' answered Christopher; 'he always does when he hears you coming.' When Christopher was irritated, his method of showing it was generally so subtle as only to satisfy himself; it slipped through the wide and generous mesh of his mother's understanding without the smallest friction.

'Nonsense, Christopher!' she said, not without a furtive glance behind the door. 'What a visitation you must have had from the whole set! Had they anything interesting to say for themselves? Charlotte Mullen generally is a great alleviation.'

'Oh yes,' replied her son, examining the end of his cigarette with a peculiar expression, 'she – she alleviated about as much as usual; but it was Cursiter who brought the news.'

'I can't imagine Captain Cursiter so far forgetting himself as to tell any news,' said Lady Dysart; 'but perhaps he makes an exception in your favour.'

'They're to go to Aldershot in a fortnight,' said Christopher.

'You don't say so!' exclaimed his mother, with an irrepressible look at Pamela, who was sitting on the floor in the window, taking a thorn out of Max's spatulate paw. 'In a fortnight? I wonder how Mr Hawkins will like that? Evelyn said that Miss Coppard told her the marriage was to come off when the regiment went back to England.'

Christopher grunted unsympathetically, and Pamela continued her researches for the thorn.

'Well,' resumed Lady Dysart, 'I, for one, shall not regret them. Selfish and second-rate!'

'Which is which?' asked Christopher, eliminating any tinge of interest or encouragement from his voice. He was quite aware that his mother was in this fashion avenging the slaughter of the hope that she had secretly nourished about Captain Cursiter, and, being in a perturbed frame of mind, it annoyed him.

'I think *your* friend is the most self-centred, ungenial man I have ever known,' replied Lady Dysart, in sonorous denunciation, 'and if Mr Hawkins is not second-rate, his friends are, which comes to the same thing! And, by the by, how was it that he went away before Captain Cursiter? Did not they come together?'

'Miss Mullen and Mrs Lambert gave him a lift,' said Christopher, uncommunicatively; 'I believe they overtook him on his way here.'

Lady Dysart meditated, with her dark eyebrows drawn into a frown.

'I think that girl will make a very great mistake if she begins a flirtation with Mr Hawkins again,' she said presently; 'there has been quite enough talk about her already in connection with her marriage.' Lady Dysart untied her bonnet strings as if with a need of more air, and flung them back over each shoulder. In the general contrariety of things, it was satisfactory to find an object so undeniably deserving of reprobation as the new Mrs Lambert. 'I call her a thorough adventuress!' she continued. 'She came down here, determined to marry some one, and as Mr Hawkins escaped from her, she just snatched at the next man she could find!'

Pamela came over and sat down on the arm of her mother's chair. 'Now, mamma,' she said, putting her arm round Lady Dysart's crape-clad shoulder, 'you can't deny that she knew all about the Dublin clergy, and went to Sunday school regularly for ten years, and she guessed two lights of an acrostic for you.'

'Yes, two that happened to be slangy! No, my dear child, I admit that she is very pretty, but, as I said before, she has proved

318

herself to be nothing but an adventuress. Everyone in the country has said the same thing.'

'I can scarcely imagine anyone less like an adventuress,' said Christopher, with the determined quietness by which he sometimes mastered his stammer.

His mother looked at him with the most unaffected surprise. 'And I can scarcely imagine anyone who knows less about the matter than you!' she retorted. 'Oh, my dear boy, don't smoke another of those horrid things,' as Christopher got up abruptly and began to fumble rather aimlessly in a cigarette box on the chimney-piece, 'I'm sure you've smoked more than is good for you. You look quite white already.'

He made no reply, and his mother's thoughts reverted to the subject under discussion. Suddenly a little cloud of memory began to appear on her mental horizon. Now that she came to think of it, had not Kate Gascogne once mentioned Christopher's name to her in preposterous connection with that of the present Mrs Lambert?

'Let me tell you!' she exclaimed, her deep-set eyes glowing with the triumphant effort of memory, 'that people said she did her utmost to capture *you!* and I can very well believe it of her; a grievous waste of ammunition on her part, wasn't it, Pamela? Though it did not result in an *engagement!*' she added, highly pleased at being able to press a pun into her argument.

'Oh, I think she spared Christopher,' struck in Pamela with a conciliatory laugh; ' "Poor is the conquest of the timid hare," you know!' She was aware of something portentously rigid in her brother's attitude, and would have given much to have changed the conversation, but the situation was beyond her control.

'I don't think she would have thought it such a poor conquest,' said Lady Dysart indignantly; 'a girl like that, accustomed to attorneys' clerks and commercial travellers – she'd have done anything short of suicide for such a chance!'

Christopher had stood silent during this discussion. He was losing his temper, but he was doing it after his fashion, slowly and almost imperceptibly. The pity for Mr Lambert's wife, that had been a primary result of Charlotte's indictment, flamed up into quixotism, and every word his mother said was making him more hotly faithful to the time when his conquest had been complete.

'I daresay it will surprise you to hear that I gave her the chance, and she didn't take it,' he said suddenly.

Lady Dysart grasped the arms of her chair, and then fell back into it.

'*You* did!'

'Yes, I did,' replied Christopher, beginning to walk towards the door. He knew he had done a thing that was not only superfluous, but savoured repulsively of the pseudo-heroic, and the attitude in which he had placed himself was torture to his reserve. 'This great honour was offered to her,' he went on, taking refuge in lame satire, 'last August, unstimulated by any attempts at suicide on her part, and she refused it. I – I think it would be kinder if you put her down as a harmless lunatic, than as an adventuress, as far as I am concerned.' He shut the door behind him as he finished speaking, and Lady Dysart was left staring at her daughter, complexity of emotions making speech an idle thing.

48

The question, ten days afterwards, to anyone who had known all the features of the case, would have been whether Francie was worth Christopher's act of championing.

At the back of the Rosemount kitchen garden the ground rose steeply into a knoll of respectable height, where grew a tangle of lilac bushes, rhododendrons, seringas, and yellow broom. A gravel path wound ingratiatingly up through these, in curves artfully devised by Mr Lambert to make the most of the extent and the least of the hill, and near the top a garden seat was sunk in the bank, with laurels shutting it in on each side, and a laburnum 'showering golden tears' above it. Through the perfumed screen of the lilac bushes in front unromantic glimpses of the roof of the house were obtainable – eyesores to Mr Lambert, who had concentrated all his energies on hiding everything nearer than the semi-circle of lake and distant mountain held in an opening cut through the rhododendrons at the corner of the little plateau on which the seat stood. Without the disturbance of middle distance the eye lay at ease on the far-off struggle of the Connemara mountains, and on a serene vista of Lough Moyle; a view that enticed forth, as to a playground, the wildest and most foolish imaginations, and gave them elbow room; a world so large and remote that it needed the sound of wheels on the road to recall the existence of the petty humanities of Lismoyle.

Francie and Hawkins were sitting there on the afternoon of the day on which Lambert was expected to come home, and as the sun, that had stared in at them through the opening in the rhododendrons when they first went there, slid farther round, their voices sank in unconscious accord with the fading splendours of the afternoon, and their silences seemed momently more difficult to break. They were nearing the end of the phase that had begun in the wood at Bruff, impelled to its verge by the unspoken knowledge that the last of the unthinking, dangerous days was dying with the sun, and that a final parting was looming up beyond. Neither knew for certain the mind of the other, or how they had dropped into this so-called friendship that in half a dozen afternoons had robbed all other things of reality, and made the intervals between their meetings like a feverish dream. Francie did not dare to think much about it; she lived in a lime-light glow that surrounded her wherever she went, and all the world outside was dark. He was going in a fortnight, in ten days, in a week; that was the only fact that the future had held for her since Captain Cursiter had met them with the telegram in his hand on the lake shore at Bruff. She forgot her resolutions; she forgot her pride; and before she reached home that afternoon the spell of the new phase, that was the old, only intensified by forgiveness, was on her. She shut her eyes, and blindly gave house-room in her heart to the subtle passion that came in the garb of an old friend, with a cant about compassion on its lips, and perfidious promises that its life was only for a fortnight.

To connect this supreme crisis of a life with such a person as Mr Gerald Hawkins may seem incongruous; but Francie was not aware of either crisis or incongruity. All she knew of was the enthralment that lay in each prosaic afternoon visit, all she felt, the tired effort of conscience against fascination. Her emotional Irish nature, with all its frivolity and recklessness, had also, far down in it, an Irish girl's moral principle and purity; but each day she found it more difficult to hide the truth from him; each day the undercurrents of feeling drew them helplessly nearer to each other. Everything was against her. Lambert's business had, as he expected, taken him to Dublin, and kept him there; Cursiter, like most men, was chary of active inter-ference in another man's affairs, whatever his private opinion might be; and Charlotte, that guardian of youth, that trusty and vigilant spy, sat in her own room writing interminable letters, or went on long and complicated shopping expeditions whenever Hawkins came to the house.

On this golden, still afternoon, Francie strayed out soon after lunch, half dazed with unhappiness and excitement. Tonight her husband would come home. In four days Hawkins would have gone, as eternally, so far as she was concerned, as if he were dead; he would soon forget her, she thought, as she walked to and fro among the blossoming apple trees in the kitchen garden. Men forgot very easily, and, thanks to the way she had tried her best to make him think she didn't care, there was not a word of hers to bring him back to her. She hated herself for her discretion; her soul thirsted for even one word of understanding, that would be something to live upon in future days of abnegation, when it would be nothing to her that she had gained his respect, and one tender memory would be worth a dozen self-congratulations.

She turned at the end of the walk and came back again under the apple trees; the ground under her feet was white with fallen blossoms; her fair hair gleamed among the thick embroidery of the branches, and her face was not shamed by their translucent pink and white. At a little distance Eliza Hackett, in a starched lilac calico, was gathering spinach, and meditating no doubt with comfortable assurance on the legitimacy of Father Heffer-nan's apostolic succession, but outwardly the embodiment of solid household routine and respectability. As Francie passed her she raised her decorous face from the spinach bed with a question as to whether the trout would be for dinner or for breakfast; the master always fancied fish for breakfast, she reminded Francie. Eliza Hackett's tone was distant, but admonitory, and it dispelled in a moment the visions of another now impossible future that were holding high carnival before Francie's vexed eyes. The fetter made itself coldly felt, and following came the quick pang of remorse at the thought of the man who was wasting on her the best love he had to give. Her change of mood was headlong, but its only possible expression was trivial to ab-surdity, if indeed any incident in a soul's struggle can be called trivial. Some day, further on in eternity, human beings will know what their standards of proportion and comparison are worth, and may perhaps find the glory of some trifling actions almost insufferable.

She gave the necessary order, and hurrying into the house brought out from it the piece of corduroy that she was stitching in lines of red silk as a waistcoat for her husband, and with a childish excitement at the thought of this expiation, took the path that led to the shrubbery on the hill. As she reached its first turn she hesitated and stopped, an idea of further and fuller renunciation occurring to her. Turning, she called to the figure stooping among the glossy rows of spinach to desire that the parlour-maid should say that this afternoon she was not at home. Had Eliza Hackett then and there obeyed the order, it is possible that many things would have happened differently. But fate is seldom without a second string to her bow, and even if Francie's message had not been delayed by Eliza Hackett's determination to gather a pint of green gooseberries before she went in, it is possible that Hawkins would, none the less, have found his way to the top of the shrubbery, where Francie was sewing with the assiduity of Penelope. It was about four o'clock when she heard his step coming up the devious slants of the path, and she knew as she heard it that, in spite of all her precautions, she had expected him. His manner and even his look had nothing now in them of the confident lover of last year; his flippancy was gone, and when he began by reproaching her for having hidden from him, his face was angry and wretched, and he spoke like a person who had been seriously and unjustly hurt. He was more in love than he had ever been before, and he was taking it badly, like a fever that the chills of opposition were driving back into his system.

She made excuses as best she might, with her eyes bent upon her work.

'I might have been sitting in the drawing room now,' he said petulantly; 'only that Miss Mullen had seen you going off here by yourself, and told me I'd better go and find you.' '

An unreasoning fear came over Francie, a fear as of something uncanny.

'Let us go back to the house,' she said; 'Charlotte will be expecting us.' She said it to contradict the thought that had become definite for the first time. 'Come; I'm going in.'

Hawkins did not move. 'I suppose you forget that this is Wednesday, and that I'm going on Saturday,' he replied dully. 'In any case you'll not be much good to Charlotte. She's gone up to pack her things. She told me herself she was going to be very busy, as she had to start at six o'clock.'

Francie leaned back, and realized that now she had no one

to look to but herself, and happiness and misery fought within her till her hands trembled as she worked.

Each knew that this was, to all intents and purposes, their last meeting, and their consciousness was charged to brimming with unexpressed farewell. She talked of indifferent subjects; of what Aldershot would be like, of what Lismoyle would think of the new regiment, of the trouble that he would have in packing his pictures, parrying, with a weakening hand, his efforts to make every subject personal; and all the time the laburnum drooped in beautiful despair above her, as if listening and grieving, and the cool-leaved lilac sent its fragrance to mingle with her pain, and to stir her to rebellion with the ecstasy of springtime. The minutes passed barrenly by, and as has been said, the silences became longer and more clinging, and the thoughts that filled them made each successive subject more bare and artificial. At last Hawkins got up, and walking to the opening cut in the shrubs, stood, with his hands in his pockets, looking out at the lake and the mountains. Francie stitched on; it seemed to her that if she stopped she would lose her last hold upon herself; she felt as if her work were a talisman to remind her of all the things that she was in peril of forgetting. When, that night, she took up the waistcoat again to work at it, she thought that her heart's blood had gone into the red stitches.

It was several minutes before Hawkins spoke. 'Francie,' he said, turning round and speaking thickly, 'are you going to let me leave you in this – in this kind of way? Have you realized that when I go on Saturday it's most likely – it's pretty certain, in fact – that we shall never see each other again?'

'Yes, I have,' she said, after a pause of a second or two. She did not say that for a fortnight her soul had beaten itself against the thought, and that to hear it in words was as much as her self-command could bear.

'You seem to care a great deal!' he said violently; 'you're thinking of nothing but that infernal piece of work, that I loathe the very sight of. Don't you think you could do without it for five minutes, at all events?'

She let her hands drop into her lap, but made no other reply.

'You're not a bit like what you used to be. You seem to take a delight in snubbing me and shutting me up. I must say, I never thought you'd have turned into a prig!' He felt this reproach to be so biting that he paused upon it to give it its full effect. 'Here I am going to England in four days, and to India in four months, and it's ten to one if I ever come home again. I mean to volunteer for the very first row that turns up. But it's just the same to you, you won't even take the trouble to say you're sorry.'

'If you had taken the trouble to answer my letters last autumn, you wouldn't be saying these things to me now,' she said, speaking low and hurriedly.

'I don't believe it! I believe if you had cared about me then you wouldn't treat me like this now.'

'I *did* care for you,' she said, while the hard-held tears forced their way to her eyes; 'you made me do it, and then you threw me over, and now you're trying to put the blame on me!'

He saw the glisten on her eyelashes, and it almost took from him the understanding of what she said.

'Francie,' he said, his voice shaking, and his usually confident eyes owning the infection of her tears, 'you might forget that. I'm miserable. I can't bear to leave you!' He sat down again beside her, and, catching her hand, kissed it with a passion of repentance. He felt it shrink from his lips, but the touch of it had intoxicated him, and suddenly she was in his arms.

For a speechless instant they clung to each other; her head dropped to his shoulder, as if the sharp release from the tension of the last fortnight had killed her, and the familiar voice murmured in her ear:

'Say it to me – say you love me.'

'Yes I do – my dearest – ' she said, with a moan that was tragically at variance with the confession. 'Ah, why do you make me so wicked!' She snatched herself away from him, and stood up, trembling all over. 'I wish I had never seen you – I wish I was dead.'

'I don't care what you say now,' said Hawkins, springing to his feet, 'you've said you loved me, and I know you mean it. Will you stand by it?' he went on wildly. 'If you'll only say the word I'll chuck everything overboard – I can't go away from you like this. Once I'm in England I can't get back here, and if I did, what good would it be to me? He'd never give us a chance of seeing each other, and we'd both be more miserable than we are, unless – unless there was a chance of meeting you in Dublin or somewhere –?' He stopped for an instant. Francie mutely shook her head. 'Well, then, I shall never see you.'

There was silence, and the words settled down into both their hearts. He cursed himself for being afraid of her, she whom he had always felt to be his inferior, yet when he spoke it was with an effort.

'Come away with me out of this – come away with me for good and all! What's the odds? We can't be more than happy!'

Francie made an instinctive gesture with her hand while he spoke, as if to stop him, but she said nothing, and almost immediately the distant rush and rattle of a train came quietly into the stillness.

'That's his train!' she exclaimed, looking as startled as if the sound had been a sign from heaven. 'Oh, go away! He mustn't meet you coming away from here.'

'I'll go if you give me a kiss,' he answered drunkenly. His arms were round her again, when they dropped to his side as if he had been shot.

There was a footstep on the path immediately below the lilac bushes, and Charlotte's voice called to Francie that she was just starting for home and had come to make her adieux.

49

Christopher Dysart drove to Rosemount next morning to see Mr Lambert on business. He noticed Mrs Lambert standing at the drawing-room window as he drove up, but she left the window before he reached the hall door, and he went straight to Mr Lambert's study without seeing her again.

Francie returned listlessly to the seat that she had sprung from with a terrified throb of the heart at the thought that the wheels might be those of Hawkins' trap, and, putting her elbow on the arm of the chair, rested her forehead on her hand; her other hand drooped over the side of the chair, holding still in it the sprig of pink hawthorn that her husband had given her in the garden an hour before. Her attitude was full of languor, but her brain was working at its highest pressure, and at this moment she was asking herself what Sir Christopher would say when he heard that she had gone away with Gerald. She had seen him vaguely as one of the crowd of contemptuous or horror-stricken faces that had thronged about her pillow in the early morning, but his opinion had carried no more restraining power than that of Aunt Tish, or Uncle Robert, or Charlotte. Nothing had weighed with her then; the two principal figures in her life contrasted as simply and convincingly as night and day, and like night and day, too, were the alternative futures that were in her hand to choose from. Her eyes were open to her wrong-doing, but scarcely to her cruelty; it could not be as bad for Roddy, she thought, to live without her as for her to stay with him and think of Gerald in India, gone away from her for ever. Her reasoning power was easily mastered, her conscience was a thing of habit, and not fitted to grapple with this turbulent passion. She swept towards her ruin like a little boat staggering under more sail than she can carry. But the sight of Christopher, momentary as it was, had startled for an instant the wildness of her thoughts; the saner breath of the outside world had come with him, and a touch of the self-respect that she had always gained from him made her press her hot forehead against her hand, and realize that the way of transgressors would be hard.

She remained sitting there, almost motionless, for a long time. She had no wish to occupy herself with anything; all the things about her had already the air of belonging to a past existence; her short sovereignty was over, and even the furniture that she had, a few weeks ago, pulled about and rearranged in the first ardour of possession seemed to look at her in a decorous, clannish way, as if she were already an alien. At last she heard the study door open, and immediately afterwards Christopher's dog-cart went down the drive. It occurred to her that now, if ever, was the time to go to her husband and see whether, by diplomacy, she could evade the ride that he had asked her to take with him that after-noon. Hawkins had sent her a note saying that he would come to pay a farewell visit, a cautiously formal note that anyone might have seen, but that she was just as glad had not been seen by her husband, and at all hazards she must stay in to meet him. She got up and went to the study with a nervous colour in her cheeks, glancing out of the hall window as she passed it, with the idea that the threatening grey of the sky would be a good argu-ment for staying at home. But if it rained, Roddy might stay at home too, she thought, and that would be worse than anything. That was her last thought as she went into the study.

Lambert was standing with his hands in his pockets, looking down at the pile of papers and books on the table, and Francie was instantly struck by something unwonted in his attitude, something rigid and yet spent, that was very different from his usual bearing. He looked at her with heavy eyes, and going to

327

his chair let himself drop into it; then, still silently, he held out his hand to her. She thought he looked older, and that his face was puffy and unattractive, and in the highly-strung state of her nerves she felt a repugnance to him that almost horrified her. It is an unfortunate trait of human nature that a call for sympathy from a person with whom sympathy has been lost has a repellent instead of an attractive power, and if a strong emotion does not appear pathetic, it is terribly near the ludicrous. In justice to Francie it must be said that her dominant feeling as she gave Lambert her hand and was drawn down on to his knee was less repulsion than a sense of her own hypocrisy.

'What's the matter, Roddy?' she asked, after a second or two of silence, during which she felt the labouring of his breath.

'I'm done for,' he said, 'that's what's the matter.'

'Why! what do you mean?' she exclaimed, turning her startled face half towards him, and trying not to shrink as his hot breath struck on her cheek.

'I've lost the agency.'

'Lost the agency!' repeated Francie, feeling as though the world with all the things she believed to be most solid were rocking under her feet. 'Do you mean he's after dismissing you?'

Lambert moved involuntarily, from the twitch of pain that the word gave him. It was this very term that Lismoyle would soon apply to him, as if he were a thieving butler or a drunken coachman.

'That's about what it will come to,' he said bitterly. 'He was too damned considerate to tell me so today, but he's going to do it. He's always hated me just as I have hated him, and this is his chance, though God knows what's given it to him!'

'You're raving!' cried Francie incredulously; 'what on earth would make him turn you away?' She felt that her voice was sharp and unnatural, but she could not make it otherwise. The position was becoming momently more horrible from the weight of unknown catastrophe, the sight of her husband's suffering and the struggle to sympathize with it, and the hollow disconnection between herself and everything about her.

'I can't tell you – all in a minute,' he said with difficulty. 'Wouldn't you put your arm round my neck, Francie, as if you were sorry for me? You might be sorry for me, and for yourself too. We're ruined. Oh my God!' he groaned, 'we're ruined!'

She put her arm round his neck, and pity, and a sense that it was expected of her, made her kiss his forehead. At the touch of

328

her lips his sobs came suddenly and dreadfully, and his arms drew her convulsively to him. She lay there helpless and dry-eyed, enduring a wretchedness that in some ways was comparable to his own, but never becoming merged in the situation, never quite losing her sense of repulsion at his abasement.

'I never meant to touch a farthing of his – in the long run – ' he went on, recovering himself a little; 'I'd have paid him back every halfpenny in the end – but, of course, he doesn't believe that. What does he care what I say!'

'Did you borrow money from him, or what was it?' asked Francie gently.

'Yes, I did,' replied Lambert, setting his teeth; 'but I didn't tell him. I was eaten up with debts, and I had to – to borrow some of the estate money.' It was anguish to lower himself from the pedestal of riches and omnipotence on which he had always posed to her, and he spoke stumblingly. 'It's very hard to explain these things to you – it's – it's not so unusual as you'd think – and then, before I'd time to get things square again, some infernal mischief-maker has set him on to ask to see the books, and put him up to matters that he'd never have found out for himself.'

'Was he angry?' she asked, with the quietness that was so unlike her.

'Oh, I don't know – I don't care – ' moving again restlessly in his chair; 'he's such a rotten, cold-blooded devil, you can't tell what he's at.' Even at this juncture it gave him pleasure to make little of Christopher to Francie. 'He asked me the most beastly questions he could think of, in that d—d stammering way of his. He's to write to me in two or three days, and I know well what he'll say,' he went on with a stabbing sigh; 'I suppose he'll have it all over the country in a week's time. He's been to the bank and seen the estate account, and that's what's done me. I asked him plump and plain if he hadn't been put up to it, and he didn't deny it, but there's no one could have known what was paid into that account but Baker or one of the clerks, and they knew nothing about the fines – I mean – they couldn't understand enough to tell him anything. But what does it matter who told him. The thing's done now, and I may as well give up.'

'What will you do?' said Francie faintly.

'If it wasn't for you I think I'd put a bullet through my head,' he answered, his innately vulgar soul prompting him to express the best thought that was in him in conventional heroics, 'but I couldn't leave you, Francie – I couldn't leave you – ' he broke down again – 'it was for our honeymoon I took the most of the money – ' He could not go on, and her whole frame was shaken by his sobs.

'Don't, Roddy, don't cry,' she murmured, feeling cold and sick.

'He knows I took the money,' Lambert went on incoherently; 'I'll have to leave the country – I'll sell everything – ' he got up and began to walk about the room – 'I'll pay him – damn him – I'll pay him every farthing. He sha'n't have it to say he was kept waiting for his money! He shall have it this week!'

'But how will you pay him if you haven't the money?' said Francie, with the same lifelessness of voice that had characterized her throughout.

'I'll borrow the money – I'll raise it on the furniture; I'll send the horses up to Sewell's, though God knows what price I'll get for them this time of year, but I'll manage it somehow. I'll go out to Gurthnamuckla this very afternoon about it. Charlotte's got a head on her shoulders – ' He stood still, and the idea of borrowing from Charlotte herself took hold of him. He felt that such trouble as this must command her instant sympathy, and awaken all the warmth of their old friendship, and his mind turned towards her stronger intelligence with a reliance that was creditable to his ideas of the duties of a friend. 'I could give her a bill of sale on the horses and furniture,' he said to himself.

His eyes rested for the first time on Francie, who had sunk into the chair from which he had risen, and was looking at him as if she did not see him. Her hair was ruffled from lying on his shoulder, and her eyes were wild and fixed, like those of a person who is looking at a far-off spectacle of disaster and grief.

50

The expected rain had not come, though the air was heavy and damp with the promise of it. It hung unshed, above the thirsty country, looking down gloomily upon the dusty roads, and the soft and straight young grass in the meadows; waiting for the night, when the wind would moan and cry for it, and the newborn leaves would shudder in the dark at its coming.

At three o'clock Francie was sure that the afternoon would be fine, and soon afterwards she came downstairs in her habit, and went into the drawing room to wait for the black mare to be brought to the door. She was going to ride towards Gurthnamuckla to meet Lambert, who had gone there some time before; he had made Francie promise to meet him on his way home, and she was going to keep her word. He had become quite a different person to her since the morning, a person who no longer appealed to her admiration or her confidence, but solely and distressingly to her pity. She had always thought of him as invincible, self-sufficing, and possessed of innumerable interests besides herself; she knew him now as dishonest and disgraced, and miserable, stripped of all his pretensions and vanities, but she cared for him today more than yesterday. It was against her will that his weakness appealed to her; she would have given worlds for a heart that did not smite her at its claim, but her pride helped out her compassion. She told herself that she could not let people have it to say that she ran away from Roddy because he was in trouble.

She felt chilly, and she shivered as she stood by the fire, whose unseasonable extravagance daily vexed the righteous soul of Eliza Hackett. Hawkins' note was in her hand, and she read it through twice while she waited; then, as she heard the sound of wheels on the gravel, she tore it in two and threw it into the fire, and, for the second time that morning, ran to the window.

It was Christopher Dysart again. He saw her at the window and took off his cap, and before he had time to ring the bell, she had opened the hall door. She had, he saw at once, been crying, and her paleness, and the tell-tale heaviness of her eyes, contrasted pathetically with the smartness of her figure in her riding habit, and the boyish jauntiness of her hard felt hat.

'Mr Lambert isn't in, Sir Christopher,' she began at once, as if she had made up her mind whom he had come to see; 'but won't you come in?'

'Oh – thank you – I – I haven't much time – I merely wanted to speak to your husband,' stammered Christopher.

'Oh, please come in,' she repeated, 'I want to speak to you.' Her eyes suddenly filled with tears, and she turned quickly from him and walked towards the drawing room.

Christopher followed her with the mien of a criminal. He felt he would rather have been robbed twenty times over than see the eyes that, in his memory, had always been brilliant and undefeated, avoiding his as if they were afraid of him, and know that he was the autocrat before whom she trembled. She remained standing near the middle of the room with one hand on the corner of the piano, whose gaudy draperies had, even at this juncture, a painful sub-effect upon Christopher; her other hand fidgeted restlessly with a fold of the habit that she was holding up, and it was evident that whatever her motive had been in bringing him in, her courage was not equal to it. Christopher waited for her to speak, until the silence became unendurable.

'I intended to have been here earlier,' he said, saying anything rather than nothing, 'but there was a great deal to be got through at the Bench today, and I've only just got away. You know I'm a magistrate now, and indifferently minister justice – '

'I'm glad I hadn't gone out when you came,' she interrupted, as though, having found a beginning, she could not lose a moment in using it. 'I wanted to say that if you – if you'll only give Roddy a week's time he'll pay you. He only meant to borrow the money, like, and he thought he could pay you before; but, indeed, he says he'll pay you in a week.' Her voice was low and full of bitterest humiliation, and Christopher wished that before he had arraigned his victim, and offered him up as an oblation to his half-hearted sense of duty, he had known that his infirmity of purpose would have brought him back three hours afterwards to offer the culprit a way out of his difficulties. It would have saved him from his present hateful position, and what it would have saved her was so evident, that he turned his head away as he spoke, rather than look at her.

'I came back to tell your husband that – that he could arrange things in – in some such way,' he said, as guiltily and awkwardly as a boy. 'I'm sorry – more sorry than I can say – that he should have spoken to you about it. Of course, that was my fault. I should have told him then what I came to tell him now.'

'He's gone out now to see about selling his horses and the furniture,' went on Francie, scarcely realizing all of Christopher's leniency in her desire to prove Lambert's severe purity of action. Her mind was not capable of more than one idea – one, that is, in addition to the question that had monopolized it since yesterday afternoon, and Christopher's method of expressing himself had never been easily understood by her.

'Oh, he mustn't think of doing that!' exclaimed Christopher, horrified that she should think him a Shylock, demanding so extreme a measure of restitution; 'it wasn't the actual money question that – that we disagreed about; he can take as long as he likes about repaying me. In fact – in fact you can tell him from me that – he said something this morning about giving up the agency. Well, I – I should be glad if he would keep it.'

He had stultified himself now effectually; he knew that he had acted like a fool, and he felt quite sure that Mr Lambert's sense of gratitude would not prevent his holding the same opinion. He even foresaw Lambert's complacent assumption that Francie had talked him over, but he could not help himself. The abstract justice of allowing the innocent to suffer with the guilty was beyond him; he forgot to theorize, and acted on instinct as simply as a savage. She also had acted on instinct. When she called him in she had nerved herself to ask for reprieve, but she never hoped for forgiveness, and as his intention penetrated the egotism of suffering, the thought leaped with it that, if Roddy were to be let off, everything would be on the same footing that it had been yesterday evening. A blush that was incomprehensible to Christopher swept over her face; the grasp of circumstances relaxed somewhat, and a jangle of unexplainable feelings confused what self-control she had left.

'You're awfully good,' she began half hysterically. 'I always knew you were good; I wish Roddy was like you! Oh, I wish I was like you! I can't help it – I can't help crying; you were always good to me, and I never was worth it!' She sat down on one of the high stiff chairs, for which her predecessor had worked beaded seats, and hid her eyes in her handkerchief. 'Please don't talk to me; please don't say anything to me – ' She stopped suddenly. 'What's that? Is that anyone riding up?'

'No. It's your horse coming round from the yard,' said Christopher, taking a step towards the window, and trying to keep up the farce of talking as if nothing had happened.

'My horse!' she exclaimed, starting up. 'Oh, yes, I must go and meet Roddy. I mustn't wait any longer.' She began, as if unconscious of Christopher's presence, to look for the whip and gloves that she had laid down. He saw them before she did, and handed them to her.

'Good-bye,' he said, taking her cold, trembling hand, 'I must go too. You will tell your husband that it's – it's all right.'

'Yes. I'll tell him. I'm going to meet him. I must start now,' she answered, scarcely seeming to notice what he said, and withdrawing her hand from his, she began hurriedly to button on her gloves.

Christopher did not wait for further dismissal, but when his hand was on the door, her old self suddenly woke.

'Look at me letting you go away without telling you a bit how grateful I am to you!' she said, with a lift of her tear-disfigured eyes that was like a changeling of the look he used to know; 'but don't you remember what Mrs Baker said about me, that "you couldn't expect any manners from a Dublin Jackeen"?'

She laughed weakly, and Christopher, stammering more than ever in an attempt to say that there was nothing to be grateful for, got himself out of the room.

After he had gone, Francie gave herself no time to think. Everything was reeling round her as she went out on to the steps, and even Michael the groom thought to himself that if he hadn't the trap to wash, he'd put the saddle on the chestnut and folly the misthress, she had that thrimulous way with her when he put the reins into her hands, and only for it was the mare she was riding he wouldn't see her go out by herself.

It was the first of June, and the gaiety of the spring was nearly gone. The flowers had fallen from the hawthorn, the bluebells and primroses were vanishing as quietly as they came, the meadows were already swarthy, and the breaths of air that sent pale shimmers across them were full of the unspeakable fragrance of the ripening grass. Under the trees, near Rosemount, the shadowing greenness had saturated the daylight with its gloom, but out among the open pastures and meadows the large grey sky seemed almost bright, and, in the rich sobriety of tone, the red cattle were brilliant spots of colour.

The black mare and her rider were now on thoroughly confidential terms, and, so humiliatingly interwoven are soul and body, as the exercise quickened the blood in her veins, Francie's incorrigible youth rose up, and while it brightened her eyes and drove colour to her cheeks, it whispered that somehow or other happiness might come to her. She rode fast till she reached the turn to Gurthnamuckla, and there, mindful of her husband's injunctions that she was not to ride up to the house, but to wait for him on the road, she relapsed into a walk.

As she slackened her pace, all the thoughts that she had been riding away from came up with her again. What claim had Roddy on her now? She had got him out of his trouble, and that was the most he could expect her to do for him. He hadn't thought much about the trouble he was bringing on her; he never as much as said he was sorry for the disgrace it would be to her. Why should she break her heart for him, and Gerald's heart too? – as she said Hawkins' name to herself, her hands fell into her lap, and she moaned aloud. Every step the mare was taking was carrying her farther from him, but yet she could not turn back. She was changed since yesterday; she had seen her husband's soul laid bare, and it had shown her how tremendous were sin and duty; it had touched her slumbering moral sense as well as her kindness, and though she rebelled she did not dare to turn back.

It was not till she heard a pony's quick gallop behind her, and, looking back, saw Hawkins riding after her at full speed, that she knew how soon she was to be tested. She had scarcely time to collect herself before he was pulling up the pony beside her, and had turned a flushed and angry face towards her,

'Didn't you get my note? Didn't you know I was coming?' he began in hot remonstrance. Then, seeing in a moment how ill and strange she looked, 'What's the matter? Has anything happened?'

'Roddy came home yesterday evening,' she said, with her eyes fixed on the mare's mane.

'Well, I know that,' interrupted Hawkins. 'Do you mean that he was angry? Did he find out anything about me? If he did see the note I wrote you, there was nothing in that.' Francie shook her head. 'Then it's nothing? It's only that you've been frightened by that brute,' he said, kicking his pony up beside the mare, and trying to look into Francie's downcast eyes. 'Don't mind him. It won't be for long.'

'You mustn't say that,' she said hurriedly. 'I was very wrong yesterday, and I'm sorry for it now.'

'I know you're not!' he burst out, with all the conviction that he felt. 'You can't unsay what you said to me yesterday. I sat up the whole night thinking the thing over and thinking of you, and at last I thought of a fellow I know out in New Zealand, who told me last year I ought to chuck the army and go out there.' He dropped his reins on the pony's neck, and took Francie's hand. 'Why shouldn't we go there together, Francie? I'll give up everything for you, my darling!'

She feebly tried to take her hand away, but did not reply.

'I've got three hundred a year of my own, and we can do ourselves awfully well on that out there. We'll always have lots of horses, and it's a ripping climate – and – and I love you and I'll always love you!'

He was carried away by his own words, and, stooping his head, he kissed her hand again and again.

Every pulse in her body answered to his touch, and when she drew her hand away, it was with an effort that was more than physical.

335

'Ah! stop, stop,' she cried. 'I've changed – I didn't mean it.'

'Didn't mean what?' demanded Hawkins, with his light eyes on fire.

'Oh, leave me alone,' she said, turning her distracted face towards him. 'I'm nearly out of my mind as it is. What made you follow me out here? I came out so as I wouldn't see you, and I'm going to meet Roddy now.'

Hawkins' colour died slowly down to a patchy white. 'What do you think it was that made me follow you? Do you want to make me tell you over again what you know already?' She did not answer, and he went on, trying to fight against his own fears by speaking very quietly and rationally. 'I don't know what you're at, Francie. I don't believe you know what you're saying. Something must have happened, and it would be fairer to tell me what it is, than to drive me distracted in this sort of way.'

There was a pause of several seconds, and he was framing a fresh remonstrance when she spoke.

'Roddy's in great trouble. I wouldn't leave him,' she said, taking refuge in a prevarication of the exact truth.

Something about her told Hawkins that things were likely to go hard with him, and there was something, too, that melted his anger as it rose; but her pale face drew him to a height of passion that he had not known before.

'And don't you think anything about *me*?' he said with a breaking voice. 'Are you ready to throw me overboard just because he's in trouble, when you know he doesn't care for you a tenth part as much as I do? Do you mean to tell me that you want me to go away, and say good-bye to you for ever? If you do, I'll go, and if you hear I've gone to the devil, you'll know who sent me.'

The naïve selfishness of this argument was not perceived by either. Hawkins felt his position to be almost noble, and did not in the least realize what he was asking Francie to sacrifice for him. He had even forgotten the idea that had occurred to him last night, that to go to New Zealand would be a pleasanter way of escaping from his creditors than marrying Miss Coppard. Certainly Francie had no thought of his selfishness or of her own sacrifice. She was giddy with struggle; right and wrong had lost their meaning and changed places elusively; the only things that she saw clearly were the beautiful future that had been offered to her, and the look in Roddy's face when she had told him that wherever he had to go she would go with him.

The horses had moved staidly on, while these two lives stood

336

still and wrestled with their fate, and the summit was slowly reached of the long hill on which Lambert had once pointed out to her the hoofprints of Hawkins' pony. The white road and the grey rock country stretched out before them colourless and discouraging under the colourless sky, and Hawkins still waited for his answer. Coming towards them up the tedious slope was a string of half a dozen carts, with a few people walking on either side; an unremarkable procession, that might have meant a wedding, or merely a neighbourly return from market, but for a long, yellow coffin that lay, hemmed in between old women, in the midmost cart. Francie felt a superstitious thrill as she saw it; a country funeral, with its barbarous and yet fitting crudity, always seemed to bring death nearer to her than the plumed conventionalities of the hearses and mourning coaches that she was accustomed to. She had once been to the funeral of a fellow Sunday-school child in Dublin, and the first verse of the hymn that they had sung then came back, and began to weave itself in with the beat of the mare's hoofs.

> Brief life is here our portion,
>   Brief sorrow, short-lived care,
> The life that knows no ending,
>   The tearless life is there.

'Francie, are you going to answer me? Come away with me this very day. We could catch the six o'clock train before anyone knew – dearest, if you love me – ' His roughened, unsteady voice seemed to come to her from a distance, and yet was like a whisper in her own heart.

'Wait till we are past the funeral,' she said, catching, in her agony, at the chance of a minute's respite.

At the same moment an old man, who had been standing by the side of the road, leaning on his stick, turned towards the riders, and Francie recognized in him Charlotte's retainer, Billy Grainy. His always bloodshot eyes were redder than ever, his mouth dribbled like a baby's, and the smell of whisky poisoned the air all around him.

'I'm waitin' on thim here this half-hour,' he began, in a loud drunken mumble, hobbling to Francie's side, and moving along beside the mare, 'as long as they were taking her back the road to cry her at her own gate. Owld bones is wake, asthore, owld bones is wake!' He caught at the hem of Francie's habit to steady himself; 'be cripes! Miss Duffy was a fine woman, Lord ha' maircy on her. And a great woman! And divil blasht thim that

337

threw her out of her farm to die in the Union – the dom ruffins.'

As on the day, now very long ago, when she had first ridden to Gurthnamuckla, Francie tried to shake his hand off her habit; he released it stupidly, and staggering to the side of the road, went on grumbling and cursing. The first cart, creaking and rattling under its load of mourners, was beside them by this time, and Billy, for the benefit of its occupants, broke into a howl of lamentation.

'Thanks be to God Almighty, and thanks be to His Mother, the crayture had thim belonging to her that would bury her like a Christian.' He shook his fist at Francie. 'Ah – ha! go home to himself and owld Charlotte, though it's little thim regards you – ' He burst into drunken laughter, bending and tottering over his stick.

Francie, heedless of the etiquette that required that she and Hawkins should stop their horses till the funeral passed, struck the mare, and passed by him at a quickened pace. The faces in the carts were all turned upon her, and she felt as if she were enduring, in a dream, the eyes of an implacable tribunal; even the mare seemed to share in her agitation, and sidled and fidgeted on the narrow strip of road, that was all the space left to her by the carts. The coffin was almost abreast of Francie now, and her eyes rested with a kind of fascination on its bare yellow surface. She became dimly aware that Norry the Boat was squatted beside it on the straw, when one of the other women began suddenly to groan and thump on the coffin lid with her fists, in preparation for a burst of the Irish Cry, and at the signal Norry fell upon her knees, and flung out her arms inside her cloak, with a gesture that made her look like a great vulture opening its wings for flight. The cloak flapped right across the mare's face, and she swerved from the cart with a buck that loosened her rider in the saddle, and shook her hat off. There was a screech of alarm from all the women, the frightened mare gave a second and a third buck, and at the third Francie was shot into the air and fell, head first, on the road.

51

The floor of the potato loft at Gurthnamuckla had for a long time needed repairs, a circumstance not in itself distressing to Miss Mullen, who held that effort after mere theoretical symmetry was unjustifiable waste of time in either housekeeping or farming. On this first of June, however, an intimation from Norry that 'there's ne'er a pratie ye have that isn't ate with the rats,' given with the thinly-veiled triumph of servants in such announcements, caused a truculent visit of inspection to the potato loft; and in her first spare moment of the afternoon Miss Mullen set forth with her tool basket, and some boards from a packing case, to make good the breaches with her own hands. Doing it herself saved the necessity of taking the men from their work, and moreover ensured its being properly done.

So she thought, as, having climbed the ladder that led from the cowhouse to the loft, she put her tools on the floor and surveyed with a workman's eye the job she had set herself. The loft was hot and airless, redolent of the cowhouse below, as well as of the clayey mustiness of the potatoes that were sprouting in the dirt on the floor, and even sending pallid, worm-like roots down into space through the cracks in the boards. Miss Mullen propped the window shutter open with the largest potato, and, pinning up her skirt, fell to work.

She had been hammering and sawing for a quarter of an hour when she heard the clatter of a horse's hoofs on the cobblestones of the yard, and, getting up from her knees, advanced to the window with caution and looked out. It was Mr Lambert, in the act of pulling up his awkward young horse, and she stood looking down at him in silence while he dismounted, with a remarkable expression on her face, one in which some acute mental process was mixed with the half-unconscious and yet all-observant recognition of an intensely familiar object.

'Hullo, Roddy!' she called out at last, 'is that you? What brings you over so early?'

339

Mr Lambert started with more violence than the occasion seemed to demand.

'Hullo!' he replied, in a voice not like his own, 'is that where you are?'

'Yes, and it's where I'm going to stay. This is the kind of fancy work I'm at,' brandishing her saw; 'so if you want to talk to me you must come up here.'

'All right,' said Lambert, gloomily, 'I'll come up as soon as I put the colt in the stable.'

It is a fact so improbable as to be worth noting, that before Lambert found his way up the ladder, Miss Mullen had unpinned her skirt and fastened up the end of a plait that had escaped from the massive coils at the back of her head.

'Well, and where's the woman that owns you?' she asked, beginning to work again, while her visitor stood in obvious discomfort, with his head touching the rafters, and the light from the low window striking sharply up against his red and heavy eyes.

'At home,' he replied, almost vacantly. 'I'd have been here half an hour ago or more,' he went on after a moment or two, 'but the colt cast a shoe, and I had to go on to the forge beyond the cross to get it put on.'

Charlotte, with a flat pencil in her mouth, grunted responsively, while she measured off a piece of board, and, holding it with her knee on the body of a legless wheelbarrow, began to saw it across. Lambert looked on, provoked and disconcerted by this engrossing industry. With his brimming sense of collapse and crisis, he felt that even this temporary delay of sympathy was an unkindness.

'That colt must be sold this week, so I couldn't afford to knock his hoof to bits on the hard road.' His manner was so portentous that Charlotte looked up again, and permitted herself to remark on what had been apparent to her the moment she saw him.

'Why, what's the matter with you, Roddy? Now I come to see you, you look as if you'd been at your own funeral.'

'I wish to God I had! It would be the best thing could happen to me.'

He found pleasure in saying something to startle her, and in seeing that her face became a shade hotter than the stifling air and the stooping over her work had made it.

'What makes you talk like that?' she said, a little strangely, as it seemed to him.

He thought she was moved, and he immediately felt his position

340

to be more pathetic than he had believed. It would be much easier to explain the matter to Charlotte than to Francie, he felt at once; Charlotte understood business matters, a formula which conveyed to his mind much comfortable flexibility in money affairs.

'Charlotte,' he said, looking down at her with eyes that self-pity and shaken self-control were moistening again, 'I'm in most terrible trouble. Will you help me?'

'Wait till I hear what it is and I'll tell you that,' replied Charlotte, with the same peculiar, flushed look on her face, and suggestion in her voice of strong and latent feeling. He could not tell how it was, but he felt as if she knew what he was going to say.

'I'm four hundred pounds in debt to the estate, and Dysart has found out,' he said, lowering his voice as if afraid that the spiders and wood lice might repeat his secret.

'Four hundred,' thought Charlotte; 'that's more than I reckoned;' but she said aloud, 'My God! Roddy, how did that happen?'

'I declare to you I don't know how it happened. One thing and another came against me, and I had to borrow this money, and before I could pay it he found out.'

Lambert was a pitiable figure as he made his confession, his head, his shoulders, and even his moustache drooping limply, and his hands nervously twisting his ash plant.

'That's a bad business,' said Charlotte reflectively, and was silent for a moment, while Lambert realized the satisfaction of dealing with an intelligence that could take in such a situation instantaneously, without alarm or even surprise.

'Is he going to give you the sack?' she asked.

'I don't know yet. He didn't say anything definite.'

Lambert found the question hard to bear, but he endured it for the sake of the chance it gave him to lead up to the main point of the interview. 'If I could have that four hundred placed to his credit before I see him next, I believe there'd be an end of it. Not that I'd stay with him,' he went on, trying to bluster, 'or with any man that treated me this kind of way, going behind my back to look at the accounts.'

'Is that the way he found you out?' asked Charlotte, taking up the lid of the packing case and twisting a nail out of it with a hammer. 'He must be smarter than you took him for.'

'Someone must have put him up to it,' said Lambert, 'someone who'd got at the books. It beats me to make it out. But what's the good of thinking of that? The thing that's setting me mad

341

is to know how to pay him.' He waited to see if Charlotte would speak, but she was occupied in straightening the nail against the wall with her hammer, and he went on with a dry throat, 'I'm going to sell all my horses, Charlotte, and I daresay I can raise some money on the furniture; but it's no easy job to raise money in such a hurry as this, and if I'm to be saved from being disgraced, I ought to have it at once to stop his mouth. I believe if I could pay him at once he wouldn't have spunk enough to go any further with the thing.' He waited again, but the friend of his youth continued silent. 'Charlotte, no man ever had a better friend, through thick and thin, than I've had in you. There's no other person living that I'd put myself under an obligation to but yourself. Charlotte, for the sake of all that's ever been between us, would you lend me the money?'

Her face was hidden from him as she knelt, and he stooped and placed a clinging, affectionate hand upon her shoulder. Miss Mullen got up sharply, and Lambert's hand fell.

'All that's ever been between us is certainly a very weighty argument, Roddy,' she said with a smile that deepened the ugly lines about her mouth, and gave Lambert a chilly qualm. 'There's a matter of three hundred pounds between us, if that's what you mean.'

'I know, Charlotte,' he said hastily. 'No one remembers that better than I do. But this is a different kind of thing altogether. I'd give you a bill of sale on everything at Rosemount – and there are the horses out here too. Of course, I suppose I might be able to raise the money at the bank or somewhere, but it's a very different thing to deal with a friend, and a friend who can hold her tongue too. You never failed me yet, Charlotte, old girl, and I don't believe you'll do it now!'

His handsome, dark eyes were bent upon her face with all the pathos he was master of, and he was glad to feel tears rising in them.

'Well, I'm afraid that's just what I'll have to do,' she said, flinging away the nail that she had tried to straighten, and fumbling in her pocket for another; 'I may be able to hold my tongue, but I don't hold with throwing good money after bad.'

Lambert stood quite still, staring at her, trying to believe that this was the Charlotte who had trembled when he kissed her, whose love for him had made her his useful and faithful thrall.

'Do you mean to say that you'll see me ruined and disgraced sooner than put out your hand to help me?' he said passionately.

'I thought you said you could get the money somewhere else,' she replied, with undisturbed coolness, 'and you might know that coming to me for money is like going to the goat's house for wool. I've got nothing more to lend, and no one ought to know that better than yourself!'

Charlotte was standing, yellow-faced and insolent, opposite to Lambert, with her hands in the pockets of her apron; in every way a contrast to him, with his flushed forehead and suffused eyes. The dull, white light that struck up into the roof from the whitewashed kitchen wall showed Lambert the furrowed paths of implacability in his adversary's face as plainly as it showed her his defeat and desperation.

'*You've* got no more money to lend, d'ye say!' he repeated, with a laugh that showed he had courage enough left to lose his temper; 'I suppose you've got all the money you got eighteen months ago from the old lady lent out? 'Pon my word, considering you got Francie's share of it for yourself, I think it would have been civiller to have given her husband the first refusal of a loan! I daresay I'd have given you as good interest as your friends in Ferry Lane!'

Charlotte's eyes suddenly lost their exaggerated indifference.

'And if she ever had the smallest claim to what ye call a share!' she vociferated, 'haven't you had it twenty times over? Was there ever a time that ye came cringing and crawling to me for money that I refused it to ye? And how do you thank me? By embezzling the money I paid for the land, and then coming to try and get it out of me over again, because Sir Christopher Dysart is taught sense to look into his own affairs, and see how his agent is cheating him!'

Some quality of triumph in her tone, some light of previous knowledge in her eye, struck Lambert.

'Was it you told him?' he said hoarsely, 'was it you spoke to Dysart?'

Every now and then in the conduct of her affairs Miss Mullen permitted the gratification of her temper to take the place of the slower pleasure of secrecy.

'Yes, I told him,' she answered, without hesitation.

'You went to Dysart, and set him on to ruin me!' said Lambert, in a voice that had nearly as much horror as rage in it.

'And may I ask you what you've ever done for me,' she said, gripping her hammer with a strong, trembling hand, 'that I was to keep your tricks from being found out for you? What reason was there in God's earth that I wasn't to do my plain duty by those that are older friends than you?'

'What reason!' Lambert almost choked from the intolerable audacity and heartlessness of the question. 'Are you in your right mind to ask me that? You, that's been like a – a near relation to me all these years, or pretending to be! There was a time you wouldn't have done this to me, you know it damned well, and so do I. You were glad enough to do anything for me then, so long as I'd be as much as civil to you, and now, I suppose, this is your dirty devilish spite, because you were cut out by someone else!'

She did not flinch as the words went through and through her.

'Take care of yourself!' she said, grinning at him, 'perhaps you're not the one to talk about being cut out! Oh, I don't think ye need look as if ye didn't understand me. At all events, all ye have to do is to go home and ask your servants – or, for the matter of that, anyone in the streets of Lismoyle – who it is that's cut ye out, and made ye the laughing stock of the country!'

She put her hands on the dusty beam beside her, giddy with her gratified impulse, as she saw him take the blow and wither under it.

She scarcely heard at first the strange and sudden sound of commotion that had sprung up like a wind in the house opposite. The windows were all open, and through them came the sound of banging doors and running footsteps, and then Norry's voice screaming something as she rushed from room to room. She was in the kitchen now, and the words came gasping and sobbing through the open door.

'Where's Miss Charlotte? Where is she? O God! O God! Where is she? Miss Francie's killed, her neck's broke below on the road! O God of Heaven, help us!'

Neither Charlotte nor Lambert heard clearly what she said, but the shapeless terror of calamity came about them like a vapour and blanched the hatred in their faces. In a moment they were together at the window, and at the same instant Norry burst out into the yard, with outflung arms and grey hair streaming. As she saw Lambert, her strength seemed to go from her. She staggered back, and, catching at the door for support, turned from him and hid her face in her cloak.

THE HOGARTH PRESS

This is a paperback list for today's readers – but it holds to a tradition of adventurous and original publishing set by Leonard and Virginia Woolf when they founded The Hogarth Press in 1917 and started their first paperback series in 1924.

Some of the books are light-hearted, some serious, and include Fiction, Lives and Letters, Travel, Critics, Poetry, History and Hogarth Crime and Gaslight Crime.

A list of our books already published, together with some of our forthcoming titles, follows. If you would like more information about Hogarth Press books, write to us for a catalogue:

30 Bedford Square, London WC1B 3RP

Please send a large stamped addressed envelope

Mark Rutherford

Catharine Furze

New Afterword by Claire Tomalin

Catharine's desires are those of every girl as she grows into womanhood – idealistic, absurd, passionate, barely spoken. In telling her story Mark Rutherford became one of the first male novelists to write sympathetically about the fate of women, and this book, along with *Clara Hopgood*, has been sought after for many years. It is his finest novel: Dickensian in its humour and pathos, exceptional in its understanding of a woman's troubled soul.

Edith Templeton
The Island of Desire

New Introduction by Anita Brookner

The Island of Desire celebrates erotic love with wit, charm
and honesty. It tells the story of Franciska Kalny,
daughter of Mrs Kalny, who with her snobbery and her
lovers sets the sort of example which requires a daughter
to rebel. So Franciska deserts the decadence of Prague
and embarks on a voyage of self-discovery through seedy
Parisian nightclubs and the haunts of millionaire
Americans, chintzy English suburbs and the romantic
piazzas of Italy. Her journey is every woman's rite of
passage: anarchic, tentative and tragi-comic, it demon-
strates an eternal truth – that the loss of innocence is
merely the beginning of the dubious rewards that adult
love so inevitably brings.

Jessie Kesson

The White Bird Passes

'Beg, borrow or steal this book' – *Norman MacCaig*

The unforgettable story of young Janie and her mother
Lisa, 'gone to the bad' in the clamorous backstreets of a
Scottish city in the days when a parent alone had no help
and the shadow of the institution loomed over all. But
Janie loves her mother, and her devotion and indomit-
able spirit carry her on against great odds.

Jessie Kesson

Glitter of Mica

'One of the literary treasures of modern Scotland . . . in
the highest traditions of European fiction' –
William Donaldson

With characteristic magic, Jessie Kesson brings to life a
world now lost – the small Scottish farming community,
from its squires to its tinkers, in which are entangled the
fates of Hugh Riddell, the dairyman at 'Darklands', his
wife Isa, his daughter Helen, and his fiercely relentless
enemy, the local politician Charlie Anson. As in the
poetry of Burns, amid hardship and tragedy spring wild
innocence and the zest of life. This is a rare gem of a
novel, in the incomparable Kesson style, colourful and
poignant, full of lingering pleasures.

Frank O'Connor
Irish Miles

New Introduction by Brendan Kennelly

Scouring the byways of Ireland on their bicycles, the famous story-teller Frank O'Connor, his wife and a friend set off in search of their country's buried past. O'Connor's discoveries range from the windswept headlands of Kerry to the mountains of Connemara, from country pubs to Cistercian abbeys – a magical journey, packed with anecdotes, strange meetings and curious characters and salted with his inimitable wit, tenderness and pungent opinions. *Irish Miles* is an enduring pleasure and an invaluable guide to an Ireland hidden from the tourist trail.